STEAM
in the
FAMILY

Avril Rowlands

Steam in the Family

Copyright © 2021 Avril Rowlands

All rights reserved

ISBN 978-0-9930080-6-1

Steam in the Family

Acknowledgements

With my grateful thanks to

The late Les Dearson, a former Great Western Railway driver, for his reminiscences about life as a driver at Tyseley engine shed.

The late Sam Essex, another former Great Western Railway driver, for his stories about his life as a driver at Didcot engine shed.

Alun Rees, former Chief Engineer and General Manager of the Severn Valley Railway, for going through the book with a fine toothcomb to ensure I did not make any terrible 'howlers' for railway afficionados to spot. Any mistakes are, of course, mine.

and finally to

My beloved husband, Christopher, whose encyclopaedic knowledge of all things relating to railways in the days of steam has been invaluable, to say nothing of his continued love and support.

Steam in the Family

Contents

Author's note

When I was a child I asked for a model railway for Christmas. I was given a model farm. In those days, girls didn't play with trains. Which probably explains a lot!

My first encounter with a real, live steam railway was when I was working for the BBC and filming a children's series, *'Carrie's War'*. The railway sequences were shot on the Severn Valley Railway in Worcestershire. My husband, a BBC film editor, was already a railway enthusiast and together we made a publicity film for the SVR, *Steam upon Severn'*.

This led to a writing career - books, and for television and the stage.

God's Wonderful Railway an eight-part children's drama series which I wrote for the BBC, and which was transmitted in 1980, was highly successful and led to the BBC asking me to write an adult drama series about a railway family whose life and work revolved around a Great Western engine shed in the mid 1930s. Sadly circumstances changed and the BBC, having commissioned the series and already commenced pre-production, never made it.

When *'God's Wonderful Railway'* was finally released as a DVD in 2017, the resulting interest from people all over the world inspired me to write *'Steam in the Family'*.

For further information about my writing, please go to my website: www.avrilrowlands.co.uk.

Chapter One

'Dammo Duw!'

Fred Watkins swore as his hand slipped and he nicked his chin on his cut-throat razor. It was only in times of stress that Fred reverted to his Welsh origins, and he frowned at his reflection in the small mirror above the stone kitchen sink. A man in his mid-fifties stared back at him. A man with a crop of black hair turning grey at the temples, disciplined into a short back and sides but standing up thickly and triumphantly on the crown of his head. A lined, well-worn face, an unremarkable face was it not for his black, deep-set Celtic eyes.

Fred was a small man, who gave the appearance of having shrunk with the advancing years so that his clothes now seemed to hang on him slightly too loosely. But if anyone was to assume that he was an insignificant person, they would soon be proved wrong. For like many small men, Fred had a formidable personality which could dominate a room or a group of people by his mere presence. He was a proud man who exuded confidence. He was a man who kept his life under tight and efficient control.

Angry at having given way to his feelings so openly, he swore again, this time in English, and felt better. It went against his strict, deeply rooted Ebenezer Baptist upbringing to swear in Welsh. Swearing in English was not, to his mind, an offence against the Lord. Glancing once more in the mirror, he saw that neither his wife nor his daughter appeared interested either in his feelings or in his cut chin, which was now bleeding profusely. A drop of blood fell on his immaculately clean shirt which he had rolled up to the elbows. Even more irritated than before, he snatched up a tea cloth and pressed it to his face.

'Now look what you've made me do,' he growled at his reflection.

His wife stopped rummaging among the dishes, cups and saucers which were piled on the marble-topped surface of the dresser, to turn and look at him in puzzled bewilderment.

'Me?' Nancy asked in vague surprise. She carried on with her search, hampered by a loaf of bread clutched to her chest. 'Now where's that blessed breadknife? I'm sure I put it down somewhere....' She looked helplessly around the room as if expecting the knife to suddenly materialise. 'It just walks off when it sees me coming.'

His daughter gave a deep sigh and turned over a page of *Picturegoer*. She moved her hand from the magazine to her cup of tea, hovering for a moment, while, with infinite care she positioned thumb and forefinger carefully around the handle before crooking her little finger in the method approved by the article in *Woman's Life* on 'How to be a Real Lady'. She lifted the cup and took a delicate sip before returning to her magazine. One of Sylvia's aims was to acquire the cool sophistication of Barbara Stanwyck, her currently favourite film-star.

Like her father, Sylvia was dark, with a determined face and expressive eyes. She prided herself on being nobody's fool and although only nineteen, had a clear idea of what she wanted out of life. For the moment she was happy with her job as usherette at The Regal Cinema, as it provided unlimited opportunity to watch her favourite film stars. She followed their lives and scandals avidly in the film magazines and dreamed of chance encounters with Kirk Douglas, while enjoying herself with a succession of boyfriends, who she treated with amused tolerance and kept well at arms' length. She looked up suddenly, wrinkling her nose in a very unladylike fashion.

'Something's burning.'

'Gracious heavens!'

Nancy flew to the stove, dumping the loaf of bread unceremoniously on the table. Blue smoke was rising from the frying pan. She grabbed the handle, flapped her hand to clear the air and looked with resignation at the charred bacon and ruined eggs.

'Couldn't you have seen to it, Sylvie?' Fred demanded, still dabbing furiously at his chin. 'Can't you see your mother's busy?'

'Mum was nearer,' Sylvia muttered, now rifling through the pile of magazines on the chair beside her. '"The He-Man Women Adore",' she read aloud. She looked up at her mother. 'Guess who?'

'Cary Grant?' Nancy left the spoilt food to peer over her daughter's shoulder.

'Douglas Montgomery.' She looked at the photograph, head on one side. 'What a charmer. I wouldn't mind canoodling with him in the back row of the cinema.'

'Wouldn't you, dear?'

Nancy was in her late forties. She had been married to Fred for over twenty years and a more ill-assorted couple would be hard to find. Taller than Fred, thin and fine-boned, Nancy's light brown hair was scraped back in an ineffectual bun from which wispy strands escaped. Her life seemed under as little control, with her cluttered and untidy kitchen a witness to her haphazard methods of housekeeping. Her family, however, were very well aware that her gentle vagueness and usual air of mild astonishment were deceptive as she effortlessly coped with the schizophrenic existence of any shift worker's wife, providing meals at all hours of the day and night while bringing up two demanding children. The marriage was a good one and, although impatient and intolerant by nature, Fred was rarely impatient with Nancy, and put up with the discomfort felt by any organised person living in a chaotic home with almost saintly tolerance. It made his outburst at the kitchen sink even more unusual.

'Stupid bloody women,' Fred muttered into the mirror.

For the third time that evening he looked at the closed door of the kitchen before throwing the bloodstained tea cloth on to the draining board with a grunt of irritation. He picked up his razor, dipped it in the water and raised it to his chin. His unease communicated itself to the others. Sylvia hunched a shoulder and turned away, burying herself more deeply in her magazine. She yawned loudly and took another delicate sip of tea. Nancy, after one quick, concerned glance at Fred, quietly busied herself with fresh bacon and eggs

'Where is the lad!' Fred exploded at last, giving vent to the real cause of his annoyance.

Nancy looked at him in mild surprise and even Sylvia glanced up.

'Give him a shout, will you Sylvie? He can't still be in his bloody bed!'

Sylvia threw down her magazine. 'No peace for the wicked.'

She left the room, crossed the hall and called loudly up the stairs.

'Tom! TOM!'

'Yes, where is Tom?' Nancy enquired gently, hovering uncertainly between the stove, her husband and the recalcitrant breadknife which she had just spotted.

'That's what dad wants to know,' Sylvia said deliberately, casting him a malicious glance as she sat down and picked up her magazine.

'I don't want to know,' Fred protested. He wiped his chin vigorously, inspected it to make sure the bleeding had really stopped, then seized his laden plate from Nancy and sat down at the table.

'It's up to him whether he's late,' he continued in an aggrieved voice. 'Let him sleep in if the job means as little as that to him.'

He dug his fork determinedly into his egg and took a mouthful.

Sylvia glanced at her mother, raised an eyebrow, then returned to her magazine.

******

It was hot in the field and Tom's back was burning as he lay breathing in the rich scents of grass and clover. Now late afternoon, the sun was still flooding the valley with its warm golden light.

He looked down the long slope of the hill. Acres of wheat stretched before him, green turning yellow, dotted with brilliant splashes of poppy red. As he watched, the wheat rippled and sighed as a warm breeze brushed across the hillside. Perhaps time would stand still, and he could lie here forever.

The valley darkened. Tom looked up towards the woods which clothed the slopes of the far hills in serried ranks of dark green. He looked higher to where a silver-rimmed cloud hid the sun. It burst out, dazzling his eyes. Half-blinded, he looked across to the fold of hills below the woods and saw, through an aureole of light, the farmhouse nestling cosily into the curve of the hillside. Tiny and freshly-washed a vivid pink, circled by a neat, newly painted white fence. White dots of sheep stood out against the green of the fields. A dusty, cream-coloured lane, no, more of a track, led down from the house. It looked like a toy farmhouse, stirring memories of half-forgotten childhood things.

I wonder who lives in that house, he thought idly. I could live there. I could be a farmer... I'd have sheep... cows... a few pigs, although pigs weren't essential. It looked... uncomplicated....

His eyes followed the path of the lane to where it met, at right-angles, four metal rails curving along the line of the valley. They glinted in the sun.

Why had he come to the valley to sit out the long afternoon? Why this valley, where the gleaming rails were a constant reminder? He shifted his position, suddenly full of nervous energy. He should have tramped off into the woods and tired himself out or stayed home and tried to sleep away the afternoon. His father suggested he should do that, but he had been stifled in his bedroom. He had slipped out when his father was busy in the garden, taking care not to be seen.

He leaned back into the hollow of ground and closed his eyes to the brilliant sky. He lay motionless, a tall, thin, fifteen-year-old with long gangling limbs, the dark hair and expressive eyes of his father, and the spare, finely-chiselled bones of his mother. He moved again, burrowing into the thick grass as if it was a hiding place. The wind dropped and the air grew heavy and still. Tom willed himself to sleep but it was no good. The railway ran through his mind as it ran through the valley. Inescapable.

There was a distant 'toot' of a whistle. Tom sat up abruptly and shaded his eyes. A hint of white steam and the sound of an approaching train, louder and louder until it burst out from behind the clump of trees far below and to his left, tiny against the background of hills. A toy train with a green engine, just like the one he had been given so many Christmases ago. The sun reflected off the copper-capped chimney and gleamed on the bright paint of the chocolate and cream-coloured coaches snaking behind.

It curved round the bend, gathering speed on a downhill gradient. Then it was gone, the sound of its final whistle remaining trapped between the hills.

Tom waited until the last echo had died away before scrambling to his feet shedding grass and seeds from his clothes. If he didn't hurry, he'd be late. He took one last look at the now silent valley with its pink-washed farmhouse, then turned and walked swiftly up the hill.

******

The back door opened quietly.

'He's here, dad,' Sylvia said unnecessarily.

Fred stopped eating and glanced round, taking in Tom's red-faced breathlessness, together with his dishevelled clothes still with bits of grass sticking to them.

'What a sight,' he commented in disgust before accepting a slice of bread from Nancy. He buttered it thickly and began to chomp his way through, his eyes fixed disapprovingly on his son. He watched in silence as Tom went over to the sink and began to wash.

'Thought you were in bed,' he said at last.

Tom glanced round. 'I can't sleep in the afternoon.'

'You'll soon have to on shift work. Take your sleep when you can get it. Can't do without your sleep.'

Nancy touched Tom's arm, a clean towel in her hand.

'Do you want anything to eat?'

Fred gave a short laugh. 'He'd better hurry if he does. I'm due on seven fifteen and I've never been late for a turn yet.'

'I don't know why you're fussing, dad,' Sylvia said. 'I thought Tom didn't have to be down the shed for ages.'

Fred bridled. 'Fussing? I'm not fussing. It's up to him entirely. He doesn't have to come down to the shed with me. No reason to. No reason at all.' He attacked his bread and

butter with renewed vigour, then glanced at Sylvia. 'And what
are you doing hanging round, my girl? Haven't you a job to go
to? Usherette in the bloody cinema. Couldn't you do better
than that for yourself?'

Sylvia grinned. 'Only following in mum's footsteps,' she
said, uncurling herself lazily from her chair. '

She looked at Tom who was anxiously staring at his father,
the towel forgotten in his hand. 'Best of luck, brother dear. Not
that you'll need it with dad hovering behind every engine, ready
to spring out and tell you what bits to clean.' She glanced at
her father mischievously. 'Dad's been like a cat on hot bricks
worrying about you.' And with a slight, malicious smile and a
graceful wave of her hand she was gone.

'Stupid girl,' Fred muttered.

'Do you want anything to eat?' Nancy repeated patiently.

Tom looked at his father.

'Not up to me, nothing to do with me,' Fred muttered,
chasing the last forkful of bacon round his plate. 'No reason
for him to go down with me. Probably better if he didn't in fact.
He's got to stand on his own two feet after all - he won't get any
favours because he's Fred Watkins' lad and the sooner he learns
it the better - eh Tom?' Triumphantly he speared the last piece
of bacon on his plate and stuffed it into his mouth.

Tom was silent.

'It's up to him,' Fred said, pushing away his plate and
glancing deliberately at his watch.

Nancy looked from one to the other.

'I'm not hungry, mum,' Tom muttered. He took a deep
breath. 'I'd better go with dad.'

Fred gave a small grunt of satisfaction at his victory.

'That's not how to begin your first day's work,' he said
sharply. 'You can't start on an empty stomach. Get him some
bacon and eggs, Nance. You've a long night in front of you

lad, and you need some ballast inside. Now stop arguing and sit down. Nance, pour the lad some tea.'

Tom sat, unresisting, and accepted the cup his mother was holding out to him. It was easier that way and, besides, what was there to resist? Tom was not, and never had been, a rebel.

******

By the age of four Tom knew that he did not want to be an engine driver when he grew up. By the age of six, he knew that was to be his destiny.

His first introduction to the railway was not auspicious. Perhaps, at four years old, he was too young to be shown his future place of work. Perhaps his father had tried too hard to instil in Tom his own enthusiasm and love for the place. Whatever the reason, the event stayed firmly fixed in Tom's mind, and this, one of his earliest memories, was not a happy one.

'Here, lad. Look. There's a fine sight!'

Tom shook his head. To look up meant danger. To look up meant to acknowledge the presence of the monster he could already hear and smell. If he did not look, he could somehow pretend it wasn't there, bearing down on him, creaking and hissing, snorting and panting.

'Tom!'

His father's voice was insistent and his hand, to which Tom clung as if to a lifeline, was shaking his arm vigorously.

Tom kept his eyes firmly fixed on the ground and desperately drank in every single detail. The cinders scrunching under his feet. His scruffy boots, cleaned to a gleaming blackness only that morning, but now coated with coal dust. One lace, half undone, trailing its long black ribbon behind him. Grimy socks, which limply encased his thin ankles. Grey shorts out of which stretched his naked, white and vulnerable legs and bony knobs of dirt-streaked knees.

Swivelling his eyes sideways while still keeping his head well down, he stared at his father's legs in their well-washed and faded trousers which ended tidily above his worn but immaculately polished boots.

Right on the edge of his vision he could see the black, oily sleepers, the grey ballast like small hard rocks, the shiny metal rails with the sun glancing off them. He could hear the sounds of the busy engine shed and the menace of the advancing engine, making the track groan under its weight, creeping closer and closer, out to crush him as it was even now crushing the sleepers hard down into the ballast. Prickles of fear ran down his back and the damp discomfort of his vest clung to his skin. He could almost hear the pounding of his heart against his small rib cage and terror, like a sick tide, rose at the back of his throat.

'Oh, please don't let me be sick', he prayed to the stern Welsh God of his father. Then, even more urgently, he added, 'and don't let me wee in my shorts!'

The day hadn't begun in fear. Tom had felt nothing but pride as he marched confidently down Station Road, his small hand lost in Fred's large one. He basked in the envious glances of his friends and felt a glow of comfortable superiority as he thought of his sister who had been left behind in floods of tears, for girls, even older sisters, were not important enough to visit their father's place of work.

But the engine shed at Acton Chalcote was more than just his father's workplace. It was the mysterious other world where his father went for long and unpredictable stretches of the day and night. It was the unimaginable black hole into which his father disappeared, returning after fighting with the fire-eating monsters who lived just beyond the end of his road. It was the place where Tom was warned never to trespass, for the monsters, called Kings, Dukes and Bulldogs, would run him down and squash him flatter than a halfpenny piece. It was the place to which he and his friends did, of course, trespass, but never further than where the trees came down to meet the fence denoting railway property, and always in fearful excitement, partly on account of the engines themselves but also in anticipation of being caught by the terrifying Mr Williamson.

For the engine shed belonged to Mr Williamson, the Shed Foreman, who lived in the big house on the other side of Station Road and had two maids so that his wife could, as he once heard his mother say in a rare cynical moment, live in the style to which she was unaccustomed. Mr Williamson, who, like Esau in the Bible, was a hairy man, with an angry beard and red whiskers sprouting out of both nostrils. Mr Williamson, who demonstrated his authority by the imposing bowler hat he wore at all times even, it was rumoured, in bed, and carried a stick topped by a real silver knob.

Mr Williamson was all-powerful. He held the engine shed for that omniscient body known as the Great Western Railway and they, in their turn, held it for God. That was the situation in Tom's four-year old understanding.

As he approached the shed, his steps faltered, and his hand grew hot and sticky in his father's grasp. For the engine shed was the focal point, the entire reason for his family's existence, the reason for everything that meant anything in his young life.

His father took him to the back of the station, along the footpath used only by railwaymen. They skirted the water column at the south end, crossed the track at the barrow crossing and rounded a corner. And there, spread out in all its enormity, lay the engine shed and yard.

It was not, in fact, a very large complex. It consisted of a straight-through shed with four roads, a lifting shop, a coal stage, a turntable large enough for a King class locomotive, the biggest of all the Great Western engines, a sand furnace, and sundry small buildings and sidings which stretched over to the allotments, covering an area locally known as 'the field'. About fifty engines were stabled at the shed with a staff of around four hundred men.

To Tom it seemed vast. He stood stock still and gazed, eyes screwed up against the sun. Suddenly the light was cut off. Tom looked up. Towering over him, too huge for him to fully comprehend, came the engine. Its wheels were twice, three times his height, its coupling rods moving up and down, up and down, relentlessly hypnotic.

'3376', said Fred. 'She's a beauty isn't she.'

It was a statement, not a question. Tom's frightened eyes travelled upwards. Up past the wheels, up to the great, green-painted body miles and miles above him.

The engine creaked to a halt.

'Want a ride in the cab, sonny?'

The voice came from an Olympian figure perched high up. Tom's free hand went to his face and his thumb sought the comfort of his mouth.

"Course he does!' his father encouraged. 'Been dying to come down to the shed. Always on at me about it.'

It was a lie, of course. Tom shook his head vigorously, but no-one took any notice. Fred lifted him up and large, rough, capable hands caught hold of him and swung him high. Tom's feet scrabbled wildly on air, then he was set down, breathless, on the wooden boards of the engine footplate. Timidly he looked around. The Olympian figure who at close quarters turned out to have a square face with a large carbuncle on one side of his nose, smiled down at him. A younger, thinner man, standing on what appeared to be a veritable mountain of coal, dug his shovel into the heap and began pulling it forwards. Tom moved hurriedly as large lumps rolled towards him.

'Careful, sonny, those pipes are hot!'

Tom shrank away from the maze of pipes and levers which bubbled and hissed with a life of their own, spurting wisps of steam and dripping water.

'Coming up, Fred?'

With the ease of long practice his father climbed up on to the footplate. The large man bent to Tom's level.

'What's your name, sonny-Jim?'

Terror prevented Tom from opening his mouth.

Fred answered for him. 'Tom. That's his name,'

'Tom, eh? That's a good name. And you want to be a driver, like your dad, is that it? You want to drive an engine like this one, eh?'

Without waiting for an answer, the man lifted Tom and carried him closer to the mass of pipes. The heat seared Tom's cheeks and he turned his head away.

'That's the one,' said the man with a wink at Fred. 'That big 'un there.' He gestured to the largest lever. 'You have a go starting her.'

His large hand imprisoned Tom's small one against the regulator and with a with a strong upward movement he lifted the lever. The world disintegrated in an explosion of noise and movement.

There was a deep-throated 'chuff...chuff...CHUFF...', the sounds of creaking, clanking, and hissing, and then a sudden lurch as the engine began to move.

With a kick, the younger man opened the heavy metal doors and, in an instant shock of intense heat, so great it was like a blow to his body, Tom saw into the very heart of the monster.

The inside was on fire with a red-hot mass of flames.

The man deftly swung a shovelful of coal through the door and the flames leapt upwards and outwards. Another shovelful then another. The flames devoured them greedily.

Tom was set down on the heaving, swaying floor and tightly held by his father.

'Like it then, do you?' Fred shouted above the noise.

The large man pulled a chain hanging from the roof of the cab and a deafening, ear-splitting whistle cut into Tom's brain. With the only form of protest open to a four-year old he screwed up his face and howled.

*****

That was Tom's introduction to the engine shed, and although the more frightening aspects of his visit eventually faded, the event left its mark. As he grew older, Tom never showed the same enthusiasm for the railway as his friends. He never kept a grubby, well-thumbed notebook of treasured engine numbers, neither was he to be seen among the groups of train-spotters who congregated like flocks of birds at the far end of Platform 2, standing for hours in all weathers just to see a Star or a Castle on the 'down' Cathedrals Express.

It was not that he consciously avoided the railway. That would have been impossible, but it intruded into his childhood only in a minor way, as part of the background of his life. But dating from that first visit there lay on his distant horizon a dark smudge, a shadow of the future, an obligation which he knew would, at some time, have to be fulfilled. From time to time there were pointers, hints, small signs that presaged what was to come. There was, for example, the model farm.

Tom was six and wanted a model farm. He wanted one very badly. Not just any model farm either. The one Tom wanted had been on display in Mr Spratt's toyshop and Tom had spent the best part of a week with his nose pressed against the window drinking in the sight of the tiny lead animals, the pink-washed farmhouse, the white fencing.

So one evening, when his mother brought him his mug of cocoa as he sat curled up in his dressing gown by the fire, and asked him what he wanted Father Christmas to bring, Tom already knew the answer. However, he did not reply immediately for he had already learnt that it did not do to appear too eager for the things that really mattered.

His sister had no such reservations. 'I know what I want,' she said importantly. 'I want a doll just like Betty Simkins. It's got a red velvet dress and real lace on its petticoat.'

After screwing up his face as if in deep thought Tom said tentatively that he rather thought he would like it if Father Christmas brought him a model farm.

'We'll have to see, dear,' Nancy said vaguely, glancing over at Fred. Engrossed in his newspaper, Fred did not look up, but Tom caught the glance, and his heart sank. He did not know what the look meant but felt, instinctively, that it did not bode well for his becoming the owner of the model farm currently in Mr Spratt's window. Although Tom still believed in Father Christmas, for whom anything was possible, he had already begun to realise that there was some sort of a connection between his parents and the fat, red-cloaked gentleman who climbed down their narrow chimney with a sackful of presents on Christmas Eve and ate and drank the two mince pies and small glass of sherry which was left out for him on the hearth.

His father had been listening. There was a moment's silence before the newspaper was thrown down with a thud.

'You want what?' Fred asked slowly.

'A...a farm....' Tom muttered. 'The one that's in Mr Spratt's window....'

'A farm!' Fred said scathingly. 'What on earth do you want a farm for?'

Tom shrank into his dressing gown. 'For... for the animals...'

Fred stood up. 'Bloody daft if you ask me,' he said and stalked out of the room.

Tom watched him go anxiously. He was always anxious where his father was concerned, dimly aware, even at that age, that his father had an image of him which did not match the reality and that no matter how hard Tom strove to remake himself to his father's satisfaction, he knew he would always fall short.

Nothing more was said about model farms and Tom resumed his guard over Mr Spratt's toyshop window. Two days before Christmas the farm disappeared, and Tom was torn between anxiety that it might have been bought by someone else and hope that a miracle would take place on Christmas morning. By Christmas Eve he had convinced himself and early on Christmas Day he lay with his eyes shut, thinking about the farm that stood, he was sure, at the foot of his bed. Each animal took shape in his mind. The horses, the cows, the pigs... would there be pigs? He could not remember whether the farm in Mr Spratt's toyshop contained pigs. No matter, he would know soon enough, and pigs were not essential.

His excitement mounted. He opened his eyes. It must be time to get up. It must be time. Light filtered through the closed curtains. With a beating heart he pushed back the bedclothes, scrambled out, ran to the window, flung open the curtains, then raced round to the foot of the bed.

In front of his eager gaze lay not a model farm, but a model railway. It was all there. A circle of track, a station, an engine, three wagons and a brake van. There was even a tunnel made from papier mâché. Disappointment rose like a tide, threatening to choke him.

'Well, how do you like it?'

Fred stood in the doorway, pleasure shining from his face. Nancy was behind him wearing a slightly troubled smile.

Tom could not speak.

'Grand, isn't it? It's only the start of course, but you can save your pocket money and build it up yourself.'

Not only was this Christmas spoiled but Tom could see his entire pocket money for years to come being mortgaged to this unwanted present. He climbed back into bed and pulled the covers tightly over his head.

'It is all right, isn't it? Nancy asked anxiously as she came further into the room. 'Your father thought...'

'I wanted a farm,' Tom muttered from under the bedclothes.

'A farm!' Fred exploded, his pleasure turning to swift anger. 'What do you mean, a farm! 'Course you didn't want a farm! Who'd want a farm when they could have this?'

'Fred, please...'

'A fortune I spent getting him that layout. A bloody fortune! I'd have given my back teeth for one as good as that his age. But it's not good enough for him, is it? Oh no, he's too choosey. He wants a bloody farm!' The contempt and disappointment in his voice were tangible. He stalked out of the room and Nancy followed telling him to stop shouting as it was, after all, Christmas.

Tom lay in cold misery. His Christmas lay in ruins. He was not aware of Fred returning and the touch of his father's hand startled him.

Fred's anger had gone. 'Having us on, were you boy? Is that it? Come on now, you didn't mean it, did you, eh?'

Tom lay rigid. Fred laughed uncertainly.

'Think I don't know my own son better than that?' He laughed again. 'Pleased as punch you are about it, aren't you? Come on boy, let's get it set up proper.'

Tom timidly poked his head out to find his father smiling at him with such appeal in his eyes that he was unable to disappoint him any further. Dutifully, hating himself, he climbed out of bed, knelt with Fred on the cold linoleum floor and began operating the railway.

Sylvia got her doll with the red velvet dress and real lace petticoat and tired of it within a week. And the dark smudge on Tom's horizon moved a little closer.

******

In 1935 Acton Chalcote was a bustling market town in the Midlands which, by a quirk of history, possessed two railway stations and two engine sheds, one owned by the Great Western Railway and the other, by the London and North Eastern Railway. The town therefore had a corporate identity in that most of the population was linked to one or other of the companies, and a split identity depending on whether one's loyalties lay with the 'Western or the 'North Eastern. The rivalry could be fierce.

Tom's childhood was therefore spent in a town which was cleanly and neatly divided into two factions. The two groups rarely met, but when they did they invariably clashed. School was a battlefield.

'London and North Eastern's better!'

'No, it ain't!'

''Tis!'

''Tain't! It's the Late and Never Early Railway!'

'It's better than your Great Way Round any day!'

'S'not!'

'Is!'

Jim Salter looked down on Tom from his superior height. 'Your dad's a second-rate driver on a second-rate railway!'

'What about yours then? If the Great Western's second-rate your dad's a driver on a third-rate railway and he's a third-rate driver too!'

'If you don't take that back...' Jim threatened.

'Well I won't...'

The two groups circled each other warily in the school playground. Children ran from all directions in order to watch.

'You will...'

'Won't!'

'Will!'

It was a losing battle from the beginning and Tom knew it. But he was used to it. He had been in many such battles and always lost them. He was small as a child and not cut out as a fighter, especially when pitted against such a sturdy enemy as Jim Salter.

Jim squared his hefty shoulders and caught hold of Tom's shirt, almost lifting Tom off his feet.

'You'll take that back...' he threatened.

'Go on Tom!' urged his supporters, whose fathers all worked for the Great Western. 'Go on, kill him, smash his face in!' they yelled, baying for blood and hopping up and down with excitement.

'A third-rate driver on a third-rate railway,' Tom repeated but with lessening confidence as Jim's hold on him tightened. Jim's face grew red with rage, and he drew back one massive fist.

Tom knew what to expect but it hurt just the same. The ensuing battle raged up and down the playground with the girls screaming and the boys rolling round the dusty asphalt, biting, kicking and punching with great enthusiasm until the bell rang, signalling the end of playtime and the beginning of further punishment. Both Tom and Jim were caned and kept in detention after school as the ringleaders of the fight.

For Tom, by virtue of his father's position at work, was the undisputed leader of the Great Western faction. Despite his known lack of interest in the railway and total unconcern about the relative superiority of either company, Tom had to uphold the honour of his father and his friends' fathers in continuous bloody battles. Jim Salter's father was of the same seniority in the LNER as Tom's was in the Great Western, therefore Jim was Tom's natural rival. The hierarchy at school was every bit as rigid as that at the respective engine sheds.

Tom accepted this without thought or question for he was not a rebel and he philosophically accepted his many beatings

both by Jim and by the headmaster. They were as inevitable as
bath nights on Friday and the remains of the Sunday joint on
Monday - a part of his life.

'Fighting again?' said Nancy despairingly as Tom arrived
home bruised and bloody. 'With that Jim Salter?'

Tom nodded.

'He's always beating you up,' said Sylvia, looking up from
her homework.

'It really is too bad! Just look at your new shirt. Torn to
shreds and those shirts don't grow on trees!' Nancy pursed her
lips and spoke with unaccustomed determination. 'I'll have a
talk to his mother.'

'No - don't... please!' Tom pleaded, already thinking of the
awful retribution that would surely follow such meddling on
his mother's part. Even Sylvia was shocked.

'You can't do that, mum!'

His father proved an unexpected ally.

'Leave it, Nance. The boy's got to fight his own battles.
Don't mollycoddle him.'

He looked at Tom proudly. 'No more'n we used to when I
was a lad. Always scrapping, we were. God's Wonderful
Railway against the rest, eh Tom?'

He winked, and Tom felt once again that he was being
drawn into a strange, uneven alliance with his father and the
person his father thought he was, and everything within Tom
shied away from this complicity, which was not complicity at
all, but a gigantic lie that rested at the heart of their relationship.
But it was too complex to put into words and too vague and
shadowy to pin down and it all meant so very much to his
father. Tom muttered something, went to the sink and washed
his wounds.

For the Great Western Railway meant everything to Fred.
One Sunday afternoon, when Tom was ten years old, Fred
reached for the heavy, leather-bound family bible and took out

a well-worn sheet of paper. It was a family tree, written out carefully in spidery handwriting.

Fred passed it reverentially to Tom. 'Here, Tom. Take a look at this. See, there's always been a Watcyn working for the Company right from the start. Look, that's the Welsh spelling of the name. I only changed it to the English when I moved to Gloucester shed. Changed my Christian name, too. Or rather it got changed for me. "Not another bloody Welshman," was how Ron Haddon greeted me. Shed Foreman he was at the time and a sour-faced man at that. "I've got two Gruffydd's already, you'll have to be Fred. Fred Watkins. Too bloody confusing otherwise."' Fred laughed. 'Poor old Ron. Only found out afterwards that he suffered from piles something chronic which accounted for his sourness. We used to wonder why it was he never sat down. Thought it was because he always liked to appear busy. Years later when I met him by chance down the 'Western he was a changed man. "Should have had the bloody operation years ago," he confessed. "The missis kept nagging, but I was plain scared of hospitals and that's the truth of it." So I became Fred Watkins and Fred Watkins I stayed, and when I moved to Acton Chalcote as a Passed Fireman the name went with me and got passed on to you.'

He ran his finger down the well-thumbed sheet. 'Did you know that your great-grandfather - his name was Thomas, too, but spelt Tomos, the Welsh way, worked for Isambard Kingdom Brunel himself in constructing the line from Paddington to Bristol? That was in 1841. He was only a platelayer, mind, but his son - your grandfather - became a driver at Rhydhafren and drivers we Watkins have remained ever since.'

Fred was something of a snob when it came to the pecking order of the Company's servants, and the engine driver was among the elite.

Tom handed it back and Fred folded it up carefully and replaced it in the bible.

'Wait there. Got something else to show you,' he said. He went upstairs and came back with an old photograph album which was filled with stern Victorian gentlemen, bearded for the most part, upright, unbending, the very essence of sobriety, respectability, and devotion to duty. Some of the photographs had been taken in groups outside the Ebenezer Baptist Chapel which, along with the railway, had played a large part in his family's history, others were of men standing solidly in front of ancient and immaculate steam engines. At the back of the album Fred brought out documents of thin, yellowing parchment paper with dust in their creases and showed Tom letters of acceptance, of commendation, of detailed conditions of work, of the approval of sections of railway property as allotments: the entire working life of these worthy figures were spread out before Tom that Sunday afternoon.

Tom never forgot that day. There was his mother, sitting in her chair beside the fire, her hands busy with a pile of mending, her hair an aureole of brightness in the firelight, a placid expression on her face, as if her thoughts were far away. Sylvia looked at the photographs and laughed at some of the people, but soon got bored and went off to play with her dolls. But Tom, just as bored, was somehow held to his father's side. Possibly because he knew instinctively just how deeply Fred would be hurt if he once displayed his lack of interest, or if he once ridiculed those fading reminders of the past. But it was more than that. Those mementoes laid a burden on Tom which he was unwilling to shoulder yet unable to evade.

As the evening drew to its close, Fred carefully folded up the fragile documents, briefly caressing each one with a hard, leathery hand. He placed them back in the album and looked at Tom.

'So you'll be following in a fine tradition, lad, a fine tradition.'

And Tom would feel the ghostly brushing of something at the back of his neck and the black spot on his horizon moved a little closer.

That was it. There was no question about it. No element of choice, no decision to be made. Tom would naturally follow his father and his father before him and his father before that as a servant of the Great Western Railway Company. It was as fixed and immutable as the existence of God or the knowledge that Jim Salter would give him a beating in the near future, or bath nights on Friday or the left-over Sunday joint on Monday. Everything in Tom's life - his education, his friends, his model railway, was fashioning him towards that one end - to make him a worthy successor to his father, and everyone knew that that was no small thing to which to aspire, for Fred was a top link driver and the most senior as well as the most respected man at Acton Chalcote engine shed.

And because Tom was no rebel, come his last day at school the black spot on his horizon had become a reality. Tom's childhood was over and his working life about to begin.

Steam in the Family

Chapter Two

At ten minutes to seven precisely - for Fred liked to be early rather than just on time - the front door opened, and he and Tom appeared. The fact that they used the front rather than the back door signified the importance of the occasion for the front door was normally only used for strangers, weddings, and funerals. Nancy stood on the doorstep and watched them walk down the short path, past the neatly trimmed hedges to the wooden garden gate.

'Good luck!' she called and Tom half-turned his head in acknowledgement. Nancy caught a glimpse of his tense, drawn face before he and his father disappeared down Station Road.

With a worried sigh she returned to the kitchen, surveyed the mess of dirty crockery and poured herself a cup of tea.

'Any left in the pot?' Sylvia had quietly entered the room.

'Oh, yes, help yourself.'

Sylvia poured herself a cup, then sat down and looked at her mother.

'He'll be all right.'

There was a long pause.

'Yes. I suppose so. Yes. It's so important to your father. I just wish...' She gave a long sigh and was silent again.

'What?'

'Oh...' Nancy sighed again. 'I suppose it'll all work out. These things usually do.' Her voice trailed away.

The walk to the shed was accomplished in silence. Fred walked briskly and purposefully, swinging his heavy black railwayman's box as if it weighed little or nothing. He was, as ever, immaculately turned out in faded but scrupulously clean railwayman's jacket and trousers, white shirt, collar, tie, drivers' cap, and gleaming black boots.

From time to time he glanced down at his slight, pale-faced son. Tom was dressed in his brand-new overalls, given to him a week ago when he was summoned to the foreman's office to sign on and be given a tour round the shed and yard. His sandwiches were wrapped in a piece of cloth which he clutched to his chest as if for comfort.

Fred's covert glances contained a mixture of ill-concealed pride, tinged with a hint of anxiety. Pride, because he had dreamt about, longed for and worried over this moment for many years. Fifteen in all... more if one counted the small grave in the corner of the churchyard with its sad reminder of Tom and Sylvia's older brother. Fred thought fleetingly of his firstborn child, who had died after just five days of life. Then there had been a long gap before Sylvia's arrival and two miscarriages soon after. Both boys. That had been the time when the first real anxieties had crept into Fred's mind. Perhaps there would be no more children, more especially, no son to carry on the family name and tradition.

But with Tom's first lusty cries all Fred's hopes and ambitions had revived and centred on this one small scrap of humanity. Precious, because the birth had been difficult and Nancy would bear him no more children, doubly precious, because Tom had been a sickly baby who fell for every childish ailment in the district and a few more besides. Fred thought back to the numerous occasions when Nancy had met him at the back door with a worried face and the news that Tom was poorly again. He thought of the long hours he had spent anxiously waiting while Tom's illnesses had run their course and of the near despair he had felt during a particularly bad bout of influenza. But Tom had pulled through time and again, showing remarkable tenacity as well as a fine pair of lungs.

It was past history now. Tom was as tough as they come, thought Fred with another surge of pride. Maybe tougher, because of what he had gone through as a child.

He glanced at Tom once more and caught the drawn expression in his son's face. For a fleeting moment Fred sensed something of Tom's terror being held in behind the barricade of the tightly held sandwiches. The vague anxieties Fred sometimes felt about his son swam to the surface, but they were anxieties to which he could never admit, for to admit to them would be to recognise truths about himself which Fred could not do, for he was not a man given to introspective thought. So, he walked confidently and surely, nodding and smiling at every passer-by and giving a cheery 'good-evening' to every acquaintance. For it was a good evening, the best in fact. Tom would be all right. He would do. Wasn't he his son after all?

They reached the bottom of Station Road, crossed over and, instead of bearing right which was the direct way to the station, they made their way down a narrow pathway leading to the footbridge which crossed the main line. The bridge was used almost exclusively by railwaymen based at the shed who were not permitted to cross through the station to and from work but had to take this more circuitous route. The paint was flaking and the wooden boards shiny with constant use.

Once over the bridge, which for some long-forgotten reason was called Barney's Bridge, a well-worn path of cinders, beaten flat and smooth by generations of locomen, led across the waste ground towards the rear of the station. A gate, similar in design to their own front gate and of a type multiplied a hundredfold on Great Western property throughout the country, marked the boundary of the Company's land and led to a walkway behind the station.

Acton Chalcote Station was of moderate size and typically Great Western in design with its distinctive fringed canopy protecting the three platforms from the worst of the weather.

Platform One, the down main line, was on the same side as the station buildings. A double, straight-through track for non-stop expresses and goods trains separated the two main platform loop lines. Platforms Two and Three formed an island which was reached by means of a long footbridge spanning the four tracks. Behind Platform Three were two goods sidings, and to the rear of those sidings was the walkway leading to the south end of the station and the engine shed beyond. The station was controlled by signal boxes at the north and south ends and the whole was presided over with tight-lipped concentration and a keen sense of duty by Mr Elmes, the small, bustling stationmaster.

That evening the station glowed dusty and weary in the late sunshine. The main onslaught of the early evening traffic had passed, leaving a battered, worn-out atmosphere enhanced by the elderly porter who was slowly and with much apparent effort pushing a large broom along Platform Two. Another porter, younger but equally tired in appearance, watered the flowers that grew in well-organised beds along the edge of the fence on Platform One.

Posters advertising holiday resorts beckoned invitingly from the station hoardings, but the few people wearily awaiting the arrival of the seven-ten were sunk into a warm, early-evening somnolence, seemingly oblivious of the many tempting offers to travel on 'the holiday route to the sun, by courtesy of the Great Western Railway'.

This lethargy continued even when the train could be seen approaching, but as it entered the station, the elderly porter abandoned his broom with astonishing speed and sprang into life.

'Acton Chalcote! Acton Chalcote! This train is for Birmingham, stopping at Bishopsholme, Matchurch and all stations to Birmingham Snow Hill. Change here for Malcester. This is Acton Chalcote!'

The train brought with it a sense of urgency. As it ran along the edge of the platform, doors were already opening in the passengers' anxiety to get home. The train came to a stand with the engine stopping close by the water column. Fred also came to a stand in order to watch 'Comet', the Duke of Cornwall class 4-4-0 engine, come to rest. It was as natural as breathing for Fred to pause and glance at any engine that happened to be in the station. The driver, a stocky figure with grizzled hair, leaned over the side and hailed him.

'"Evening, Fred!'

'"Evening Chalky,' Fred nodded at the engine. 'Isn't the old girl due for Swindon?'

Chalky nodded agreement. 'About bloody time they had her in. She's riding rough and knocking in the boxes.' He glanced at Tom, standing behind his father. 'Your lad?'

'Aye.' Fred was unable to keep the pride out of his voice. 'He's starting work today.'

Chalky stared critically at Tom. 'Can see the likeness,' he pronounced at last. He smiled suddenly, exposing startling front teeth that stuck out like fangs. 'You'll do all right, lad. Have to, seeing who your old man is. All the best, eh?'

'Thanks,' Tom muttered.

The sun was touching the bank leading to the coal stage as he and Fred approached the yard. Tom looked down at the shed and drew in his breath sharply. For an instant only it was transformed. In those few seconds until the sun slipped behind the bank, the engines seemed creatures of another world, beautiful and majestic as their copper-capped chimneys flamed with sudden gold. Spirals of white steam climbed high into the still air, tinged with pink from the dying sun, while the pall of soot and smoke that always hung over the yard was touched with magic as a million particles of coal reflected back the light and shone like an iridescent veil.

'Beautiful, isn't it,' said Fred with quiet satisfaction.

Tom glanced at his father and saw, in a sudden moment of closeness, that Fred had seen and felt as he had. The moment was as fleeting as the transformation of the yard. A small tank engine at the foot of the ramp leading up to the coaling stage suddenly reversed with a loud clank of metal on metal as the coal wagons pushed each other on their slow way up the hill towards the coal stage. The metallic sound broke the spell and, as if on cue, the sun dropped swiftly out of sight and the engines were only engines, the dust only dust and the pall of soot and smoke no longer a magic veil, but a dark, smothering cloud.

The engine shed was a busy, noisy, dirty place. Here the locomotives reigned supreme, their needs being attended to by an army of people who swarmed in, on and around them, preparing them for work or stabling them for cleaning or boiler washouts. The place hummed with an activity of which Tom was only dimly aware. Later, this kaleidoscope of sights, smells and sounds would resolve itself into the myriad jobs which make up the working of a busy shed, and later still those same engines of which he was only vaguely conscious would take on identities as individual and idiosyncratic as the men he worked with, but that was all in the future.

As they passed down the yard, Fred commented on the engines, but his remarks were incomprehensible to Tom, who felt as distanced as ever from his father. The shared moment by the coal stage might never have taken place. He shivered, although the evening was mild, and clutched his parcel of sandwiches more tightly.

He could not help noticing, however, how Fred seemed to expand with every step they took. His footsteps, firm at any time, became firmer, his eyes brighter and his greetings to all within hailing distance became louder and more cordial. It was as if he were coming home, and Tom glimpsed a side of his father that he had rarely seen. He did not realise that much of

Fred's intense pleasure that evening came from having his son beside him.

They crossed the barrow crossing and walked round the side of the sand furnace. There they almost collided with a man staggering slightly under the weight of two buckets full of sand.

'Sorry about that,' said the man cheerfully, in a strong Welsh accent. He put down the buckets and wiped his brow with an oily hand. 'Fine evening, Mr Watkins.'

But Fred, who had treated everyone within earshot with a good-natured friendliness, ignored the apology. His face set in hard lines and he merely grunted before brushing past the man and walking on towards the shed. His father's behaviour was surprising, so uncharacteristic of everything that had gone before, that Tom turned to look.

He saw a man in his late twenties or early thirties, sturdily built but with a certain lithe grace about him. Dai Davies had the dark hair and features of the Welsh but was taller than the average. His face was sensitive and intelligent and his habitual expression one of faintly amused cynicism. Now, however, he just looked astonished. He caught Tom's glance and grinned ruefully.

'Now whatever did I say?' he murmured, before lifting the heavy buckets and continuing on his way.

Tom entered the engine shed. The air struck cool after the warmth of the evening. It took his eyes a moment to adjust to the darkness, but then Tom could see row after row of engines, some cold and dead, some in light steam. Tom looked up, following the thin trails of smoke which drifted up to the air ducts high in the roof.

The shed was built on massive lines, not of human size, but to accommodate the largest locomotives. It seemed to stretch away to infinity. At intervals along the wall closest to Tom were a number of doors, tiny and out of all proportion, looking for all the world like entrances to rabbit holes in some vast mountainside. The sheer size and immensity of the place overwhelmed Tom, and he remained just inside the entrance, half fearful of taking another step.

Fred turned. 'Right. This is where we part company.'

He hesitated, strangely ill-at-ease. He glanced at his son, and Tom's face stared back at him, solemn, pale, with eyes that darted nervously from one object to another. Fred felt a wave of compassion, a desire to protect, to help, to set him right. There was so much he could explain. But Tom would have to learn the hard way, just as he had done.

'Why don't you go down to the cleaner's cabin as you're early?' he said, and his voice sounded almost brusque in his effort to hide his feelings. 'I expect Alf'll be along soon to sort you out. He's Chargeman Cleaner.'

'Right.'

'It's down there,' Fred said, waving a hand towards a closed door. 'Well, you know that don't you? I expect it was pointed out when you came.' He hesitated once more and cleared his throat. 'Well - I won't go giving you a lot of advice - you wouldn't take any notice if I did. You've got to stand on your own feet and learn by your own mistakes - right? You just do what the gaffer tells you and no messing.' He paused. 'If I hear you've been cheeking your betters, you'll have me to deal with - understand?'

'Yes dad.'

Fred's face softened as he looked at his son.

'Not that you're that sort of lad, I'll say that for you.' He hesitated again. Words were so inadequate. 'Well, all the best then. Not that you'll need it, mind. You'll do all right.'

With that he gave a slight nod, turned, and went in through a door which led to the booking on lobby. Tom just had time to see a room full of people and hear Fred's loud greetings before the door closed behind him.

He took a deep, almost relieved, breath, stood still for a moment looking around before he slowly made his way down the shed to the cleaner's cabin. He paused outside the door, took another deep breath, and opened it wide.

He was confronted by a row of upturned, grinning, nervously expectant faces. He took a step over the threshold and, in an instant, a bucket of dirty oil, water and ashes emptied itself neatly over his head and began trickling down his neck, making black rivulets down his new clean clothes. His mouth and nose were full of the taste and smell of the vile mixture, and he was momentarily blinded. Coughing and spluttering, he wiped a hand over his eyes, blinked rapidly, and was just able to make out a group of eight or so people in the room, most of them his own age and known to him.

A roar of laughter and cheers greeted his entrance, swiftly followed a hail of oily cotton waste. Seconds later he was surrounded by boys, well pleased with themselves, thumping him on the back, laughing at his discomfiture and generally making him welcome. There was Ginger, his flaming mass of carrot-coloured hair at odds with the gentle, almost anxious, expression on his plain face. Les was next, small and sharp-featured, both friends from school and both senior to him as employees of the Great Western Railway by a matter of weeks. There was Billy and his brother Bob, whose father, like his own, was a driver at the shed. Tom's eyes slid past the grinning, self-conscious cleaners and took in his surroundings as he tried to assimilate the shock of the practical joke that had just been played.

The cleaner's cabin was a sordid place, inhabited by lads who had neither the slightest idea nor the remotest inclination for keeping the room in any semblance of order or cleanliness. It was a depressing room containing a vast amount of broken-down items which, in better days, had been furniture, engine parts and other objects which had long since outlived any usefulness. These items arrived by way of the engineman's cabin, after the drivers and firemen had discarded them. As they only went to the enginemen after they were of no further use to the Company, and as the Company was scrupulous in exacting the greatest possible use from all its possessions, the state of the objects in the cleaner's cabin can well be imagined. The only recognisable items of furniture consisted of a couple of wooden benches, much scarred, a carriage seat with stuffing and springs hanging out, and a table with two of its original legs missing which leant drunkenly against a wall, propped up with bits of old wooden sleepers.

Despite the repeated efforts of the Chargeman Cleaner to get the lads under his authority to keep the place clean and tidy, grubby overalls were strewn around the room, left where their owners had wriggled out of them, lunch boxes were piled on every available surface, and dirty cotton waste lay in indiscriminate heaps.

Although never overly fussy himself, the cabin did nothing to raise Tom's spirits, dampened as they were by dirty oil and water which was even now seeping through his clothes.

There was a sudden movement from a corner of the room. Tom looked and saw an ancient stove belching forth black smoke. A figure stepped from behind the stove and Tom saw, with a second shock almost as great as the first, the well-known features and solid shape of Jim Salter standing apart from the rest, a malicious smile on his face.

Tom stared in disbelief. Jim Salter, that staunch supporter of the rival railway company, that implacable enemy of himself, his friends, and all things Great Western. How could Jim ever have made his way so far into hostile territory as to be standing in the cleaner's cabin of the Great Western Railway's engine shed at Acton Chalcote?

'Jim?'

'The same,' Jim said, enjoying Tom's confusion.

Ginger took his arm. 'You get cleaned up over here,' he said, guiding Tom towards a bucket. Tom bent over and plunged his head into the cold water while a babble of different conversations began to fill the air.

'You liked my little welcome then?' Jim's strident voice spoke above the general noise.

Tom straightened up, took the piece of clean cotton waste that Ginger was holding out to him, and began to wipe his face.

'Take no notice,' Ginger advised in a low voice. 'They did the same to me when I started - they do it to everyone. It's just one of those things.'

Tom did not answer, and Ginger found his silence unnerving.

'Honestly - they do it to everyone and if they don't do that, they do even worse. They stripped old Bob starkers and smothered him with engine grease - didn't they Bob?'

'They did that,' said Bob, smiling with pride at the recollection, but Tom was not listening.

'You work here?' he asked Jim.

'Any reason why I shouldn't?'

'But your dad's with the North Eastern.'

'So?'

'You always said....'

'What? That I'd never work for the Great Way Round Railway?'

Tom was silent and the talk among the boys in the room stopped, for the tension between the two was tangible and stretched back over the years.

'The 'Western gave me a job and I didn't get it handed on a plate on account of who my dad is,' Jim said mockingly, glancing at the cleaners ranged round the room.

Everyone shifted uncomfortably, for most had family connections with the Great Western, but none of them would challenge Jim. They left that, as they had always done, to Tom.

Tom reached for another piece of cotton waste and began wiping the worst of the oil from his clothes.

'I like to make my own way in life, and I fight my own battles,' Jim continued, his eyes fixed on Tom. He was provoking, attacking, hitting out first as was his custom. Tom suddenly felt very tired.

'Yes,' he said quietly. 'You always were a bully.'

The room was totally silent now. Jim stood in the centre, large, solid, a fixed smile on his face. The boys looked from one to the other, just as they had done time after time in the school playground when the two protagonists squared up for a fight. Weariness dragged at Tom like a great weight, dulling his senses. It was all so unfair.

Why had no-one told him? Ginger, Les, Bill, Bob, Doug... they all knew. Why hadn't they prepared him? And why did they now apparently accept Jim, looking up to him, treating him with deference? At school the opposing groups had never met except in battle in the playground. Tom shook his head. It was as if the rules of the game had been changed without anyone telling him, leaving him following a childhood antipathy that had long since been discarded.

He looked at Jim, seeing how his mouth hardened and his eyes coolly calculated the form his reprisal would take. No, the game had not changed, Jim had not changed, but his friends had. He felt resentful. How could they make Jim welcome? How could they, knowing how contemptuously Jim felt about them, their fathers, the Company? And the supreme irony being that Tom was to be the one left fighting for a cause which meant nothing to him at all.

Jim laughed suddenly and turned his back. The tension eased.

'Fancy a cuppa?' Ginger asked nervously.

'No thanks.'

Ginger glanced uncertainly at Tom, then moved away. More cleaners drifted in as the day and night shifts mingled. Glances were thrown in Tom's direction and one or two attempts made to draw him into various conversations. Their talk swirled incomprehensibly past him.

'...down the nick he was, honest...'

'No!'

'Honest. Other side of Chalcote bank...'

'There I was, giving the old girl a nice dry wipe when along comes the gaffer and he says, "Where's your oil, Jones?"'

'...the steam pressure'd dropped right down...'

'...3205's left hand injector...'

Waves of talk surfaced, eddied and sank, leaving Tom stranded, alone and lonely.

Then Jim's voice, confident, assured, cutting across the rest.

'Heard the latest about Billy?'

A chorus of voices answered.

'He's refusing to give Sammy White any oil until Sammy apologises for calling him a squint-eyed Brummy bastard for not letting him have any more cotton waste. Sammy's going to complain to the gaffer.'

'Wouldn't be Sammy's mate today. Mad as fire he'll be.'

Exclamations and comments. Everyone flocked across to Jim who glanced at Tom, an arrogant glance, daring him to dispute his authority. Tom looked away and Jim smiled.

'Billy says he may be squint-eyed and he was born in Birmingham, but he doesn't allow anyone to question his parentage, and if Sammy'd like to make the trip to Balsall Heath he'll see it all written up in the church register. They were at it just a moment ago, having a right old ding dong.'

Roars of laughter greeted this. Tom walked across to the broken carriage seat and sat down on the cushion with its gaping hole oozing stuffing, black and disgusting from contact with the grimy backsides of countless cleaners.

Nobody so much as glanced in his direction as the day shift went home and the night shift prepared for work.

Chapter Three

The film was half-way through when Sylvia's attention began to wander. She had already seen the same film all last week and five times this - six if one counted the matinee on Tuesday. And although a fan of Clark Gable, even the most ardent fan might tire after such repeated exposure.

She glanced over at Florence and wrinkled her nose. 'Not one of his best films is it?' she hissed.

Florence grinned, then put her finger to her lips. They'd get into trouble if they were caught whispering on duty.

Sylvia leaned against the wooden partition at the back of the stalls and slipped her feet out of her shoes. That was better. What on earth possessed her to wear her new pair tonight? It wasn't as if she was meeting Cyril after the show.

Florence shook her head warningly.

'Watch it!' she mouthed, and nodded towards the office where Mr Wilson sat, the back of his head with its sparse strands of white hair clearly visible through the glass partition. Sylvia pulled a face at Mr Wilson's head and wriggled her toes luxuriously on the carpet. Mr Wilson wouldn't come out until the closing titles. He never did. She gave a fleeting thought to the elderly manager who had been there for as long as she could remember, long, even, before the time when her mother played the piano at the cinema. He must be near retirement.

Her mind wandered. What would Cyril be like when he was near retirement? The thought made her giggle and Flo shot her another warning glance. Would he still be as correct, as formal, as pedantic as he was now? Would he still choose plaice when dining out at Sid's? She giggled again and stuck her tongue out at Flo's frown of annoyance.

What right had Flo to be so superior? It was she, after all, who had made that first joke about Cyril. It was the night they'd all gone to Sid's for late fish and chips after the show. They used to go regularly, Flo and her steady Walter, Sylvia and Cyril, and it was the same every time. Cyril would keep everyone waiting while he read through the menu with absorbed interest, despite knowing, as they all did, Sid's limited range of meals off by heart. Eventually he would put the menu carefully down on the table, aligning it precisely alongside the salt and pepper. Then he would stare into space, purse up his mouth and pronounce, in a tone of great deliberation, 'I think… I think… I'll have the plaice.'

Time after time. Always the same. 'I think… I think… I'll have the plaice.' The three would wait in an agony of mounting hysteria as they willed themselves not to look at each other in case they started to laugh. It would be unkind to laugh for Cyril was very sensitive. It grew so bad that in the end they were forced to abandon Sid's and as there was no-where else to eat out late in the evening they stopped going out as a foursome altogether.

Sylvia felt a flicker of anger at Cyril who, all unwittingly, had broken up those evenings. This was followed by a feeling of guilt. Poor Cyril, with his slicked-down hair firmly parted on the left, his high-pitched voice, his small mouth pursed into an 'o', his safe job at the bank. It wasn't his fault. But it was high time she got rid of him and found someone else. It was a shame really, for he surprised her many times with small, unobtrusive kindnesses - and large doses of boredom, she thought firmly.

She shrugged her shoulders and discarded Cyril with as much ease and as little compunction as she had discarded Joe and George and Ronald and all the other young men who had been dazzled by her abundance of dark hair and large, mischievous eyes.

She looked down the length of the cinema, past the rows of backs of heads, some attentively watching the screen, some engrossed in one another, one or two slumped down in sleep. It was a full house. She strained her eyes to see whether the seat at the back of the stalls on the extreme left had been taken, but it was impossible to tell. She considered flicking her torch briefly over the area but that would only disturb the audience, incur more disapproving looks from Flo, and, if he was sitting there, he would know why she had done it. She would hate that. Besides, he couldn't possibly be in the audience again. He wouldn't have the nerve after the brush-off she had given him only yesterday.

At first, she had barely been aware of him, other than mentally marking him down as one of the regulars. But then she had noticed him staring at her as she showed people to their seats. He had an appraising look in his eyes and smiled, a lazy, mocking smile with a hint of complicity, as if they both shared some secret joke. Sylvia had turned away, confused and a bit angry, both with him and with herself for her sudden awareness of his dark good looks and her own shiny nose in need of powder.

The following evening, he had been there, in the same seat, and most evenings after that. The seat had been chosen, it seemed, not for its uninterrupted view of the screen but for its uninterrupted view of herself. She found herself missing him on the evenings when he did not come and was angry with herself for that as well.

She asked Flo who he was and Flo, who knew everyone and everything that happened in Acton Chalcote said that he was a railwayman who worked at the same shed as Sylvia's father. Flo said his name was Dai Davies and that he came from Wales which explained, Sylvia thought, his dark good looks.

From then on she had tried to ignore him, to live up to her avowed intention never to get involved with a railwayman. But he showed a steadfastness in his pursuit which demonstrated both his arrogance and his determination. It was both flattering and irritating.

The film came to an end and curtains swept across the screen. The audience stirred, when the spell was broken, as if out of a long sleep. Sylvia put on her shoes and stood with the audience while 'God Save the King' was played. The house lights came up and the audience began making their way to the exits. Flo saw them out of the foyer while Sylvia walked up and down the aisles checking for belongings left behind.

'Hello my lovely.'

The quiet voice made her jump and she whirled round.

'You, again!'

Dai smiled deprecatingly.

'You've got a cheek!' Sylvia went on warmly.

'I live in hope. And I happen to be a devotee of the cinema.'

'Well, the performance is over, so would you kindly leave the auditorium' Sylvia said in her most repressive voice.

'Very nicely said.' The man held out his hand. 'How about a cup of tea and fish and chips at Sid's, or would you prefer something stronger?'

'Look,' Sylvia began, dropping her air of formality. 'You're wasting your time.'

'Going to the cinema? I don't think Mr Wilson would like to hear you say that. You're not supposed to put off ardent cinemagoers like myself. Anyway, I enjoyed the film. Not as much as I did the first time round. Only the best films, I think, stand up well to seeing them five nights running - wouldn't you agree?'

As this echoed Sylvia's own feelings so precisely, she wisely said nothing. Dai glanced at her with understanding.

'I don't know how you girls manage to keep awake seeing the same thing night after night. When does the programme change?'

'I don't go out with railwaymen.'

'That must restrict you enormously in a town like this,' Dai commented. 'I mean, who else is there?'

Sylvia thought fleetingly of Cyril but said nothing.

'It's either us handsome, virile men of the Great Western or those North Eastern lot. Which do you prefer?'

'That's none of your business.'

'What's wrong with railwaymen anyway?' Dai asked with interest.

'I'm not marrying anyone who works that sort of barmy hours,' Sylvia blurted out and blushed bright red.

A slow smile spread across Dai's face.

'Aren't you being just a little bit premature?' he asked gently. 'I'd be honoured, of course, but this is the longest conversation I've had with you so far so I think we should get to know each other a little more before we start thinking of marriage. Which brings us back to Sid's.'

Sylvia turned away. 'Flo... Flo... wait for me.!' She turned back, well in control of herself. 'I'm sorry, sir, I'm still on duty. If you don't mind....?'

Dai smiled at her, a warm, understanding smile. '"Til tomorrow then. Sleep well, my lovely.'

Sylvia watched him go. She was suddenly tired, deflated, and depressed. She glanced at her watch. Nearly eleven o'clock. Her feet in their new shoes throbbed and ached and she wanted to go home.

****

An hour later Police Constable Herbert Grant flashed his torch at his watch, thought longingly of a nice strong cup of tea and cheese sandwich and turned into Station Road.

He glanced along the street and was reassured by the quiet. Not that he really expected anything else. Apart from the odd foolishness late on Saturday nights after the pubs had closed when some drink-fuelled hotheads from the two engine sheds had squared up to one another, Acton Chalcote was a mainly law-abiding town.

P.C. Grant shivered. Despite the warmth of the day, the temperature had plummeted within the last hour and a cool wind had sprung up. He moved briskly to keep his circulation going and cast experienced middle-aged eyes from one side of the road to the other, from one blank, anonymous house to the next, their windows, for the most part, tightly shut against the night air. It was very still, and the silence enveloped him like a cloak.

Gas lamps cast their creamy-yellow light at intervals up the street, creating faint pools which illuminated the pavement and road around them and reflected back from the neatly trimmed hedges. A bicycle, parked by the kerb, was trapped within the radius of one of the lights.

The sound of several small stones pattering against glass abruptly shattered the quiet. P.C. Grant stopped and listened. The sound of more stones followed, and he moved swiftly towards the source. He paused for a moment and shone his torch on the bicycle. It was a well-used machine painted dark brown. Its tyres were worn, and the words 'Great Western Railway' had been painted along the crossbar in cream letters, with many curls and flourishes.

P.C. Grant straightened up in time to hear a disembodied voice shouting from behind the hedge of an adjacent house.

'Driver Jones! Driver Jones!'

An upstairs window was suddenly flung wide, and a man's night-capped head appeared in the opening.

'Driver Jones, one fifteen shed pilot!'

'Ta very much,' said the man and the window banged shut.

The policeman waited until Tom emerged into the street, then shone his torch full in his face. Tom flung up his arm to shield his eyes.

'New, aren't you? asked the policeman in a conversational voice. He switched off his torch.

Tom, somewhat shaken, crossed to his bicycle.

'Yes.'

'What happened to the other lad, the ginger one?'

'I've taken over from him,' Tom explained.

P.C. Grant stared at Tom in silence, committing his features to memory. He saw a thin lad with a scared face dressed in oil-streaked clothes. Over the years the policeman had seen many such lads as Tom. He felt inclined to chat.

'Seems bloody daft, doesn't it,' he said. 'You'd think the railway'd buy their staff alarm clocks instead of using you lads. What's your name, sonny?'

'Tom. Tom Watkins.'

'Mmm. Your dad's a driver, isn't he?'

'Yes.'

'Thought I'd seen him down the pub a couple of times. And how old are you, Tom?'

'Fifteen.'

'Well then lad, there's a cup of tea down the station if you've a mind.'

Tom looked at his long list of calls. 'I haven't time,' he said regretfully.

'All right. Some other night, eh?' And with that P.C. Grant continued his stately progress up Station Road.

Tom shivered slightly, picked up his bicycle and rode off in the opposite direction. He cycled along streets he had known since childhood, streets which were as familiar to him as his own bedroom. But they were now unfamiliar, alien places filled with the desolation of lost identity which falls on a town in the early hours of the morning.

As he cycled, he thought back over the long evening. But tiredness had made time shift and Tom could remember nothing other than isolated incidents that remained vividly imprinted on his mind.

There had been Alf Wittall's arrival at the cleaner's cabin. When the gaunt, elderly man, leaning heavily on his stick, had opened the door, the crescendo of noise had ceased as if by magic, for the Chargeman Cleaner did not just exude an air of authority, he was authority personified. With a minimum of words, some of them bitingly sarcastic, Alf had dispatched the cleaners to their jobs and the room had emptied in seconds.

Finally he had turned to Tom, who was standing fearfully pressed against the wall.

'Fred Watkins' lad, isn't it?'

'Yes, sir.'

Alf subjected Tom to a brief, piercing scrutiny.

'Your father fired to me when I was still driving,' he said at last, and Tom, relieved at the mild words, had felt again the burden of being his father's son.

'You shouldn't have started on night shift but we're short-handed. A couple of lads off sick. I spoke to Fred and your dad said he'd speak to you, but he was sure you wouldn't mind.'

Tom felt a moment's resentment. His father hadn't spoken to him about it, but then, he thought wryly, he wouldn't have expected him to.

'You'll be helping Billy Hughes in stores,' Alf went on, 'but mainly you'll be calling up. Go and book on, then report to Billy.'

Booking on. Tom cycled through the dark streets while a vision of the booking on lobby rose in his mind. A bright, large, bustling, noisy room with a counter at the far end and rows of free-standing notice boards forming a series of aisles down the entire length. The lobby had been full of men, booking on and off duty, reading notices, exclaiming at rosters, complaining, chatting, laughing.

Tom had joined the end of the queue which stretched down to the counter.

'Watkins. Tom. I'm new,' he said when his turn came to speak to the time-keeper on the far side of the glass partition.

'Watkins, eh? Wouldn't be old Fred's son, would it?'

'Yes.'

'Fancy that now. Old Fred's lad.' A brass disc was pushed towards him. 'Here's your number. Don't go losing it. You hand it in when you book off and collect it every time you book on. Got it?'

'Thank you.'

Clutching the small rectangular disc with the number 188 stamped in the centre, Tom turned to go, then hesitated.

'What you after son?' asked a man directly behind him.

'Stores. Billy Hughes in stores.'

The man laughed. 'Here, listen to this, lads. Here's someone wanting Billy Hughes.'

Those in the immediate vicinity laughed. Tom looked uncomprehendingly from one person to the next.

'Just follow the sound of his voice, lad. You can't miss it.'

'It's next door,' said the first man.

As Tom puffed and panted his way up the steep hill to the back of the town he thought of the round face, thick pebble glasses, small eyes, and precise mouth of Billy Hughes.

'You weigh out this cotton waste for me and make sure you weigh it out proper, mind, into half pounds and quarter pounds, because I've got to account for it and, if you're not careful lad,

57

these drivers'll have you giving them more than their share. And I know what they get up to 'cos I was one of them myself. The trouble I've had with some of them now, you wouldn't believe. Sammy White for instance, now there's a villain for you! Quarter pound of waste he's entitled to, being on relief turn, and don't tell me he doesn't know it because he does...'

Accompanied by this unending voice Tom had weighed out the cotton waste, handed oil and paraffin to drivers, firemen and cleaners, sorted lamps and engine spares and placed them on their allotted shelves. And all the while Billy had talked and talked and talked...

'...a mouthful of abuse is what I get. So I refuse to give him any oil until he's apologised and now he's threatening me with the gaffer, and I don't know what else besides. Threaten as much as he likes, he won't scare me. "Listen son", I said, "you don't know the half of it. Billy Hughes was driving the runners when you were still soiling your nappies!" He didn't like that, I can tell you! But you've got to be firm with them, lad, you've got to be firm...'

Life to Billy was a single-handed crusade against the drivers and firemen receiving stores to which they were rightfully entitled. King of his small domain he jealously guarded the Company's property to the extent where it became an achievement to get anything from him at all.

It was past eleven o'clock when Billy handed Tom a list of names and addresses.

'Now these are the drivers and firemen you've to call up. Call 'em in good time and it's important that you make sure they're really awake as they're up to all the tricks and will swear blind you didn't give 'em a knock if you're not careful.'

He nodded towards the bicycle standing in a corner.

'There's your bike. Go on, off with you. And don't say I didn't warn you!' he added as Tom wheeled the bicycle out of the door and thankfully made his escape.

That had been well over an hour ago. Since then he had crossed and recrossed the sleeping town glad, at first, to be out of the shed and revelling in the quiet of the dark streets. But as the night wore on Tom grew anxious. His list of calls seemed as long as ever, his legs were aching, and time appeared to be racing past.

'Driver Southcombe! Two thirty Leominster!'

Silence.

Tom knocked again. 'Driver Southcombe! Two thirty Leominster!'

Silence again. Tom hammered on the door.

'Driver Southcombe! Two thirty Leominster!'

His voice echoed harshly in the quiet night. The window of a neighbouring house was suddenly thrown violently open, and an elderly man leant out.

'If you don't shut your bloody noise, I'll come and shut it for you! I've just had a bloody rough trip back from Newport and I'd like to get some bloody sleep!'

Tom hurried up the road and along the alley which led to the path running behind the backs of the houses. There was no light and he groped along carefully, counting the black outlines of the houses he passed to make sure he stopped at the right one. He opened the gate into the garden and walked straight into George Southcombe's chicken run. Startled chickens began squawking and an elderly dog who had been asleep in his kennel began to bark and strained on the end of his chain in his attempt to repel the intruder.

A light went on in an upstairs room, and from the outdoor toilet in the yard, the placid, portly figure of George Southcombe emerged, not a bit put out by the chaos around him. He carried a copy of the 'Great Western Magazine' in one hand and a railway lamp in the other, which he held up high in order to see the cause of all the commotion.

'Why, it's Fred Watkins' lad, isn't it? This is a nice surprise. Wasn't you shouting back there, was it?'

'I was trying to call you up,' Tom explained apologetically.

'Oh dear, oh dear, sorry about that.' George waved his copy of the magazine. 'I was deep in this - you know how it is - you need a bit of peace and quiet to read the magazine.'

He opened it and held his lamp close to the page. 'Look at this now. "Mr Joseph Evans, a Gloucester City Magistrate, has retired from his position as passenger train driver after forty-four years' service. He was presented by his fellow employees with an armchair as a parting gift."' He closed the magazine and beamed at Tom. 'Isn't that nice now? I know Joe Evans well. Big man you know, bigger than me. Hope it's a big armchair they got him.' He chuckled. 'Well, it's been nice having a chat with you lad, but I mustn't keep you standing about, got a lot more calls to make I expect.'

'You're on two thirty Leominster, Mr Southcombe,' gabbled a desperate Tom.

'Thank you, lad, but I knew that already,' George said placidly. 'Don't bother to call me up in future. Albert next door, well, he's a bit of a light sleeper and he gets cross if he's woken... we've had one or two words about it... not angry ones, you follow me, so I went and bought myself an alarm clock. Does the job beautifully...'

Tom cycled recklessly back across town, missed a cat on the prowl by inches, found the next house on his list, flung down the bicycle, raced to the front door and pounded heavily on it.

'Fireman Marshall! Fireman Marshall! Two thirty Leominster!'

The door was thrown open by an irate Jerry Marshall who glowered at Tom, a rag held against a nick in his chin where he had shaved himself too hastily.

'Why didn't you bleeding well call me on time then?' he growled. 'It's past two now!'

He slammed the door in Tom's face.

****

5935 Norton Hall, one of the 4-6-0 Hall class of engines, thundered through the night, a train of passenger coaches snaking behind. It passed through towns, through suburbs and along the backs of houses, the rhythm of the wheels providing a familiar and comforting background to the dreams of the people asleep within. Then the train thundered out into the country, speeding past fields and woods, a dark shape under the starlit sky.

The thin trail of steam emerging from the engine's chimney was suddenly tinged with a red glow as the firebox doors were opened and the light from the fire reflected upwards. Red-hot glowing sparks and cinders were blown into the night.

Charlie examined the state of the fire, threw a couple of shovelfuls of coal first to one side of the firebox then to the other and clanged the doors shut.

Fred, from his position on the right-hand side of the cab, glanced across but did not speak. There was no need. He and Charlie had worked as mates for many years and together they formed an efficient and harmonious team, working round each other with the minimum of words and the minimum of fuss, crisp in their actions, decisive, anticipating each other's needs and the needs of the engine with the ease of long and accustomed practice.

Fred eased down the regulator and applied the brake and the engine responded, its wheels slowing. He dropped down the lever and watched for the forty mile an hour speed restriction in force on this stretch of the main line.

Fred was in his element on the footplate. It was his natural home. He was part of the machine, at one with it. He drove with the skill of years of experience, but it was more than that, much more. He drove with the responsiveness to the individual requirements of each engine that was intuitive. It was a skill which could not be taught. It was, as Fred himself would say, 'in the blood'.

The speed restriction past, Fred opened the regulator and notched up the lever. The train sped on through the night.

'Tea, Charlie?'

Charlie nodded. He was a short, stocky man in his late forties, an abundance of hair turning grey, a broad, rather vacant-looking face and a strong Black Country accent, denoting his North Midlands origins.

He lifted the square whisky bottle from its place on the ledge above the firebox, poured out two mugs of strong tea and liberally spooned in sugar. He carried one steaming mug over to Fred.

'Tea as mother makes it.'

'Ta.'

Fred took a long swig, opened his railwayman's box and rummaged inside. He brought out a packet of sandwiches, unwrapped them and offered one to Charlie.

'Cheese 'n pickle.'

Charlie shook his head regretfully. 'Mustn't I'm afraid.'

'Same trouble?'

'Aye. Guts been playin' up something shockin'. The missus blames it on the shift work.' He laughed. 'I blames it on her cooking.'

Fred nodded. Charlie's ulcer had been a continuing source of conversation over the years.

Charlie took a drink of tea. 'The missus wants me to pack it in,' he said.

'Pack it in?' Fred was surprised.

'She thinks I could get some cushy job behind a desk. Pen pushing.'

Fred frowned and Charlie chuckled. 'Don't worry, mate. It'd take a lot to get Charlie Pearce off the footplate and it wouldn't be for a soft salaried number either.'

Fred laughed, relieved.

'Besides, I couldn't let my mate down,' Charlie continued. 'Not after all these years.'

'Glad to hear it,' Fred said dryly.

The relationship between the two men was of mutual respect, friendship within the strict confines of the job, and a shared enjoyment of chess. But it was not an equal relationship. Charlie stood in considerable awe of Fred. He was grateful for his friendship, but never presumed upon it or forgot for an instant that Fred was his superior both on and off the footplate. He would say, quite simply, that he didn't have half old Fred's brains. But, to a great extent, Fred's reputation at the shed, although deservedly won, had been fostered by Charlie who would talk to all and sundry over a pint of beer or two down the Railwayman's Club about the greatness of Fred Watkins.

Fred in his turn took Charlie's devotion for granted, treated his faithfulness as a matter of course and used him as a foil whether at work, in company, or playing a quiet game of chess. He valued Charlie as a mate but had grown so used to Charlie's quiet professional skills that he thought them nothing out of the ordinary. The relationship between the two men was that of liberal boss and devoted servant and both were content that it should remain so.

'When's your lad start?' Charlie asked.

'He has already. Tonight.'

'Calling up?'

'I expect so.'

Charlie chuckled. 'I bet he was rarin' to go, eh? Just like his old man.'

The image of Tom's white, taut and nervous face floated into Fred's mind and he felt a momentary disquiet. The feeling was gone in an instant, but it left a slight aftertaste.

'He'll do,' he said abruptly.

He downed the rest of his tea, wiped his hands on a bit of cotton waste and moved back to his side of the cab.

'Watch out for the back 'un,' he said curtly.

Charlie moved to the side of the engine, a little surprised at Fred's sudden change of mood. He hung over the side of the cab watching for the distant signal that heralded the approach into Willston. His stomach rumbled slightly as his ulcer fought against the tea that had been drunk too quickly and too hot and he thought, with regret, of the cheese and pickle sandwich Fred had offered.

He caught sight of the flickering green light of the distant signal.

'Right away, mate!' he called.

Fred opened the regulator once more and the train began to speed up.

Chapter Four

Daylight was beginning to filter into the engine shed as Bert Bradshaw stopped to check the state of 2784's fire. It was Bert's job to check the boilers and keep the fires stoked enough to keep them alight before raking round to make sure the night's ashes had dropped through then building up the fire for the fireman booking on for the engine's shift.

As Bert bent down to the firebox, his sharp features were briefly illuminated by the glow from within. The fire was burning through nicely. He carefully positioned a shovelful of coal on to the fire, closed the firebox doors and rubbed a grimy hand across his face.

With a sigh of relief, Bob Jones the cleaner, who was standing on the handrail of 3283 'Comet', blew out his flare lamp and put it down. It was light enough not to need it and he could devote both hands to the hard job of scouring the copper-capped chimney with brick dust in such a way as would satisfy the exacting standards imposed by Alf.

One by one across the shed the individual flare lamps, those metal vessels reminiscent of Aladdin's lamp, which gave out a dim yellow glow and a mass of choking black smoke, were blown out.

It grew lighter, and the engines turned from brooding monsters of darkness into recognisable objects.

An engine shed was never a silent place, and nights could be as busy as days. But there was a period in the hours before dawn when something approaching peace would descend. The few sounds there were would be accentuated: the occasional shovelling of coal; the intermittent chink of metal against metal as the fitters did running repairs; the odd comment; the distant whistle of a passing train. With the growing light the level of noise rose and a sense of urgency pervaded the shed.

But one sound remained constant. The steady, unvarying tones of Billy Hughes could be heard throughout the shed, carrying on, regardless of day, regardless of night, relentlessly issuing forth from the direction of stores and only ceasing when he was off-duty.

It grew lighter still and the shed came to life. There was a steady stream of men travelling in the direction of the booking on lobby, some to book on for their early shifts, some to book off, eager for their beds.

Ben Goodey, the Day Foreman, arrived to relieve Geoff Willis, and the two soberly dressed, bowler-hatted gentlemen exchanged words about various matters relating to the shed before Geoff departed on his bicycle for his home, his wife and his five children.

Engines returned to the shed from their nights' journeys as dirty as their crews. They were left on the ashpits to be dealt with by the fire-droppers, while their weary firemen and drivers made their way to their own cabin prior to booking off. And all around the yard engines were being moved, turned on the turntable, coaled up, watered, oiled, and driven off shed to their new destinations.

After a final glance at the gauge glass to check on 2784's boiler water level and then the steam pressure gauge, Bert collected his unused firelighters and the remainder of paraffin-soaked rags and climbed off the footplate.

In stores, a very weary Tom slowly filled a can with oil while Billy carried on spirited conversations with anyone who came within earshot and with Tom if no one else was around.

'Well, that's right enough Frank, but it isn't up to the gaffer, now is it? I mean if it comes from the top there's not a lot Joe can do about it, is there?'

Tom carried the heavy can over to the counter and Billy lifted it across.

'There you are then Frank.'

An upright, soldierly-looking man took it.

'Thanks Billy.'

Frank nodded and was gone. Billy turned to Tom.

'Know who that was? Frank Bateson. One of the top-link drivers like your dad. Why, I can remember when I was....'

'Got the locker keys to 1861 Billy?' shouted an impatient voice. It belonged to a short-cropped, ginger-headed man in his mid-thirties.

'Just coming Joe.' Billy looked at Tom whose face was drawn with tiredness.

'You knock off lad,' he said kindly. 'You haven't done too badly for your first night I will say, but then I wouldn't have expected any different from Fred Watkins' lad.'

'It's Tom,' Tom said quietly. It was his one small assertion of himself after what had seemed an endless night of anxiety and exhaustion.

'What's that?'

'My name. It's Tom.'

Bill stared at Tom for a moment, incomprehension in his round, bespectacled face.

There was an impatient tapping on the counter. 'Billy! The keys to 1861! Don't take all bloody day about it!'

Incomprehension turned to righteous fury. Bill turned sharply to the counter. 'And you keep a civil tongue in your head Joe Stratton!' he rapped out and darted away.

Tom came out of stores and leant for a moment against the wall, closing his eyes, letting tiredness flow unchecked through his body. It had been every bit as bad as he had anticipated, but he had survived. He had survived.

'*"In every rank, or great or small,*
'*Tis industry supports us all."*

Or perhaps I should say, 'tis Billy Hughes supports us all'.

Tom's eyes flew open. Dai Davies was standing in front of him, a slightly sardonic smile on his face.

'Fred Watkins' lad, isn't it?' Dai asked.

'Yes,' said Tom wearily.

'I can see you're suffering from a surfeit of the redoubtable Billy, God bless him,' Dai said sympathetically. He held out his hand. 'Dai my name is - Dai Davies - failed poet and passed fireman.'

Tom shook his hand. 'Mine's Tom.'

Dai chuckled and shook his head. 'Not here, Fred Watkins' lad. Not here. Don't you know your old man's a living bloody legend at this shed? You'll be Fred Watkins' lad for some time to come whether you like it or not.'

He nodded lightly and was gone.

****

The 7.40 train from Acton Chalcote slowed at the speed restriction before the bridge and embarked with care upon the cast iron structure spanning the River Charl. Not that the bridge was in any danger of collapse. It had stood since the line was built in 1860 and would, no doubt, stand for many years to come, bearing the weight of the 7.40 'up' passenger with its eight coaches and Hall class engine as well as the countless other trains through the day and night.

Not one of the hundred or so passengers on the train that morning so much as lifted their heads from their morning newspapers as the train passed over the bridge. If they had glanced out of the windows, they might have seen the slight figure of the boy stripped to his underpants as he stood poised at the waters' edge, arms raised to dive in.

Tom dived, and the train, safely over the bridge, gathered speed. The water was cold and clean. It flowed like silk against his skin and he felt tiredness dropping from him as his body was shocked into wakefulness in the icy water. He swam strongly then came up for air. He turned, duck-dived, and swam to the opposite bank, fighting hard against the swift current.

As he surfaced for the second time the sun shone directly into his face, dazzling him. He blinked, dashed drops of water from his eyes, and saw the slight figure of Maggie standing on the far bank. He waved and Maggie waved back. She waited while he swam across.

Maggie looked about twelve but was in fact just two months younger than Tom. She had straight hair which framed a heart-shaped face, a button nose, freckles, and gentle, dreamy, grey eyes which sat oddly above the determined mouth and jaw. She was dressed in a black skirt that was too long, an unattractive white blouse cut to accommodate a figure altogether more rounded than Maggie's undeveloped boyish shape, white socks, schoolgirl shoes and an oversized black handbag. She looked as if she were dressed in her elder sister's cast-offs, which was not the case as she only had one, much younger, brother.

She stood on the river bank and her rounded shoulders only accentuated the unsuitability of her clothes and the air of defencelessness that clung to her. Everything about Maggie was small and vulnerable, arousing protective or bullying instincts in those she encountered.

'You're all goose pimples,' she said, wrinkling her nose as Tom clambered out of the water.

'It's smashing in there,' Tom enthused between chattering teeth. He grabbed hold of her arm with a dripping hand. 'Come on in.'

'Leave go! You're all wet!'

Tom laughed, released her arm, and began to dress.

Maggie was not an obvious choice of friend for Tom, despite the fact that she lived in the same street and her father was a railwayman, albeit a signalman. But their friendship spanned the years and its origins lay in their first days at school.

A five-year old Maggie, smaller than her classmates, timid and shy, was frequently used as a butt for the aggression of the older children. Jim Salter was her especial tormentor and made her life miserable until the day when Tom had watched, with not a great deal of interest, as Jim and his friends pursued Maggie out of the school building and across the playground. Jim had hold of Maggie's satchel and was hitting her round the legs with it, not hard, but relentlessly.

Maggie ran off, but Jim gave chase, easily catching up with her. Again and again she broke free until finally, like a cornered rabbit, she had turned and stood her ground, her face white and impassive.

Something about her attitude - perhaps it was her lack of tears, perhaps it was the dignity with which she confronted her tormentors - whatever it was, something touched the five-year old Tom. He abandoned his game of marbles, ran over to Jim, and caught the satchel out of his hand just as Maggie was flinching in anticipation of a further blow. Surprised by his success, Tom aimed an inexpert punch which managed to catch Jim off balance and send him sprawling in the playground, grazing both knees on the sharp asphalt. It was the first and last time that Tom ever beat Jim in battle. In the ensuing fight Jim exacted full retribution and Tom had his first taste of the persecution that was to become a regular feature of his schooldays.

But Jim never tormented Maggie again and, from that day, she became Tom's slave, a small shadow hovering on the edge of Tom's world, ready to obey his every wish.

Tom at first found this devotion embarrassing, then he began to tolerate and finally accept it. He now regarded Maggie almost as a younger sister, someone who would listen to anything he cared to say, who would run all kinds of errands, become involved in any dangerous pursuit he and his friends devised and who could be ignored with impunity when he felt disinclined for company. Someone, in short, who would remain loyal, steadfast, and faithful whatever he did.

Maggie of course no longer hero-worshipped Tom. She had long passed that stage, knowing him too well to be blindly devoted. For her, Tom had become the elder brother she had never had, and she revelled in her position. She never abused it and never made demands on Tom's time with her own wishes. Tom would confide in her as in no one else, but she never made the mistake of trying to reciprocate.

She knew Tom's feelings about the railway and knew, in part, something of what he felt about his father, as much as he was able to express out loud. With her more mature eyes she was able to see past Fred's possessive ambitions for Tom to the simple, wholehearted love he had for his son. She was able to see this love and understand it, for it mirrored her own feelings. She could see, but she kept silent, for her role was not that of judge or even adviser. It was that of sympathetic listener, of confidante, and she was careful not to overstep the invisible bounds imposed for fear of damaging or even severing a relationship that increasingly she could not do without. For Maggie, despite her youthful looks, was growing up considerably faster than Tom.

'What are you doing here? Shouldn't you be at school?' Tom teased, throwing on his clothes as quickly as possible.

Maggie drew herself up to her full height.

'School? I'm a working girl now I'll have you know. Got a job at Purvis & Purvis.'

'Nobody'd believe you're old enough. Did you have to take your birth certificate with you?'

Maggie did not answer, and Tom finished dressing in silence. Maggie could see the dark circles under his eyes, the strain in his face. She felt an overwhelming desire to put her arms around him, to gently kiss away the tiredness and stroke the lines in the thin face. Instead, she looked away and demanded, in a voice that was unusually abrupt,

'Well? How was it?'

Tom shuffled uncomfortably, reluctant to discuss it even with Maggie.

'How was what?'

'Don't have to act daft even if you are,' Maggie said tartly.

Tom stooped down, picked up a stick and flung it far into the river. He watched the current take it swiftly downstream.

'After what you said the other night...'

'It was - all right,' Tom said, his voice non-committal.

'Was it?'

Tom shrugged. 'No.'

'Why?'

"Cos 'y's a crooked letter,' Tom said impatiently. 'Stop asking questions. What's it to you anyway? You wouldn't understand. You're only a child...'

Maggie turned abruptly and walked off. Tom stood still for a moment watching the small figure disappearing down the path. She looked so... small... so...pathetic... He sighed and ran after her.

'Maggie,' he said, pleading. 'I'm going to have to put up with enough questions when I get home.'

Maggie turned on him angrily. 'I do understand! And I'm not a child. You didn't think so the other night!'

As soon as she had said it, she could have bitten off her tongue. It was hurtful to watch Tom's face as he screwed up his eyes in an effort to remember.

'The other....? Oh that... that was nothing... just messing about...' he finished lamely.

It was even more painful to have it dismissed so lightly.

'So that was all it was,' she said.

'It was only a kiss,' Tom hedged. 'And you asked me to...'

Maggie stood silent for a moment, her face burning. It had only been a kiss, a fumbled, adolescent, unsatisfactory kiss.

It had been a warm early September evening and she had met him while walking home with a bag full of shopping. Tom had taken her bag but instead of walking her straight to her door had turned off to take the longer route beside the river. He had sat on the bank and she had sat beside him, both staring at the sun glinting off the water, the ducks swimming in and out of the reeds, the fronds of the willow tree gently brushing the surface of the swift flowing river. They hadn't talked, just sat in companionable silence. Then, with a sigh, Tom had got to his feet and put out his hand to raise her. They had stood still for a moment, faces close, staring into each other's eyes. 'Will you?' she had said, moving closer until her lips had touched his.

She had misunderstood the situation, she thought, turning away, misread something she had imagined she had seen in his face, in the way he had looked at her. But she had been wrong, quite wrong. It had been nothing at all... just messing about...

'Well don't worry, I won't ask you again.'

Tom hesitated, then abruptly walked off, unable to cope with any more changes in his life, angry with Maggie for confusing things, for refusing to remain the one constant in his unsettled world, angry with himself for upsetting her.

His journey home was as slow as he could make it in order to put off the hour when he would have to face his father. He slipped quietly into the house, hoping that Fred would have gone to the allotment or to bed. It was a vain hope. Fred was sitting in his chair by the kitchen table as if he had been there for hours. He had a newspaper in his hands and looked up sharply as Tom entered. Then he ostentatiously returned to his reading, rustling the papers noisily as he turned a page.

Tom paused in the doorway.

"Lo dad.'

Fred did not so much as glance up. 'You took your time,' he muttered into the paper.

Tom entered the room.

'I didn't know you were waiting for me.'

'I wasn't.' Fred threw down his paper and went to the door. 'Nance - Nance! The lad's back and wants food!' Then he returned to his seat and his newspaper and silence fell.

'I didn't hear you come in,' Nancy said apologetically as she hurried into the kitchen. 'You look tired. Come and sit down.' She put her hand on his shoulder.

'Your clothes - they're all wet!'

'Get the boy some food and stop fussing woman,' Fred remarked to the inside page.

Nancy ignored him. 'How did you get all wet like that?'

'I went for a swim.'

'You must want your head examining,' Fred said, giving up any pretence at reading. 'The current in that river's dangerous. I've told you before.'

'He's a good swimmer, dad,' said Sylvia from the doorway. She had just got up and was wrapped in an elegant dressing gown.

'And I'm a good driver, but I don't take foolhardy risks,' Fred retorted. He looked at his daughter in disgust. 'And what do you think you're doing coming down here dressed like that my girl?'

Sylvia shrugged and came into the room. 'Give us a cup of tea, mum, will you?'

'Well boy, what happened?' Fred said, turning eagerly to Tom.

'Spare the grilling 'til I've gone please,' Sylvia pleaded.

Nancy poured out two cups of tea and handed one to Sylvia. 'There. Will you have a bite to eat?'

'No thanks. There's a League's display on Saturday and I can't run out in front of a couple of hundred people bulging out of my black shiny knickers, can I?'

For some reason Sylvia's membership of the Women's League of Health and Beauty irritated her father, which was why, of course, she had brought it up. She sat back with enjoyment to await the explosion.

'Will you women keep quiet!' Fred thundered. 'I want to talk to Tom!'

Sylvia leant over and patted his hand. 'But does Tom want to talk to you, dad?' She glanced at Tom. 'He looks as if a puff of wind would blow him away.'

'I should hope he's a bit tougher than that, eh Tom?' Fred retorted. 'Now then... what happened?'

Tom shrugged. 'Nothing much.'

Nancy, lost in her own thoughts as she cracked eggs into a bowl, looked up, a worried frown on her face.

'Sylvia, will you be home for tea?'

'It all depends. I'll be home unless something more interesting presents itself.'

Fred looked at her sharply. 'If you mean that Dai Davies, you can think again.'

'Dai Davies?'

'Don't play the innocent with me, girl. I know he's been hanging round that cinema of yours making sheep's eyes.'

'Your spies must have been working overtime,' Sylvia said lightly. 'What's wrong with him?'

Fred looked stubborn. 'I won't have you going out with him and that's flat.'

Why ever not?'

'Because I say so, that's why not.'

'Oh, come on dad, what's wrong with Dai Davies? Apart from him being a railwayman of course.'

'He's no good for you,' Fred said.

'Why?'

Fred hesitated and Sylvia laughed. 'It's no good, dad, you've got to tell me. We're not living in the Victorian age when children did what their parents said without question.'

'More's the pity,' Fred grunted.

Sylvia put down her cup. 'Well?'

'The man's a fraud, a boaster,' Fred said angrily, with the air of having been cornered. 'Thinks himself so high and mighty, does Dai Davies which is no wonder considering where he comes from. You mark my words, girl, nothing good ever came out of the Rhondda.'

'Oh dad, how can you be so prejudiced!'

'Prejudiced? Me? I'm not prejudiced. I'm not prejudiced, am I Nance? No-one's ever called me prejudiced.'

Sylvia laughed. Fred looked at her suspiciously, marshalling further arguments.

'And if that's not enough, there's his bloody poetry. Thinks he'll be Wales's latest Bard to hear him go on. Oh, he's got a very fine opinion of himself has Dai Davies!'

'Poetry? Well, well. Poor Dai. Perhaps I've been a bit hard on him. I've never met a poet before...'

She stood up and went to the door. 'Thanks dad.'

'You're not to go out with him - you hear?' Fred called after her.

'Don't shout, Fred,' Nancy gently expostulated.

Fred snorted and drew his chair closer to Tom's. 'Now then...'

'Let him have his meal Fred,' Nancy insisted, putting a plate in front of Tom. 'The lad's worn out.'

'Will you get out of the kitchen and leave us in peace Nance!' Fred exploded. 'It's like Paddington Station this place - can't hear yourself think!'

'Don't let him keep you up too long,' Nancy said gently to Tom. Her hand brushed the top of his head, and she quietly left the room.

For a moment there was silence.

'Oh go on then, eat your bloody breakfast!'

Fred re-opened his newspaper and stared at it in disgust. Tom meanwhile picked over his meal, his father's burning curiosity destroying his appetite. He pushed his plate away and Fred looked up sharply.

'I heard you had a bit of bother calling up. Albert can be a difficult man, especially after a long trip. Old Southey was telling me about it.'

'It was all right.'

A weight of tiredness and depression enveloped Tom. Something of this communicated itself to his father who fell silent, gazing searchingly into his son's face.

'Don't let Billy Hughes get you down,' he said at last. 'He's a good enough man when all's said and done, but he'd talk the hind leg off a donkey any day. I should have warned you.'

'He didn't bother me.' Even speaking had become an effort. Fred stared at him and Tom felt the familiar anxious tension welling up. Then Fred smiled.

'I know what it is. You thought you'd go straight on to the locos.'

Tom shook his head.

'"Course you did,' Fred insisted. 'And you're disappointed. It's only natural. Well, don't you worry about it. It'll happen soon enough.' And having thus explained Tom's inexplicable mood to his own satisfaction, Fred relaxed and expanded.

'I was lucky when I started you know. They were short-handed so the first thing they put me on was cleaning. I was never call-up boy. 1128, the Duke of York. That was my first. One of the 2-2-2 Queen class. Beautiful locos they were. Just one single bloody great driving wheel. You don't see them now, of course, they were all scrapped before the war, more's the pity.' He glanced at Tom. 'But you don't want to hear my old stories. You'll be full of your own soon as Alf Wittall lets you on an engine.'

Tom stood up. 'Think I'll turn in.'

'Yes. Of course. You do that. I'm going up to the allotment. You wouldn't want to come, I suppose...?'

'I'm a bit tired...'

'Right you are.' Fred started for the back door, then paused and turned. 'And Tom - listen - if there's anything I can help with, you've only to ask. Anything at all.'

There was a long pause.

'Thanks.'

'Don't forget now. Just ask.'

Tom hesitated for a moment then nodded slightly and went out. Out in the hall he could hear Nancy playing the piano. He listened for a moment while she played the same refrain over again, then he crossed to the stairs, walked halfway up, stopped, returned to the hall and went over to the parlour door. He paused for a moment then turned the knob and went inside.

The net curtains had been pulled right back, bathing the parlour in sunlight. Motes of dust danced in the air and dust lay in a thin cover across the surfaces of the heavy, dark furniture. The parlour was seldom used by anyone except Nancy. Kept as the 'best' room for state occasions such as weddings and funerals, it had long been known as Nancy's room and her personality could be seen everywhere, by the chairs pulled out of their regimented order and the sheets of music spread around her at the piano. She was practising a light classical piece, a frown of concentration on her face as she played and replayed every stanza, each time with greater confidence as her fingers learnt the notes. Her hair was sticking up wildly where she had run her fingers through it in exasperation.

There was something comforting to Tom in her complete absorption in what she was doing. She was as oblivious of her surroundings as she was of him, and he stood leaning against the door watching her play for quite five minutes before she sensed his presence. She glanced up and smiled but continued to play.

'Dad's gone to the allotment,' Tom said eventually.

Nancy nodded.

'And I'm going to bed.'

She stopped playing. 'Leave those damp clothes outside your room and I'll have them dry before you wake up.'

She resumed playing, starting at the beginning of the piece, still slightly hesitant. The tune came through, slowly but clearly.

'That's nice.'

'It came this morning. I'm still learning it.'

She reached the end then turned to Tom, giving him her full attention.

'Did you have a talk? Your father's been so anxious for you to come home.'

Tom was silent.

'He's so proud, you know.'

'Proud?'

'Of course.'

'I don't see why. He's in the top link. What's he got to be proud of me for?'

'You're his son.'

The words seemed to hang in the bright sunlit room along with the motes of dust.

'I hated it, mum.'

Nancy nodded, unsurprised. 'I hope you didn't tell your father that.'

'If I had he wouldn't have believed me,' Tom said moodily.

She smiled. 'Go to bed. It's been your first night's work and you're tired out. Things always look worse when you're tired.'

'I suppose so.' Tom was unconvinced.

'It'll be fine tomorrow. You'll see.'

He gave her a fleeting smile and was gone. Nancy turned back to the piano but did not begin to play immediately. She sat still for a long time.

Chapter Five

Before the building of the original line from Springswell to Matchurch, Acton Chalcote was no more than a small rural village with a population of around seventy to eighty. The coming of the railway changed all that as it changed so many other communities, especially with the decision to make Acton Chalcote the junction for the line to Besham, necessitating the construction of an engine shed on the edge of the village. By this time the original railway company had been swallowed up by the Great Western who, with customary thoroughness, built a number of houses for their employees, a medical centre and a meeting hall. It was not comparable to the GWR's extensive building at its headquarters at Swindon by any stretch of the imagination, but it increased the population of the village and put an indelible stamp on the character of the embryo town.

By 1861 the population had risen to just under three hundred and it continued to rise steadily until it became the small town that Tom grew up in during the 1920s and 30s. Its increasing prosperity and growing importance as a railway junction naturally attracted the attention of speculators anxious to reap their share of the profits to be made in the lucrative new railway business. Their eyes focused greedily on the Great Western's thrust into the heart of the wealthy industrial Midlands, and throughout the 1860s various schemes were projected for other lines. They all failed due mainly to the determination of the Great Western not to let anyone else muscle in on their territory and ride on the back of their success.

However, by 1874 Acton Chalcote had found itself with another line, although with no connection to the Great Western. The small East and West Junction and South Wales Mineral Railway Company (E&WJ & SWM) with big ambitions but little money, built itself a temporary terminus on the edge of the town. Their plan was founded on the fact that by the 1860s the blast furnaces in South Wales had used up their local stocks of iron ore and it seemed highly probably that iron ore from the Northamptonshire mines would be used instead. A railway would be needed to transport the mineral from one side of the country to the other and the E&WJ & SWM proposed to bridge that distance by building such a line, both as an economic necessity and as a means of providing their shareholders with handsome dividends.

Sadly for them, the expected traffic never materialised due to the importation of cheap iron ore from Spain. So the line, begun with such great expectations, was built no further than Acton Chalcote and never extended further west into Wales.

By 1901 the E&WJ & SWM was in a sorry state. Somehow it had weathered one financial crisis after another but at the cost of its day-to-day operations. Its two ancient engines were both worn out. Its track was in a shocking state of disrepair and the small engine shed which had been built as a temporary measure in 1874 to house the two engines blew down in a gale. In 1902, the Great Central Railway, reviving plans of a connecting spur to the Great Western, thereby gaining access to Birmingham via Matchurch through running powers, bought up the ailing E&WJ & SWM, much to everyone's relief.

The Great Central built an engine shed on the site of the E&WJ & SWM's temporary terminus and a station, Acton Chalcote Central, although there was nothing central about it as it was on the eastern fringes of the town. They then began lengthy negotiations with the Great Western and quickly came unstuck. The Great Western was as determined as it had been in the 1860s that no connection should be made between them and the Great Central at Acton Chalcote. Despite cordial relations between the two companies on other ventures, the Great Western did not feel that it would be advantageous to themselves to allow the spur wanted by the Great Central, let alone give it running powers over the GW line. The Great Central was therefore left on the outside of the town, forever cut off from the link it so anxiously sought, and the seeds of later conflict between the two rival sheds were sown.

In 1923, with the grouping of the railway companies after the First World War, the Great Central became part of the London and North Eastern Railway. Only the Great Western retained its full identity together with its name.

Time passed, and in Acton Chalcote the increased prosperity brought about by the two companies gave rise to new building which gradually pushed out the town boundaries to encompass the LNER line. By the 1930s Acton Chalcote was firmly established as a railway town with a corporate identity in that most of the population was linked to one or other of the two railway companies, and a split identity depending on whether one's loyalties lay with the 'Western or the 'North Eastern'.

*****

Tom's first days at the busy, bustling engine shed passed in a bewilderment of faces, Great Western practices, rules and regulations.

Every evening he pounded his way round the familiar streets at the mercy of the weather and irate drivers and firemen who he had just woken out of sleep. His legs discovered new muscles as he tried to make the old Great Western bicycle keep pace with the long list of calls he had to make. When he had made his calls he would return to the unlikely sanctuary of stores, to fulfil a host of tasks under the exacting eye and monotonous voice of Billy Hughes. He began to match faces to names on his lists and learn the various idiosyncrasies of the drivers and firemen he called up.

Driver Jones, for example, left a piece of string snaking down from his upstairs window to the front door. A label was attached to the end reading: 'Caller-up - pull hard!'. Tom pulled hard and was rewarded by the sound of a loud thud followed by a yell. The upstairs window was flung open and Driver Jones stuck his grizzled head outside.

'That's some pull you've got there lad,' he called. 'Nearly took off my big toe. I ties the other end of the string round it, you see. Nothing else wakes me.'

Calling up meant a reprieve from the engine shed and Tom felt himself in a state of limbo, cycling through dark, deserted streets, his only contact being the brief 'Morning,' or 'All right lad, I can hear you - not bleeding deaf yet' and similar remarks from half-asleep firemen and drivers. The only other person he talked to during those early autumn nights was P.C. Grant, who took a liking to the thin young lad with the perpetually worried expression on his face. P.C. Grant took to turning up unexpectedly at some point or other during Tom's round with comments of heavy humour, such as, 'And how many houses did you burgle last night when I was off duty?' and offers of cups of strong, heavily-sweetened tea which Tom gratefully accepted, time permitting.

During those weeks Tom lived an unreal, twilight existence, his time at the engine shed, apart from his duties in stores, were confined to booking on and off, and a few minutes in the cleaners' cabin where he was careful to avoid the other cleaners, not just Jim, his old enemy, but old friends like Ginger and Les. He didn't know why he was acting like this, but for a short while he was almost able to put his new job out of his mind, and even pretend that he hadn't begun his lifetime's career. But this state of mind could not last and ended abruptly with the arrival of Norman.

Norman was an undersized youth with outsize freckles. Tom was present while he was initiated into the fraternity of the cleaners' cabin in the same manner as himself, but Norman, unlike Tom, had no confusing loyalties to resolve and quickly became accepted in a way that Tom was not. Tom felt slightly envious of the ready acceptance of the newcomer by the other cleaners.

Norman took over Tom's duties as caller-up and in stores, while Tom was put on a cleaning team under Jim's leadership. Their object was to render 3283 as spotless as was possible in the allotted time in order to pass the eagle-eyed inspection of Alf Wittall.

Jim collected the cotton waste and oil from stores then joined Ginger, Tom and Les who were already waiting by the engine. Jim threw a handful of waste to Tom.

'Right,' he said briskly, 'I'll take the motion.'

Tom, unaware of the protocols of engine cleaning, said nothing, but Ginger and Les both protested.

'That's not fair!' said Ginger hotly, while Les, in a more conciliating manner said,

'We ought to toss for it.'

Jim ignored this and continued with his orders. 'Ging, you take the left side out and Les, you take the right.' He threw Tom a mocking glance. 'His lordship here can take the cab and boiler.'

He waited for Tom to speak, but Tom said nothing. With a sidelong smile Jim vaulted neatly down into the pit underneath the engine. Les retreated to the right side of the engine, but Ginger hesitated.

'Know what you've got to do?' he asked awkwardly.

'I think so.'

Ginger rubbed his upturned nose, something he did when he felt uncomfortable and glanced down to where Jim could be heard whistling tunelessly.

'He ought to have told you,' he said. 'It's his job as he's in charge of the gang.'

Tom shrugged and put his foot on the bottom rung of the ladder.

'Given you the worst job, he has, in full view of Witty. Know why he took the motion? It's the best job of all 'cause you can have a quick smoke or a kip and you're well hidden. Witty doesn't often check down there because of his arthritis.'

Tom was silent.

'Well,' Ginger still hesitated. 'Anything you want, just ask.'

'Thanks.'

'Tell you one thing for free,' he said, pouring a small amount of lubricating oil and paraffin on to a piece of cotton waste.

'What's that?'

'Witty's red hot on finding the bits you've missed, so watch out.'

Tom sighed, looked up at the engine looming over him, climbed carefully on to the frame and began work.

He was soon hot and sweating profusely as he polished the copper-capped chimney. He had left, what seemed to him, the best part until last, and was quite enjoying himself working up a shine until he could see his reflection, small and golden, in the chimney. Suddenly aware that Jim's tuneless whistling and Ginger's more tuneful humming had stopped, he glanced down, to see, far below him, the upturned faced of Jim, Ginger and Les together with the slight, but formidable figure of Alf Wittall.

'You've only two hours each on the bugger, not all morning,' Alf said caustically.

Tom flushed and scrambled down.

'Right,' said Alf. 'Let's have a look.'

Alf Wittall was a spare-looking man in his mid-sixties. Forced to come off the footplate due to bouts of chronic arthritis, Alf was in charge of rostering the thirty or so cleaners, administering jobs, and ensuring that each engine sent off shed was in pristine condition and a credit to the Great Western Railway. A big man in his time, constant pain had caused him to shrink and necessitated his walking with the aid of a stick, which he used to good effect when inspecting the cleaners' handiwork. A stickler for work well done, Alf was both feared and respected and the days when he was especially difficult were recognised by everyone as days when his arthritis was playing him up. Today was clearly one of those days for Alf had a sour expression on his face as he watched Tom make a slow and careful descent.

When Tom was safely on the ground, Alf gave a grunt and began walking round the engine, glancing over the oiled workings which made the paintwork shine even in the gloom of the shed. The four boys watched him. He stopped abruptly, took a rag out of his pocket, tied it to the end of his stick and, with a sudden thrust, poked it between the wheels and twisted it sharply. It emerged coated with grime and oil. Alf glanced at the boys grimly, prowled round to the other side of the engine then climbed laboriously into the cab to inspect Tom's work. He seemed to remain there for an age before slowly descending.

'Hmm. Not bad for your first effort,' he said as he climbed down. 'But you're not polishing your mother's priceless candlesticks you know. You'll have to speed up.'

Jim and Les exchanged grins. With surprising speed Alf turned on them and levelled his stick in their direction.

'And you two can wipe those silly grins off your faces for a start,' he said with some asperity. He pointed his stick at the dirty wheel then produced the grimy rag from his pocket and held it under Jim's nose.

'Not good enough, Salter. Don't think you can hide from me by choosing the motion. I know that's considered a cushy number, but when you're in charge of a gang it's known as abusing your authority. Do you know what I mean by that?'

'Yes, sir.'

'You can clean that wheel again,' Alf said. He turned to Tom, ignoring Jim's angry scowl.

'Fred Watkins' lad, isn't it?'

'Yes, sir.'

'I knew your dad when he was still firing. A good man, Fred Watkins.'

Leaning heavily on his stick as though it had no other purpose than to support his pain-wracked body, Alf made his careful way to where another gang had just finished cleaning.

Tom turned to find Jim staring at him.

'No marks for guessing who the blue-eyed boy round here is, eh Fred Watkins' lad?'

He turned to the offending wheel and began attacking it viciously, and, for the remainder of the shift both Tom and Jim studiously avoided one another.

Tom also avoided Ginger and Les and hurried off alone, to the cleaner's cabin to collect his lunch. Ginger watched him go.

'Don't know what's got into him,' he said, shaking his head.

Les agreed.

Ginger sighed. 'It's no good. I'll have a word.'

He accosted Tom as they collected their lunchboxes from the cleaner's cabin at the end of the shift.

'Look, I know Jim's a pain and doing everything he can to make things hard for you, but you don't exactly help, do you?'

Tom shrugged.

'I mean, you don't mix with any of us - not even your mates. Some of the lads are saying you're snotty-nosed because of your dad.'

Tom gave a short laugh.

'You're just not doing anything to help yourself,' Ginger continued, keeping pace with Tom as he walked to the lobby to book off. 'Look, you and me used to be mates, didn't we? Why don't you come down to the Rec once we've booked off? I'm going there with Les and a couple of the lads for a game of football.'

'Not just now, thanks,' Tom said shortly. He reached the front of the queue, handed in his brass pay-check, and was booked off. He half turned. 'Thanks for trying anyway,' he said and set off alone out of the shed, walking fast to stop Ginger from following.

He crossed the barrow crossing, hardly looking to see if there were any trains approaching and almost ran along the track that led behind the station.

Why, he wondered, was he behaving like that to Ging, his old schoolfriend, his closest mate? Why was he brushing him off, him and Les and everyone he'd known all his life? What was so different now that they were at work and not at school? Let's face it, he thought, Alf Wittall bears more than a passing resemblance to old Foxy Smith, the history teacher, even to the cane, although Foxy used to use that on bare legs rather than the inside of wheels.

As Tom hurried along the path, he felt angry, an impotent anger - at himself, at his circumstances. Trapped, that was what he was. Trapped. Rage spurred him to walk straight past his house and up into the High Street. He was still walking fast, head bent, oblivious of the shops and passers-by when Maggie called him.

'You're in a hurry.'

She was just coming out of the side door of the haberdashery shop and fell into step beside him.

'I had to work late tonight,' she said conversationally. 'Stocktaking. It's so boring. Mr Sneller seems to think that unless it's all done and accounted for in one day then something dreadful'll happen. Like Maisie stealing a dozen pairs of silk stockings or something. He nearly went berserk because we were short of a liberty bodice.'

She glanced at Tom, who hadn't heard a word.

'Sorry,' she said contritely. 'You're off somewhere and I'm holding you back. I've got to get home anyway, got to babysit, as per usual.'

She turned to go, but Tom held out his hand. 'Don't go. Come down to the river.'

'I've got to babysit,' she repeated, but even as she spoke, she knew she would go because that was the way she was. Tom could pour out all his troubles and feel the better for it, but he would never once see her as someone with troubles of her own for that was the way he was. She sighed. It wasn't fair, but neither was life.

They reached the river and had walked as far as the bridge before Tom spoke.

'I hate it.'

They walked on in silence for a moment before Maggie summoned the courage to ask what had always puzzled her.

'Look - why did you take the job in the first place if you knew you wouldn't like it?'

'What else is there?' Tom answered impatiently. 'The only work for a man in this town is with one of the engine sheds. You know that. But I never thought it'd be like this - not once I'd started.'

They turned at the bridge and began walking back to town.

'I'm not a person there. I'm Fred Watkins lad. And if only they knew...'

'What?'

'I didn't get the job 'cos of dad, whatever they might say. I really wanted it. I wanted to prove to dad...' Tom paused, trying to put his jumbled thoughts into order. 'But it's all more than

just a job for him. It is for all of them. And I'm not like that...
I'm not like any of them. I'm just - just - not interested...'

'Does it matter?' Maggie said reasonably. 'I mean, it's just
a job, isn't it? I'm not interested in haberdashery, but I sell it.'

'It does matter,' Tom insisted. 'It matters to dad.'

They were silent again.

'Can't you tell him?' Maggie said at last. 'Tell him how you
feel about it.'

'You daft or something?' Tom said incredulously. 'Tell dad?
I tried, but he wouldn't listen. He never listens. I could holler
things at him and he wouldn't listen. Besides, he'd never have
got over it if I hadn't gone on to the footplate.'

'Well, why don't you try for a job at the North-Eastern shed
then?' Maggie said reasonably. 'No one knows you there.'

There was a long silence. Tom strode on, his eyes fixed
somewhere far in the distance. Maggie walked beside him,
knowing she had said the wrong thing but not knowing how to
unsay it. At last Tom spoke quietly.

'I think it would break dad's heart.' He paused, trying to put
into words something he had always known but never voiced.

'You just don't understand. My great-great-grandfather
worked for Daniel Gooch in 1840 on the Paddington to Bristol
line and dad's never forgotten it. He never lets me forget it
either. The 'Western's everything to him. I couldn't have got a
job with a rival company.'

'Jim did,' Maggie began.

There was another silence.

'Well, I'm not Jim,' said Tom shortly. 'I'm not dad either.
I'm me - Tom Watkins. for all the bloody use that is.' He
looked at her for the first time. 'Come on. Didn't you say
you've got to babysit?'

****

Sidney Silverthorne's Fried Fish Shop - 'Fish like you've never tasted it' - otherwise known as Sid's, had been a popular place in Acton Chalcote since it first opened in 1923. Strategically placed on the corner of the High Street and Station Road, it attracted after-cinema customers from The Regal as well as hungry customers pouring out of the Alhambra Dance Hall. It was popular with railwaymen from both the Great Western and North Eastern sheds and early in its life, Mr Sidney Silverthorne realised the potential of a late-night eating establishment both for courting couples in a town where most activities other than shift work closed at 10.00 p.m. and for the many shift workers on the railway. Mr Silverthorne quickly found that by the addition of half a dozen tables and chairs his clientele and popularity soared. Sid's became the regular meeting place of the young, where romances began, flourished, and sometimes ended amid the smell of frying oil and vinegar. It had changed little from its early days, apart from the acquisition of the next-door property in 1930 and the furnishings were very basic, although oilcloths now covered the tables and white enamel lampshades hung from the ceiling. Sidney Silverthorne had passed away, but the business was still very capably run by his son Dick, and his ample wife, Joan, and the name had never been changed. 'Dick's' did not have the same ring as 'Sid's', and, besides, the name, as the shop, was a landmark.

That particular evening the place was unusually empty. Only one table was occupied. Most of Sid's custom was late evening and this was still early. Dai and Sylvia sat at the end table. They were eating the standard fare of the café, or rather Sylvia was eating, while Dai was watching her. Sylvia glanced up and flushed.

'Have I got a smut on my nose?'

Dai smiled. 'You know you haven't.'

'Well what are you staring at then?'

'You.'

Sylvia had expected the answer, almost angled for it, but now it had come she felt embarrassed. Dai was different from the run-of-the-mill youths she had been out with before. He was older, for a start, and disconcerting. It was as if he could read her mind. She was not at all sure whether she liked it, or him.

'I don't know why I agreed to go out with you,' she said, almost petulantly.

'Yes you do. You couldn't resist my peculiar Welsh charm any longer,' Dai said calmly.

Sylvia grinned, enjoying a private joke. 'It wasn't that.'

'Oh?'

'It was something dad said.'

'What did dad say?'

Sylvia took a mouthful of fish and chips and ate them slowly before replying. 'I'm not telling you. You've got a big enough head already.'

Dai frowned, trying to work it out. 'I thought your father didn't approve of me,' he began cautiously.

'He doesn't,' Sylvia said, then laughed. She smiled to herself as she finished her meal and drank her tea. 'I must get home.'

'I'll walk you back,' Dai said, but made no move to get up and neither did Sylvia.

'How's Tom getting on?' Sylvia asked, more to break the sudden silence. The way Dai was staring at her made her feel gauche, as if out on her first date.

'I wouldn't know,' Dai replied, enjoying looking at her wide brown eyes, firm chin and mass of dark hair, bobbed in the latest fashion.

'He's never really been interested, you know,' Sylvia went on, opening her bag and rummaging inside. 'Not like dad.'

She took out her powder compact, frowningly examined her reflection before applying a spot of powder to her nose. It gave her something to do and took her mind off the effect Dai was having on her. After all, they couldn't sit in Sid's cafe just staring into each other's eyes, could they? It was too uncomfortable.

'The two don't necessarily go together,' Dai replied.

'What? Who?' Sylvia had lost the thread of the conversation.

Dai smiled. 'Tom and your father,' he said gently.

'Oh yes.' Sylvia made a great business of putting away her compact. 'No, but it helps I should think. Especially with dad...'

'You know, I have the greatest respect for your father, and I like your brother, the little I've seen of him, but I'd much rather talk about you.' Dai stopped. 'You've got lovely eyes.'

'I bet you say that to everyone.'

Dai smiled. He had a nice smile, Sylvia thought. It started in his eyes, crinkling the edges, then spread slowly to his mouth until his whole face lit up.

'No I don't. I never say it to Ben Goodey - he's the foreman. I never say it to my driver either, come to think of it.'

'Do you always joke?' Sylvia asked abruptly.

'That was a very poor one,' Dai confessed. 'But I try to. It eases difficult situations like this.'

It was a game they were playing, Sylvia felt, a game of words, light and bantering on the surface, with undercurrents that made her heart beat faster.

'Why is this difficult?'

Dai took his time answering.

'Because I'm a railwayman of course,' he said at last, lightly, then leaned across the table and sketched a kiss on her forehead. It was a light touch, little more than a caress, but the hard-bitten Sylvia who knew her own mind and could keep any number of boyfriends well in hand, felt a hot tide of red rush into her face and hated herself for the childish display.

'And you never go out with railwaymen.' With infinite gentleness, as if understanding her distress, Dai outlined her face with his finger, from forehead to chin.

> *'"Who is Sylvia?*
> *What is she?*
> *That all our swains commend her?*
> *Holy, fair, and wise is she;*
> *The heaven such grace did lend her,*
> *That she might admired be."'*

There was silence while they stared at each other. Sylvia, her colour, and some shreds of composure returning to normal, said, with a slight smile, 'Dad said you were a poet.'

But her composure was jolted once more when Dai threw back his head and laughed.

'I'm flattered,' he said, 'but I didn't write it.'

'Oh,' said Sylvia flatly.

Dai, seeing her discomfort, smiled, a warm, understanding smile. And Sylvia smiled tentatively back.

Despite his occupation he and Sylvia continued to see one another and Dai was no longer required to sit through the same film evening after evening in order to have a few words with her at the end of the show. They met now by pre-arrangement, either for a meal at Sid's, or for a walk or a dance at The Alhambra. Once or twice they went for a drink, but Sylvia found the almost exclusive railway talk and the jokes and innuendoes aimed at Dai by his friends uncomfortable.

What was it about Dai that was so different from Joe and George and Ronald and Cyril, she wondered, as she watched the sixth showing of a rather boring Western from the back of the stalls. She smiled. Between Cyril and Dai there could be no comparison. Dai would never dither about ordering food or anything else. He was older than the other men she had dated but that did not explain the pull of attraction which she knew was not just on her side. He was sometimes teasing, but always quick to understand her feelings when she was hurt. He was... she hunted for the right words. A soul mate. That was it. Increasingly she felt that there was a deep, unspoken, understanding between them. Pity he had such an impossible job. She sighed loudly, then caught Florence's eye and straightened up ready to smile and sell ice creams during the interval.

Chapter Six

As time passed Tom grew accustomed to life in the engine shed. The cleaner, he found, was at everyone's beck and call, quite apart from their main job of keeping the stable of locomotives at Acton Chalcote looking immaculate for when they went out on the line. He learnt about the different engines, the bits that were hard to access when cleaning, and was told about their various idiosyncrasies by the firemen and drivers. The fitters kept the engines in prime working order, while the cleaners kept them looking pristine.

Tom began to understand the many different jobs and the strict hierarchy that permeated the whole of the Company, and after a while, he began to relax with his mates, go off with them to the Railwayman's Club and although he was too young to legally have a beer, he could have a lemonade and try out the occasionally cigarette. But he could not dismiss the thought that he lived in his father's shadow, that he would never be anything other than Fred Watkins' lad, someone who could never aspire to an identity of his own, someone who would always fall short, would always fail to live up to the legend that was Fred Watkins, for the feelings that have been ingrained in childhood can never be fully eradicated.

But although he became good at cleaning and took pride in the work, and although he liked being able to present his weekly pay packet to his mother and receive her smile of approval and a few coppers to spend for himself, he never expressed any longing to be taken on the footplate and have a turn as an acting fireman, as did Ginger and Les and the other cleaners. The very early memory of being taken on to the footplate of an engine in steam and the feelings that engendered remained and he wondered fearfully how he would cope.

Ginger, Les, Jim and those senior to him duly had their first firing turns and came back full of excited talk and a lot of bravado about the experience. His turn came sometime later.

'Watkins!'

He was crossing the yard on his way to the booking on lobby, walking briskly against the early-morning chill, blowing on the fingers of one hand while swinging his lunch box with the other, when the shout made him stop. He couldn't see who was calling because engine 5705 was creaking, clanking and groaning past him, as if protesting at being taken out on to the main line. There was a hiss of escaping steam and a deep-throated chuff...CHUFF, and Tom was blanketed in a cloud of steam.

'Watkins!'

'Me sir?'

Once the steam had cleared, he saw Alf Wittall and Ben Goodey looking in his direction. Alf waved his stick irritably.

'You, yes you. Who do you think I meant? Book on double quick. You'll have to do a firing turn.'

Tom looked about him. 'But isn't there anyone...?'

'No-one else. Young Salter's not turned up for duty.'

'Don't look so worried lad,' Ben spoke encouragingly. 'You're not going on the main line. It's only shunting. Your driver's waiting for you on the tankie over by the coal stage.'

Tom hesitated.

'Get a move on Watkins, we're short-handed this morning,' Alf said testily before following Ben back into the shed.

Firing turn, Tom thought as he went reluctantly over to the coal stage. Firing turn. His heart began to thump. He wasn't ready for it. He would never be ready for it. What was he meant to do?

Dai was waiting for him at the bottom of the slope leading to the coal stage. He was looking upwards to where the coalman was getting ready to upend a skip full of coal.

'One more!' Dai shouted. Coal showered down into the engine's bunker.

'That's enough mate!'

Dai turned to Tom.

'Well and if it isn't young Watkins. Am I glad to see you. Thought I was going to have to drive and fire single-handed.'

Another skipful of coal cascaded down, narrowly missing both of them.

'You stupid bloody prat! Trying to kill me are you?' Dai shouted up.

'Sorry mate!'

'I should bloody well think so!' He turned back to Tom. 'Come on up.'

'Watkins.'

Tom stopped climbing up to the cab and turned. Jim was hurrying across the yard towards him.

'That's my turn you're taking.'

'What...?'

'It's my firing turn. I'm senior to you.'

Dai leaned out of the cab. 'What the hell's going on?'

'It's my turn,' Jim insisted. 'Get off that engine!'

Tom hesitated.

'Are you doing to get off that engine, or am I going to pull you off? Just 'cos your old man's top driver at this shed doesn't mean you can pinch other people's turns. Now get off!'

'Salter!' Ben Goodey spoke quietly from behind him.

Jim wheeled round.

'Just what do you think you're playing at?'

'I'm senior to Watkins, sir. It should be my firing turn,' Jim insisted angrily.

'Salter, have you any idea of the time? It's a quarter past seven. You were due on at seven, not a quarter past.'

Jim flushed. 'I – I'm sorry. I can explain...'

'I haven't time for explanations. I've a busy shed to run here, we're short of staff so you can think yourself lucky you're not being sent home for the day. I won't tolerate unpunctuality Salter. Now go and report to the Chargeman and let's have no more nonsense. As if we haven't enough problems this morning.' He nodded to Tom. 'All right Watkins.'

He walked off and Tom finished climbing into the cab, conscious of Jim watching his every move.

'Some of us don't have it as jammy as you, Watkins,' he muttered. 'Some of us don't have their dads to pull strings for them. But you wait. I'll get you for this. You just wait.'

He turned and abruptly walked off.

'Well there's a fine display of temper for you,' Dai said thoughtfully. 'What's wrong with your friend?'

Tom shrugged.

'Never mind. Ever fired before?'

'No.'

'Nothing to it. You just do what Uncle Dai tells you and you'll be fine.' He handed the shovel to Tom. 'Now first thing is to level off that coal so we don't lose half a ton when we move.'

Dai drove the tankie forwards on to a train of mixed vans and wagons which was parked in one of the sidings, waved on by Bob, the shunter.

'Right, boyo, we're off,' he remarked to Tom. 'You just keep an eye on the fire, Tom and watch the water level – don't let it drop.'

Bob coupled up the train and Dai reversed the engine and pulled it out of the siding with the familiar clanking sound as the loose-coupled wagons pulled apart. Bob put up his hand when the rear of the train was clear of the points and Dai stopped. Bob swiftly changed the points, uncoupled the brake van and a couple of wagons, and signalled to Dai, who pushed the whole train towards the next siding. When Bob signalled again, Dai shut off steam and the train stopped, leaving the brake van and the two wagons to roll on. Bob dropped the brakes down to stop them hitting the buffers, while Dai reversed the remains of the train back past the points ready for the next move.

'The ferret's in good shape,' he said as he watched Bob reset the points for the third siding, uncouple a single wagon at the end of the train and wave Dai forwards once more.

'The ferret?'

'Watch the way he ferrets in and out of those wagons. It's a real treat.'

Bob changed the points once more to the siding chosen for the next wagons.

'Got to keep your wits about you to keep up with him – and not run him over of course.'

'How does he know which siding the wagons should go in?' Tom asked as he leant over the side to watch.

'Each wagon is labelled,' Dai explained as he moved the reversing lever ready to bring the remainder of the train forwards. 'Simple really.' He opened the doors of the firebox and glanced inside.

'A couple of shovelfuls, Tom, towards the front.'

Tom dug his shovel into the pile of coal, swung the shovel round and emptied the coal into the fire. Dai watched him.

'Not bad for a first time – could be a bit further back though. You'll get used to it, it's just a knack.'

He leaned out to watch Bob.

'Close 'em up!' Bob called and Dai pushed the train forwards.

It was a long, slow process moving the wagons into their allotted sidings, despite the speed at which Dai and Bob worked. Tom, keeping one eye fixed on the water level and the other on the state of the fire, found to his surprise that he was enjoying himself. Dai was a good instructor, keeping up a running commentary about what was going on, answering his questions, and giving him due praise when he managed, for the first time, to get the coal to the right spot in the firebox.

It was past lunchtime before Dai brought the engine back to the shed and stopped it over the pits. He and Tom climbed down.

'Not bad for the first time. Enjoy yourself?'

'Mm. Thanks.'

'What for?'

'Well... showing me what to do...and that...'

Dai laughed. 'Think nothing of it. Everyone's got to learn. Trouble when I started was I thought I knew it all see, but my first firing trip soon put that right. I picked up a shovelful of coal, missed the firebox altogether and showered it over my mate! He never let me forget it even when I became...'

He stopped when he saw that Tom was looking towards a group of cleaners busily at work on an engine, Jim among them.

'Don't you let yourself be bothered by that young fire-eater,' Dai advised. 'He's probably forgotten all about it by now.'

But Jim had by no means forgotten and over the following few days he put his threats into practice. It was like school all over again, Tom thought, when he used to dread the end of the day and the protection of the classroom as he anticipated Jim waiting for him in the school playground. Now Jim's methods were more subtle.

'Who's brought a bad smell in here then?' Jim asked, sniffing the stale air of the cleaner's cabin when Tom arrived for his break. 'You smell it Les?'

Les looked uncomfortable while a couple of the other cleaners laughed. Tom silently picked up his lunch box took it over to where Les and Ginger were perched on a rickety bench. He sat down beside them, keenly aware of Jim's watching eyes and amused expression. Tom opened his box. His sandwiches were gone. In their place was a mess of oily waste.

Jim stood up. 'Reminds me of the farmyard,' he said casually sauntering out of the room.

Ginger thrust out a sandwich. 'Here – have one of mine.'

Tom shook his head. 'I'm not hungry.'

Quietly he began cleaning out his box, watched by the others.

Then there was the afternoon in stores. Tom had spent some time arranging the pay tins in numerical order on a tray. As he picked up the tray to take it to the Wages Clerk, his elbow was jogged and the tray with its contents went flying.

'Oops, sorry mate,' Jim said from behind him.

'You finished with those pay tins?' Billy Hughes said bustling up. 'Hurry up with them now, they want to make up the wages.'

Tom knelt to pick up the tins from the floor as Jim went off, whistling.

Little things, nothing big enough to challenge Jim with, but all adding to a feeling of helplessness. Tom would almost have welcomed an open fight as in their schooldays rather than this drip, drip of small bullying tactics.

Les and Ginger watched in silent sympathy but could not intervene and Tom wouldn't have wanted their sympathy. He hated to be pitied. But, he thought, he would get his own back. Oh yes, he would get his own back.

The following night he was putting the finishing touches to the cab of the heavy freight engine 2843 when Jim's voice broke in.

Right you lot. Grub.'

'About bloody time too,' Les grumbled as he followed Ginger off the engine. Jim climbed down after them. Tom gave a final wipe to the regulator and glanced round the interior of the cab. It looked good. Satisfied, he swung himself out to begin climbing down the steps – and nearly slipped on the first one. He looked down. The step was liberally smeared with grease. Slowly he began to clean it off.

He entered the lobby to find Les and Ginger standing in front of one of the notice boards, deep in conversation.

'..it was when Barney had just finished cleaning Norton Hall's coupling rods,' Ginger was saying.

Jim hurried out, brushing past Tom.

'Where's he off to in such a hurry?' asked the Time Clerk, pushing his glasses for the umpteenth time back up his nose. He repeated this action continuously, having a narrow face and a very thin, straight nose, and was, not surprisingly, nick-named Nosey. He had been given the name from the moment he had arrived at the shed, twenty-six years ago, and there were few who remembered his real name, Jimmy Prior.

'Probably gone to have a kip in a warm firebox,' Joe remarked, handing over his disc to book off.

'Strictly against the rules,' said Nosey mildly, pushing his glasses up again.

Les shivered. 'Can't say I blame him. Bloody freezing in here.'

'Anyway,' Ginger continued, 'Witty threw his stick at him, yelling that the rods were filthy. Couldn't have been cleaned for God-knows how long, but it wasn't really Barney's fault for it wasn't one of our engines, it came from Newport.'

'Yeah, well, what did Witty expect,' Les commented. 'Lazy lot down at Newport.'

Tom hesitated for a moment, then went out. He glanced round the shed and caught sight of Jim climbing up into the cab of 2843. Tom glanced round again. There was no-one in sight.

He waited patiently. Five minutes, ten minutes. He walked quietly over to the engine, climbed the steps, and peered cautiously into the cab. There was no sign of Jim. He bent down to look in the firebox. Jim was neatly curled inside, using his jacket as a cushion for his head. It was warm in there even though its fire had been dropped some hours earlier and Jim was fast asleep and snoring gently. Hardly daring to breathe, Tom closed the doors and latched them together before straightening up. He looked both ways before climbing down from the cab and hurrying over to the cleaner's cabin.

He arrived to find Ginger and Les huddled over the stove. Tom took out his sandwiches and began to eat.

'Want to come in on the game?' asked Ginger, looking up from the card game they were playing.

'No – no thanks.'

He watched the game for a moment before getting up to pour himself a mug of tea.

'Put some more coal on, will you?' Les said, without looking up. 'It's real brass monkey weather.'

'Righto.' Tom filled the stove then sat munching his sandwiches, although they tasted like sawdust. He shivered in a moment of excitement and fear. Mad, he thought, he must have been mad.

He looked up at the clock. Like everything else in the cleaners' cabin it was a reject from a station clock. The end of the minute hand was broken off and it had a tendency to move jerkily forwards for one minute then backwards for two. The cleaners were used to it and would joke about it being like the job of a cleaner, one step forwards, two steps back, especially if Witty was on the warpath!

Tom put down his sandwich. Perhaps he should go and unlatch the firebox doors. But he stayed rooted to his seat and watched, un-seeing, as the card game progressed.

At last Les put down his cards, yawned and stretched.

'Nice while it lasted. Oh well, back to the grindstone.'

Ginger looked up. 'Do you think someone ought to wake Jim? Not like him to have overslept.'

'I'll do it,' Tom said quickly and rushed from the room.

He was too late.

As he approached the engine, he saw Alf Wittall and Jim staring down at him from the footplate.

*****

'It was a bloody stupid, dangerous thing to do and I won't have that kind of horse-play going on in this shed – do you understand? Both of you?'

'Yes sir.'

Jim and Tom were in the foreman's office, standing, caps in hands, in front of a grim-faced Geoff Willis, the night foreman, who was sitting behind his desk. Alf was standing behind them like a jailer.

Geoff turned to Jim. 'Let this be a lesson to you, Salter, that you don't catch up on your beauty sleep inside a locomotive firebox, however cosy and warm it is. If you're that tired, I suggest you get more sleep at the proper time not during the Company's time. The Great Western pays you to work, not to sleep.'

He turned to include Tom.

'I know there's been a bit of bother between you two. I don't want to know what it's about; I'm not interested. I don't care what either of you do when you're not at work, but when you're here you leave your private quarrels outside this shed. Understand?'

'Yes, sir,' they chorused in unison.

'And as for you, Watkins, I'm disappointed in you and I know your dad will be too. You're not messing here you know, you're not back at school. If you want to end up a driver like your dad you've got to understand what this job's about.' He leant forwards. 'It means growing up, lad, and not shutting your mate in the firebox for a joke or for any other reason. And if you can't do that pretty fast, you'd better think seriously whether you're really suited for this job.'

He looked from one to the other. 'You can both book off straight away and I'm suspending you tomorrow. You'll lose a day and a half's pay.' He sighed and bent his head to the mass of paperwork on his desk. 'I've wasted enough time already, now clear out, both of you.'

*****

'See you, Charlie,'

'Righto mate.'

Fred walked briskly off to the pathway leading to the footbridge across the main line. Once on the bridge he paused to look across to the station. A number of passengers were standing on Platform Two, huddled into themselves against the chill wind as they waited for the 7.30 Birmingham train and the day's work. One man rustled the morning newspaper, another stamped his feet irritably up and down, a lad porter was balanced precariously on a ladder, cleaning a light. Even at that distance Fred could hear his tuneless whistle. Two porters were busy manhandling a laden cart to one end of the platform.

There was the whistle of the approaching train and Fred turned to watch its arrival. His eye was caught by a lonely figure seated at the far end of the platform. He sighed and made his way across the bridge.

'Acton Chalcote! Acton Chalcote Station!' the porter shouted. 'Birmingham train stopping at Crosley, Matchurch and Birmingham Snow Hill! Platform 1 for the next train to Oxford and Paddington! This is Acton Chalcote Station!'

Tom jumped as he felt a hand on his shoulder.

'You shouldn't be here you know,' Fred said. 'Railwaymen aren't permitted to go through the station.'

He sat on the bench beside Tom and glanced at him.

'So, what happened?'

Tom shrugged. 'I got suspended.'

'How long for?'

'Rest of today and tomorrow.'

'I heard what you did. It's not the end of the world. We've all done daft things in our time,' Fred said cheerfully. 'Not that I'm condoning it, mind. Bloody stupid thing to do.'

Tom bit his lip.

'Mr Willis said I ought to think about whether I'm suited for the job,' he began slowly, tentatively.

''Course you're suited,' Fred was dismissive.

The train doors slammed shut, the engine whistled and the train departed. Fred watched it go.

'I don't know if I am suited,' Tom mumbled.

'What's that?' Fred turned back to his son.

'I said I don't know if I am suited.'

'Don't talk such rubbish, of course you are.' Fred stood up. 'You're my son, aren't you?'

Tom hunched into himself. 'Don't see what that's got to do with it.'

Fred sat down again. 'Look, just what is this?'

'Perhaps,' Tom began, summoning his courage, 'perhaps I shouldn't have got a job on the railway in the first place. I – I just don't fit in…'

Fred snorted. 'Don't fit in? I never heard such a load of nonsense!'

'But I don't!'

A train pulled in and stopped at Platform One with a hiss of steam and squeal of brakes.

'Acton Chalcote! This is Acton Chalcote! This train's for Gratton, Beesham, Oxford and London Paddington!' Change here for Shrewsbury. Acton Chalcote Station!'

Doors opened and a few passengers emerged. Parcels were loaded into the guard's van.

Fred watched the activity before turning back.

'Know what the trouble with you is? You're over-tired, that's what. Come on. Let's get you home.'

He stood up.

'You don't understand!'

Fred made an exasperated noise. He was rapidly losing his temper. 'Understand? Of course I bloody understand! I understand a lot more about you than you think. Just like me you are, and I know what this job means to you...'

'I'm not like you and I never wanted to work for the railway!' Tom blazed out. 'I never did!'

In the tense silence that followed, the train on Platform One departed.

'Well that's the first I've heard of it then. So you never wanted to work for the railway? Don't give me that! Weren't you mad about engines as a nipper? Didn't you used to beg me to take you down to the shed? Why you bawled your head off the first time I took you when it was time to go home. Well, didn't you?'

'Once I went to the shed with you – just once – and I loathed it. It's all – all in your mind. I'm not like you and I never have been! Oh, what's the use!'

He stood up and began to hurry off. Fred followed.

'So you never wanted a job on the railway? You expect me to believe that? Go on – pull the other one, it's got bells on it! And if that's the case then you must have put up a pretty convincing show when you went to Swindon for your interview because, let me tell you lad, jobs with the Western don't grow on trees. The Company can pick and choose who they want, and they don't take on lads who don't want to work for them. So why did you bother, eh? Why – when you didn't want to work for the railway in the first place?'

'Stop it – stop!' Tom shouted. 'You never let me explain...never! It's all so – so complicated!'

Fred laughed. 'Complicated? Strikes me as bloody simple. You get a bollocking from Ben, get scared what I'll say, so you make up this rubbishy story. Next you'll be saying that I pushed you into it. That it? Is that what you mean?'

'No! Yes – not in the way you mean!'

'Well, that's gratitude I must say! That really is. So it turns out to be all my fault!'

Tom stopped and turned to his father. 'I didn't mean that!'

'Well you should say what you bloody mean!'

Tom turned and walked on, while Fred took a deep breath, trying to control his anger.

'Look son – Tom – look... Nance and me have never tried to make you do anything you didn't want. We've never pushed you into anything. We've had our plans... it's only natural... all parents have... but we've never pushed you. But when you decided you wanted to come on to the footplate – and it was your decision, make no mistake about that – well, I don't mind admitting that we were proud, very proud.'

He put a hand on Tom's shoulder. Tom glanced at him briefly, then down. He felt defeated. The gulf between them was too wide.

'You see,' Fred went on as they carried on walking, 'you're carrying on a long tradition in this family...'

Tom shook his father's hand off violently. 'For God's sake, dad, is that all it's ever meant to you? The family tradition?'

'What's wrong with that? It's a fine tradition and a fine job and a fine Company to work for and I'm not ashamed to have followed my father and his father, yes and his father before that on to the footplate!'

'That's not what I said!' Tom shouted. 'Stop twisting things!'

They walked on in silence, rounding the water column before stepping on to the walkway behind Platform 3. A couple of railwaymen passed, glancing curiously from one to the other.

'Evening Fred,' said one of them, nodding to Tom.

Tom started to speak, then stopped. What was the use, he thought despairingly. What was the use?

'You'll never bloody understand!' he cried before breaking away and rushing off. Fred stopped and watched him go.

******

It was peaceful on the allotment, despite its proximity to the main line. The only sound was the occasional noise of a passing train and a tuneless whistling from one of the railwaymen working on his plot of ground. Built on land owned by the Great Western, Acton Chalcote's allotment ran alongside the shed and was for the use of its railway workers.

Early morning sun slanted across dozens of marked off plots of earth, many with freshly turned soil already showing shoots of winter vegetables. Each patch contained a shed, some newly painted, others in need of repair.

Dai Davies came out of his rather dilapidated shed, spade in hand, and was hailed by Frank Bateson, one of the senior drivers. Frank had stopped to catch his breath after turning over a section of soil prior to planting spring cabbage. They exchanged a few words before Frank bent his head once more to his work. Dai surveyed his own patch, gave a sigh and was about to start digging when he saw Tom sitting on a tree stump at the edge of the allotments. Dai regarded him in silence for a moment then stuck his spade firmly in the soil and made his way over.

'D'you fancy a drink?'

Tom looked up and shook his head.

'Me neither. Mind if I join you?'

Tom shrugged.

'I'll take that for acceptance,' Dai said wryly, sitting on an adjacent stump. He got out a packet of cigarettes and offered it to Tom who shook his head.

'You're probably wishing I'd bugger off and leave you alone,' Dai said, shaking out a cigarette. 'Right?'

Tom didn't reply.

Dai lit up and inhaled deeply. 'You're probably also working out what you'll say to the gaffer when you hand in your notice. Right again?

What do you want?' Tom muttered.

Dai regarded him with sympathy. 'I know what happened this morning. The whole shed does - probably the whole town as well by now. If you must have a row with your dad I'd advise you to choose a less public spot than Acton Chalcote Station in the morning rush hour,' he added wryly.

'I didn't start it.' Tom said defensively.

'No - I don't suppose you did. You didn't start all that trouble with the young fire-eater either. I was there, remember?'

There was a moment's silence.

'It's not just that,' Tom muttered.

'I know.' Dai thought for a moment. He looked reflectively at his cigarette before continuing. 'Look Tom, I didn't come from a railway family like you. My father's a miner. So are my brothers - well Gareth and Alun are. Owen was killed in the war. So why didn't I follow the family tradition and go down the pits you might be asking?' He glanced at Tom. 'But then again you might not. Well, I won't bore you with the story of my life, but I didn't go on the railway because I'd a burning ambition to be a driver. Far from it. I wanted to be a poet.' He gave a short laugh. 'What I suppose I'm saying is that there's all sorts of reasons why men go on to the footplate and it's not always because they were keen train spotters when they were lads. For many of them it's just a job, same as any other. There's nothing wrong with that.'

There was a long pause before Tom said quietly, 'It's more than a job to dad.'

'I know that, so does everyone else, but why should you let it bother you?'

'I don't know. Because he expects so much and I just can't…'

'Live up to it? Of course you can't and why should you?' They sat in silence while Dai finished his cigarette. He threw away the butt-end and ground it into the soil with his foot. 'It's not a bad job taken by and large you know. Oh it's got its ups and downs of course, especially if your mate happens to be one of the few miserable buggers who like to give their firemen a hard time. Most of them are all right though.' He glanced at Tom. 'You've not really given it a fair chance, have you?'

There was silence. Frank, having finished planting and put away his tools, locked up his shed and walked over to them.

'You two coming to the MIC tonight?

Dai looked up at him. 'Trying to drum up support Frank? You couldn't keep me away.'

Frank glanced at Tom, waited for a moment before shrugging slightly.

'Well…see you later then.'

He nodded and walked off. Dai stood up.

'I found out, by the way, what made Jim late that morning. When you were given his firing turn.'

Tom also rose but did not reply.

'It was because of his dad. He's a driver with the North Eastern. Was a driver I should have said. He just heard he's been taken off the footplate. For good. Got a burning cinder in his eye. That's something we all fear,' Dai said seriously. 'Not having A1 eyesight. Anyway, it shook young Salter up no end. His dad's something of a hero to him.'

'Well,' he added after a moment's silence. 'Digging will keep I suppose. Must go and have a bite and clean myself up for the MIC.'

He walked back to his patch, leaving Tom staring after him.

******

The MIC or Mutual Improvement Classes held regular meetings for educating and training the more junior staff in all aspects of the profession. They were run by senior drivers in their own time. Fred was often one of the instructors but that evening it was Frank Bateson. The Acton Chalcote classes were held in an ancient railway carriage with a clerestory roof placed in one of the sidings. The interior had been gutted and wooden forms ran around the inside. In the centre of the carriage stood an old round stove with a pipe sticking out of a hole in the roof, emitting minimal warmth and maximum smoke. At one end of the carriage was a blackboard perched on an easel with a well-worn table beside it. On the table rested a brass model of an engine, cut through to reveal its working parts.

The carriage was full of drivers, firemen and cleaners when Tom, washed, changed, and looking better after a meal and a sleep, opened the door and paused on the threshold, blinking to adjust his eyes to the dim lighting and haze of thick smoke coming from cigarette smoke and the stove.

'Over here mate!' called Ginger who was perched on a bench alongside Les.

Tom raised his hand in acknowledgement. He was about to go over to them when he caught sight of Jim sitting in a corner of the carriage. After a moment's hesitation he crossed over.

'Sorry about your dad...' he mumbled awkwardly. 'I didn't know...'

Jim looked at him but didn't speak.

'And sorry about what happened...' Tom shrugged and his voice tailed away.

There was another moment of silence.

'That's all right,' Jim mumbled.

Tom hesitated, but when Jim turned to talk to the cleaner next to him, he re-crossed the carriage to sit down on the bench in the space left by Ginger and Les who had squashed together to make room for him.

Frank came in and walked over to the table in a purposeful manner. He looked around and waited until there was silence.

'Right then lads - let's begin. This evening I'm going to talk about the vacuum brake, and I'll start by asking a question. What is vacuum?'

After a pause, a voice called out, 'It's - well - it's space isn't it?'

There were one or two laughs and Frank waited a moment but no-one else spoke.

'According to the book - and I'd better teach you by the book else you won't pass those exams - vacuum is space devoid of air. Now complete vacuum is registered at thirty inches, but we never work a complete vacuum for the simple reason that the system wouldn't work. We work on twenty-five inches of vacuum...'

A passenger train passed at speed on the main line alongside the siding, rocking the coach violently from side to side. Frank raised his voice slightly and continued talking.

*****

The strains of a piano sonata floated round the house. Fred listened for a moment, his hand on the knob of the parlour door before quietly entering the room. He walked over to the piano. Nancy glanced up at him then back to the music and finished the piece. Fred put a hand on her shoulder and she put her own hand up to meet his. She looked up and they smiled at each other.

'I've put the kettle on,' he said.

'Thanks. What was that row with Tom about?'

'What row?'

Nancy gave him a quizzical look.

'Did he say anything to you?' Fred asked casually.

'He didn't have to.'

Fred shrugged. 'It was nothing Nance. Nothing at all.'

Nancy stood up. 'I'll make tea.'

'No. You stay there. I'll do it. Play something else. I like hearing you play.' He went to the door, then hesitated, trying to appear unconcerned. 'Is the lad about?'

Nancy smiled. She wasn't fooled. 'He rushed through his tea, dashed up to change, muttered something about the Mutual Improvement Class and fell fast asleep. He must have woken in good time because I heard him go out a short while ago.'

Fred expelled his breath as if suddenly released from a burden. 'Did he? Did he really? Good. Good.' He opened the door. 'I thought that's where he'd be,' he said as he went out.

Nancy smiled, turned a page, and once more began to play.

Chapter Seven

The town hall clock struck six-thirty. It was a cold winter's morning and the town was shrouded in darkness. Was there a faint streak of light towards the east? Fred gazed up at the sky. To judge by the way the temperature was going down, dawn couldn't be far off. He blew on his hands to warm them.

'Bit of a rum do, when you think of it,' Charlie observed.

They were sitting on a bench in the municipal square under the fitful light of a gaslamp and a statue of an eminent benefactor of the town. Both men were in their working clothes and their lunch boxes were beside them on the seat. Fred blew on his hands again.

'What do you mean?'

Charlie was staring across the square at the dark outlines of the houses opposite. A dim light came on in an upper room, becoming suddenly brighter as the occupant drew back the curtain.

'Well, here's us, finished our day's work and there's all those buggers just waking up and getting ready to start theirs.'

'I wouldn't change it,' said Fred.

It was the time when barriers were let down, when it was good to talk, good to ease cramped limbs and let the body adjust to being on firm ground and not moving to the swaying motion of the engine's cab, good to think of a hearty breakfast followed by a few hours' sleep, albeit in a strange bed.

'Me neither,' Charlie agreed, after a pause.

Both men fell silent.

'It was a good run that,' Fred remarked, still feeling the wind against his face and the engine responding to his touch as Berrington Hall thundered through the dark countryside, the plume of steam rising high above them. He had seen such a sight a thousand times but somehow last night it had been special. He stretched out his legs. Yes. It had been a good run. He looked around. The darkness was slowly beginning to lift and unrecognisable objects were gaining shape.

'Funny old job this,' he remarked. 'I wonder how many times we've spent wandering round strange towns at strange hours of the day and night.'

'Yeah,' Charlie shivered suddenly. 'Right now I'd rather be tucked up nice and cosy with the missis.'

They watched as the growing dawn made objects recognisable. One or two people appeared, all with pinched, early morning faces. A couple walking their dog, a few men hurrying to work, a woman with a harassed look, tucking her scarf more tightly round her neck.

'I'd rather have my job than be one of those poor sods. Just look at them. Doing the same thing, day in, day out...'

'Oh I don't know,' Charlie countered thoughtfully. 'There's a lot to be said for a job with regular hours.'

'Not for me there isn't'.

'Contented bugger aren't you?'

'Aren't you?'

'Me? I suppose I would be if it wasn't for me digestion.'

'A brisk walk's what you need,' Fred said firmly. He stood up. 'Come on mate. Tilly's Café should be open by now and I could do with a good breakfast.'

*****

At Acton Chalcote it was light enough to see the goods train with nine wagons and a brake van gently move up to the signal and stop. Alfie, the guard, walked back, checking the wagons, before climbing into the brake van.

Tom hung out of the cab, watching for the signal. It changed to 'clear'.

'Right the board, mate!' Tom called over his shoulder.

George Southcombe began easing the train forwards while Tom watched for Alfie's wave. The train eased its way out of the sidings and on to the main line.

'Right the guard, mate,' Tom called, acknowledging the guard's green signal from his lamp.

George pulled on the whistle, opened the regulator, and glanced at the fire as Tom picked up the shovel.

'Get a bit around her Tom. We've quite a load to pick up.'

Tom nodded. He was visibly nervous and strained over each shovelful. George watched him with sympathetic amusement.

'No need to kill yourself lad. There's a long day ahead.'

Tom didn't answer.

'First trip on the road?'

'Yes.'

'Thought so. Don't worry. I'll see you right. Have you reversed the dampers?'

To begin with, George's large, comforting presence was reassuring. It became less so, as the morning progressed. As more wagons were taken on, Tom became acutely aware of George watching his every move, and then passing comments. It grew increasingly irritating. Tom remembered that George's name among the cleaners was Southey the Fusspot. With good reason, he thought, thrusting his shovel resentfully into the pile of coal.

'Keep the back end well up, Tom,' George advised, inspecting the fire.

Tom gave the shovel a tremendous swing, hit the side of the firebox and coal spewed across the footplate. George gave him an amused look but said nothing while Tom flushed and began clearing up the mess.

The job of picking up wagons continued and, as the train lengthened, Tom was kept hard at work keeping the balance between enough fire and sufficient water. Despite the cold wind, he was sweating profusely by the time they were diverted into a loop just outside Crosley Station to be held until an express passenger train had passed by on the main line.

George brought the train to a stand with a hiss of brakes and mopped his brow with a large red and white spotted handkerchief.

'Now you put the feed on and hose that shovel down while I get myself organised,' he instructed Tom. 'Then I'll cook you a George Southcombe special. I expect the missis has given me enough to feed an army, she usually does...'

He rummaged in his lunch box, took out a clean cloth and spread it on the seat. He followed this by diving again into his box and bringing out thick slices of buttered bread, eggs, sausages, mushrooms, and tomatoes. Tom watched in awe. It reminded him of a magic show he'd been taken to as a child when the magician had produced item after item out of a top hat.

George glanced up. 'I like my food, Tom, I'll not deny that, but if I was to eat my way through half what my Elsie gives me, I'd be three times the size I am now.' He chuckled richly. 'And I'm no light-weight am I?' He dived once more into his box and brought out, with a flourish, thick rashers of bacon with fat smeared between the slices.

'There we are... just polish that shovel off with a bit of waste will you? That's it...'

He took the shovel from Tom, laid the bacon and sausages on it, and cracked the eggs before placing the shovel just inside the firebox, balancing it carefully.

'It's an art, Tom. Once lost my whole breakfast by knocking the shovel against the side.'

As if by magic, footsteps could be heard on the steps.

'Timed that nicely, Alfie. Care for some grub?'

'Not 'arf! I was hoping you'd ask. Brought along some of Gladys' fruitcake for afters.'

George withdrew the shovel, tested the sausages with a fork, then added the tomatoes and mushrooms.

'There's salt and pepper in my box, Tom. Get them out will you?'

Tom and Alfie exchanged grins. Alfie sat down on the fireman's seat while Tom perched on an upturned bucket.

George meanwhile had taken out the shovel and begun making giant-sized sandwiches.

'This is the life, eh?' he said happily as he took a large bite.

******

Fred and Charlie, on their second mug of tea after a hearty breakfast, were playing a game of chess with Fred's pocket chess set. Tilly's Café had filled up with late and early workers and the air was fuggy and warm. Condensation streamed down the windows.

'Check,' said Fred, moving his queen into position.

Charlie quietly moved his knight to block the move and the game progressed.

'Bit of a daft move there Charlie,' said Fred, taking the knight.

'Mmm. Not thinking. Your game I think.'

Fred began to reset the pieces.

'That makes it one each. Best of three?'

'Not right now.' Charlie yawned. 'I could do with some shut-eye.'

'Me too if Molly Parkins'll let me.' Fred laughed. 'She's a talker that one.'

He carefully wrapped up the chess pieces in a clean piece of cotton waste and put them away.

'You should try my lodgings,' Charlie said. 'Old Ma Jones is all right.'

Both men stood up.

'Got the bill, love?' Fred asked the waitress. 'It's that smell of kippers I can't abide,' he said to Charlie. 'It's even in the sheets.'

Charlie laughed. 'Better'n some smells I could name on other double home turns. You shouldn't be so fussy mate.'

They left the café and began to walk together down the road.

'Anyway, I've something to do before I kip down.'

'Something for the missis?'

Fred nodded. 'I like to get her something when I'm on double home turn. Only small things, a bit of chocolate, some knick-knack or other…nothing fancy… just something…'

'My missis would think I've something to hide if I started buying her presents.'

'I've always done it. Broke one of her teeth on a stick of rock I got her at Torquay when I took 4088 down to Devon. Before your time, Charlie. But I never know whether or not she likes me doing it,' Fred finished, almost to himself.

'Doesn't she say?'

'Oh yes, she seems pleased… but I never really know…'

'Why do you do it then?' Charlie asked, suppressing a yawn.

Fred shrugged. 'Because I'm away from home so much… because she gets out of the house so little… I don't know…'

They stopped at a crossroads.

'I'll turn off here.'

'Don't forget, we're off shed at six ten,' Fred replied, suddenly brusque.

'I'll be there early just to make sure,' Charlie reassured him. 'Those Laira men'd have your pants off soon as your back's turned. I wouldn't put it past them to nick the headlamps off your loco if they felt like it, just to save walking down the stores.'

Fred laughed. 'They're not that bad. Still, suit yourself.' He nodded as Charlie turned to go. 'Have a good sleep mate.'

'You too.'

Fred walked briskly towards the shops, annoyed with himself for sharing his concerns with Charlie. He and Charlie had, over the years, shared a great deal, but never his deepest worries, worries that he only half admitted to himself. Did Nancy really like the small presents he bought her? Did he really know anything at all about his wife? She was too good for him, he knew that. He'd been lucky, he knew that too. So lucky. Or perhaps it was divine providence looking after him. He glanced for a moment up at the slate-grey sky, as if half-expecting to see a benign face peering down at him, although, he thought ruefully, the Almighty wouldn't be gazing at him in friendly fashion, not after the way he had neglected him for years.

Suddenly physically tired but with his brain as active as ever, Fred was not yet ready for what would be Molly Parkins effusive welcome which he would escape, as soon as was polite, to a lumpy bed and a few hours' sleep. So he sought refuge on another bench, this time outside an imposing church.

His mind wandered back to the Ebenezer Baptist Chapel which had played such a large a part in his childhood. Chapel on Monday with Bible Study, Chapel on Wednesday with Choir Practice. Saturdays were always devoted to some fund-raising or other, where he and his brothers and sisters would be energetically involved in setting out tables and chairs, washing up endless cups and saucers and being polite to the chapel elders and their wives. Sundays of course saw three visits to

Chapel – the morning and evening services and Sunday School in the afternoon. He hadn't minded it, any of it. His father had been Deacon of the Chapel and Fred could remember sitting, enthralled, as the tall, commanding figure read the lesson: 'Put on the whole armour of God, that ye may fight to stand against the wiles of the devil...' He could still quote whole passages from the Bible from memory if he put his mind to it.

He had thought, at one time, that he had a vocation and remembered how uncomfortable his over-zealous piety had made everyone at the time, even his devoutly religious parents. For a while thought of serving the Almighty had vied with a life serving the Great Western Railway. What, he wondered, had tipped the balance? Probably something in the blood, as he had told Tom many a time. It was something you couldn't get away from, no matter how hard you tried. He thought back to the long talks he had held with his father on the subject.

'Well, Gruffydd, we've never had a Minister in our family and if you feel called to service in this way then your mother and I would be proud that the Almighty has singled you out to do his holy work,' his father had said with a great deal of solemnity. His father had been a solemn, God-fearing, and often formidable person. 'But we'd also be proud if you followed in the family tradition and worked for the railway. All you can do is pray that the good Lord shows you which path you should take and all your mother and I can do is pray for you.'

And he had prayed. Night after night Fred remembered kneeling by his bed on the uneven wooden floor, asking God, pleading with him, demanding some sign to show whether he should truly abandon a job which he ached for with every fibre of his being – that of becoming an engine driver on the Great Western Railway - to take a very different path. Sitting on the hard bench, his knees ached now with the remembrance of the hard, uneven surface of the floor.

'Can't you go and pray somewhere else?' Morfudd, his sister, had said. 'Whenever I come up here, I trip over you.'

Morfudd was courting at the time and the only place she and her intended could be alone in that small, overcrowded house, was the back bedroom.

'You know what our mam would say about you carrying-on with Alun like you do?' Fred had replied solemnly. 'Downright wicked, that's what she'd say.'

'And are you going to tell her then?' Morfudd had retorted sharply. 'There's priggishness for you! Oh, go and talk to God somewhere else for goodness' sake!'

She had flounced off, and Fred had transferred his venue in wrestling with the Almighty in the relative peace of the privy at the bottom of the garden. That was until he had been driven from there by his younger brother, who was suffering from a surfeit of stolen, unripe plums and needed the place urgently.

'Retribution, that's what it is,' he had told Evan self-righteously as he emerged from the privy in order to make way for his brother. 'Serve you right for stealing.'

'Bugger off Gruffydd and polish your halo somewhere else!' Evan had retorted before rushing in and slamming the door.

Gruffydd, Fred thought reflectively. No-one had called him that for a long time now. His parents were dead, taken during the flu epidemic in 1919. Morfudd had married, not Alun, a shunter on the railway, but Edward Jones, a very respectable bank clerk from Pontypridd. They never saw each other now. His other sister, Ceri, younger than him and the bright darling of the family, was also dead, taken in the same terrible pandemic that came upon the world after the war had ended – as if it had been a judgement from God on the evils of war-mongering, as the preacher had once thundered from the unadorned pulpit in the Ebenezer Baptist Chapel. Evan, his cheeky brother of the stolen plums, had died somewhere on the

Western Front. His only remaining brother, Huw, was on the other side of the world and only wrote occasionally. Well, Fred thought, that's the way it goes nowadays with families.

Whether it was the Almighty's answer to his youthful prayers, he had ended up on the railway and Gruffydd Watcyn had become Fred Watkins, largely, he thought wryly, due to the shed foreman's acute case of piles at Gloucester's engine shed. When he moved to Acton Chalcote as a passed fireman the name had gone with him and was a part of him now, part of the man he had become.

He remembered how lonely he had been to begin with at Acton Chalcote, missing his home and the tight-knit communities of the engine shed and chapel. At the Gloucester shed there had been friends from Wales and it had not been too far to have a ride home on the cushions on his days off. In any case, he had often travelled through Rhydhafren, on goods trains. It was familiar territory.

Acton Chalcote, however, was alien territory, deep in the heartland of England. He was able to get home less often and the landlady of his digs had been cold and unfriendly. Almost as cold and unfriendly as the room he rented from her. Now what was her name? Mrs...oh yes, Mrs Ellington. A widow, having lost her husband and two boys on the Somme. Separated now by a gulf of years he could think of her with pity, but to the young passed fireman she was an additional trial. He had yet to prove himself at his new shed and his uncompromising Christianity threw up a barrier between himself and his workmates. The reputation he later acquired had yet to be built. There was no non-conformist chapel in Acton Chalcote and Fred found himself adrift for the first and only time in his life.

He remembered wandering round the streets one evening, unwilling to go back to his digs. He had wandered into the Anglican St. Peter's Church, kneeling to pray in the pew at the back, but the elaborate architecture and glowing colours of the alter cloth offended his puritan soul. Used to the Baptist Chapel's stark simplicity, Fred found it hard communicate with the Almighty in such surroundings.

Funny, Fred thought. It was a St. Peter's church where he and Nancy had got married.

Nancy. That reminded him. He had yet to find a suitable present for her. A bit stiffly he got to his feet and began to wander up the High Street, looking cursorily into the shop windows. Nancy. His meeting her was, in a sense, when the first chapter of his life ended. Not in his decision not to enter the ministry, nor in Ron Haddon's arbitrary re-christening of him in the Gloucester shed, Nancy signalled his break with chapel and all that that entailed. Not, he thought, that he was not still a God-fearing man. He hoped he was. But it had signified his homecoming to a new home in the centre of England. It signalled the start of his real dedication to his job and a new contentment based on a pride in himself, a growing reputation among his colleagues, a wife he adored and eventually a son to follow in his footsteps, to do even better things and aspire to greater heights. And it had all begun with a major tussle with his conscience.

It had been another of those long, lonely evenings, he remembered, evenings that, in retrospect, had always seemed cold. He was off-duty, and shunned the temptation of the Great Western pub, the haunt of off-duty railwaymen, for Gruffydd had been brought up strictly teetotal, regarding public houses on a level with cinemas, theatres and brothels as yet further manifestations of the devil. Fred had not quite shaken off this upbringing as he walked the streets of Acton Chalcote, trying to steel himself to return to his joyless room and write a long-delayed letter to his mother.

It had begun to rain, and the lights of The Regal Cinema beckoned temptingly. A burly commissionaire, all gold braid and crimson uniform, moved out of the rain to the shelter of the canopy and looked down his long nose at Fred.

'Only seats left are in the one and nines,' he said majestically.

Fred had looked past him, through the massive double doors to the deep red plush of the interior, glowing with golden light which reflected the polished brass of the fittings and reminded him of the polished brass of the steam locomotives. Surely, he had remembered thinking to himself, it could not be so very sinful to go to the cinema – depending on the film of course. He examined the billboard. Charlie Chaplin in a film called 'The Kid'. The blurb read that it was a film about an abandoned child. It could not be that wicked and Fred had heard of Charlie Chaplin.

It had begun to rain, and he had turned up the collar of his coat. The thought of his room seemed even less appealing than before and without any further conscious thought Fred found himself through the double doors and into the foyer. The doors had swung together behind him with a faint sigh and this sound seemed to mark a definite break with something. A pang of conscience smote him, but he smothered it as he walked to the cashier sitting in her glass booth.

And that was how he had met Nancy. Not the cashier who had taken his proffered one shilling and nine pence and issued a ticket. He had been shown to his seat and sat in comfort, looking around slightly guiltily at the audience before focussing his gaze on the deep red curtains in front of the screen.

And then it had happened. A woman appeared, walked on to the stage and seated herself at the impressive piano which was placed to one side. A tall, slim figure in a long dark-green gown, a mass of unruly light-brown hair framing a fine-boned face. There was a smattering of applause from the audience. Nancy raised her hands and began to play the opening music for the film. The curtain swept apart, the British Board of Film Censors certificate appeared, and the film began.

To this day Fred had no memory at all of the film. His eyes were fixed on the pianist, who was watching the screen intently in order to play the relevant music as the scenes changed. It was a virtuoso performance which moved from sad to comic, from danger to fear, according to the action being played out silently on the screen. Nancy's eyes were focussed, and her hands moved over the piano keys as if with a mind of their own.

The film ended, the heavy red plush curtains swept across the screen and Fred, together with the audience, rose to stand in silent attention as Nancy played 'God save the King'. When it had ended the audience began to move towards the exits. Fred remained in his seat, but his view of the stage was obstructed by the people pushing past. Once they had left, he saw that Nancy had gone.

The following days, shifts permitting, Fred haunted the cinema, waiting patiently by the side entrance both before and after the performances, paying to see the film again and again. It was no good. Nancy was like a will-o-the-wisp or a creature from another world who appeared on the stage at the start of the film and disappeared at the end.

It was two weeks before he saw her in any guise other than in the cinema and it was, surprisingly, in Station Road, which he walked down daily on his way to and from the shed. She was just coming out of a large house, one of half a dozen nearest the railway, which were inhabited by the upper echelons of the railway hierarchy. He discovered later that her father was the District Locomotive Superintendent, and that Nancy was so far above him as to be unobtainable, for at the time he was a very newly passed fireman, just one step up on the ladder towards being a driver.

Why she ever looked twice at me I'll never know, Fred reflected humbly. But she did. He remembered speaking to her before she turned into the road.

'You're the one who plays the piano at The Regal,' he had said, removing his cap and twisting it in his hands.

She turned a bright-eyed gaze on him. Her eyes were large and dark brown.

'Did you like the film? I love Charlie Chaplin, don't you?'

He blushed bright red. 'I didn't see it,' he admitted. She waited, her head on one side.

'I was watching you,' he mumbled.

Nancy burst out laughing.

And that had been it, Fred thought. Mentally he shook himself. No point going back over the past. He must be more tired that he knew. Time he retraced his steps to Molly Parkins' digs and a bit of shut eye. He glanced at the shop he was passing and stopped.

Tucked into a corner of the window was a small wooden box, intricately carved, its lid encrusted with tiny sea shells which glowed in the light that illuminated the shop window. That was it. That was it. Without hesitation Fred pushed open the shop door and went inside.

Chapter Eight

George swallowed the last bite of cake and took out his pipe.

'Mmm. Very nice, Alfie. Proper tasty I must say. I do like a nice slice of fruit cake.'

'Not bad,' Alfie agreed. 'We have our ups and downs, Gladys and me, but she's a grand cook.'

'Well, you can't say fairer than that.' George lit his pipe and took a contented puff.

'You're not such a bad cook yourself. First-rate, that fry-up.'

'Nothing to beat bacon and eggs off the shovel I always say, although the missis don't agree. Dirty way of cooking, she says, but then she's very particular. "Look girl," I tell her, though she's no more a girl now than I'm a lad, being at least as big as me.' George chuckled. '"Look girl, I've been eating food off the shovel for more years than I care to remember and it's not done me much harm now has it?" "Well," she says, giving me a prod "it's made you a good bit heavier in bed than when I married you." Talk about the pot calling the kettle black!' he added.

Tom, half asleep on his upturned bucket, let the talk swirl round him. His eyes closed.

And flew open when 2920 St. David went past on the main line.

'Find out from the bobby how long we're going to be held here Tom.'

Tom blinked, jumped to his feet and set off for the signal box. He soon returned.

'Another express due in five minutes then it's us.'

George tapped out his pipe and Alfie walked back to the brake van while Tom, under George's instructions, tidied away the remains of their meal. Five minutes later the express thundered past, the points were changed, and the goods train came out of the loop and on to the main line.

The signalman came hurrying down the steps of the signal box to meet them.

'Quick as you can George, there's a passenger behind you.' He handed the token to Tom. 'I'd have left you in the loop myself, but Control wants you away. You've got a margin but it's tight.'

Tom showed the token to George who glanced at it and nodded.

'We've a full load on so I hope they don't expect miracles.'

'They always do,' the signalman grinned, climbing back to his box.

Tom leant over the side of the cab, waiting for Alfie's signal.

'Right away, mate!'

George opened the regulator and the train moved off.

Once past the station the train began its slow climb up the steep incline towards Crosley Tunnel. George glanced at the steam pressure gauge.

'The clock's walking back, Tom.' He looked at the fire and shook his head. 'You've too much in front. Get the pricker out and pull the fire back until it gets hot,' he ordered. 'You've got to keep her thin at the front else she won't steam and we don't want to have to stop for a blow-up on the bank. All right lad?'

Tom put down his shovel and picked up the long metal pricker, with its vicious spike at one end. With difficulty he manoeuvred it into the firebox and began pulling the fire back.

It was hard, heavy work and he was soon sweating despite the cold wind blowing through the cab.

The train crept onwards, still losing speed and Tom, exhausted, began working more slowly. George glanced over at him.

'Here, come out of the way,' he said brusquely. He took the pricker from Tom and began to rake the fire efficiently. Tom watched.

'Always was a rough old drag up here,' George commented, 'but we don't usually have a passenger up our backsides.' He glanced at the water level.

'Put your feed on, Tom.'

Tom wearily put on one injector. He moved to the second.

'Only one, or you'll knock her back too far!'

Tom bit his lip and continued to watch as George concentrated on the fire.

The engine picked up a little speed, wagons clanking and banging behind, and George, after a final rake through, examined it and put the pricker away.

'That's a bit more like it,' he said, satisfied. He glanced round at Tom.

'Don't worry lad – it's a bit of a gamble but I've been in worse spots. We'll get through the tunnel all right.'

They carried on up the incline, with the engine working hard and Tom wondering how he was to get through the remainder of the journey. George looked at the fire once more.

'Right Tom, a bit up each side but don't get too heavy-handed or you'll smother her.'

Eager to redeem himself, Tom picked up the shovel and began shovelling coal enthusiastically into the firebox. He soon slowed down.

'Put that shovel down!' George said irritably.

'No...' Tom gasped. 'I'm all right...'

'Do as you're bloody well told!'

George examined the fire, used the pricker once more then shut the firebox doors.

'There. Now leave that fire alone until I say!'

Tom looked over the side of the cab. The black hole of the tunnel was in front of them.

'Keep your head in Tom!' George called.

Darkness swept over them as the train entered the tunnel. The only light came from a crack where the firebox doors were not quite closed and the dim red glow of the gauge lamp. The noise was tremendous.

The train topped the head of the incline, burst out into daylight and began to coast down the bank. George chuckled.

'Downhill all the way – I knew we'd do it. All right, Tom?'

Tom stared at the floor of the swaying cab.

'Here, don't take it to heart, lad. It's happened to the best of us, especially on Crosley Bank. Put the feeds on and get the boiler up, then put on the handbrake.'

He turned back to look out of his side of the cab. Tom, rooted in misery, remained where he was.

'Tom! Wake up lad! It's not the end of the world!'

Tom started. 'I – I'm sorry... what did you say?'

George sighed. 'Put the feeds on and get the boiler up, then start rubbing the handbrake. And jump to it!'

He waited until Tom had moved then turned away.

The remainder of the journey passed in a blur of misery for Tom. He agonised over his mistakes and grew increasingly worried that he was just not strong enough. What if he had been firing an express passenger train to Paddington?

Once the majority of wagons had been offloaded, the train made its way home and came to rest at the south signal box of Acton Chalcote Station. Rob, the signalman, ran down the steps to take the token from Tom.

'Back inside, George,' he said.

'Righto mate.'

George pushed open the regulator and the train crept forwards.

'Inside, Alfie,' Rob advised.

'Righto.'

Having cleared the points George closed the regulator and stopped the train, waiting for the ground signal to be pulled off. Alfie gave them a wave and Tom who had been leaning out of the cab watching for the signal, turned back inside.

'We've got the dummy,' he told George.

'Watch for Alfie's signals, Tom. It's my blind side.'

Tom turned and leaned out again.

Positioned on the main line, George got ready to back the goods train into the sidings. Half-way down were a couple of stationery wagons. A shunter was waiting to signal the train back. Tom leant further out so that he could see both the shunter and Alfie. The whole of the south end of the station was also in view.

The shunter waved the train back and Alfie duplicated his signals.

Tom turned his head. 'Right back mate.'

He copied the hand signals given to him and George carefully began to move the train, watching Tom's hand signals all the while.

On Platform One a passenger train was waiting to depart southbound. Dai was leaning out, chatting to one of the drivers. They stopped talking to watch the goods train, as did a fireman, balanced on the tender of 2263, holding the leather spout as the engine took on water. The tank now full, water began to cascade over the tender. A couple of cleaners were halfway over the barrow crossing. Tom took all this in at a glance and Dai gave Tom a nod.

His attention taken, Tom did not notice that both the shunter and Alfie had changed their signal to 'slow down'. The shunter raised both hands to 'stop', but it was too late. The train ploughed into the two stationery wagons, sending them flying back hard against the buffer stop. The shunter leapt out of the way while Alfie was knocked backwards in the brake van.

George swore under his breath and applied the brake.

The train stopped and the shunter, much shaken, came rushing up to the engine.

'What the bleedin' 'ell do you think you're playin' at? Tryin' to pension me off early are you?'

George, also shaken, climbed down on to the track. 'Well why didn't you tell me there was a couple already in there half-way down?'

Alfie came up. 'The kid knew. He should've told you.'

'And what the 'ell were you doing ignoring my signals?' the shunter persisted. 'I give you a caution and a stop and so did Alfie, I saw him! Frightened the daylights out of me you did!'

'The kid was watching out. It wasn't George's fault,' Alfie insisted.

'I don't care whose bleedin' fault it was! Never saw such a rough shunt in my life – bleedin' disgustin' I call it!'

'Well, let's go and look at the damage,' George said peaceably. 'Is there any?' he asked Alfie.

'Yeah, taken ten bleedin' years off my life!' growled the shunter.

Mr Elmes, the stationmaster, hurried along the track.

'What happened driver?'

'We're just going to take a look,' George replied, and they began moving off. Tom started to climb down from the cab.

'You stay there,' George told him curtly.

Tom watched as the men walked back down the length of the train. When they returned Tom was sitting on his seat, staring into space. He jumped up as George swung himself into the cab.

'George, I...'

'It's not that bad – made a bit of a dent in the buffer blocks that's all.'

'George…'

'I know what happened, you don't have to tell me. I'm not as daft as I look lad. Think I haven't had youngsters like you before? Think you're the first to make stupid mistakes?'

Tom was silent.

'Now I've a deal to say to you but we've a job to be finished. I told Alfie we'd hook off. So off you go.'

Tom began climbing down. George poked his head over the side.

'Put a couple of brakes down and don't forget the tail lamp.'

Tom dutifully unhooked the remaining wagons and placed a tail lamp at the rear of the engine. In silence he returned to the cab and in silence George drove on to the ashpit in the shed yard. They picked up their lunch boxes and climbed down. George led the way to the base of the coal stage, stopped and turned to face Tom.

'Look Tom, two things happened today and they're quite different,' he began. 'What happened on the bank was just inexperience. You were a bit over-keen, a bit heavy-handed and then you couldn't sort out the mess after. No blame to you and nothing to go making a mountain out of. I told you that at the time, but you wouldn't listen.'

Tom looked down at his scuffed boots and didn't speak.

'I've watched you this afternoon and you've been miles away and that's why you never told me about those wagons on the road and never gave me the stop signal. You were so busy worrying about the cock-up on the bank and wondering which of your mates would get to hear of it that you weren't bloody concentrating on the job in hand. That's it, isn't it?'

'I'm sorry…' Tom began miserably.

'I don't want your apologies, Tom, I want you to understand. You can't afford to let your attention go for one

137

single second on this job. You can't afford to let your own feelings take over. This job's not a game. Oh, aye, I can see you thinking that I'm a bit of an old woman and you're not the only one as thinks that... I know what they call me behind my back... but you've not got a clue, lad... you're still wet behind the ears far as I'm concerned. I tell you Tom, I don't know whether or not you'll ever make a driver, but I do know that if you don't stop thinking the world revolves round you and your troubles you'll not get anywhere in life, whether it's on the railway or off it.'

He began to walk away.

'Come on, let's book off.'

In silence they walked to the shed. George stopped before they reached it.

'And Tom, what happened just now will be all round the yard and you'll have to face your mates and their comments. But far as I'm concerned, what happened on the bank is just between you and me see? All right?'

Tom nodded.

'But don't ever let me down like that again,' George finished. Tom nodded again. George looked at him for a moment, gave his shoulder a slight squeeze and walked off. Tom remained where he was, watching him go.

******

Nancy lifted a batch of freshly baked scones out of the oven and sniffed. They smelt good. Flushed with the heat and with her hair rapidly unravelling from her bun, she carried the tray over to the table. Sylvia was sitting on the other side, a bottle of bright red nail varnish in front of her and an undrunk cup of tea pushed to one side. She was gazing into the distance.

'Penny for them.'

Sylvia started. 'What?'

'You're miles away.'

Sylvia took a sip of tea. 'Uggh… it's cold.'

Nancy took the cup from her. 'Here, kettle's just boiled. I'll top it up.'

'Mum… can I ask you something?''

Nancy topped up Sylvia's cup and poured one for herself. She sat down at the table. 'Ask away.' She pushed the tray of scones towards Sylvia. 'Want a scone? They're still hot.'

'No thanks. Mum, does it bother you – dad working shift?'

Nancy nursed her cup in her hands. 'Not really – not now – I'm used to it.'

'But to begin with,' Sylvia persisted. 'When you first got married.'

'Well, I can't say I wouldn't have preferred your father to be home nights – especially when you were small. And of course it was hard trying to keep two toddlers quiet during the day so he could get his sleep.'

'I wouldn't put up with it,' Sylvia said decidedly, reaching for a scone. 'I wouldn't!' she reiterated when Nancy gave her a look. 'I think if you marry someone then that should come first – your marriage – and the job second. I mean, if you marry someone who works shift then everything has to be fitted round his job and I don't think that's right.'

Nancy smiled at Sylvia's muddled thinking.

'It's not like that Sylvie,' she said, gently.

'With dad it is. His job's more important than… well, than anything. It's… it's an obsession…'

Nancy laughed. 'If it had been another woman I could have tried to compete, but it's hard to do that with a hundred tons of steam engine!'

'It's not a joke, mum!'

'Oh Sylvie. Almost everyone has some sort of interest. Call it obsession, or passion, if you like. More than one perhaps. Music's my great love but it doesn't get in the way of what I feel about your father, or about you and Tom for that matter. And what about the King? His passion is for stamps, and I must say I'd rather have your dads for his engines than for books of musty old stamps.'

'I'm not going to come second to anyone's job,' Sylvia said defiantly.

'You do see things in black and white, don't you, love?' Nancy took a sip of tea. 'It's not a matter of coming second. It's more... when I decided I wanted to marry your father, his working shift and his interests never entered my head. Those things don't. It just – didn't matter. Anyway, I don't think your young man would be as obsessed with the job as your father.'

Sylvia flushed red. 'He's not my young man!'

Nancy gave a small smile.

'And what about your career?' Sylvia demanded. 'Didn't that matter?'

'What career?' Nancy began taking the scones off the tray and on to a plate.

'Your music. You gave that up when you married dad.'

'My career indeed! Pianist at The Regal Cinema! Fine career that was.'

'But you were good, mum.'

'No I wasn't. Not really. And I still play.'

'It's not the same,' Sylvia insisted.

'Well, I did enjoy it, I can't say I didn't, but the job would have come to an end anyway when the talkies came in.'

Sylvia didn't reply.

'Will you be in for supper?'

'I don't know. We're doing a show at Gratton this afternoon. And afterwards...' she broke off, shrugged, shook the bottle of nail varnish vigorously, removed its brush and began painting her nails.

Nancy watched her in sympathetic amusement. Her daughter was, she thought, very young and very transparent. She sighed suddenly, hoping she wouldn't get hurt.

******

'...and Mr Southcombe was so nice about it, that's what made it worse in a way.'

Tom was in the lane that ran along the backs of the gardens. He was leaning against Maggie's garden fence, moodily picking away at peeling bits of paint. Maggie had listened in silence to the edited version of his story while she pegged up a basketful of washing. He had not told her exactly what George had said. That was too painful.

'He's a nice man. Reminds me of a cuddly teddy bear,' she remarked when he finished.

Having offloaded his story, Tom began to feel better. 'I don't know about a cuddly bear, but he's certainly a big man. Don't know how he manages to be so nimble on the footplate.' He grinned in sudden remembrance. 'He made us, Alfie and me, a smashing breakfast on the shovel. Won't need to eat again for a week.'

Maggie concentrated on hanging up the last few items of clothes.

Tom suddenly straightened. 'Here, do you want to come fishing? I'm going. Ging said I could have his old rod and I'm just off to pick it up.'

Her face lit up. 'Just let me get my coat.'

There was a shrill voice from inside the house. 'Maggie! Maggie, you finished?'

Freda, Maggie's mother, a vision in mauve afternoon frock, patterned with bright yellow sunflowers, a tiny mauve and yellow hat perched at a rakish angle, hat and gloves in hand, came to the back door.

'Just coming mum!' Maggie called, picking up the empty basket and turning towards the house. 'Won't be long!' she said over her shoulder to Tom.

Maggie's mother was sure that life had treated her badly and signs of her dissatisfaction were apparent in her face. Despite heavy make-up and liberally applied lipstick, lines of age and resentment couldn't be easily erased. Having lost her father in the first world war and her mother soon afterwards in the epidemic of Spanish flu, Freda had been brought up by an uncaring aunt and uncle and rushed into marriage at the age of 18 with Len, a hard-drinking signalman who worked on the railway. An early pregnancy followed by two miscarriages before giving birth to her youngest, Freda felt that someone, somewhere owed her a living and she got out of the house whenever she could.

'You took your time,' she commented, 'and I can see why,' she added, flashing a brief, dismissive smile at Tom. 'Look, I've got to go out, so I've left the cutlets for your dad's supper on the draining board and the veg are done and in a pan on the stove. He can have the remains of that pie for afters. Don't go giving him the one I got today, mind, that's for you and Joey.' She began struggling into her coat. 'Oh, and Joey needs collecting from Mrs Rider. She said she'd have him 'til eight so you'd better get the meal first as you know how your dad carries on if his food's not on the table the instant he gets in.'

The bright look on Maggie's face vanished.

'I was going out, mum.'

'You can go out later, can't you? It's little enough I get out. I told Amy Gibson I'd go with her down the W.I. I'd have thought you'd have been pleased to give your mother a hand now and again the things I do for you. Now just make sure Joey goes to bed the minute you get him home and tell your father he's to stay with him and not go down the 'Western 'til one of us is back. Do him good to have to babysit for a change.

Better still, you stay with Joey 'til I'm home. It won't be much after 9.0. Can't trust Len not to leave him alone in the house.'

She buttoned up her coat. 'Brr, chilly isn't it? 'Bye, sweetheart, be good.' She blew a kiss in Maggie's direction and disappeared inside the house. They heard the front door slam shut.

Maggie turned to Tom.

'Sorry' she muttered.

Tom shrugged. 'I'll see if Ging is free. He'd probably like to try out his new rod. 'Bye!'

He hurried off down the path that ran along the back of the gardens. Maggie stared after him for a long moment, shoulders slumped in disappointment, then turned and went slowly into the house.

******

The village of Gratton, about twelve miles from Acton Chalcote, boasted two pubs, a church, a post office, a shop, a railway station about a mile from the village and a large, modern village hall. From inside came the sound of music and the stamping of many feet.

Dai hesitated outside the hall. He was late for the performance. Would it be better to go in, now that it was half over, possibly causing a disturbance, or wait outside? He thought for a moment then made up his mind. Sylvia might forgive him for arriving late, but she might not forgive him at all if he just did not turn up. Mind made up, he pushed open the swing doors and went in.

The hall was full of an appreciative audience, mostly middle-aged parents of the girls who were engaged in an intricate dance routine on the stage. Dai found it hard to distinguish Sylvia from the rest as they were all identically dressed. Then he spotted her at the end of the row as the Acton

Chalcote branch of the Women's League of Health and Beauty finished the display, bowed to enthusiastic applause, and danced off the stage.

Dai went out with the audience and made his way over to where a Dudley's coach was parked on the other side of the road. He lit a cigarette and waited.

Ten minutes later a stream of girls came chattering out of the back entrance to the hall, crossed the road and piled on to the coach, many of them glancing his way. Sylvia, talking animatedly to a tall, elegant girl, was one of the last to leave.

'Sylvia!'

She looked round.

'So you did come. I couldn't see you in the audience. What did you think of it?'

'Amazing... stupendous... exhilarating... In fact the sight of all those beautiful naked legs proved almost too much for me.'

Sylvia looked at him steadily for a moment.

'You weren't there!'

'You wrong me – oh how you wrong me!'

Sylvia gave him a look and Dai sighed. 'All right. My mother said I'd never make a good liar. I was there but only at the very end. I was unavoidably detained.'

While they were talking, Sylvia's friend had got out her powder puff and was making running repairs to her face, while casting covert glances at Dai. She decided it was time to intervene.

'Aren't you going to introduce me to your friend then Sylv?'

'Sorry. Carol, this is Dai. Dai Davies. Carol Brewer.'

Carol looked at Dai with cool appraisal and he returned her gaze. Carol looked, and was, slightly older than Sylvia. A small green cloche hat with an upturned brim was perched at a becoming angle on top of her long, blonde hair. Her make-up was immaculate and her elegantly tailored suit with its wide, boxy shoulders fitted her like a glove. Beside her, Dai thought, Sylvia looked fresh, young, and absurdly appealing.

'With a name like that you've got to be Welsh,' Carol drawled.

Dai bowed very slightly. 'What a perceptive lady you are.'

The coach driver lent out. 'You coming with us or not?' he called.

'Yes, come on Sylvie, you're holding up the works!' called one of the girls who was leaning out of the window and watching and listening avidly.

'We've plenty of room for your fella!' another one called.

'We'll all squeeze up, won't we girls?' the first one called back into the coach. There was a chorus of agreement.

Sylvia turned pink with embarrassment.

'Let me take you home,' Dai said quietly.

'I came on the coach,' Sylvia demurred.

'We'll go home on the train. It's more reliable.'

'Oh. All right. 'Bye Carol.'

Languidly Carol mounted the step. At the top she turned to stare at Dai, opening her eyes wide.

'Sylvia, I approve. I adore Welshmen.' She went inside, the door swung shut and the coach roared off to hands flapping out of the windows and a chorus of 'Byee!' 'Be good!' 'Don't do anything I wouldn't do!'

Sylvia and Dai began to walk up the road.

'What a terrifying lady.'

'Who, Carol?' Sylvia laughed. 'She's only like that when there's men around. Otherwise she's quite normal.'

'She probably eats them for breakfast. *"He that kills me some six or seven dozen of Scots at a breakfast, washes his hands and says to his wife, 'Fie upon this quiet life! I want work!'"* A female Hotspur, that's what she is.'

'Who?' Sylvia asked.

'Your friend. Shakespeare my lovely.'

'Oh.'

'I'm sorry,' Dai said contritely. 'I really don't mean to do it.'

'Do what?'

'Quote at you all the time.'

Sylvia didn't answer.

'Tired?'

'A bit.' She walked on. 'Why couldn't you come to all the show?'

'Oh, one thing and another,' Dai replied. 'Your brother started it.'

'Tom?'

'Yes. We were late getting away and that had a sort of knock-on effect you might say.' He laughed. 'What a dreadful pun.'

'Why?'

'Nothing. It wouldn't be fair to your brother to tell you.'

There was a silence.

'You are in a funny mood,' Sylvia remarked.

'I'm not. I'm my usual good-natured self.'

'You're not.' She topped. 'You're smug and ... and conceited. Quoting things I don't understand and not explaining jokes.'

'You <u>are</u> tired, aren't you?'

'I'm not! Oh... go away...!'

She hurried away from him, up the lane. Dai followed. 'Look, Sylvia, if I've upset you I honestly didn't mean to and I'm sorry. How shall I make amends? Shall I go down on my knees and beg forgiveness?'

'Don't be ridiculous.'

'Well, shall we just start again then and pretend we've only just met?' He walked away a couple of paces and turned.

'Sylvia – how lovely to see you! Whatever are you doing in Gratton? May I take you home as I see that your coach has gone?'

'You fool...' Sylvia was laughing. They walked on up the lane and into the station.

'Are you very tired?' Dai asked as they went on to the platform.

'That's the third time you've asked. Why?'

'Too tired to go dancing?'

'It depends...'

'On what? There's a good band playing at the Alhambra.'

'It's awfully expensive.'

'Isn't that my problem?' Dai replied, amused. 'Us passed firemen aren't totally impoverished you know. Tell you what – I'll even stand you fish and chips at Sid's first.'

Sylvia laughed. 'How can I resist?'

The waiting room was warm, friendly and empty when Dai and Sylvia entered. A bright fire was burning in the grate. Sylvia sat down and was silent, deep in thought. Dai watched the firelight playing on her cheek.

'Dad doesn't like you, does he?' she suddenly said abruptly.

'Whatever put that idea into your head?' Dai replied.

'But he doesn't, does he?'

Dai thought for a moment. 'I have the most enormous respect for your father. He's a formidable man and a first-rate driver... but no, he doesn't seem to like me.'

'Why?'

Dai sighed. 'Sylvia, I don't know. I'm eager, hard-working, and have no particular vices that I'm aware of. You'll have to ask him yourself.'

Sylvia turned to look into the fire.

'I – I don't know much about you...' she began shyly, 'except that you're clever of course...'

'Don't confuse an ability to reel off quotations at the drop of a hat with cleverness. One has nothing to do with the other.'

He glanced at Sylvia, who remained silent.

'What do you want to know? I'm thirty-one, clean-living and hail from the Rhondda Valley. My dad's a miner. At some tender age I decided I'd either be a poet or die tragically and heroically in the war. I'd read Dylan Thomas and Dafydd ap Gwilym...' he stopped at her bemused look. 'Dafydd ap Gwilym was one of the greatest Welsh poets there's ever been, Dylan Thomas notwithstanding. Anyway, I was hooked on poetry. I was too young to be called up and the poetry didn't go down well with my family as nothing like that had ever happened before. So they held a conference to which everyone was invited, and I mean everyone, the aunts, the uncles, the cousins, anyone who was in any way remotely related, as well as a sprinkling of friends and neighbours – it's a very tight community in the Valley. After a lot of discussion one of my uncles, who's a track inspector, suggested I get a job on the railway as it would get the poetry nonsense out of my head faster than if I went down the pits. I never could see why myself.'

'So that's what I did. Went on the railway and eventually landed up here. I knew before I was twenty that I'd never make a poet, although I do dabble in my spare time. My family, all of them, to say nothing of the friends and neighbours, heaved a collective sigh of relief. According to my mam I've a good steady job with prospects and all she wants now is for me to find a fine, pink-cheeked Welsh lass and settle down.'

Sylvia continued looking fixedly into the fire. Dai smiled.

'I found one once, but she decided she preferred a bank clerk with a stammer to a handsome, virile, romantic Welsh fireman.'

He stopped. 'Well?'

'Well, what?'

'Does the potted history satisfy you? My past is an open book – nothing hidden.'

They both looked up at the sound of the train entering the station. Dai held out his hand.

'Come on – it's our train.'

She remained where she was for a moment, then took his hand and allowed him to pull her to her feet.

******

It was early morning when Fred, carrying his shoes in his hand, quietly opened the bedroom door. He hung up his jacket and walked softly over to the bed.

'Fred?' Nancy murmured, half asleep.

'Go back to sleep Nance.'

'What time is it?'

'Just after four.'

Nancy propped herself up and switched on a bedside light.

'How was the trip?'

'Same as usual,' Fred said, sitting on the bed and taking off his socks.

'Did you find the sandwiches I left? I forgot to put them on the table.'

'I found them.'

'What time do you want waking in the morning?'

'Oh... ten o'clock'll do. That'll give me a chance to plant those sets of onions.'

He stood up and began to undo his braces.

'Everything all right here?'

Nancy snuggled back into bed. 'Tom had some sort of to-do at work. I didn't understand the half of it, but I expect he'll tell you all about it,' she said sleepily.

'Yes,' said Fred after a pause. 'I expect I'll hear about it down the shed.'

He carried on undressing, folding his trousers neatly and hanging them over the end of the bed rail. He padded across the room and fished in the pocket of his jacket which he had hung on a hook on the back of the door.

'I got you something, Nance... nothing much...' He took out the small parcel, carefully wrapped in brown paper, and placed it gently down on the bedside table.

Nancy had turned from him. She was fast asleep. Her hair, released from its ineffectual kirby grips, was spread out across the pillow. Fred watched her for a long moment.

'It'll keep 'til tomorrow,' he said quietly before slipping into bed and turning out the light.

Chapter Nine

It was a bright day with the promise of spring in the air when the pannier tank 2035 and three wagons came round a bend and began meandering at a leisurely pace along the valley, a thin trail of steam floating above it.

Seated on the driver's right-hand side of the cab, Dai contentedly watched a patchwork of fields roll past. Some were brown with rows of well-ploughed soil, others had green shoots poking up in regimented lines, yet others were of grass. Sheep and their new-born lambs scampered away from the shadow cast by the train and the sound it made. Tom, after sweeping away some dust and a few small pieces of coal, looked across to Dai.

'Dai...'

'Mmm?'

'Can I ask you something?'

'Ask away. Dai the Counsellor that's me.'

'How do you go about body building?' Tom said diffidently.

Dai looked at him, startled.

'Body building?'

'You know, building up your muscles and strength...' his voice trailed away.

Dai grinned. 'You really want to know?'

'Yes, you see...'

Dai got off his seat, suddenly business-like.

'Well, if you're sure...' He opened the regulator wide and dropped down the reversing lever. Clouds of black smoke emerged from the chimney as Dai worked the engine very hard, sending most of the fire straight up into the air. The noise filled the valley, making the sheep flee even faster and a few startled rabbits dive headfirst into their burrows.

'There you are,' he said, sitting down once more. 'Get your backside off that seat and start firing. That'll soon build your muscles!'

Tom picked up the shovel resignedly and began rebuilding the fire. Dai knocked back the regulator.

'Mustn't overdo it,' he said conscientiously. 'She doesn't like being driven rough and we don't want Sammy having a heart attack at the back.'

They resumed their leisurely pace, now into a cutting, then through more woodland before the scenery opened out once more into fields and the occasional cottage.

'This is the life,' Dai said happily. He closed the regulator and began to apply the brakes. The train slowed.

'Why are we stopping?'

'You'll see.'

The train rounded a bend, then came to a stand at a crossing. An elderly lady was waiting there, a coal bucket in her hand. She was tall and thin, with a frizz of white hair framing a face criss-crossed with lines. She was wearing a long grey skirt and yellow blouse, protected by a floral pinafore. A man's jacket was thrown around her shoulders.

'Well then, Dai, and how are you?' she asked forthrightly.

'All the better for seeing you my lovely.'

'Oh, get along with you, flatterer!'

She held up her bucket and Dai reached down to take it from her. He passed it to Tom. 'Fill this for Mrs White, would you, Tom?'

He turned back. 'And how are you keeping, sweetheart?'

'Can't complain, Dai, can't complain.'

'And Joe?'

'Him! I've no patience with him. Lazing round all day like a great baby. Moan, moan, moan that's all he does!'

'There's hard-hearted you are.'

'No good ever came of mollycoddling a man, and it's his own fault, silly old fool. Won't help himself and won't take the medicine from the doctor. He's only himself to blame, stuck in that chair of his day in, day out.'

'Poor Joe,' Dai said, trying not to smile.

'And what about you? How's that young lady of yours?'

Tom handed back the bucket, now brimming with coal.

'Must be careful what I say. This is her brother.'

Mrs White stared at Tom. 'Is he now… hmm… I hope she's a bit better looking than him.'

'Oh much,' Dai replied easily.

'I'll carry it home for you, Mrs White,' Sammy called, walking up the side of the train from the brake van.

Dai shook his head. 'Tom can do it. Part of the job. Hop down now Tom. Mrs White only lives in that cottage over there.'

Mrs White tut-tutted in disapproval. 'What do you think I am, Dai – and you, Sammy? Made of china?'

'You're as tough as nails, my lovely. Be good now and give my regards to Joe.'

Tom climbed down, took the bucket and he and Mrs White set off across the field.

'What's your name, lad?' she asked

'Tom. Tom Watkins.'

'And you're a fireman.'

'Well …. learning to be.'

'Your father's on the railway, isn't he?'

'Yes.'

'Thought so. My Joe was too. Fifty-two years as a platelayer and never a day off sick. Then he retires and it's one thing after another. I wish he'd never left. So does he. Can't be much fun for him, me nagging all day,' she added with grim humour.

They reached the small cottage with its immaculate front garden. Mrs White opened the gate and sighed.

'I've taken to doing the garden now. Joe says it makes his knees bad. I keep telling him that if he exercised a bit more they wouldn't be bad, but there's no telling him anything. Stubborn as a mule.' She led the way round to the back door. 'Just set it down here will you Tom. Thank you.'

'Can't I take it in for you?'

'No. If Joe sees you, you'll never get away. He misses railway talk you see.'

Tom turned to go but she stopped him.

'Wait a minute. I've something for you.'

She disappeared into the house. Tom glanced across the field to where the train was patiently waiting. Then came a couple of sharp whistles from the engine.

'I must go!' Tom called in a panic.

Mrs White came out with a basket of eggs.

'Laid this morning.' She handed it over to Tom.

The engine whistled again.

'Thank you,' Tom said, backing away down the path.

The engine gave a deep-throated chuff, CHUFF. Tom glanced round and saw the train begin to move.

'Careful with them now!' Mrs White called. 'Don't break them!'

'Yes. I will be.'

'And come again when you've a bit of time. Joe would like to meet you. Very lonely he gets and he'd be glad of the company, especially from the railway.'

'I will,' Tom called back, in an agony to be gone. 'Yes. Thank you. Goodbye.'

'Goodbye now.' She waved her hand after him.

Tom raced across the field. He reached the crossing, leapt over the gate without opening it and ran along the track.

'Hi! Wait! Wait for me!'

The train disappeared round a bend, then began to slow.

Dai was grinning broadly as he shut off the regulator.

As Tom reached the brake van, Sammy put out his head.

'There's another one along in a minute,' he grinned.

Tom hurried past him, along the line of wagons and climbed up as Dai opened the regulator and the train began to move.

'Thought you said you needed the exercise,' Dai grinned.

Tom leant against the side of the cab, trying to get his breath.

'You shouldn't have stayed chatting to Mrs White, Tom. You're supposed to be working.' He picked up the basket. 'Are those eggs a present?'

Tom nodded.

'I'm glad you didn't break any. Mrs White's hens lay the best eggs the English side of the border. Sheer poetry they are. To eat them is an experience in itself. Goodness knows what she feeds her hens on.' He looked through the front glass. 'Nearly at Hampton Lacey.'

The goods train pulled into the platform and Tom handed the token to the signalman.

'Passenger's on time, Dai.'

'Right you are.'

Tom checked the fire, put the injector on, swept the footplate then hosed it down with the pet pipe to lay any dust. Dai watched him, before climbing down on to the platform.

'Come on. Let's get some fresh air.'

He led the way to a bench and sat down.

'She's a lovely lady you know, Tom.'

'Mrs White?'

Dai nodded. 'And Joe. Did you see Joe?'

'No.'

'He's a real character. Very kind to me they both were when I first came to Acton Chalcote. I lodged with them for a while you know. Treated me like their own son they did.' He sighed. 'Their son was killed in the war. Photos of him are all round the house. I don't think they've ever got over it.'

He fell silent for a moment.

'There's a poem, 'Youth Calls to Age', expresses it perfectly. It's by Dylan Thomas, to my mind the greatest living Welsh poet.' He sighed. 'I met him you know. Couple of years back, just before he moved to England. It was in a pub in Swansea. We talked poetry to each other and got roaring drunk... and then I went home and tore up everything I'd ever written. He's younger than me too...' he added, wryly.

He looked at Tom.

'Oh, don't mind me.' He grinned. 'Now then, what's all this about body building?'

'Oh... nothing.'

Dai was silent.

'Well... you know the mess-up the other day..'

'I watched every moment of it with total delight. Never seen Southey move so fast before. I didn't know he could.'

'It was my fault,' Tom admitted. 'But it wasn't just that... we nearly had to stop for a blow-up on the bank. I couldn't cope,' he said, after a pause. 'I never thought firing would be so hard.'

'You're managing today all right,' Dai said encouragingly.

'It's only a tankie and we're not out to break any records or go up Crosley Bank. Oh, I know I was firing all wrong but...'

'You just want to know that if you're asked to fire a forty to Paddington and back you can do it, is that it?'

'Yes,' Tom said eagerly. 'That's it. I just thought if I could get a bit of muscle...'

The passenger train slid into the station and stopped.

'I wouldn't worry. You can't help but develop muscle in this job. But...' a slow smile spread across Dai's face.

'What?'

'Nothing.' Dai stood up. 'You'll be all right.'

*****

The following day Tom was met by a grinning group of cleaners as he entered the shed.

'Something for you in stores, Tom.' Ginger said, trying not to laugh.

Puzzled, Tom went to the stores counter, followed by all the cleaners, now openly sniggering.

'Billy! Billy!'

Billy appeared, a box of cotton waste in his hands.

'So there you are Tom and about time too! Let me tell you that I am not the Parcels Office nor the Lost Property and if you have any more parcels would you kindly arrange for them to be left somewhere else!'

With that he pushed a large parcel towards Tom. Much of the paper had been torn away, revealing a pair of dumb-bells. Tom took it, mystified, and read the label. 'Tom Watkins. For his personal use.'

Ginger felt Tom's arm.

'Hmm. Bit on the flabby side.'

Tom flung his hand away.

'Just wait 'til I see Dai Davies!'

He hastily re-wrapped the dumb-bells, and parcel under his arm, walked out of the shed, accompanied by ironic cheers. He reached home to find Fred in the kitchen, reading the newspaper. He glanced up as Tom put the parcel down with a thump on to the kitchen table.

'What's that?'

Fred poked at the wrapping and looked at Tom in surprise. 'I'd have thought you get enough exercise without going in for those things. Not cheap either. Whatever did you pay for them?'

'Someone lent them to me.'

'Bloody daft if you ask me.' He returned to his paper, then looked up once more. 'Know how to use them?'

'I'll learn,' Tom said grimly.

'You can do yourself a mischief if you don't handle them right,' Fred commented. 'I used to do a bit when I was a lad. Let's see...'

He abandoned his paper, picked up the dumb-bells and weighed them in his hands. 'Eight pounds or so...quite light...' He handed them over to Tom. 'Well - let's see you have a go.'

Tom took hold of them self-consciously and swung them up. Fred winced.

'Not like that.' He took them from Tom. 'Look...'

He demonstrated. 'These're called shoulder presses...'

He changed the exercise. '...and this is dumb-bell curls...'

He changed the exercise once more. '...this is rowing...'

The kitchen door opened. Nancy and Sylvia stood transfixed in the doorway.

'Fred! Whatever are you doing?' Nancy exclaimed.

Feeling rather pleased with himself, Fred put the weights down on the table and resumed his seat, breathing only slightly faster than usual.

'Well fancy me remembering after all these years. How about that, eh Nance?'

'We'll have you in the League yet,' Sylvia grinned. 'I can just see you kicking up your legs in black knickers and white blouse.'

'Don't talk so daft girl,' Fred said mildly. He picked up his newspaper and noisily turned the pages.

'You're coming to see us at the fete, aren't you, dad?'

'Won't get any peace if I don't,' Fred grunted.

Sylvia gave him a pat on the head. 'That's right. You won't get any peace.' She turned to Tom. 'Well come on Tom - let's see if you can do better than dad.'

Tom picked up the weights. 'No-one can do that,' he said bitterly.

There was a moment's silence. Fred looked up from his paper.

'Oh, come on...' Sylvia coaxed.

'No. Later. After tea.'

He went up to his room, put the dumb-bells down on the floor, sat on his bed and stared at them. After a moment he got up, took off his jacket and wedged a chair against the door. He was enough of a laughing stock already down at the shed, he thought, and didn't want any unwanted interruptions at home. He picked up the weights and began, tentatively at first, to try the shoulder-presses.

******

The following Saturday, which turned to be a sunny, spring-like day, much to the great relief of the organisers, the Acton Chalcote fete was in full swing. The entire town, it seemed, had turned out for this popular annual event which was supported by the GWR and LNER companies and raised money for various local charities. The rivalry between the two engine sheds was, for the day, suspended.

A sudden brisk wind made the pennants on the tops of the two large blue and white striped marquees flap wildly. Inside were the stalls containing locally grown vegetables of all shapes and sizes, large displays of flowers artistically arranged in an assortment of vases, pots of home-made jams and pickles, and tables groaning under the weight of enticing home-made cakes, all of which would be judged and sold off later in the afternoon. Coloured flags flapped around the edges of the many sideshows and stalls. The white tablecloths covering the tables outside the tea tent blew upwards and struggled to break free from the cups and saucers, plates of cakes and small jars of flowers and go sailing over the town. A chair blew over, and those sitting at the tables held on to their cups with one hand and their hats with the other.

Grouped around the 'Test your Strength' machine was a large group of people, mainly railwaymen, among them Dai. He and Sylvia were nibbling on sticks of candyfloss.

'Roll up, roll up...test your strength on this unique apparatus...! Hit the bell at the top and your money back... three tries for only threepence a go... Come on now ladies, see how strong your men really are... and all for threepence a go and your money back if you hit the bell...! You sir...?'

Dai handed the remains of the candyfloss to Sylvia, and, amid cheers and catcalls, paid his threepence, spat on his hands, picked up the mallet and brought it down hard on the peg. The striker shot three-quarters up the machine then fell back, to groans from his mates and cheers and caustic comments from everyone else. Dai grinned apologetically at Sylvia.

'See what a weakling you're going out with,' he commented before taking up his stance once more and hitting the peg. This time the striker hit the bell. Dai put down the mallet and, to cheers and laughter, received his threepenny bit and took back his candy floss.

'Tom ought to have a go at this,' he said as they watched Jerry Marshall try his luck.

'Why Tom?'

'Oh... because...'

Sylvia narrowed her eyes. 'Did you have anything to do with those dumb-bells he came home with?' she asked suspiciously.

Dai grinned. 'Oh look!' he said, hurriedly steering her over to one of the stalls. '"Hook a duck and win a goldfish,"' he read out loud. 'Come on, I'll treat you with my hard-won threepence.'

'But I don't want a goldfish,' she protested.

'Who said you'll be able to hook a duck?'

Laughing, they pushed their way through the crowds.

A sack race was taking place in the arena area at the centre of the field, watched by doting parents, while over-excited children with sticky toffee-apple smeared hands and faces raced around the rest of the field. Along the rows of sideshows, a red-faced Alfie was being egged on by his four children as he tried to hit an Aunt Sally, while two stands further down, Fred and Charlie were attempting to knock coconuts off their perches on the Coconut Shy.

'I reckon they're stuck on,' grumbled Charlie after his fourth unsuccessful try.

In another part of the field, George and his equally large wife were roaring with laughter at the 'Tip a Lady out of Bed' stand, and Ginger, Les and Jim, with a group of cleaners, together with their girls, were happily crashing into each other on the dodgems.

Over in the tea tent, ladies from the W.I were dispensing sandwiches and cakes, while Nancy, wielding a large brown teapot, poured tea into an inexhaustible row of cups, which were constantly being replenished by Girl Guides who had undertaken washing up duties. A queue for refreshments stretched out of the tent and down the field.

After the sack race in the main arena came the egg and spoon race, swiftly followed by the three-legged race. In the lull that followed, Ben Goodey, who, alongside his LNER counterpart, had been acting as Master of Ceremonies, picked up the microphone and stepped on to the make-shift wooden dais.

'Ladies and gentlemen, don't miss the members of the Acton Chalcote and District Town Band who are about to entertain you with a selection of popular music, after which the ladies of the Women's League of Health and Beauty will give their display in the centre of the field. Teas and light refreshments are still being served in the marquee near the entrance!'

He stepped down as the Acton Chalcote and District Town Band marched smartly into the arena playing 'Entry of the Gladiators'. Their music could be heard over the babble of voices in the crowded tea tent.

'We're on next, I'd better go.' Sylvia hastily finished her tea and stood up.

'I'll come and cheer,' Dai said, standing up with her.

'Polite applause is all that's required.'

'I'll applaud politely then.' They smiled at one another, then Sylvia hurried off.

Dai looked around and spotted Tom. He made his way over.

'How's the body building going?'

Tom glowered. 'I guessed it was you.'

'Well you did ask for my help.'

'I didn't ask you to let the whole shed know.'

Dai sat down beside him. 'You know perfectly well you can't keep anything secret down the shed. And when I think of all the trouble I went to finding a mate who'd lend them to me, I do think it's a bit ungrateful,' he added in an injured voice.

Tom gave a reluctant grin, then caught his breath at a twinge of pain.

'Just you wait, I'll get even with you!'

'I'll look forward to it.' Dai stood up. 'Mind you don't damage those dumb-bells now - my mate wants them back in one piece. Must go, or I'll be in Sylvia's black books if I miss the display.'

He ambled off and Maggie, who had been clearing away dirty crockery, approached him hesitantly.

'Enjoying yourself?'

Tom shrugged 'Not really.'

She sat down. 'There's a dance on tonight in the Town Hall. Are you going?'

Tom shook his head.

'You working then?'

'No,' Another twinge of pain shot down his back and he winced.

'You all right?'

'Fine. Just a bit of back trouble. Nothing really.'

'Oh. I'm sorry,' she said with ready sympathy. 'It's my feet that are killing me – it's been that busy here. I don't suppose I'll be going to the dance either.' She laughed uncertainly. 'Unless we went together and sat out the dances like a couple of old crocks.'

She waited, hopefully, but when Tom didn't reply, she stood up. 'Must go or mum'll be after me.'

To a burst of applause, the band marched out of the arena and the Women's League of Health and Beauty ran in to more applause. A wind-up gramophone was brought on and placed on a chair. Sylvia took a record carefully out of its paper sleeve, put it on the turntable, positioned the needle in the groove and ran to join the others. They all linked arms, and to the tune of 'Keep Young and Beautiful', the display began. A growing and appreciative audience applauded the sequence dancing and keep fit exercises. At the end of each piece of music Sylvia detached herself from the group and changed the record.

Dai was waiting at the exit to the arena and took the records from her.

'You should have put me in charge of this. Dab hand, I am, changing records.'

'How was it?' Sylvia asked breathlessly.

'You looked like a black and white dryad.'

Sylvia aimed a cuff at his head. 'Not me, the whole thing.'

'I only had eyes for you.' He looked round. 'Quick, over here. Your friend Carol has her eye on us. Another cup of tea?'

Sylvia nodded. 'Yes please. But I must change first.'

Dai ran an appreciative eye over her figure. 'I don't see why, you look delectable as you are.'

They walked together over to the changing tent.

'What's a dryad?'

Dai laughed. 'It's a spirit who lives in trees and takes the form of a beautiful woman.'

'Flattery will get you everywhere,' Sylvia said dryly. 'Oh dear. There's dad over there glowering at us.' She smiled across at him, gave a cheeky wave and blew him a kiss.

'There's pity it is, all these people we have to avoid,' Dai said lightly. 'Too tired to go to the dance tonight?'

'Just try and stop me.'

They walked arm in arm across the field.

*****

3376 was waiting under the water column while the engine took on water. As the tank began to overflow, Tom turned off the water and swung the standpipe and spout away from the engine's tender. As he did so, George walked up and climbed into the cab. Tom followed and glanced anxiously round.

'Back all right now Tom?' George asked, sliding his lunch box into its accustomed place.

'I think so.'

'Never tried dumb-bells myself and it's a bit late now for that sort of exercise.' He gave a comfortable laugh but stopped when he saw Tom's worried expression.

164

'Don't worry lad. You'll cope all right,' he said, reassuringly.

He opened the doors of the firebox and glanced inside.

'That's all looking fine,' he added approvingly.

Tom began to relax.

'Take it easy now, Tom and we'll have a good trip,' George added. He grinned. 'Just you wait 'til you see what comes out of my lunchbox. The missis has done us proud after I told her you needed feeding up.'

He opened the regulator, and the engine began to move away from the water column and off shed.

Tom grinned, leaned out and began watching for the signal.

Steam in the Family

Chapter Ten

Afterwards nobody could remember who had first made the suggestion. It began in the cleaners' cabin when a crowd of cleaners had been having lunch. It was an unusually warm day, and everyone was hot and tired after an early start and engine cleaning to the exacting standards demanded by Witty.

Whoever had made the suggestion met with general approval although in the end it was only Tom, Ginger, Les and Jim who had, with a certain bravado and a certain amount of trepidation, left the cabin and crossed the tracks. Few people were about, and it was unusually quiet apart from a rhythmic banging of metal on metal in the boiler shop, the distant sounds of shunting taking place over in the far sidings and, as always, the ceaseless murmur of Billy Hughes in stores.

'Wouldn't be Chalcote engine shed without good old Billy,' Les remarked.

They walked along the front of the coaling stage to the water tower. Mounted on a massive plinth, the tank towered over them, filled with more than seventy-four thousand gallons of water.

Tom licked his lips and looked round apprehensively. What had seemed a good idea in the cleaners' cabin didn't seem so good now.

Come on lads, last one up's a cissy,' Jim began untying his shoelaces. If he felt nervous, he didn't show it. He removed his shoes, socks and grubby overalls then ran, stark naked, up the narrow metal ladder to the tank. Once at the top he dived in before putting his head over the metal frame.

'It's great in here!' he shouted down.

Half scared, half excited, the other three soon stripped off, throwing their clothes on top of Jim's. Soon they were all splashing round inside the tank, showering each other with water, yelling and halloo-ing at the tops of their voices.

A short while later, Ben Goodey, perspiring freely under his bowler hat, came out of the shed. He stopped, frowned, looked across the tracks and began to make his way purposefully over to the tank. He reached it in time to see a row of naked dripping legs and bottoms descending the ladder.

'All right lads,' he said resignedly. 'The fun's up.'

Half guilty, half grinning, the four cleaners looked down at him from varying heights.

'I was beginning to wonder why it was so quiet round the shed. Now I know.'

They finished their descent and stood in a naked dripping huddle at the base of the tower.

Ben's lips twitched.

'What a sight! If the Company had thought anyone would have been bloody stupid enough to swim in the tank, they'd have strictly forbidden it, and anyway that water's going to end up in a loco boiler and I don't want it contaminated by you lot.'

A few firemen and drivers, attracted by the scene, drifted over, and began laughing.

'All right. Make yourselves decent then report to my office.'

Mindful of his dignity, he stalked off, and the cleaners turned to where they had left their clothes.

'Where's our things?' Ginger demanded.

Tom rounded on the sniggering railwaymen. 'Who's pinched them?'

'Showing off your assets, lads?' Joe Stratton murmured. He was leaning, arms folded, against the side of 4962 Ragley Hall, while Ted, his driver, grinned down from the footplate.

'Did you take our stuff?' Jim asked angrily.

'Stuff? What stuff?'

'We left our clothes here!'

Joe slowly looked around then shook his head, 'I don't see any clothes. Do you Ted?'

'Not me,' Ted grunted.

'But they were here a minute ago!'

The watching railwaymen, hugely enjoying the unexpected entertainment shouted with laughter and made ribald comments.

'Perhaps the gaffer's spirited them away,' Joe said reasonably, 'or maybe they just vanished in a puff of smoke...'

He looked up to the smoke rising from the chimney of 4962.

'You never...!' Tom began wrathfully.

The four of them moved threateningly towards Joe, who laughed and climbed swiftly and nimbly into the cab.

'Now watch it lads... don't want to do yourselves an injury, do you? Not with your crown jewels on display!'

Ted pushed open the regulator and the engine began to move forwards. Suddenly it blew off and the four cleaners disappeared under clouds of steam.

A short while later Jim, Tom, Ginger and Les, dressed in an assortment of tatty, ill-fitting overalls, knocked tentatively on the foreman's door and filed sheepishly inside. Waiting for them were Alf Wittall and Ben Goodey, both trying hard to conceal their grins.

'Well, as you're so nice and clean and lily-white, Alf and I've thought up some nice, clean jobs for you, haven't we Alf?'

He nodded at Ginger. 'Coaling up.'

He turned to Les. 'Tube cleaning.'

He looked at Jim. 'Salter, you can clean out the pits.'

And finally turning to Tom. 'And you can have a spell helping Ernie with the stationery boiler. It's wash-out day.'

The faces of all four of them fell.

'And as you've wasted so much time already, lazing round in the tank, you'll get no extra pay for those labouring turns. Now go on – hop it.'

'The filthiest jobs,' Jim complained once they were outside the office.

'And no extra pay,' said Les, gloomily.

'Well, they didn't really have any option,' Ginger said fairmindedly. 'We did ask for it.'

'Yeah, though it was good while it lasted,' Tom put in.

Jim turned to him. 'You've bagged the worst of it, mate,' he said maliciously. 'I'd rather clean out the pits any day than help old Ernie down the black hole.'

'Me too,' Les agreed.

Tom looked from one to the other. 'Why?'

Jim glanced at the others. 'You'll soon find out.' He tapped his head. 'Short of a bob or two.'

'Or three or four,' Ginger added.

The three of them laughed and walked out of the shed. Tom hesitated for a moment before walking through to the far end.

He knew about the stationery boiler of course. He had walked past it from time to time but apart from knowing that it was there to supply steam for washing out boilers, he had never given it a thought. As he walked round the side of the repair shop towards a line of engines waiting for their boilers to be washed out, he wondered why Jim had called it the black hole and what he and the others meant about Ernie.

He reached the front of the queue of locomotives, to where a large, sweating red-faced man was busily engaged in boiler washing. Ahead of him was a brick building with the top part of an engine sticking incongruously out of the front, complete with funnel which was extended with a very tall stove pipe to carry the smoke high into the air.

Tom paused, went inside, and was instantly hit by the heat. It was like walking into a furnace. Sweat coursed down his body and within seconds his shirt was wringing wet. It was dark, too, and it took him a moment for his eyes to grow accustomed. The glowing red hole of the firebox dominated the area but as his eyes adjusted to the gloom, he could see a large pile of coal in one corner. A figure was bending over the fire, shovelling coal with practised ease. The man straightened up.

'Come in, son, come in... hard work today... there's five engines down for washout.'

Ernie Patch put down his shovel and came towards Tom. Ernie was a short, wizened man who walked with a pronounced limp. As he drew closer, Tom could see deep, livid scars running down one side of his face and disappearing under the collar of his shirt. His thinning hair grew sparsely leaving glistening bald patches of his skull, which was also scored with deep scars.

'Come on up mate.'

Ernie mopped his shining face with a piece of cotton waste as he returned to the boiler. He put the injector on and handed over the shovel. As Tom took it, he wondered what Jim had meant. Ernie seemed welcoming, friendly, and eminently sane.

'Just keep a good, thick bed of fire, that's what the old girl likes... and keep an eye on the water... it drops down like a drink in the desert when the wash-outs on,' Ernie instructed.

Tom nodded. He examined the fire and began shovelling coal. It was a minute or two before he realised that Ernie was standing behind him, half hidden in the shadows. Startled, Tom stopped firing and, for a moment they stared at one another in silence.

'Did you check the detonators and red flags like I said?' Ernie asked. His voice sounded different, sharp and business-like. 'I told you last week. You mustn't forget to check the detonators and flags.'

Tom swallowed nervously.

'And have you filled the sandboxes? It's a damp morning and we can't have the old girl slipping on Crosley bank.'

He came closer and Tom backed away. With a sudden movement, Ernie grabbed the shovel from him.

'You watch out for the right-away, mate, and I'll just build up your fire a bit... a good thick bed of fire, that's what the old girl wants.'

Tom watched him, half scared, half fascinated. Ernie fired for a minute or two before stopping to take out an ornate watch. He screwed up his eyes to read it in the dark.

'We'll be late away if we're not careful... and we'll have a job making up time with this load on...'

He put the watch away then looked deep into the firebox, deflecting the flames with his shovel.

'There, that's good now...'

He handed the shovel back to Tom.

'We've got to look after the old lady haven't we? Her and me... both of us put out to grass.'

Tom checked the water, keeping a wary eye on Ernie who watched his every move. He turned to dig into the pile of coal.

'Not like that lad, put your back into it... here, give it to me.'

He grabbed the shovel from Tom.

'You clean the footplate, mate, and get her all squared up before we knock off for a cuppa... and don't forget to trim the coal... we don't want any falling off and hurting the passengers on the platform...' He smiled at Tom, his face a livid red in the light from the fire, his scars standing out sharply.

'And don't forget now, anything you want to know, you just ask... there's not a lot Ernie Patch doesn't know about locos...'

He glanced at the boiler pressure gauge.

'Steady on, lad, she'll be blowing off in a minute...'

He began to work furiously at stoking the fire before glancing at the water level.

'Come on, mate, put the injector on then bring up the coal from the back – it's a load of rubbish and dust up front... come on now... jump to it...'

After a final glance at Ernie Tom picked up another shovel and began to rake the coal forwards from the back of the pile.

He jumped as Ernie's hand touched his shoulder.

'Don't mind me lad...' Ernie said gently, his eyes screwed-up against the heat and dust. 'I get a bit confused at times... go on... you get outside for a breather... it's hot as Hades in here.'

Tom staggered outside and leant against the wall, brushing the sweat from his eyes with a shaking hand. The boiler washer glanced at him.

'Like the black hole of Calcutta in there.'

He jerked his head towards the boiler house. 'Don't know how old Ernie stands it, day after day.' He shrugged. 'S'pose he's got used to it, and it's a job after all.' He spat on his hands, wiped them on his filthy overalls and turned back to the boiler he was washing out.

******

'Morning, Nosey,' Dai said cheerfully as he booked on and collected his brass disc. 'How's things?'

Without waiting for an answer, he went over to the notice boards and ran his eyes over the information sheets pinned there. He stopped at the names of the crews.

'Dammo duw,' he swore under his breath.

'What's wrong?' asked Jerry, who was standing beside him.

'Oh, nothing.' Dai moved away from the board. Jerry leaned across and glanced rapidly down the sheet.

'So, your Fred's mate on the Swansea run, are you? That'll make sparks fly,' he said, slightly maliciously. 'Wonder what's wrong with poor old Charlie?' He raised his voice. 'Is Charlie ill or something?'

'Something to do with his guts,' Nosey called back.

'There's always something wrong with his guts, poor bleeder,' Jerry commented.

'Reckon it's down to his missis' cooking,' muttered someone in the queue.

Dai made his way over to stores. Of course it was inevitable that everyone at the shed knew of his involvement with Sylvia and Fred's opposition to it. You couldn't keep secrets for long in an engine shed. You couldn't keep secrets at all in an engine shed!

'Keys to 2928 Billy if you don't mind,' he said on entering.

'You're going to have fun today Dai, with Fred Watkins as your mate,' Billy commented as he handed over the keys.

'First rate driver, Billy. I'll learn a lot from him,' Dai said mildly, refusing to rise to the bait.

'Here's your lamps and spare cans and your waste. Fred's already been in for the oil.'

'Has he? Then I'd better get my skates on.'

'Here, you heard about old Arthur Beckett...?'

'Sorry, Billy, haven't time now.'

Fred was already checking and oiling the lubricators and reservoirs when Dai hurried up.

'Took your time didn't you,' he said laconically.

'Morning Fred,' Dai replied cheerfully as he climbed up to the cab. He stowed away his lunch box, lamps, and oil cans, checked the fire, water and steam pressure and began pulling coal forwards from the tender.

'You filled the sandboxes?' was the only remark Fred made in the hour it took them to prepare the engine. When they'd finished, Fred moved the engine off shed to take on water before coupling up to the eight coaches waiting in Platform One and begin the journey down to Swansea.

'Charlie's bad again, is he?' Dai asked in a lull between firing.

Fred grunted.

'Sorry to hear that,' Dai murmured, returning to his task. He was soon hard at work, the engine working against an uphill gradient as the train thundered up the bank. Once over the top he straightened to find Fred staring at him before deliberately turning his back. Dai gave a slight shrug and pulled out the pep pipe to hose down the floor of the cab.

'Watch for the Laxford back board,' Fred said sharply.

Dai was surprised. 'But it's on your side.'

'Do as I bloody well tell you.'

Dai crossed over to Fred's side of the cab and looked out. The distant signal which they were fast approaching was showing clear.

'You've got the board mate.'

He crossed back to his side of the footplate as the train passed the signal, before a gentle descent to Laxford Junction Station where some passengers got off, and others got on.

'You remembered the tea?' Fred asked brusquely as they moved off once more.

'Yes.'

Dai hesitated a moment.

'Fred,' he began.

'What?' The word was a challenge.

Dai sighed. 'Oh, nothing.'

'I don't think we've anything to say to each other, have we?' Fred said deliberately.

'What have you got against me?' Dai asked, puzzled. He genuinely wanted to know.

'Against you? Nothing. Nothing at all. Just do your job and keep your mouth shut and I won't complain.'

'Is it because of Sylvia?' Dai persisted.

Fred was silent for a moment.

'Sylvia knows my feelings on that score and I don't propose to discuss them with you,' he said at last.

He crossed to the firebox and peered inside.

'Back end's burning hollow,' he said.

Dai picked up his shovel and grinned, his sense of humour reasserting itself.

'You old bugger,' he muttered under his breath as he dug into the pile of coal.

******

The booking on lobby was crowded when Tom entered and joined the queue to book off.

'How d'you get on with Ernie then?' Ginger asked.

Tom didn't answer for a moment.

'Well?'

'It was – all right,' Tom said reluctantly.

The door opened and a very weary Dai came in.

He was instantly hailed by Joe Stratton. 'Dai! Over here! This'll be up your street!' He began to read out loud from a notice on the board. '"In connection with the centenary celebrations of the Great Western Railway, staff will be interested to know that the Company has made a film with sound…"'

'I'm not interested if it hasn't got Jean Harlow in it,' said Jerry from the back of the queue.

'Doesn't sound like my cup of tea either,' muttered Len, another fireman.

'You'll want to go, Dai,' Joe encouraged.

'Why?'

'Well, history and that. And you're interested in films, aren't you – well, you've got an interest in the cinema – especially in the staff!'

There was general laughter.

'It'll be right up old Ernie's street, too.' Bert came across to read the notice. 'Very historically-minded Ernie is.'

'Ernie?' Tom asked.

Bert nodded. 'Proper walking encyclopaedia.'

'He was at Swindon, wasn't he?' asked Joe.

'That's right.'

'But isn't he...' Tom hesitated.

'Bit soft in the head? Well, sometimes he is and sometimes he isn't.' Bert tapped his head. 'But he's still got a lot stored up here.'

Dai was reading the notice. 'It's going to be on at The Regal.'

'That's where your girl works, isn't it?'

'Yes.'

'Think any of the blokes from the North Eastern'll go to see it?' asked Jerry.

Bert grunted. 'Might teach them something if they did.'

Everyone laughed.

'You won't get me going to see it,' said Jerry decisively. 'Not unless they paid me.'

Dai grinned at him. 'Oh, what a philistine you are Jerry! Why a film is art man!'

His voice was drowned out by good-humoured comments.

'Put a sock in it, Davies!'

'Watch out lads, he'll be spouting poetry next!'

A voice cut in above the rest.

'Bloody pansy!'

There was a startled silence as everyone looked from Fred, who had just come in, then across to Dai.

Dai shrugged slightly.

The silence in the booking on lobby lengthened and a couple of men departed. Fred caught sight of Tom, still wearing the ill-fitting assortment of clothes he, Ginger, Les and Jim had found that morning.

'What the hell do you think you're wearing then, eh? Think yourself a bloody circus act?'

'What...?'

'Wasn't there a pile of old rags down by the coal stage, Ted?' Joe remarked, moving away from the notice. 'Of course, they might have walked by now...'

There was general laughter, tinged with relief as Tom and Ginger made a dive for the door. Fred glanced sharply at Joe then booked off in silence. The men made way for him as he walked out.

'What's up with old Fred then, Dai?' asked Joe. 'Apart from you taking out his daughter?'

'Give him a rough trip did you?' Jerry asked.

'I wouldn't rate your chances with his lass very high mate,' grinned Sammy White.

'When I want your opinion Sammy, I'll ask for it, thanks all the same – mate!' Dai said angrily and walked out, leave those remaining in the room looking at one another in surprise.

'Not like Dai to lose his temper,' someone commented.

'Don't know about Dai giving Fred a rough trip, reckon it was the other way round,' Jerry murmured.

******

Sylvia heaved a sigh of relief as she hurried out of the back door to the cinema. It had been a tiring evening with a full house. Halfway through she had to try and quieten and then evict a small handful of rowdy lads who had had too much to drink and were trying to impress their girls. The film had been dull too, when she had had time to watch. Mind you, she had been watching the same film all week. She turned the corner and found Dai lounging against the railings.

'Sorry I'm late,' she smiled, 'it's been quite a night and I couldn't get away earlier because Mr Pilger was fussing.

'What about?'

'Oh… he's like that. He was all right when he was under-manager but now he's boss he's impossible. Just because Gertie added up the money wrong. He made us all stay until she'd sorted it out. As if we could do anything about it!'

She chattered on until they reached Sid's.

'Tea?'

'Please.' Sylvia sat down with a sigh of relief and undid her headscarf.

'Anything to eat?'

She shook her head and Dai went to the counter. It was quiet at that time of the evening and they were the only customers.

'D'you know what he did – when he got promoted?' she asked when Dai returned.

Dai handed over a cup and saucer and sat down. 'I can't imagine.'

'He gave all his suits to the Welfare and had new ones made, more fitting to his position.'

Dai laughed.

'He did – honestly. Silly little man.'

'He must have more money than sense.'

Sylvia considered this. 'Well he can't be doing badly.' She took a sip of tea and wrinkled her nose. 'Uggh. Stewed.' She took another sip. 'At least it's hot and wet. It was a rotten film too and we had some drunks to evict.'

'How did you do that?' Dai asked amused. 'Throw them over your shoulder and hurl them outside or just strong-arm them up the aisle?'

'Spoke nicely to them at first and when that didn't work I had to bring on the heavy brigade.'

'Mr Pilger?'

She giggled. 'Him? He's so weedy he couldn't swat a fly even if it lay down and flapped its wings. No, I had to get Rob

– he's the commissionaire and an ex-prize fighter – to do it. Had his feet up and was having a nice cup of tea and chat with Gertie when I called him and he wasn't too pleased.' She thought for a moment. 'That's probably why Gertie got the money wrong – she spent the evening with Rob. Sweet on him, she is.' She took a third sip of tea. 'I'll be glad to get away.'

Dai put down his cup. 'You're leaving?'

'Only going on holiday.'

'It's a funny sort of time to be having a holiday.'

'You can thank dear Mr Pilger for that!'

Dai was silent for a moment. 'When are you going?'

'Next week.'

'Where to?'

She shrugged. 'Don't know yet. Torquay maybe... or Paignton...it's cheaper.'

'Are your parents going?'

Sylvia looked across at him, surprised. 'Look, what is this? Some sort of inquisition? I'm going with a friend.' She paused, then said teasingly. 'A girl friend.'

'Would you consider going away with me instead?' Dai said suddenly.

'You?'

'Why not?'

'Well... I can't... it's all arranged...' she replied, flustered.

'You just said it wasn't.'

'Yes, but... I didn't mean that... and besides...' she felt herself blushing.

'Besides what?'

'I couldn't...' she muttered, 'not just the two of us...'

'Why?'

Sylvia snatched at the first excuse she could think of. 'Whatever would dad say.'

'Ah...' Dai said quietly. 'Fred.'

'And mum...'

'What's it got to do with them?'

'They'd be horrified.'

Dai sighed. 'What about you? Are you horrified?'

Sylvia traced a pattern on the oil cloth with her finger. 'Well... it's just... not done, is it? I mean, it's not as though...' she broke off, near to tears. It wasn't fair, she thought. It just wasn't fair Dai saying things like that when she wasn't prepared. When she'd had such a rotten evening as well. She made a move to stand up.

'I think I'd better go home...'

Dai caught her hand. 'Sylvia, would it help to tell you that I've no designs on your virtue – well, no, that's not strictly true, but it's not the reason I asked you. I asked because I want to get to know you better. I've only ever seen you over hurried cups of tea in Sid's or at the occasional dance, and every time we meet I feel that there's someone standing behind me, breathing disapproval down my neck.'

'I don't know what you mean.'

'Isn't it obvious?'

Sylvia shook her head, puzzled and unhappy.

'I'm sorry,' Dai said. 'I've had a pretty rough day firing to your father.'

'Did you have a row?'

'Oh nothing so ungentlemanly.' Dai grinned wryly. 'He just made sure I worked my backside off.'

He looked at her. 'Won't you change your mind?'

Sylvia hesitated. She picked up her cup, then set it down again, and shook her head.

'All right. Don't look like that,' he added gently.

'Like what?'

'Bewildered... like a child that thinks it's lost something.'

She bit her lip. 'Do I?' she asked in a small voice.

He put out his hand and gently stroked her hair back from her face. 'Sylvia... I think I love you, but I'm not sure.'

She said nothing, not trusting herself to speak.
Dai stood up. 'Come on, I'll see you home.'

Chapter Eleven

'… and dad says there's pheasants.' Ginger explained as he, Tom and Les walked briskly up Station Road.

'Don't they belong to Mr Jenkins?' asked Tom.

'If they stray into the woods they're fair game for anyone, dad says.'

Les was uneasy. 'I thought there was some law to say they couldn't be shot after the first of February.'

'I don't suppose for a moment we'll bag one,' Ginger replied cheerfully. 'It's just a bit of fun.' He glanced at Tom. 'Here, give me that gun. The way you're waving it around you'll do someone a mischief.'

Tom handed it over. 'I thought it wasn't loaded.'

''Course it's not. Dad says you should never load a gun until you're going to use it. But that's not the point.'

'Yes, it is.'

'No, it's not.'

'If it's not loaded then it can't hurt anyone.'

''Course it can. You could bash someone on the head with it.'

'Or poke their eye out,' Les agreed.

They continued to bicker amicably as they made their way up the road.

'Hello Tom.'

Maggie was manoeuvring a pram through her front gate. Two bags of shopping dangled from the handlebars.

''Lo Maggs.'

'Whose gun's that?'

'It's Ginger's dads.'

'Is it loaded?' she asked, looking at it doubtfully.

Ginger laughed. 'Not much use if it isn't.'

'No, it's not loaded,' Tom assured her. 'Not yet. We're off to the woods to bag a pheasant.'

Maggie looked from one to the other. 'Can I come? I've just got to put Joey down for a sleep, but it'll only take a minute.'

Ginger shook his head. 'This is serious stuff, Maggie.'

'It's for men, not for girls,' Les added, grinning.

'Can I, Tom?'

Tom hesitated.

'It's not up to him,' Ginger asserted. 'It's my gun, well, my dad's, and that's the next best thing and I'm in charge of this trip and I say you can't. You might be frightened by the bang.'

'Oh, dry up!' Maggie pushed the pram angrily on to the path.

'Want a hand with that?' Tom asked diffidently.

'I can manage,' she said abruptly.

'Trouble with Maggs is she thinks she can do everything we can,' Ginger commented as they strolled off.

'Well she used to, didn't she,' Tom said fairly. 'She always went round in our gang.'

'Yeah, but that was before. We were only kids then.'

'She's still just a kid.'

Les screwed up his eyes as he turned to watch Maggie round the corner of the house. 'You think so? I don't know so much...'

Ginger grinned at Tom. 'You'd better watch out mate, 'cos she's after you.'

'Me?'

'S'obvious.'

Les nodded. 'Sweet on you she is.'

'Don't talk daft!'

They carried on in high spirits until they reached the woods. Tom pushed open the gate and they went inside, following a well-worn path which was thick with last year's leaves. Following the heavy rain of the night before, their boots left little pools of water as they squelched over the sodden undergrowth. The quietness of the woods seemed to close around them and they stopped talking.

Although the streets and houses of Acton Chalcote had been sprawling ever outwards until the town now pressed hard up against Chalcote Woods, once inside they could be in another world. The ground on either side of the path was carpeted with the deep blue and white of bluebells and wild garlic which spread out under the canopy of trees and disappeared into the dimness of the woods as far as the eye could see. A green mist seemed to be stealing over everything. The leaves on the trees were beginning to unfurl, and the air was redolent of the sharp smell of wild garlic mingling with the more subtle scent of the bluebells.

'Mmm. I love the smell of wild garlic,' Tom said happily, sniffing the air.

Ginger stopped, loaded the gun and handed it to Tom.

'Here mate, see what you can do.'

The three of them were quiet, watching for any movement in the shadows of the trees.

'There's one,' Les whispered.

Tom aimed the gun, took a deep breath, and fired. The sound ricocheted round the woods.

'You missed, you stupid bugger!' Les shouted.

'No I didn't! It's here somewhere!'

Tom hurried off, tramping down bluebells and garlic and pushing through thorny bushes in his excitement. The others followed.

A sudden sound made Tom whip round. Branches parted to reveal Ernie's frightened face.

'Ernie!'

Ginger and Les came crashing up.

Ernie stood up and abruptly limped away.

'Ernie! Wait!' Tom called.

Ernie turned. His face was blank and devoid of any recognition. He turned and made off further into the woods and the three of them watched him go.

'Nutty as a fruitcake,' Les said, shrugging his shoulders.

'What do you think he's up to?' asked Ginger. 'He had a gun.'

'Same as us, probably,' Tom said uncertainly.

'Yeah, and I'm a blinkin' fairy,' Les snorted. 'He's up to no good, you mark my words. Blokes like him ought to be put away. Come on Tom, give us that gun. Your aim's about as good as a one-eyed sailor.'

He took the gun and turned to go back the way they had come. Tom hesitated for a moment, staring into the dimness of the trees. There was no sign of Ernie. Tom shrugged and followed the others.

******

A couple of hours later Tom was on his way home. It had been a good afternoon, he thought, although none of them had bagged a pheasant – or anything else come to that. He turned down the path which led along the backs of the gardens. He was hungry and ready for his tea. He opened the gate in the fence and went inside.

'Tea's not ready yet,' Fred grunted. He had been hard at work pruning some of the bushes, and piles of branches and twigs were strewn across the path. He was now digging and weeding.

'You can give me a hand 'til it is.'

Tom obediently picked up the dead branches and took them over to a larger heap in the corner, while Fred carried on digging.

'We'll have a bonfire soon.'

He handed Tom the spade.

'Go on – you're younger than me.' He picked up his jacket which was hanging over the fence. 'So how did you find Ernie?'

'Ernie?'

'You've been on the stationery boiler, haven't you?'

Tom nodded.

'So, how d'you find him?'

'All right,' Tom said uneasily. He didn't know whether or not to mention their sighting of Ernie in the woods.

'He's quite harmless, you know. Wouldn't hurt a fly.'

For a moment, Tom concentrated on digging.

'Was he ever a driver?' he asked at last.

'Yes, and a bloody good one.' Fred shrugged himself into his jacket. 'He had an accident. Run-away goods.'

'Why's he still working then? Shouldn't he be pensioned off or something?'

'Is that what you'd do with him?' Fred asked sharply.

'Well, he's not really fit, is he?'

''Fit? What do you know about fitness?'

Tom stopped digging and stared at his father in surprise.

'I only meant...' he stammered.

'You don't know what you mean half the time, that's the trouble with you youngsters,' Fred said roughly. 'Here – give me that.' He grabbed hold of the spade. 'Can't even dig two spits properly.' He drove the spade viciously into the soil. 'So you'd condemn a man who's given his life to his job just because his mind wanders a bit. Is that what you'd do?'

'I never said...'

'Thank God the Company don't see things the way you do. They don't throw blokes like Ernie on the scrapheap after a lifetime's service. That's why they're such a fine company to work for Tom, and don't you forget it. They care for their staff, they look after them.'

'I don't think it's very caring making him work in the black hole,' Tom muttered. 'He ought to be in hospital or something.'

'You know nothing about it, nothing at all!'

'All right, I don't! I never said I did! You started it, not me!'

Fred carried on as if Tom hadn't spoken. 'They gave him a job, didn't they? A responsible job. A job within his capabilities. He's still got his self-respect, hasn't he, he's still got his pride. And that's what's important!'

'Would you do it then?' Tom demanded. 'If you had to come off the footplate, would you do Ernie's job?'

It was the wrong question to ask. Fred abruptly stopped digging and stared at him. 'Don't talk so daft. The question doesn't arise.'

'But if it did?'

Fred took a deep breath, then nodded towards the pile of wood waiting in the corner.

'You can burn that lot after tea.' He dug deeply into the soil until he had reached the end of the row, then cleaned off the spade, wiping it with a handful of weeds. Tom watched him anxiously.

'Of course, Ernie's lucky in a way,' Fred went on. 'He doesn't really know what's happened to him... not really... it's a lot harder for the blokes who've had to come off the footplate and who haven't had knocks on the head... blokes who know what's happened.' Fred was silent for a moment. 'Come on,' he said abruptly. 'Tea'll be ready.'

******

Every Wednesday, after tea, Charlie would come round for a game of chess. He and Fred were both keen players and belonged to the Chess Club held in the Railwayman's Club.

'You better now, Charlie?' asked Nancy, putting a cup of tea down in front of him.'

'Ta, thank you Mrs Watkins. Good as I'll ever be, but it was a nasty turn.'

He and Fred settled down and Tom went into the garden to light the bonfire. When he returned, the wireless was playing dance music, and Nancy was sitting by the fire, sewing.

Tom rinsed his hands at the sink. 'I got it going, dad, but it was a bit of a job – everything's sodden with all that rain we had.'

'That's good,' Fred said absently. He made a move. 'Check.'

Charlie hastily moved his king. Fred made another move. 'Mate.'

Charlie sighed. 'I'll never win against your husband, Mrs Watkins.'

'You're improving, Charlie, you're improving.'

Charlie stood up. 'Well, it's been a pleasant evening…'

'Another cup before you go?' Nancy asked, also getting up.

'No, ta. Missus'll fret if I'm not home soon.'

'Not even a last game?' Fred asked, resetting the pieces.

'No, really. Your lad'll give you one.'

Fred laughed shortly. 'Never could interest him in chess, could I, Tom? Pity. He could have come along with us to the Club.'

'It's no fun playing against someone who always wins,' Tom said, an edge to his voice.

'Now, that's not the right spirit, is it? Eh Charlie? What do you think?'

'I think I'd better be running along before the missus sends out a search party,' Charlie said hastily. 'Thanks for the tea and the hospitality Mrs W.'

'A pleasure, Charlie.'

Fred put away the chess pieces and stood up.

'I'll give you a hand with that fire in a minute, Tom. I've built up a few fires in my time, haven't I, Charlie?'

'True enough there, mate.'

'Don't bother, dad,' Tom said curtly.

'It's no bother...'

Nancy looked up. 'Tom can deal with it, Fred,' she said with quiet authority.

Fred looked nonplussed. 'Oh... well... all right.' He turned to Charlie. 'How about a quick jar at the 'Western then Charlie? It's on your way home.'

'Go on,' Charlie said after a moment's hesitation. 'Twist my arm.'

******

It was busy in the yard early the next morning with engines being made ready. Tom crossed the yard and was about to go to the booking on lobby when he hesitated for a moment before walking round the outside of the shed building. He passed a line of engines waiting for their boiler washouts, reached the entrance to the boiler house and peered inside.

The fire had been lit and the floor swept. The large pile of coal was stacked in one corner and the row of tools cleaned and arranged with precision along the wall.

Tom went inside. Noticing some dirty marks on the front of the boiler he picked up a rag and automatically began wiping them off.

'Good lad. That's the ticket.'

Tom spun round to find Ernie standing in the doorway.

'Can't work on a dirty footplate.'

He came inside. 'You my mate today?'

'I don't know,' Tom said slightly nervously.

'Six engines down for washout. That'll keep us busy.'

'I've got to book on.'

'You do that. But be quick now. We've a tough old day ahead.'

Tom sidled past Ernie.

'And bring back the tea!' Ernie called after him. 'We're going to need it!'

Tom booked on then went to the cleaners' cabin. Alf Wittall looked up from the clipboard he was carrying, glanced ostentatiously at the clock, and frowned.

'You're chancing it, Watkins,' he commented.

'I'm not late, am I?'

Alf sniffed. 'Only just made it in time.' He carried on issuing instructions to the cleaners in the room.

'Your gang, Jones, can take 2379. You've got an hour and a half on it.'

'Oh come on Mr Wittall...'

'And I don't want you skimping it either. Harris, your gang can take 3376. And I've three labouring turns.' He looked round at Ginger, Tom and Les. 'You three are senior. There's...' He consulted his list. 'sand drying... cleaning out the pits... and helping with the boiler washouts. Extra pay of course.' He waited. 'Well, don't all speak at once will you.'

'I'll help Ernie if you like,' Tom offered.

******

By the end of the morning Tom was hot, tired and longing for a break. To his surprise, Ernie seemed as fresh as ever.

'Not a bad morning's work, considering. You get some grub, mate, and I'll stay here.'

He began to hum as he opened his lunchbox and brought out a neatly wrapped packet of sandwiches.

'Can't leave the footplate unattended.'

Tom hesitated. 'Ernie...' he began.

Ernie looked up, his eyes sharp. 'What do you think would happen if that gauge glass blew?' he asked briskly, indicating the water gauge glass on the front of the boiler.

'I – I don't know... Would all the steam escape?'

'Ha! That's what most people would think,' Ernie said triumphantly. 'But you wouldn't get the full boiler pressure. Know why that is?'

'No.'

Ernie went over to it. His limp seemed less pronounced, his movements were crisp and incisive, and his manner was that of an instructor before a class.

'There's two valves fitted inside,' he said, taking off the protective cover. 'Come over here, Harry.'

Tom looked round, but no-one else was in the room. He went over to the boiler.

'The valves are inside here. The escaping steam would push them into position which would reduce the force of the steam... it's as simple as that,' Ernie explained. He began to replace the protective frame. 'That water level,' he pointed, 'that's about halfway up the glass. That means the boiler's half full of water. It's steam on top but you can't see it because it's superheated. You watch an express loco running on a warm, sunny day. Look at the chimney. You won't see the steam coming out of that chimney. It not until some way after it leaves the chimney that the steam becomes visible. On a cold day of course, it'll show straight away...' his voice slowed, then stopped. He shook his head as if to clear invisible cobwebs from his mind. 'Used to be instructor at the MIC once... not any more though... they said I confused them...'

192

Tom bit his lip, moved by Ernie's vulnerability. 'It's not confusing… it's interesting…'

Ernie gave him a straight look but said nothing. He patted the gauge glass and moved away.

'Ernie… do you… do you mind…? Tom asked, hesitantly.

'Mind?' Ernie began to unwrap his lunch. 'Mind what?'

'Being taken off the footplate.'

Ernie froze in the act of unwrapping his sandwiches, then looked up at Tom. His eyes were blank.

'I don't know what you mean. I'm not off the footplate.'

He bent his head and took a bite out of his sandwich. Tom watched him for a moment, then left. Once outside, he took a deep breath.

******

Sitting comfortably in the third-class compartment as the train thundered through the countryside on its way to Devon, Sylvia was dozing while Carol was flicking through a movie magazine.

'Sylvie – hey Sylv, look at this.'

Sylvia opened her eyes.

'Clark Gable. My dream man. Don't you think he's too much?'

She handed over the magazine.

'Much too much,' Sylvia said dryly. 'Not really my type.'

'Well, we all know what your type is, don't we?' Carol said archly as she took back the magazine. 'Did you see Clark in "China Seas"?'

'Twice nightly and matinees Tuesday and Saturday,' Sylvia said wearily.

'You're spoilt, that's your trouble. Wish I had your job.'

'You could always ask Mr Pilger. Get him on a good day, throw in a few compliments about how well he runs the cinema.' Sylvia giggled. 'Runs it like the army. Flo says we should stand to attention and salute when he speaks to us. Perhaps we should,' she said thoughtfully, 'just to see how he reacts.' She grinned at Carol. 'He's not married, you know. At least, I don't think so. You smile and bat your eyelashes at him and he'll be eating out of your hand in no time at all. You could be in with a chance.'

'I might just do that,' Carol said, considering the matter seriously. She took out her compact, powdered her nose and re-applied some lipstick. 'Terrible the smuts you get on the train,' she complained.

Sylvia looked at her with affection and a little envy. Carol was stylish as ever in a three-quarter length pink and green floral dress with a wide cream collar. Her green jacket and hat had been bought to tone in with the dress and her cream shoes, gloves and bag finished the ensemble. Sylvia sighed. She would never look as chic.

'You look just fine,' she said. 'Wish I could look half as good as you.'

Carol grinned and returned to her magazine and Sylvia looked out of the window. She felt... out-of-sorts... that was what it was. Out-of-sorts. She wondered why. It was good to get away from the cinema. Good to get away from Mr Pilger. She was off on holiday to the seaside, to somewhere she'd never been. Her swimming costume was packed, although it might be too early in the year for a swim. It would be a good holiday. She was looking forward to it, she said firmly to herself. Or was she? She sighed and traced a face on the window with her gloved finger. Damn. Now she'd made her new gloves grubby.

The door to their compartment suddenly slid open. Carol lifted her head from her magazine and Sylvia looked up. Dai was standing in the doorway. He looks, Sylvia thought suddenly, like a small boy caught in the act of stealing an apple, half sheepish, half pleased with himself. The thought, and the sight of him, warmed her.

'Well, and if it isn't the adorable Welshman,' Carol purred. She smoothed her hair, smoothed down her skirt, and crossed her legs.

'Dai, what on earth are you doing here? Are you working?'

'I'm on holiday. May I come in?'

Carol looked reprovingly at her friend. 'Sylv, you never told me.'

'I didn't know, that's why,' Sylvia retorted. She looked up at Dai. 'You shouldn't have come.'

'Shouldn't I? Where are we going, by the way? Torquay is it – or Paignton – I hear that's cheaper.'

'Goodrington,' said Sylvia beginning to smile.

'Ah, Goodrington. Of course. I've always wanted to go to Goodrington.'

He returned her smile while Carol glanced suspiciously from one to the other.

'I think you planned it between you, Sylv, and if you imagine I'm going to play raspberry to you both...'

Dai's mouth twitched.

'... well I'm not, see.'

'Of course you're not. Or gooseberry, come to that,' Dai said soothingly.

Sylvia stood up. 'Dai, I want a word with you... outside.'

'Of course, my precious.' He turned to Carol. 'Excuse us, won't you. I think I'm about to be told off.'

He let Sylvia proceed him out of the compartment and slid the door shut behind her.

They walked down the corridor, past a couple who were holding hands and gazing, not at the scenery, but at each other.

'Sorry,' Sylvia apologised as she squeezed past. Dai followed. 'Excuse me.' The couple sprang apart, looking embarrassed.

'Perhaps they're off on an illicit holiday to Goodrington,' Dai murmured. 'Or Paignton, or even Torquay. Wonder if they've also got a raspberry stuck back in the compartment.'

'You shouldn't make fun of her,' Sylvia said.

'She shouldn't be so silly.'

Sylvia said nothing more until they were inside the dining car.

She sat down and Dai sat opposite. An attendant hurried over.

'Sir? Madam?'

'Tea, or something stronger for shock?'

'Honestly, Dai... oh, tea'll do.'

'Well I need something stronger. Pot of tea for one and a pint of bitter please.'

The attendant left.

'Phew!' Dai took a deep breath. 'Glad that's over. Took all my courage to accost you back there. You might have screamed or pulled the communication cord.'

'Have you ever had anyone pull the communication cord?' Sylvia asked curiously.

Not yet, but I live in hope.'

'Have you been on this train all the time?' she asked suddenly.

'Only since Exeter.'

'Why Exeter?'

'Because, sweetheart, the crews change at Exeter and I'd be less likely to be spotted.'

Sylvia wrinkled her nose. 'Why would that matter?'

'I love it when you do that,' Dai said. 'Makes you look about twelve.'

'Dai...!'

He sighed. 'If it became known, as it undoubtedly would, that Dai Davies, who was believed to be visiting his loving parents in Wales, had boarded a Devon-bound train accompanied by the beautiful Sylvia Watkins…'

'And Carol.' Sylvia put in.

'I didn't know about Carol at the time. Anyway, there would have been hell to pay when the news reached your father. He'd probably have come after us breathing fire and brimstone.' He thought for a moment. 'I'm not entirely sure what brimstone is, but it doesn't sound very pleasant. And I didn't want that.'

The drinks arrived and they were silent for a moment.

'You really shouldn't have come,' Sylvia said at last. She looked down at the table. 'I don't like all this… subterfuge…'

'Don't you?' Dai said lightly. 'I'm rather enjoying it myself.'

Sylvia tried not to smile. Dai could always make her laugh. She suddenly felt light… happy.

'Dad's all right. He's only like that because he cares about me.'

'I know, and it's greatly to his credit.'

Sylvia considered this for a moment.

'How did you know we'd be on this train?' she said at last.

'I didn't. But I guessed you might be. If I'd been wrong, I'd have got off at Dawlish and waited for the next one.' He hesitated. 'It's only for a few days. I've got to be back on Thursday. Can't you put up with me 'til then? I'll carry your bags, walk a few paces behind you and try not to make a nuisance of myself.'

'Don't be ridiculous.'

She fell silent.

Dai put a hand over hers. 'Angry with me?' he asked, slightly anxious.

'No, you idiot. How could I be? But what about Carol?'

'What about her?'

'It's a bit unfair on her.'

Dai pulled a face. 'It's more likely to be a bit unfair on me,' he said. 'Why, for heaven's sake, didn't you say it was her you were going away with.'

Sylvia looked up and smiled mischievously. 'I didn't want to put you off.'

Chapter Twelve

Tom had been feeling guilty ever since Ginger had been so dismissive of Maggie. He was used to thinking of her as a younger sister and felt that his mates had been unkind. And he should have stood up for her, he thought. She could have come with them. She had always trailed along with them when they were young.

Rarely sensitive to the feelings of others he had felt protective of Maggie since they were children. He didn't like to see her hurt. As for what Les had said, about her being sweet on him, Tom dismissed it.

So that evening he had waited outside the shop until she finished work. She was surprised to see him and even more surprised when he said he would walk her home. They went the long way by the river path because he wanted to tell her about Ernie. Maggie had always been a good listener.

'He's funny,' Tom said, after explaining about his time in the boiler-house.

Maggie laughed.

'No – I don't mean like that. At times he's quite normal and times he isn't. Sometimes, when he thinks he's on the footplate of a loco that's moving he makes it all sound so real I almost believe him.'

'Sounds like you're as daft as he is.'

I thought he was round the bend at first, but he's not. He knows about all sorts of things.'

'What things?'

'Well science and stuff – and about the railway. Especially about the railway. But it's all jumbled up in his head, see. It's weird.'

Maggie glanced at him.

'He's sad... no... he's not sad, not in himself, except when he knows he's confusing things. Most of the time he doesn't realise, but when he does, a sort of blank look comes into his eyes. He can switch so quickly, it's a bit hard to keep up. He called me Harry once – perhaps that was his mate. Half the time he thinks he's on an engine footplate, but sometimes he's lecturing like an MIC instructor.' Tom walked on, lost in thought. 'He's... gentle...' he said at last, rather surprised at the thought that had come to him. 'You know, I think he's one of the nicest blokes I know.'

A train passed on the opposite bank of the river. Tom stopped to watch it go past and Maggie watched Tom.

'You've changed,' she said.

'Have I?'

'You've got quite wrapped up in it – the job, the railway.'

Tom shrugged.

She felt a surge of tenderness towards him.

'Tom...' she began, then stopped.

'What?'

'Oh – nothing. I must get home. Mum's out tonight and I've got to get tea.'

They resumed their walk at a brisker pace.

'It was nice of you to meet me,' Maggie said shyly.

'Thanks for listening.' He smiled at her. 'Sorry I banged on about old Ernie.'

'No need to apologise.' She moved closer to him and took his arm but when he didn't respond, she sighed and moved away.

******

A couple of brave swimmers ran down the beach at Goodrington Sands and dashed, yelling, into the sea. They splashed about for a few minutes, shouting and screaming, then came hurriedly out of the water and raced back to one of the bathing huts.

Other than the swimmers, a brisk east wind had kept most people off the beach. A few brave souls were huddled into one of the many shelters along the promenade, among them Dai, Sylvia and Carol.

Dai was reading aloud from a book.

'"…£54,000 has recently been spent on an improvement scheme including cliff gardens, promenades, seaside cabins, up-to-date bathing machines, putting greens, a large boating lake, Peter Pan playground…"' He looked up. 'The list is endless. Why have I never discovered this jewel of a place before, I ask myself?'

'Perhaps because you'd never heard of it until yesterday,' Sylvia said dryly.

'That might just be the reason.'

'Where did you get that book?' Carol demanded.

Dai closed it. '"GWR Holiday Haunts, 1935". I borrowed it. Along with "Rambles in South Devon", "Glorious Devon", and "Winter Resorts served by the GWR". Not that it's winter, although with this wind you wouldn't believe it's May. You see, Carol, I like to come well prepared.'

'You sound like a walking advertisement for the Company's publicity department,' Sylvia teased.

'I think it's nice to come prepared,' Carol said archly, smiling up at him. 'I like a man to be prepared.'

Dai sighed. 'I'm sure you do.'

'Well, it's cold here, so shall we go and see all these recommended improvements?' Sylvia said brightly.

And see the sights they did. The weather got better so they ate ices on the promenade, had a putt on the putting green – Dai won although Sylvia said he cheated. They took a boat out on the lake, scrambled over the cliffs, hired a bathing machine but only used it to leave their clothes in as they raced down to the sea. Afterwards, Sylvia and Carol relaxed in deckchairs while Dai sat on the sand, intent on making a sandcastle with a borrowed spade, only it wasn't a sandcastle at all, Sylvia realised when she went over to look at it. It was a rough outline of an engine. A small group of children had gathered round him, watching his every move. He added four wheels and a wavy line of smoke and the children cheered. Dai looked up and smiled.

It should have been an idyllic holiday. It would have been an idyllic holiday, Sylvia thought, if it hadn't been for Carol who had decided that rather than playing gooseberry, she would try to lure Dai away.

But things began to improve after they became acquainted with Eddie. He accosted Carol and Sylvia the following afternoon as they sat outside a café waiting for Dai to return with ice-creams.

'What are these two lovely ladies doing, sitting all on their lonesome?'

Eddie was a short, solidly built man, a vision in tartan waistcoat, tartan trousers, and to complete the ensemble, a flat tartan cap on his head.

'We can't have that now, can we?' He vaulted over the white railing surrounding the tables and chairs.

'Eddie "call-me-Jock" MacCauley, at your service.' He bowed and took off his cap before fanning himself with it. 'Warm, in't it?' He sat down.

Dai came out of the café with three large ice-creams and Eddie jumped to his feet.

'Just trying to entertain your two beautiful charmers, mister. No offence meant.'

'None taken.' Dai handed over the ices and sat down.

'This is Eddie "call-me-Jock" MacCauley,' Sylvia told Dai.

Carol smiled at Eddie. 'Why don't you sit down and tell us all about yourself?' she purred.

Dai and Sylvia exchanged amused glances.

'You seen my show at the Winter Gardens?' Eddie asked. 'If not, you're missin' the event of a lifetime. Two lifetimes. Once seen, never forgotten. I'll get you some tickets. On the 'ouse.'

'You're an entertainer?' Carol asked, opening her eyes wide.

'Star turn,' Eddie said. 'Keep 'em rollin' in the aisles wiv me Scottish jokes.'

Sylvia was intrigued. 'But you're not Scottish.'

Eddie crossed one tight trouser-leg over the other. 'Well, it's a funny thing, see. Tell 'em jokes in me native vernacular, which is down Bermondsey way, east end of London, and nobody laughs. Not a titter. Put on a Scottish accent, get rigged out like this and tell 'em the same jokes an' they fall about. That's why I call meself Jock.'

'Is MacCauley your real name?' Dai asked curiously.

''Course not. It's Smith. But the Eddie's real enough. Named after me grandfather. He was in the entertainment business too. Magician he was and sawed ladies in half. Went to a show when I was a nipper and I was hooked.'

'But you didn't become a magician?' Sylvia asked.

'Naaw. That's a mug's game. Tried it once, but me rabbits, what come out of me hat, ran off when I was in Whitby an' you can't get performing rabbits in Whitby. Not for love nor money. Fish, but who ever heard of a performin' cod?'

Sylvia laughed.

'And you're on tour?' Dai asked.

'Yeah. Booked to play all along the coast. Nice digs, nice weather – all I need is a nice girl to walk out with.' He winked at Carol, then stood up. 'But mustn't keep botherin' you, ladies. You're a lucky man, squire,' he added to Dai. 'I'll leave tickets at the box office.'

After that they were no longer a threesome, but a foursome. Eddie, well-meaning, genial and apparently totally besotted by Carol, seemed to pop up everywhere they went. True to his word, tickets had been left for them that evening and, also true to his word, the audience loved his jokes, told with a mock Scottish accent.

'He's a nice "wee" man,' Sylvia said as they dawdled along the promenade behind Carol and Eddie.

'He's a pain,' Dai said forcefully. 'I thought he'd take Carol off our hands but we've just been lumbered with him as well.'

'He probably wants company. And the holiday hasn't really been fair on Carol so far, has it?'

Dai sighed. 'The trouble with you is that you've too nice a nature.'

'That's why you like me,' Sylvia replied with mock complacency. She giggled. 'At least Carol's stopped making a pass at you.'

Dai took her hand. 'And I'm devoutly thankful for small mercies.' He suddenly stopped. 'I have a plan.'

******

Early the following morning found Dai and Sylvia walking hand in hand across a deserted beach. They reached the waters' edge and stopped. Sylvia shivered.

'Cold?' Dai asked, putting his arm round her.

'Not really.'

'I shouldn't have dragged you out so early, but it seemed such a good idea. What time's breakfast?'

Sylvia pulled a face. 'I'm quite happy to miss it. I think our landlady made all the toast for the season in January. Goodness knows what it'll be like in September.'

They stood for a moment, staring out to sea, then began walking along the waters' edge.

'I like this time of day,' Dai said. 'And I like the seaside. Especially at this time of the year.'

'Why?'

'There's a special sort of atmosphere.'

'Everything opening up you mean?'

'Yes. It's the anticipation. Freshly painted, bright and shining, looking forward to the summer. It's as if the place gives a great collective sigh, shakes off its winter sleep in preparation for the hordes of holidaymakers. When we come, of course, we think we own the place, but we don't. We're the interlopers.'

Sylvia didn't answer.

'I'm talking rubbish,' Dai said wryly.

'No you're not.'

'Yes I am. I'm a fake.'

He stopped walking and fell silent, watching a train skirting round the bay, small against the early morning sky, leaving a trail of steam as it went on its busy way to Kingswear. Then he sighed and began to speak, so softly that Sylvia had to strain to hear him.

> *'"Had I the heavens' embroidered cloths,*
> *Enwrought with golden and silver light,*
> *The blue and the dim and the dark cloths*
> *Of night and light and the half-light,*
> *I would spread the cloths under your feet:*
> *But I, being poor, have only my dreams;*
> *I have spread my dreams under your feet;*
> *Tread softly because you tread on my dreams."*

I have to use other people's words, see. I'm groping, right now, for the right words to say to you.'

'It's lovely. Who wrote it?'

'W.B. Yeats.'

'Is he Welsh?' she asked tentatively.

'No. Irish.'

'I'm very ignorant,' she said humbly.

Dai looked at her. 'No you're not. You've just never steeped yourself... You'll know far more about films than I do.' He shook his head impatiently. 'Why am I finding this so difficult...?'

Sylvia looked at him enquiringly.

He began again, hesitantly, 'You told me once, that you would never marry a railwayman. Do you still mean it?'

She bit her lip and bent to pick up a shell that had been washed clean by the sea.

'I love collecting shells,' she said, inconsequentially. 'I could live by the sea and walk along the beach early every morning just to collect the shells. Every one is different.'

'What would you do with them?'

'Oh, I don't know. Keep them for a while, then bring them back and scatter them on the beach.' She fell silent, then, shyly. 'It would depend...'

'On what?' he asked gently.

She didn't reply, just stared out to sea.

'Sylvia, the job isn't as important to me as it is to your father, but it is important. It's all I've been trained for and it's become a part of me,' Dai stood beside her and looked far out to the horizon. 'There's something very satisfying about it despite the bloody awful hours and hard work. Every engine's different, you know, and everyone has its own peculiarities, its own idiosyncrasies. I like that.'

'Dad would agree with you.'

'We've a good deal in common, Fred and I, although he doesn't realise it. We're both loyal to the Company for a start. It's a good company to work for. It's individual, it's flamboyant and it's got a strong streak of eccentricity.' He grinned deprecatingly. 'Like me in fact.'

They began to walk on.

'It stands for the sort of things both Fred and I would agree with.' He stopped abruptly. 'I'm sorry. We're on our own for the first time and all I do is bore you to death spouting poetry and talking about the job.'

'And dad,' she added.

'And your father,' he agreed. 'Why does he seem to come into everything?'

'You're not boring me,' Sylvia said abruptly.

'You only say that because you're kind.' He looked at her. 'You're very beautiful.'

'And you're very biased.'

'All right,' Dai agreed. 'I'm very biased.'

They stopped walking and stared at each other. Dai bent his head and gently kissed her. 'Sylvia...'

'Coo-ee! Sylvia! Dai!'

Carol was running across the sand towards them.

Dai swore under his breath.

'Sorry to break up the party but you'll miss breakfast, Sylvie, if you don't get a move on.'

******

'Tom! Here, Tom!'

It was early in the morning and Tom was on his way to the cleaner's cabin when Bert called to him from the footplate of 2202.

'You working down the black hole today?'

'Far as I know,' Tom called back.

'Well you won't find Ernie there.'

'Why not?'

'He's off duty. Compassionate leave. His missus has just died.'

'I didn't know he was married.'

'Oh yes. Been married for years. Devoted to one another they were.' Bert looked into the firebox and closed the doors. 'That's another one burning through nicely.'

He climbed down off the footplate and made his way over to engine 1455. 'Only another three to light up then it's home for a good fry-up.'

******

Tom worked mechanically that day, his mind elsewhere. His mate was a big man, previously unknown to Tom, who spoke in grunts and was clearly unhappy at having to work in the stationery boiler house.

Once Tom had booked off, he had made up his mind. He walked up Station Road then turned right into Jubilee Close. He went past the row of houses that also belonged to the Company and stopped outside Number 29. He looked past the neatly trimmed hedge, the tidy garden, and up to the freshly painted window frames, the sparkling windows. Perhaps he shouldn't have come. Perhaps Ernie wouldn't want a visit. What do you say to someone whose wife had just died? After another moment's indecision, he took a deep breath and knocked.

He hadn't long to wait before the door was thrown abruptly open. Ernie looked much the same as always, dressed neatly but not in uniform.

'Hello mate – nice of you to call! Come in, come in, don't stand there on the doorstep.'

He ushered Tom inside and into the parlour. It was very clean, almost oppressively so, and clearly rarely used. The walls were painted dark green and the dark, heavy Victorian furniture soaked up the sun that shone in through the window. The walls and most of the surfaces were covered with framed photographs and pictures.

Tom pulled off his cap. 'I just thought I'd drop by and see how you did...' he said awkwardly.

'Well, that was nice of you... very nice. You'll stay for a cup of tea won't you? It's all brewed.'

'Oh, don't bother.'

'No bother.'

He limped out of the room. Tom put down his lunch box and stared around. All the pictures were of engines – Cities, Saints and Star classes. A painting of 'The Great Bear' took pride of place on the wall above the fireplace. The mantlepiece held framed photographs which had been arranged with care. Tom picked up one of them.

'Looking at my collection, are you?' Ernie asked, a tray of tea and biscuits in his hands. He pushed the door closed with his behind before setting the tray down on the oval mahogany table in the centre of the room.

'They're very good,' Tom said uncertainly.

'They are that.' He nodded at the one in Tom's hands. 'Know who that is?'

Tom shook his head.

'Mr Churchward. Mr George Jackson Churchward. Here...' He poured out a cup of tea with a slightly unsteady hand. '...have some tea. You must be ready for it. Us railwaymen are always ready for a cuppa.'

Tom put the photograph back on the mantlepiece and took the cup. 'Thank you.'

'Yes. Mr Churchward – finest British locomotive engineer for my money.' Ernie waved his hand at the photographs round the room. 'He designed all of these... beautiful engines they are... driven all of them...' He pointed to the painting of 'The Great Bear'. 'Even that one.'

He fell silent, staring at it.

'Ernie…' Tom said at last. 'I… I'm sorry about your wife.'

'Gladys? She's out now but she'll be back soon.' He glanced at Tom. 'Drink your tea while it's hot. Can't abide cold tea.'

He joined Tom at the mantlepiece and picked up another photograph of Churchward.

'This one now… taken – oh, before the war… this is very good – very much like the old man…' He handed it to Tom.

'You knew him?' Tom asked, surprised.

'Oh yes. I was at Swindon when he was Loco Superintendent. Here…' he limped over to the table and proffered the plate. 'Have a biscuit.'

Tom shook his head. 'No thank you.'

'Go on. Gladys baked them…' he stopped for a moment. '…just before she died.'

Tom silently took one.

'Sit down… sit down.' He gestured to a chair and sat beside him. 'Started work in 1886 you know… third of January 1886. That makes me 64… not bad eh?'

He got to his feet, went over to the massive sideboard that ran almost the entire length of the room, opened a drawer and rummaged inside. He took out a photograph album, brought it back to the table and began turning the pages.

'That's my dad. He was a platelayer. Very pleased he was when I got taken on as cleaner. "An engine driver's the finest profession a man can have" he said, "barring a doctor, and let's face it Ernest, you'd never have made a doctor"'.

Ernie turned to a photograph of a grinning group of platelayers.

'That's him again,' he said, pointing a finger. 'That was taken when they changed the line from broad to narrow gauge. I could never understand why they changed it – seven foot wide the track was, and you should have seen the locos… fine engines they were, Harry, very fine... Go on, have a look through it.'

He fell silent and Tom turned over a page.

'Here, let me top you up.' He refilled Tom's cup.

''Course it was different then – when I started work. Run like the army it was and no worse for that. Didn't do us any harm and the Company looked after us very well... very well... Here, have another biscuit.'

Tom took one.

'Twenty-one I was when I went to Swindon,' Ernie continued. 'Wonderful I thought it. The Company built all the houses – nice they were – Gladys and me had one when we got married... and they built the school and the hospital. Then there was the Mechanics Institute... they used to put on classes there in the evenings - marvellous things you could learn.'

He shook his head and blinked as if trying to blow away the mist that fogged his brain. 'Forgotten most of it now... I get confused you see, Tom.'

He turned another page of the album. 'Gladys and me met at a dance at the Institute... that's her, there.' He pointed. 'And there's the church... St. Marks... see, that's us on our wedding day. Looked beautiful she did. Fair took my breath away.' He frowned, as if trying to remember. 'There was the park on one side of the church, and the main line on the other. I'd have liked my boy to have been buried at St. Marks but they said it wasn't possible. Just turned sixteen he was. My Harry. Big lad and mad to go. Nothing Gladys and me said would change his mind.' Ernie sighed. 'I was in a reserved occupation and Harry, he said he'd go on behalf of the family. Full of big words and big ideas, he was. "Dad", he said, "no time at all I'll be back. Like a bad penny. You'll see".'

Ernie fell silent. The room was quiet, apart from the ticking of the grandfather clock in the hall.

211

'So off he goes to the recruitment place and pretends he's eighteen. Big lad, he was, and they believed him. Just sixteen and been working as cleaner... Look Tom, here's a picture of him. Him and Gladys. Took it on a vest pocket camera I'd saved up for. Mad on photography I was in those days. On holiday we were... see... that's them on the beach. The Company put on a special train every year to...where was it now? Weymouth, that's it. Weymouth. "Swindon by the Sea" we called it during the works shut-down.'

Ernie stared down at the photograph. 'Died somewhere abroad. Flanders... some field in Flanders... Pity really, he'd have liked to have been buried at St. Marks. Every birthday Gladys takes a bunch of flowers and puts them propped up against the wall in the graveyard... Pity not to know where he's buried... he was going to be a driver like his old man...that's what he wanted... "I'll be back, dad," he said. "You don't get rid of me that easy."'

Tom glanced at Ernie and saw that tears were coursing down his scarred face.

A clock in the hall struck six. Ernie had been silent for some time, his hand gently stroking the photograph of his wife and son. He closed the album and looked up at Tom.

'Mr Churchward now, he was a real gentleman. Not that he was stuck-up or anything – not a bit of it. He'd swear like a trouper with the best of us if something had gone wrong. But a gentleman none the less and a very great man... big man he was and dressed in tweed suits... he always wore a trilby hat too, not a bowler... "If a man wears a bowler, he's the boss and to be respected" my dad used to say but Mr Churchward wore a trilby and we all respected him.'

'He said to me once, he said, "You stick up for the Great Western, Patch, for it's a fine Company" and he was right at that.'

'I drove him on a test run of a '43. After the trip he came up to the cab, shook me by the hand and said, "Thank you very much Ernie. A bloody good run." That was praise you know – coming from the old man.'

'They were great days you know, Harry. Not like that now of course, although I'm still proud to work for the Company.'

Tom put down his empty cup.

Off are you?' Ernie said, blinking up at him. 'Sorry you couldn't wait for Gladys... round at her sisters I think... she's got six sisters you know – her father, that's my father-in-law, said he wouldn't give up 'til he had a son, but he had to in the end... We only had Harry...' He was silent for a moment. 'Tell you about the accident I had, did they?'

'Well, something...'

'Run-away goods. They said it wasn't my fault, but it must have been. After all, if you're the driver, you take the responsibility don't you? That's what I always believed – you take the responsibility and the blame and that goes with the job. My mate was killed... in the accident... don't remember much about it now but they said I was lucky to be alive. Well so I was really but only for Gladys' sake... I've been very lucky, Harry. Never looked at anyone else after I met Gladys.'

He sat, lost in thought.

'I've seen many changes, Harry, and not all for the best... but you know, when you get to my age you get a bit tired... and then it's been a bit on the quiet side here the last few days... Gladys has been away – staying with her sister. Ever so sorry she'll be to have missed you. We don't get many visitors you see... not now...'

'I must go,' Tom said, rising awkwardly to his feet.

'What's that? Oh yes...' Ernie stood up. 'Well, thanks for dropping in – nice of you... pop in again if you're passing, but you're probably busy with your girlfriends and such. I know you young lads.'

He picked up the photograph of Churchward once more.

'Shook my hand he did and said, "Thank you very much Ernie. A bloody good run... oh yes... a great gentleman..."'

******

'We're going to miss you, Dai – aren't we Sylv?'

Carol, Sylvia and Dai were standing on the platform at Goodrington Sands waiting for the train.

'That's very kind of you Carol, but Eddie'll look after you.'

'Eddie! Told me his wife and three kids would be coming today for a bit of a holiday.' She shrugged. 'Never liked those flashy tartan clothes he wore anyway.' She looked up at Dai soulfully. 'Couldn't you take the rest of the week off?'

'Regrettably, no.'

The signal came off with a clang.

'Carol, would you do me an enormous favour?' Dai asked.

'What's that?'

'Well, it's a long journey and I've nothing to read, see? You wouldn't be an angel and get me a paper, would you?'

Carol glanced at Sylvia who was standing silently, a little apart.

'Please?'

'I wouldn't do it for anyone else,' she sighed theatrically, and walked off.

'Thank the Lord.'

'Poor Carol,' Sylvia murmured as the train pulled alongside the platform.

'Put it down to experience. It'll be good for her.'

'Mmm. I've rather gone off her I'm afraid.'

'Have you my sweetheart? I'm so glad because when we're married I wouldn't really like to entertain her, but of course if she's still your friend I suppose I'd have to.' He walked

214

towards a compartment. 'I could always make an excuse, mind, and go down the pub.'

'When we're what?' Sylvia demanded.

'Married.'

'Train's about to depart sir,' called the guard.

'Thanks for telling me.' Dai opened the compartment door.

'Are we going to be married?'

'Of course.'

'But you haven't asked me.'

'Haven't I? Oh dear.'

The guard waved his flag, the engine gave an answering whistle and Dai jumped in as it began to move. Dai leaned out of the window.

'Sylvia... will you marry me?'

'Yes, you fool, but couldn't you have chosen a better moment?' she called, walking alongside.

The train picked up speed and Sylvia walked faster.

'Not with that man-eater about!'

'Dai..!' Sylvia was running now, to keep up.

'What?'

'Don't tell anyone 'til I get back...Dai!'

'All right...' Dai shouted, leaning far out. 'I love you...!'

Sylvia stopped at the end of the platform, waving her hand as she watched the train curve round the bay.

'Me too, you idiot,' she said softly.

Steam in the Family

Chapter Thirteen

'Found on the main line just south of Chalcote Tunnel. Dead.'

Jerry had burst into the shed, big with news. Tom, Ginger and Les stopped cleaning 5705 to listen, as railwaymen gathered round Jerry.

'Dead?' Tom echoed.

'Killed outright they reckon.'

'How?' asked Ginger.

'Knocked down by the 9.10 "up" fast and found by the driver of the following goods.' Jerry shrugged. 'What he was doing wandering about on the main line at night is anyone's guess.'

Everyone was silent, shocked.

'Poor old Ernie,' Ginger said at last.

'Well, perhaps it's for the best,' Les said practically as he returned to his cleaning.

'Probably is.' Ginger agreed.

Tom climbed down off the engine and made his way through the shed and out the other end. It was very dark outside and Tom shivered, although it was a mild night. He walked along the row of engines which were waiting until morning for their boilers to be washed. Long shadows flickered in the light of the flare lamp he carried. When he reached the stationery boiler house he peered inside. The boiler itself looked like some squat dead animal. Who would operate it now, he wondered?

'Here... what you doing kid?'

Tom started and turned abruptly. 'Who's that?'

Bert stood in the entrance, holding up his lamp. 'Oh it's you Tom. Sorry if I startled you. Thinking about Ernie?'

Tom nodded.

'Doesn't seem possible, does it?'

They both stood silent for a moment.

'You was friends wasn't you?' Bert said as they began to walk back.

'No – not really. I hardly knew him.'

'Well he talked of you as his friend... talked a lot about you he did.'

******

The audience in the cinema was mostly made up of railwaymen, their wives and girlfriends. They were watching *'The Romance of a Railway'*, a film made by the Great Western Railway to celebrate the company's centenary. There were dramatised scenes showing the railway's history: the original meeting in Bristol; the line being built; its opening from Paddington to Maidenhead; the building of the Severn Tunnel to shorten the journey from London into Wales. It ended with a survey of the Swindon locomotive works and the overhaul of a King class engine.

The Company had taken over The Regal on an afternoon when there was no matinee. There was no admission charge and the place was packed. Even railwaymen from the LNER shed had come out of curiosity.

The film finished with an address by the Great Western Railway's Chairman, Viscount Horne.

'The picture of those powerful, modern locomotives rounds off a century of history rich in development and experience, beginning with the day when a group of far-seeing men embarked upon an epoch-making enterprise the extent and

importance of which have far exceeded their most sanguine hopes. During the passage of the years, many eminent people have contributed to the results which we see today, but in this historic year we cannot fail to pay a special tribute to those outstanding men whose names are written large in the history of the Great Western Railway.

'At the end of one hundred years of effort and achievement, the pioneering spirit still possesses us in facing the new problems of these trying times. We aspire to the same vision and courage and determination as characterised our earliest predecessors, and we recall with gratitude and with admiration the unquenchable confidence which they displayed in entering upon this great undertaking dedicated then and for ever to the high service of the British people.'

The lights came up, and, after a moment's silence, the appreciative audience began to applaud before standing for the National Anthem.

Fred, Tom and Nancy joined the throng of railwaymen moving towards the exit.

'First rate, that was,' Fred said enthusiastically. 'Did you see 6013 Tom, coming out of the works? Beautiful loco that was. I'd love to have driven it.'

'What did you think of 6014 and its new streamlining?', asked Sammy who was just behind them.

Fred snorted. 'Trying to be like Gresley's latest locos on the LNER. Bloody ridiculous I call it with that bullet-shaped nose. They say it's better for wind resistance, but I'm not so sure.'

'Made me quite nostalgic, seeing Swindon again,' Sammy said, reflectively.

'Were you at Swindon, Mr White?' Tom asked.

'Thought everyone knew,' Sammy replied. 'Only came here a couple of years back. 19th December 1933 it was and cold enough to freeze the balls off a brass monkey – begging your pardon, Mrs Watkins, I didn't see you there. Same day as Mr Churchward was knocked down and I was sorry because I was on days and couldn't get back for his funeral.'

'Mr Churchward? Knocked down?' Tom asked.

'Didn't you know? Run over by the "down" Fishguard. Killed outright. Never forget that day, dreadful it was. The wife and I'd had a hell of a bust-up and two of the nippers were in bed with the measles or chicken pox or something...'

Tom wasn't listening to the end of his speech.

'Just like Ernie,' he said.

'What's that? Oh yes – never thought of it like that. Ernie was knocked down by a train wasn't he?'

'Tom! Hey Tom!' Les and Ginger pushed their way past the crowds. 'Wait for us!'

Tom waited for them to catch up.

'We're going to that dance tonight, remember?'

'What dance?'

'Come on mate – wake up!' Ginger shook his arm vigorously and marched him up the road. 'You can't have forgotten! Good band playing.'

'Lots of lovely crumpet!' enthused Les.

'And us three handsome young railwaymen...' Ginger went on.

'With plenty of money thanks to the generosity of the Great Western Railway!' Les finished.

Ginger stopped and removed his cap. 'Thank you, Great Western Railway,' he said with mock solemnity.

Les nudged him. 'Got to hurry if we're to catch the train.'

They walked on faster, overtaking Jim and Maggie standing at the street corner, Maggie looking obstinate, Jim angry.

'Tom!' Maggie called.

The three of them stopped.

'I'm sorry about your friend,' Maggie said awkwardly. 'You know, the one you were telling me about.'

'Oh... well...' Tom shrugged.

'You two coming with us?' Les asked.

Maggie glanced at Jim. 'I'm not..' she began.

'If you mean to the dance, I've been trying to persuade her,' Jim said with some annoyance.

'Do come,' Les pressed.

'Yes, do,' Ginger added.

Maggie looked at Tom, but he was silent. She sighed. 'Oh all right then.'

She smiled at Tom, who smiled back and Jim, watching them closely, narrowed his eyes.

'Come on then,' he said brusquely, taking her arm.

He bustled off with her and the other three followed.

'Why's she going with Jim?' Tom asked.

Ginger shrugged. 'Think they've been walking out for a bit.'

'She never said anything to me.'

'Why should she?'

Tom fell silent. Why should she indeed? He was surprised to find himself a little annoyed that she hadn't told him and more than a little annoyed to find her going with Jim. He stopped. He didn't want to be with his friends. He didn't want to go to a dance.

'I think I'll go home,' he said. Les and Ginger looked at him.

'You can't do that,' Les said, scandalised. 'We've got to celebrate!'

'Why?'

'It's the railway's birthday,' he explained.

'And you know something else?' Ginger said, looking at his watch. 'We'll miss the 6.20 if we don't get a move on!'

They raced down the road, Tom pulled along between them. Ginger and Les began to sing 'Happy birthday to you' at the top of their voices. Still singing, they ran into the station, across the footbridge and caught the train by the skin of their teeth.

******

The entire Watkins family were sitting at the kitchen table having finished the excellent roast beef followed by apple crumble served up by Nancy. No-one had been able to do justice to the meal which had been eaten in a strained atmosphere.

Tom was restless and uncomfortable and anxious to get away. Sylvia, dressed in her usherette's uniform, was rebellious and upset after having delivered her bombshell of an announcement. She delivered it at the precise moment that Nancy, dishing out the food, was flushed with triumph at having for once managed to co-ordinate all the elements of the meal, so that the vegetables weren't over-cooked, the beef undercooked or the gravy full of lumps. Nancy now sat at the table with a worried frown, gazing sadly at the congealing and rapidly cooling food on everyone's plates. And Fred? Fred was sitting in his usual seat at the head of the table, looking round in apparent unconcern, but his fingers were drumming the edge of the table.

'But dad...!'

Nancy got up to refill the teapot.

'And another thing...' Fred said loudly. Sylvia subsided into silence.

'And another thing, my girl, you're far too young to know your own mind...!'

'I'm nineteen!'

'Nineteen! You'll fancy you're in love with someone else before you're twenty!'

'I won't! I love Dai and want to marry him!'

222

'Love!' Fred said contemptuously. 'You don't know the meaning of the word! Neither does Dai Davies! You don't think for one moment that he's serious, do you? That man's not serious about anything!'

'He is!'

'And if he was serious,' Fred steamrollered on, 'why didn't he do the decent thing and ask my permission before proposing to you? Eh? Why didn't he do that?'

'Because he knows what you'd say!' Sylvia replied passionately. 'You've always disliked him, you've always been prejudiced...!'

'Prejudiced? Me? Don't talk daft! You're under-age and it's me he should have come to!'

'Don't be so bloody archaic!'

'And don't you use language like that girl! You're not too old to have your mouth washed out with soap!'

'Mum...!'

Nancy looked up but said nothing.

'We should never have let you go off on that holiday,' Fred went on. 'Just you and that flighty friend of yours. So Dai Davies just happened to go to the same place did he? When he was telling everyone at the shed he was off to see his family? There's deceit for you. That shows what he's really like!'

'It's impossible trying to talk to you!' Sylvia said hotly. 'You just don't listen!'

'Oh I'm listening all right. I hear you loud and clear. Coming out with it just now, upsetting your mother just as she was giving us that lovely meal. Thinking only about yourself, no concern for anyone else. Just a child you are!'

'I'm nineteen, dad,' Sylvia reiterated between clenched teeth. 'And I've been working for years...!'

'Yes, and what sort of a job is that, eh? Usherette at the cinema! That's no sort of a job for a decent young girl! I was against it at the time but, no, you wouldn't listen, would you?

Now you listen to me. When you're twenty-one you can do as you please, but until then you'll do as I say or you'll pack your bags and clear out of my house!'

Sylvia jumped up.

'Serve you right if I did!' she shouted and rushed out of the room. For a moment there was silence.

'Pass us another cup of tea Nance.'

Nancy put down the teapot and went after Sylvia.

There was a long silence.

'Did you hear Sammy got into a bit of bother yesterday?' Fred asked Tom, striving for normality. 'He was on a job with 3448 when the main steam pipe joint blew. They had to drag him in.'

'I must be off,' Tom said, standing up and picking up his lunch box.

Fred looked at him. 'Don't you worry about your sister now. It might seem hard but I'm doing the right thing Tom, believe me.'

Tom stopped at the door and turned. He was about to make some biting comment but when he saw Fred sitting upright and complacent at the table, he just shrugged and went out. What was the use, he thought, despising himself. What was the use?

Fred got up, poured himself a cup of tea, returned to his seat, added milk and two teaspoons of sugar and stirred it slowly. But he did not drink. He sat silent for a moment, then suddenly the façade began to crumble as he put his elbows on the table and pressed his hands over his eyes.

******

Tom raced down the road, anxious to get away. He caught up with Maggie, trudging slowly along, a heavy basket of shopping in her hand.

'Late for work?' she asked.

'Just glad to get out. Here, give me that.'

He took the basket and they walked in silence for a while.

'He's just like some heavy Victorian father!' Tom burst out suddenly.

'Who is?' Maggie said, lost in her own thoughts.

'Dad, of course.'

Maggie didn't reply. Tom glanced at her.

'Shouldn't you be at work?'

She shrugged, her face expressionless. 'Mum's away so I had to have the time off to look after dad and Joey.'

'How long's she away for?' Tom asked, without any real concern.

'Don't know.'

'Oh.' Tom began to walk faster. 'He's just told Sylvia she can't marry,' he said bitterly. 'He won't give his permission for her to marry Dai... Dai Davies you know.'

'I know.'

'No reason, oh no, dad never gives reasons! It's just "you do what I say because I know best". That's dad.' He stopped for a moment to draw in a breath. 'He's so, so smug about it! So smug and complacent! So sure he's right!'

'Perhaps he is.'

'Maggie!' Tom was hurt. 'He's not! He's just... just... stupid and stubborn. Wants his own way in everything and expects everyone to jump to his tune!'

Maggie walked on.

'He's never in the wrong... he doesn't even know what it's like. You know what I wish? I wish, just once, that he'd be wrong and know it. I wish he'd fail at something, just once, then perhaps he'd realise that he isn't God!'

By the time they reached Maggie's house Tom had calmed down.

'I'm sorry, I shouldn't have said all that.'

'I don't mind. I must go in – dad'll be home soon for his tea.'

She took the basket. 'Thanks for carrying it.'

'Well... 'bye then... I'm sorry I said...'

'You needn't be. 'Bye.'

He hurried off and Maggie watched him go. Then, with a dispirited shrug, she turned and opened the gate.

******

As Tom walked past a row of empty wagons on his way to the shed, Ginger's voice echoed from inside the last wagon.

'Here, give us a hand out will you?'

Tom climbed up the side of the wagon and peered in to find Ginger lying flat on his back, head resting on a small pillow of sand. His eyes were closed.

'How d'you know it was me?' Tom asked.

'I'd know that clod-hopping walk of yours anywhere,' Ginger replied, his eyes remaining shut.

'What're you doing in there?'

'Having a rest. I'm worn out.'

Tom laughed and Ginger sat up and began to shake the sand from his hair.

'I've been doing your work I'll have you know.'

Tom helped him out.

'It's all Witty's fault,' Ginger explained as they walked towards the shed.

'He tells me to unload this lot of sand, right? He says it's urgent, right? So, because I'm a hard-working, willing sort of chap I near kills myself emptying the lot. And when I finish, guess what happens?'

'You've shifted the wrong load?'

'Worse than that! Witty comes past and what do you think he says?'

'Tom! Here, Tom!' Dai came hurrying over. 'Have you seen Sylvia? She was meant to meet me.'

'No,' Tom began awkwardly. 'Not since lunch... I think she's gone to work...'

Dai looked at him sharply.

'What happened?'

'There was an awful row...' Tom said reluctantly.

'Row?'

'With dad. About you.'

'Dammo duw! I told her to leave it to me!'

He turned and rushed off.

'Well,' Ginger went on, determined to finish his story. 'Witty said, in a surprised voice, "Finished already? I'd booked Watkins to clear the rest of it tonight". See?' He dug Tom in the ribs. 'So I reckon you owe me one, mate.'

'What's that?' Tom said, staring after Dai. 'Oh... yes...'

Ginger stared at him, then shook his head and stalked off into the shed.

******

It was late afternoon when Dai walked up Station Road. He stopped outside Tom's house, took a deep breath, opened the gate, and walked round to the back. Fred was weeding at the far end of the back garden.

Dai stopped and watched him for a moment.

'Fred... could I have a word?' he said at last.

Fred stood up slowly. Without saying anything he brushed past Dai and went into the house. After a moment's hesitation, Dai followed, his eyes adjusting to the dim light in the kitchen. Fred was at the sink, washing his hands.

'Fred...'

'I didn't invite you in.'

227

'Look Fred... I was coming to see you. I told Sylvia to leave it to me...'

'So, you give orders to my daughter, do you?'

'No, of course not.'

Fred dried his hands then came closer to Dai. He peered up at him.

'I've told Sylvia and I'll tell you. While she's under-age I'll not allow her to throw herself away on some half-baked, cocky young Welshman. I'll not allow her, do you hear? She's my daughter and she'll do what I say. Now get out of my house.'

'Can't we sit down and talk about it...?'

'There's nothing to talk about. Nothing at all.'

'But...'

'Get the hell out of my house d'you hear!' Fred shouted.

He turned from Dai, staggered, and put his hand out to the kitchen table to steady himself. The door to the hall opened and Nancy came in.

Dai looked across to her. 'Good evening, Mrs Watkins. Sorry for the intrusion. I'm just going.'

He went out the way he had come.

Fred looked up. 'Nance? That you?'

Nancy switched on the light.

'You saw that Welshman here, making a fool of himself?'

'I saw him. But he's not the only Welshman making a fool of himself, is he?' she said gently, as if to a child. She sighed. 'Oh Fred...'

Fred sat down heavily. 'What? What do you mean?'

She didn't reply, just came and sat beside him and took his hand.

******

228

The last customers had gone, the house lights were up and Sylvia was walking along the rows of seats checking that no-one had left anything behind. She looked strained and unhappy.

'Sylvia.'

Dai was standing at the back, watching her.

'How long have you been there?'

'Not long.'

She turned away as Dai walked down the aisle to meet her. He cupped her face in his hands.

'Crying?'

'Don't. Mr Pilger'll see.'

'Let him.' He kissed her. 'Besides, I've every right. We're engaged.'

Sylvia turned away.

'It's all right,' he said. 'I know what happened.'

He guided her to a seat in the back row and sat her down.

'Why did you tell him, silly girl?' he asked. 'I said leave it to me.'

'It wouldn't have made any difference,' she said. 'He's just...' she fell silent.

The house lights began to be switched off.

'We'd better go, or we'll be locked in.'

'I wouldn't mind. Could be nice and cosy.' Dai got up and hauled her to her feet. 'Come on. A cup of tea at Sid's is what you need.'

Once seated in the café, Dai began to speak then stopped.

'What?' Sylvia asked.

'I – I couldn't have chosen a worse time to tell you but... there's a vacancy come up for a driver at Bristol.'

'Bristol?'

'Yes. And I'm next in line.' He paused. 'I can't really refuse it.'

There was a long pause.

'I see.'

'But now this has happened it might be all for the best.'

'For us to break it off?'

'Nothing of the sort! I mean to be away from this shed so I'm not under your father's feet all the time.'

'Absence making the heart grow fonder?' Sylvia said wryly.

'Something like that.'

They were both silent.

'I'm sorry. It's what happens if you marry a railwayman. I honestly don't have a choice.'

Sylvia made patterns in the sugar bowl with her teaspoon. 'It's funny... when I was little I used to be able to twist dad round my little finger... he spoiled me rotten... He's always been full of bluster and that, but – he's really soft underneath. I just don't understand...' She looked up at him. 'He's never been like this...'

'Sylvia...' Dai began hesitantly. 'Have you ever thought... is he quite well?'

'Why? Dad? What do you mean?'

'I don't know... it's just... something...'

'Because he's taken against you?'

'No, not that. I can understand that. It's just...'

'What? Tell me.'

Dai shook his head. 'No, nothing. Just my fertile imagination running riot.' He took her hand. 'You're much too good for me.'

'Me?'

'I thought you'd want to break it off when I told you about Bristol.'

'Well...' she gave him an impish look. 'I might not find anyone else who'd be daft enough to want to marry me.' She stood up. 'Better get home else they'll think I've gone for good.'

Chapter Fourteen

Bright lights were shining on the Great Western Travelling Post Office, lighting up the three distinctive carriages with 'Royal Mail' lettering on the side. The TPO, together with a rake of seven chocolate and cream liveried passenger coaches headed by the engine Saint Dunstan, was standing by the platform in Bristol Station waiting to depart on its night-time journey to Shrewsbury.

The area was a scene of great activity. Post office workers and porters, working under the eye of the Post Office Supervisor, were busy moving bags of mail from vans to the train to be sorted on the way. Everyone worked quickly and efficiently, for speed in getting the mail to its correct destination was of the essence.

On the footplate, driver Harry Wills was having a long swig of tea while Geoff, his fireman, pulled coal forwards from the back of the tender.

'What was wrong with 4010?' Geoff asked.

Harry shrugged. 'Both injectors failed, I was told.'

Geoff looked anxious. 'We've quite a load on. Bit more than 2921's used to.'

Harry grinned reassuringly. An experienced driver in his late fifties, he took life as it came and didn't look for trouble.

'We can only do our best.' He poured out some tea and passed it over. 'Here, have a drop.'

Once the mailbags were safely stowed and the doors closed, the guard gave the 'right away' and the train moved out of the station and began its journey.

Inside the sorting carriage, men were standing in a row in front of a long, padded wooden counter which extended the full length of the coach. Behind the counter was a rack with hundreds of pigeon holes. Sacks of mail were emptied on the counter, the addresses read and the letters thrown into the appropriate pigeon hole for the district. Bags of sorted mail hung on pegs behind the sorters, ready for delivery. The sorters worked swiftly, swaying effortlessly to the motion of the train as it began to speed through the night.

Post office mail vans were beginning to arrive at mail exchange apparatus along its route. These were the collection and drop-off points. The post office workers waiting at the trackside would suspend their pouches of mail on to the trackside apparatus to be caught in large nets hanging out from the side of the train. Once caught, they were be transferred to the sorting carriage for the men to begin work.

On the train bags of sorted mail had been sealed into leather pouches. These were suspended out on a steel arm and released at the correct time, sending them sweeping through the air to be caught by the net at the side of the track, collected by the workers on the trackside who would deliver them to the local post offices. The train never had to slow down and the whole exchange was fast, efficient, and relied on split-second timing.

In the stowage van a post office worker strapped a pouch inside the train on to the steel arm, ready to swing it out to the waiting net. The supervisor glanced at his watch.

'She's running late,' he commented and soon all the post office workers began to notice that the train had started to lose speed.

Inside the cab, Harry glanced at the pressure gauge. It was dropping. He eased down the regulator.

'She won't make it up the bank.'

Geoff nodded. He stopped shovelling and wiped his hand across his sweating face.

As they approached Chalcote signalbox, Harry put in the brake and stopped the train. He told Geoff to request the signalman to turn them off the main line into the loop and then summon assistance. Geoff jumped down and ran up the steps.

******

In the booking on lobby at Acton Chalcote, Fred was leisurely reading the notices before going to the engineman's cabin. He had been rostered as 'spare' and was in no hurry.

'Fred!' Geoff Willis, the night foreman, hurried in. 'The down Mail's in trouble. The Chalcote signalman has put them in the 'down' loop. He's just been on the blower and asked us to assist the TPO up the bank.'

'Righto.'

'You can take 5935. She's just come in off the Circuit. Drop on the bars and glands and she's ready to go.'

Fred nodded and started for the door.

Geoff stopped him. 'Would you take your lad as mate? He's the only one around.'

'Of course.'

'I wouldn't ask as a general rule, you know that. Sure you don't mind?'

'It'll be good to see how he's shaping,' Fred said as he went out.

Tom had just finished filling Norton Hall's tank and was swinging the pipe away from the tender when Fred arrived.

'Tom? That you Tom?'

Tom climbed down. 'Here dad.'

Fred looked at him in silence for a moment. He was secretly pleased at the thought of working with his son, but he wasn't going to show it.

Don't want to give the lad a big head, he thought, as he climbed up into the cab.

'Well, so you're my mate,' he said evenly.

'Yes, dad.'

Fred grunted. 'Don't expect any allowances from me. You'll pull your weight same as any other mate or I'll see the guvnor about you.'

Tom didn't answer.

'Look lively then!'

Tom climbed into the cab and they set off.

By the time Fred's engine came past on the main line the Post Office train had been moved into a loop by the signalman. After the points had been changed, Tom waved the engine back into the loop to form a double-headed train. As he coupled the two engines, Harry climbed down from his cab.

''Lo Fred.'

Fred leant over the side of the cab. 'What's the trouble?'

Harry shrugged. 'Too big a load. She's been struggling on the hills and I don't want to risk stalling on the bank. See us over the top and we'll be all right.'

'Righto.'

The double-headed train was soon on its way, speeding through the night as it tried to make up for lost time. Inside the cab Tom was working hard as the train thundered up the bank. After they had breasted the summit, Tom stopped firing and let out a sigh of relief.

'All right mate?'

'I'll just turn on the pep pipe,' Tom said, slightly nervously, afraid of doing the wrong thing. Fred nodded and Tom watered the coal in the tender to lay any dust.

The Automatic Train Control inside the cab gave advance warning of an approaching distant signal, with the horn sounding for caution, and so Fred immediately cancelled the warning signal, closed the regulator and gently applied the brake. The identical warning signal was simultaneously cancelled by Harry in the cab of his engine who also shut off steam.

Fred leant out of the cab and peered into the night as he looked for the home signal. Where was it? He moistened his lips and narrowed his eyes. Damn it, where was it? Tom, seeing his hesitation, hurriedly crossed to Fred's side and looked out.

'It's red dad!' he called. 'Can't you see it!'

'Don't teach me how to drive this train!' Fred snapped.

'We'll run by it!' Tom shouted.

Harry, looking out of the cab behind Fred's engine, was also watching for the signal.

'What's Fred think he's doing?' he muttered as he slammed in his brake.

The train instantly slowed and the sorters inside the sorting carriage were thrown violently off their feet.

'What the bloody hell...!'

The mail waiting to be sorted flew on to the floor and the bags of sorted mail fell off their pegs. Envelopes slid out of pigeon holes and the carriage was filled with flying paper and choice language from the sorters.

The train came to a stand by the signal. Harry climbed down from his cab and hurried up to Fred.

'What the bloody hell's the matter with you Fred?' he called, shaken out of his usual imperturbability. 'What're you playing at?'

'Sorry mate,' Fred said slowly. 'Must have been dust in my eye.'

Harry shrugged. 'Fair enough.' He hesitated for a moment before going back to his engine.

Fred turned to find Tom staring at him.

'Water that coal down,' he said roughly. 'Must have been some dust.'

'Didn't you see it dad?'

'I said wet it down!'

'I just have!'

'Do as you're bloody well told!'

Tom stood motionless as Fred turned away, then reached once more for the pep pipe.

They returned to the shed without another word being exchanged. Once Fred had brought the engine to a stand over the ashpit he climbed down but missed his footing and half stumbled, half fell on to the track. Tom was beside him in a flash.

'Dad...'

'Too bloody dark to see your own feet!'

He shook off Tom's helping hand and walked towards the shed. Tom watched him go.

******

There was no sign of Fred when Tom finally came off shift the following morning. Nancy was humming a dance tune while hanging out the washing as Tom trudged wearily up the path and rounded the corner of the house.

'Is dad back?'

'I don't think he's come in. He's probably gone to the allotment. Do you want anything to eat?'

Tom shook his head. 'Think I'll turn in and get some shut-eye.'

'A hard night?' Nancy asked sympathetically.

'Mmm.' Tom turned to go into the house, then turned back. 'Mum... is anything wrong with dad's eyesight?'

'Wrong?'

'I was booked with him last night and he nearly ran by a signal. I don't think he saw it.'

'What does your father say?'

Tom shrugged. 'Blamed it on me of course.'

Nancy gave him a sharp look.

'I'm not making it up, honestly!' He picked up a shirt and handed it to her. 'Haven't you noticed anything? Hasn't dad said anything?'

Nancy shook her head.

'Mum... will you talk to him? He'll listen to you. He won't listen if I say anything.'

Nancy pegged up the shirt and reached down for a pair of trousers.

'Tell him there's something wrong...' Tom urged. 'Tell him he ought to get an eye test.'

'You go in. I won't be a moment and then I'll make you some tea.'

'Mum! It's important! And I don't want any tea.'

'All right.' Nancy said reassuringly. 'Leave it with me.'

******

Later that evening Nancy was sitting at the piano. She had been playing a piece of music by Chopin but had now stopped and began to turn over some music. She wondered what to say, how to broach the subject. Once or twice she glanced at Fred, who was sitting in his armchair, staring into the fire.

'Fred...' she began at last.

'I know what you're going to say, Nance, and the lad's wrong.' Fred said firmly.

Nancy was silent.

'It was a bit of dust in my eye... could have happened to anyone.'

'Tom was worried...'

'There's nothing wrong I tell you, nothing!' Fred spoke a shade too loudly. 'Sorry, Nance,' he said in a quieter voice. 'I'm a bit tired.'

He looked across at her, almost pleading. 'There's nothing wrong... you've got to believe me...'

'If you say so,' Nancy said, after a moment's silence.

Fred picked up the newspaper. 'Lad's got a bee in his bonnet for some reason,' he said in his usual voice. 'He'll soon get over it.'

He opened the paper and appeared to bury himself in it. Nancy watched him for a moment or two then turned back to the piano and began to play once more. Fred put down the paper and stared into the fire.

******

Along with the Regal Cinema, the Alhambra Dance Hall was the most popular place for entertainment in Acton Chalcote, and the resident band, Sid Waller's Rhythm Orchestra, was kept busy from 6.00 pm to 11.00 pm six nights of the week, with tea dances at 4.00 pm on Wednesdays and Saturdays.

That evening the hall was, as usual, packed, the glitter balls hanging from the ceiling reflecting light down on the heads of the dancers through a haze of cigarette smoke. After having tango'd, swung and jitterbugged for the last couple of hours, Dai and Sylvia were recovering, drinks in hand, at one of the many tables ringing the dance floor.

'Aren't you on early shift tomorrow?' Sylvia asked.

'My last as a fireman.'

'Shouldn't you have an early night?'

'You sound like my mam,' Dai smiled. 'I'll be fine.'

'And then you're off to Bristol,' she said sadly.

'Will you come and see me go?'

Sylvia nodded.

On the other side of the hall, Ginger and Les were also sitting over drinks, enjoying themselves by eyeing up and commenting on the unattached girls while secretly wondering whether they would be able to pluck up enough courage to ask them to dance. Tom was sitting with them, but he was watching Maggie, who was dancing with Jim. The music came to an end.

'Ladies and gentlemen, there will now be a short interlude,' called the conductor and the band thankfully put down their instruments and took up their pint glasses. Tom stood up and walked purposefully across the floor.

'Maggie. I want to talk to you.'

Jim thrust Maggie to one side.

'Wherever did they teach you manners Watkins? In the farmyard?' he said contemptuously. 'The lady's with me.'

Tom ignored him. 'Maggie... please... just for a minute...'

Surprised and a bit flattered, Maggie touched Jim's arm. 'Will you get me a drink, please?'

'All right...' Jim said reluctantly. 'But I won't be long.'

'Why on earth are you going out with him?' Tom asked, watching Jim cross the dance floor.

'What's it to do with you?'

'You ought to be more careful. He's no good.'

'I'll thank you to let me make up my own mind about that,' Maggie said coldly. 'As I said, it's none of your business. What did you want to talk about?'

'Let's sit down. Away from this crowd.'

He led the way to a vacant table by the door. Maggie followed.

'Well?'

'Maggie… it's about dad… there's something wrong…'

'And you drag me away to tell me that?' Maggie said furiously.

'But I've got to talk to someone and I've…'

'Well you can jolly well talk to someone else! Tom Watkins, you're the limit, you really are!'

'But Maggie…!'

'I don't care about your dad and I don't care about you and if you ever thought any different, you're wrong, see! Quite, quite wrong! And as from now on you can stop using me as someone you can pour out your troubles to because I'm fed up with it, see, I'm fed up with it!'

She was shouting now, and people seated at the tables around them were staring, some curious, some amused. Maggie took a deep breath, jumped to her feet and rushed across the dance floor.

'Maggie!' Tom called after her.

The band picked up their instruments and the dancers returned to the floor.

'I think my little brother has just created a scene,' Sylvia remarked, looking across to them.

'Little brother can fight his own battles.' Dai pulled her to her feet. 'Ah, that's more in my line,' he said as the band began to play a slow waltz. 'Something slow and easy. Your dancing puts me to shame.'

'Nothing puts you to shame, Dai Davies,' she retorted, as she rested her head on his shoulder. He held her close.

******

Two days later Dai and Sylvia were on a bench on Platform One. A suitcase was at Dai's feet and he was looking unusually smart. Meanwhile Sylvia was staring into space, and sighing

240

every now and then, which tickled Dai's ready sense of humour.

'Don't look so tragic, sweetheart. It's only Bristol I'm going to, not Timbuctoo.'

'I know.'

'I'll write as soon as I've fixed myself up some digs and be back to see you on my first day off.'

'Yes.'

'Well then...'

'It's all right for you, you're the one who's going. I wish I was.'

'And present yourself to the shed foreman as the new driver? I'd love to see his face.'

'It's not a joke.'

'Oh you know me, Dai the Comic...' Dai said easily.

Sylvia turned away.

'Sylvia...' he said coaxingly.

'You haven't got to live with dad. He's become impossible. I wish I could come with you.'

'And have Fred tearing down to Bristol out for my blood?'

'Coward!'

Dai nodded. 'Dai the Coward, that's me.'

Sylvia began to giggle and they smiled at each other.

'Dad would go after you, you know.'

'I'm certain he would.'

'You like him, don't you?'

'No need to sound so accusing!' Dai thought for a moment. 'Let's say I can understand how he feels. I think I'd feel the same if I thought my daughter had fallen for some worthless sort of chap.'

'You are funny.'

'Am I?'

'I don't see how you can take his side.'

'It's not a question of "taking sides". I can just see his point of view, that's all.' He laughed. 'That's my trouble. I can always see the other fellow's point of view.'

He fumbled in his pocket.

'Before the train comes.' He took out a small box. 'This is for you. Just so you won't forget me and get tied up with some other worthless fireman.'

Sylvia looked at him then took the present and opened it. Inside was a thin gold chain with a deep blue stone pendant hanging from it.

'Oh Dai... It's... it's lovely...'

'It's nothing much, nothing to cry over,' he said gently, brushing away a tear. 'I wanted to get you a ring, an engagement ring, but thought you wouldn't want to wear it without me to protect you when your father saw it. Anyway, I don't know your size, and it's something we should get together and...' he stopped suddenly, as if embarrassed, then laughed. 'Never known a Welshman lost for words before.'

They moved closer...

'Hey Dai!'

'Thought we'd missed you!'

Jerry Marshall and Joe Stratton came racing up the platform. At the same moment the train came in and stopped, the driver acknowledging Dai with a wave of his hand.

Dai gave Sylvia a rueful glance. 'First Goodrington, now here!'

Sylvia laughed. 'At least there's no Carol.'

He turned to the firemen. 'Well lads, this is nice.'

'We just wanted to make sure you were really going,' Jerry panted.

'As you can see.' Dai raised his voice. 'But I don't know how far we'll get with old Eric driving. The way he bangs them...'

A lump of dirty cotton waste was thrown at him from the engine's footplate.

'Hey, mind my smart clothes!'

'Perhaps we'll get some peace at the shed now.' Jerry grinned.

'With no more flaming poetry!' Eric called from the cab.

Dai laughed and called out,

"Parting is such sweet sorrow
That I shall say goodbye 'til…"'

He got no further for another lump of waste was thrown in his direction and the fireman blew the whistle.

'Philistines! Let's hope the lads at Bristol are more civilised!'

'Better send a wire down to tell them what they've got coming,' Joe advised.

'Done it already,' said Jerry.

The guard began moving down the train, closing the compartment doors.

Dai turned to Sylvia.

'Take care of yourself my precious.'

'And you.'

'Oh I will. We Welshmen excel in taking care of ourselves.'

He gave her a hurried kiss as the engine whistled once more. The guard held the door open for him with mock ceremony. Amid raucous comments from his mates Dai picked up his suitcase and jumped on to the train. The guard blew the whistle, waved his flag and the train departed.

******

George Southcombe eased his bulky figure to a more comfortable position as he lent against engine 2784 and continued.

'…So there I was, down in the pit, wedged tight under that fifty-six, not able to move an inch. Well I was just wondering what to do, Tom, when along comes old Tic-Toc – we called him that on account of how he was always looking at his watch, you won't remember him, he's at Laira now – he comes along and I shouts to him to give me a hand. Well, old Tic-Toc was a big man and has me out in no time, but that's why you won't get me oiling up under a fifty-six or anything else again, not if I can help it.'

Tom laughed as he climbed out of the pit, oil can in hand.

'Finished have you? Good lad,' George said approvingly. He climbed up into the cab and Tom followed. George took off the brake, eased open the regulator and the engine began to move slowly away from the shed. Tom was leaning out of the cab, watching the road ahead. Suddenly he stiffened.

'Dad! Dad get out of the way!' he yelled.

Fred, having just climbed down from his engine was taking his usual care in crossing the tracks, but he hadn't seen George's engine on the converging line. He glanced round and jumped out of the way. George put in the brake.

'Dad, are you all right?'

'"Course I'm all right!'

'Sorry about that Fred,' George said, leaning out of the cab.

'Wasn't your fault mate,' Fred replied shortly.

'Didn't you see us, dad?' Tom asked anxiously.

Fred stared at him for a moment before turning and walking off.

******

Once his shift had ended, Tom caught up with his father in Station Road.

'Dad!' Dad!'

Fred pretended not to hear and Tom ran to catch up.

'Dad, you've got to do something about your eyes!'

'Nothing wrong with my eyes.'

'There is! What happened back there...'

'What happened could have happened to anyone.'

'What about the other night then, on the Post Office...'

'What happened then was nothing more than a bit of dust in my eye because you didn't water the coal.'

'It wasn't. You know it wasn't!'

Fred turned to face him. 'So you'd argue with me would you? If you weren't my son I'd have reported you that night for disobedience of orders!'

'Well, why didn't you?' Tom shot back at him.

Fred didn't answer.

'You didn't report me because you knew I'd tell them you would have run by the home because you didn't see it!'

'And you think they'd believe you?' Fred asked scornfully.

'They'd believe me when Harry tells them that he had to put the brake in, not you, otherwise we'd have run by!'

'It was the dust...!' Fred insisted.

'It wasn't! You know as well as I do that I'd just watered the coal. There was no dust!'

Fred was silent.

'Dad... it's for your own good...'

'My good! Listen lad, when I want your advice, I'll come and ask for it, but it'll be some time before I ask advice off a jumped-up bloody cleaner who's not been doing the job more than two minutes and thinks he knows it all! You make me laugh!'

'All right! If you won't tell them, I will!'

Fred stared at him.

'I never thought my own son would be so disloyal,' he said bitterly.

'Disloyal! You're a fine one to talk of being disloyal! How loyal to the Company are you being, now your own job's at stake?'

'My job's not at stake! There's nothing wrong with my bloody eyesight!' Fred spat at him.

'Prove it then! Go on, prove it! But you won't, will you?' Fred was silent.

'All my life I've been scared of you. I wanted to be like you so much but I always failed.' Years of pent-up feelings poured out of Tom. 'But you never failed, did you? Not at anything. Always right, always certain that what you said was for the best. And I believed you. I could never come within a mile of you. You've always made me feel so... so... inadequate. But not any more... oh no! You, who've always been so loyal to the Company, such an upholder of the rules, where's your loyalty now? What about upholding the rules of safety then – what about it? How safe are your passengers now, being driven by someone whose eyesight might be failing but who won't do anything about it?'

Fred stood in the street, as if turned to stone.

'If you're so sure you're in the right you'll go and have an eye test just to prove me wrong. But you won't, will you?' Having worked himself up, Tom was unable to stop. 'You won't because you can't even admit to the possibility of being wrong. What gives you the God-given right to be so sure about everything?'

There was silence. Tom, triumphant, appalled at himself and scared of Fred's reaction, felt his breathing return to normal. Still nothing was said. Fred looked at him, stricken. Then he rallied.

'Look, just what is this, eh? Just what do you think you're playing at? Eh? What are you trying to do? Get me taken off the footplate is that it? Want your old man off to make more room for you? You want me to end up like Ernie Patch, stoking the stationary boiler? Is that what you want? Is it?'

'You're always bloody twisting things!,' Tom shouted, touched on a raw spot. 'You... you stubborn old fool!''

Fred hit him, hard, across the mouth.

'Don't you ever speak to me like that again! Ever!'

He turned and walked off up the road. Tom stared after him.

******

'He's got to see someone, mum. He's got to be made to!'

Tom was pacing up and down the kitchen. Nancy put down her mending and looked at him in silence for a moment.

'Tom, your father is the most conscientious man in the world when it comes to his job,' she said at last. 'He would never do anything to endanger his passengers. Never. So if he says there's nothing wrong I believe him.'

Tom came to the table. 'He's hoodwinked you like he has everyone else.'

'Hoodwinked?'

'To believe everything he says.'

Nancy smiled. 'You think that?'

'What about Sylvia and Dai then? He's wrong there, isn't he?'

Nancy sighed. 'Fred says a lot of things in the heat of the moment which he doesn't always mean,' she said slowly. 'Surely, you must know that...' She looked at him, puzzled. 'But what I don't understand is, what business it is of yours?'

'He could be a danger, mum – to himself and his passengers,' Tom replied earnestly.

Nancy thought for a moment. 'Have you thought what would happen if he had to come off the footplate?' she asked. 'Have you thought what it would mean for him? It's his life,

Tom. Take that away and you take away all his pride, all his respect in himself.'

'I'm concerned about dad too!' Tom fired back, defensively.

'Are you?'

Tom opened his mouth to speak, then closed it. Without another word he turned and walked out. Nancy watched him go.

******

After a sleepless night Tom had come to a decision. The following day he crossed the yard, entered the shed and walked up to the foreman's office. For a long moment he paused outside before knocking on the door.

When he was called in Ben Goodey was standing by the window, looking out. He turned as Tom entered. For a moment neither of them spoke.

'Well?' Ben asked at last.

'I think I should tell you, sir, that... that...' he faltered and stopped. There was a long pause. Tom took a deep breath. 'I'm sorry, sir. It's nothing. I shouldn't have troubled you.'

He turned to go.

'Wait a minute.'

Tom turned back.

'Sit down.'

If it's about your dad, Tom, you don't have to tell me. I know.'

'How?'

Ben sat down behind his desk. 'He came to see me. But I knew something was wrong. Word gets round. Sooner or later I get to hear most things.'

'What'll happen?' Tom asked, after a pause.

'I've sent him to Swindon for an eye test and medical.' Ben looked at him with sympathy. 'It might not be as bad as you think.'

But if it is...?'

'Well, we'll just have to see, won't we. We'll find a job for him.'

Tom swallowed and looked away. Ben watched him in silence.

'I've known Fred a long time, you know. Long before you were born. He wouldn't want to be anything less than first rate at the job. He's not like that.' He stopped for a moment. 'You know, and he knows, that you have to have A1 eyesight for this job, Tom.'

'But...'

Don't go crossing bridges 'til you come to them.'

Tom said nothing. He stared, unseeing, round the room.

'Fond of him aren't you?' Ben asked quietly.

'I, I don't know... I've never thought...' Tom swallowed and fell silent. The feeling of self-righteous revenge which had buoyed him up drained away, leaving him desolate and bewildered. He swallowed hard as tears pricked his eyes. 'Yes...' he said at last. 'Yes I am...'

'I wish my son cared as much for me,' Ben said gently.

Tom didn't answer.

'Off you go now.'

******

Tom walked slowly, reluctantly, up Station Road and stopped outside his house. He looked up. The paintwork shone in the sun and the windows gleamed. In the garden the soil was freshly turned in the beds and Fred's tenderly cared-for roses were a riot of gold, white and pink. He opened the gate and closed it carefully behind him. He walked up the path, rounded the corner of the house and stopped again.

Should he go in or should he go off somewhere, a walk along the river, into the woods, anywhere so that he didn't have to see his father... didn't have to speak to him... didn't have to know ...

He took a deep breath and slowly opened the back door. The sun had gone from the back of the house and the kitchen was dim. Fred was standing beside the sink. His eyes were closed. Tentatively, with outstretched arms, he began to grope his way across the room.

Tom watched from the doorway as Fred hesitantly took one pace, then another, then another, touching objects as he passed. He walked into the edge of the table and his eyes flew open.

He and Tom stared at one another for a long moment.

'They're taking me off the footplate,' Fred said at last.

Tom didn't speak.

'I'm going blind, Tom. I'm going blind.'

As Tom stood, rooted to his spot in the doorway, Fred sat down heavily and put his head in his hands.

Chapter Fifteen

A slight, dark-haired girl was half-lying, half-sitting on the station platform at Acton Chalcote. She was cradling her right arm close to her chest. Her coat, which had been slung round her shoulders, had fallen off. She looked pale and was shivering. She had a red mark just below her left knee and on her right shoulder was a lump.

Seventeen-year old Isobel was the centre of a wide circle of intent spectators, most of them railwaymen from both the Great Western and L.N.E.R sheds, but there were others in the crowd, among them Sylvia and Maggie.

Dr Lansdowne, a tall, thin man of minimal words, was judge of this year's St. John Ambulance Inter-Railway Challenge Competition (Acton Chalcote Branch). He was reading aloud from a card.

"'While attempting to alight from a moving train, the patient falls forwards on to the platform. There are no bystanders. First aid equipment is situated in the Stationmaster's Office. There is a doctor at the local hospital, two miles away. First aid to be rendered within fifteen minutes.'"

There was a moment of silence, then a whistle was blown. A team marched purposefully through the crowd. Dai was Superintendent and No. 1, Len Thomas (No. 2), Alfie Jones (No. 3), Tom (No. 4). Jim Salter, who was reserve, stood to one side. The team were all wearing St. John Ambulance badges but were not in uniform. Dai glanced round the scene of the 'accident'.

'I can see no further danger,' he said to Dr. Lansdowne. He looked at his team. 'Number 3, get first aid equipment and blankets. Number 2, comfort the patient.'

Dai knelt beside Isobel and Alfie went off to the booking office. Dr Lansdowne, meanwhile, walked around the scene, marking a test paper on his clipboard.

'Where does it hurt?' Dai asked.

'My shoulder... my leg...'

Dai gently touched her shoulder and she winced convincingly.

'I'm sorry.' Dai looked at her leg. 'Is the bleeding severe, sir?' he asked, looking up at the doctor.

'Yes.'

'And the colour?'

'Scarlet,' the doctor replied, writing furiously.

'Is it spurting?'

'Yes.'

'Number 4, get me that case,' Dai ordered.

Tom picked up Isobel's suitcase which lay near her on the platform and slid it under her leg to raise it while Dai applied pressure to the artery. Dai smiled at Isobel.

'Don't worry. We'll soon have you safely tucked up in bed,' he reassured her. He again looked up at the doctor. 'I am applying digital pressure to the femoral artery after having raised the patient's leg and supported it.' He glanced round at Len and Tom. 'Number 2, will you telephone the doctor. Number 4, will you support the patient's arm.'

Doctor Lansdowne was watching closely.

'Is the bleeding controlled, sir?' Dai asked him.

'Yes.'

Tom knelt beside Isobel and gently lifted her elbow.

Dai gave it a brief look. 'I would suspect a fractured clavicle. Number 4 will you examine the state of the injury...'

Isobel gave a theatrical shudder.

'...and keep the patient warm,' Dai added.

Tom picked up Isobel's coat and placed it carefully around her good shoulder.

'Is that better?' he asked.

'Thank you.'

'Are you in much pain?'

'Yes,' she said composedly, smiling up at him. Tom noticed that her eyes were a deep dark blue. Thrown off balance he began to smile back at her, then looked away.

Alfie returned with the first aid equipment. He took out a tourniquet and handed it to Dai who applied it to Isobel's leg.

'I am applying the tourniquet to the femoral artery to stop the bleeding,' he reported.

'Can you show me exactly where it hurts?' Tom asked solicitously.

She pointed to her shoulder.

'Does your arm feel helpless?'

Isobel sighed. 'Oh yes.'

She leant back against Tom, who suddenly became conscious of her slim body.

'Is the bleeding controlled, sir?' Dai asked, still ostensibly applying the tourniquet to Isobel's leg.

'Yes.'

Dai glanced round. 'Number 3, will you keep a check on the tourniquet while I pad and dress the wound.'

Tom gently felt Isobel's shoulder under her thin summer dress.

'Is there any irregularity, sir?' he asked the doctor.

'Yes.'

'Does the bone overlap?'

Dr Lansdowne, who was now watching Tom closely, nodded.

'Is there swelling?'

'Yes.' He beckoned to Len. 'The doctor has been called to an urgent case, therefore directs that the patient be taken to hospital in a motor ambulance.'

Dai, who was dressing the wound, spoke to Len. 'Number 2, will you test the stretcher and prepare it. Number 4, will you take the patient's pulse while I am applying this dressing to the wound and bandaging it tightly over a pad of cotton wool to prevent further loss of blood.'

Dai's team, well- practised for the competition, worked smoothly and efficiently.

'I'll have to take your pulse,' Tom told Isobel.

'Of course.' She held out her wrist and Tom took it carefully. He was very aware of her closeness to him, of the paleness of her face - make-up surely - of the faint perfume surrounding her. He sniffed. Lily of the Valley, he thought. Sylvia used something like that. Her pulse beat warmly under his fingers and Tom was finding it hard to remember what he was supposed to be doing. He made himself concentrate.

'What is the nature of the pulse, sir?' he asked Dr Lansdowne.

'Feeble,' said the doctor.

'And the colour of her face?'

'Pale.'

Tom rummaged in the first aid bag, took out some smelling salts and tested them before wafting them under Isobel's nose. She sneezed.

Dai glanced up.

'Number 4 is giving the patient smelling salts before securing the injured limb.'

He finished bandaging. 'Release the tourniquet,' he said to Alfie.

'Is the bleeding still controlled?' Dai asked Dr Lansdowne.

The doctor bent down and checked the tightness of the bandage.

'Yes.'

Tom was lifting Isobel's arm in order to place a pad underneath. Isobel drew in her breath sharply.

'Did I hurt you?' Tom asked anxiously.

'No,' she said, smiling at him. 'You're very gentle.'

Tom swallowed hard and turned away to find Dai behind him, ready with the bandage. Dai gave Tom the merest ghost of a wink.

*****

The meeting room in the Great Western Hotel, a more modest, privately-owned establishment than the imposing railway hotels which had been built by the Company at principal railways stations such as Paddington, Exeter, and Bristol, was crowded with people, but the conversation was desultory as everyone waited for the results. The two teams stood a little apart and there was a tangible tension in the air.

Dai caught sight of Sylvia in the crowd. She was waving and mouthing 'Good luck!' He smiled back at her. Tom glanced round the room. Maggie was standing in the front, but Tom's glance swept past her. Maggie sighed and turned away.

There was a sudden stir as the official party entered the room and made their way to the platform. The Chancellor of the Order of St. John led the way, together with Lady Mansell who was to present the prize. Behind them walked the Secretary General and other dignitaries, both from St. John Ambulance and from the two competing railways. Doctor Lansdowne was among the party, with his daughter, Isobel beside him. She had changed out of the summer frock which she had worn on the platform and was now dressed in a matching dark-blue linen skirt and jacket. With dark curls peeping out from under her pale blue cloche hat, framing an elfin-like face, she looked like a child, small and fragile beside her tall father. Tom saw her come in and watched her avidly.

There was a moment's hush, then the Secretary General, a big man who seemed on the verge of bursting out of his suit, stepped forwards. He fingered his small moustache nervously and cleared his throat.

'Ladies and gentlemen. It is very good to see so many of you here today, giving your support and encouragement to the competing teams. We are fortunate in having Lady Mansell here with us to present the trophy.' He half bowed in her direction and she graciously inclined her head.

'Before reading out the results, however, I would just like to pay tribute to the 'patients' – members of the Girl Guides and Boy Scouts, as well as Dr Lansdowne's charming daughter - who all played their parts so ably. I would also like to thank Dr. Lansdowne, well-known to all of us for his work in the Ambulance movement, and to the Great Western Railway for allowing us to stage this event on their premises.'

He stopped, to allow for the applause.

'Railwaymen attach great importance to first aid and rightly so as accidents do happen. The standards set by the two companies has been, as ever, of the highest, and the competition has been fierce. Copies of the reports, citing both the good points and the areas where there could be some improvement, will be given to the superintendents of each team.'

He paused again before picking up a sheet of paper and clearing his throat.

'The results are as follows: out of a maximum possible score of one hundred and eighty points in the team test, the London and North Eastern 'A' team have gained one hundred and fifty-five points...' There was a smattering of applause, quickly smothered. '...and the Great Western Railway have gained one hundred and sixty-two points.'

This time the applause was much louder.

'Therefore the winners of this years' Inter-Railway Ambulance Challenge Competition are the Great Western 'A' team, and it is my pleasure to ask Lady Mansell if she will present the trophy to the winners.'

He sat down to more applause and mopped his brow.

'Great Western 'A' team, attention!' Dai called.

The team, including Jim, stood to attention.

'Forward...march!'

With Dai leading them, they marched up to the platform where Lady Mansell presented Dai with the trophy and shook hands with all the team in turn. Tom glanced at Isobel, but she was chatting to her father and wasn't looking.

After the prize-giving came tea and buns. The small room off the main hall was crowded and buzzed with talk and laughter and Dai and his team were surrounded by well-wishers offering congratulations. Jerry Marshall pushed through the crowd and laid a hand on Dai's shoulder.

'Dai, you old fraud! Shall I tell the judge that you're a Bristol man now and shouldn't have been competing?'

'Special dispensation – my team couldn't manage without me.'

'Still the same old Dai – big-headed as ever. How's the job?'

Maggie came past, a cup of tea in each hand.

'Congratulations, dad.' She gave Len a kiss and handed him one of the cups.

'What about me?' Jim asked, coming up behind her. 'Don't I get a kiss too? I was part of the team too, even if I was only reserve.'

Maggie turned, slightly flustered. 'Oh... Jim...'

Tom caught sight of Nancy wielding a tray with plates piled high with buns.

'I'll do that mum,' he offered, trying to take it from her.

'You will not! You'll stay where you are and be congratulated!' She smiled proudly at him.

The noise level in the room went up. Snatches of conversation could be heard above the general hubbub.

'... a fractured tibia was it, or a fibula... I forget...' an earnest lady was saying to a flummoxed member of the L.N.E.R team who was trying to look interested while gazing, with a hunted expression, round the room for a way of escape.

Nearby, Dr Lansdowne was deep in conversation with another medical man. '...well of course, my dear fellow, it is generally recognised that morphine is the gold standard for post-operative pain relief but the incidence of addiction and abuse is shocking, quite shocking...' Both men solemnly nodded their heads in agreement while Isobel, who was standing beside her father, looked faintly bored.

More tea was drunk, more buns eaten and the air grew thick and stale with cigarette smoke.

Jim was trying to talk to Maggie, but she wasn't paying him much attention.

Dai, meanwhile, had been taken over by the Secretary General, who, red-faced and beaming, was coming to the end of a long monologue about past competitions. He finished in a very complementary manner.

'... and you held it together nicely... very nicely indeed...'

'Thank you, sir,' Dai replied politely.

The Secretary General paused to light a cigar then began again. 'I remember once in a similar situation...'

Sylvia rushed up to Dai and flung her arms impulsively round him.

'Dai... oh Dai well done!'

The Secretary General choked on his cigar, looked startled, then indulgent.

'Young people today,' he murmured as he moved discreetly away.

'You interrupted the Secretary General in full flow,' Dai said reprovingly.

'I'm so proud of you!'

As Nancy passed with yet another laden tray, Sylvia grabbed her arm.

'Sylvie! Mind out!'

'Mum... mum this is Dai.'

'Let me relieve you of that tray, Mrs Watkins.' Dai took it from her and placed it on a nearby table.

'Have we met...?' Nancy asked vaguely.

'Once. Briefly,' Dai replied, thinking back to the discomfort of that situation.

'It's hard to hear yourself think in here,' Nancy frowned, brushing a stray lock of hair off her forehead. 'Yes, of course. Congratulations.'

'Thank you.' There was a slightly awkward pause. 'How is... Mr Watkins?' Dai asked quietly.

Nancy did not reply. She looked from Dai to Sylvia.

'Sylvia... you must bring Mr Davies round to tea...' she said on a sudden impulse. 'Yes. Bring him to tea.'

Sylvia looked at him.

'Are you sure?' Dai asked gently.

'Oh yes...' Nancy said hesitantly. Then, more firmly, 'Yes. When you're next up this way... Sylvia, you'll arrange it, won't you?'

She gave them both a brief, distracted smile, picked up the tray and disappeared into the crowd.

Isobel tugged at her father's sleeve.

'Daddy...'

He turned from the two St. John Ambulance ladies he had been talking to and frowned.

'You mustn't be so rude Isobel...'

The two ladies moved away.

'Daddy...please...!'

She dragged him off to where she had spotted Tom, who was standing on the far side of the room, surrounded by his mates. As the doctor followed his daughter, he passed Dai and stopped to shake his hand.

'Congratulations my dear chap. Very good effort.'

Isobel, meanwhile, had reached Tom.

'Congratulations,' she said, smiling in a friendly way.

'Thanks,' Tom said gruffly, feeling suddenly conscious of his scuffed shoes and dirty trousers, the result of kneeling on the platform.

Isobel put out her hand. 'My name's Isobel. Isobel Lansdowne.'

Tom swallowed hard and shook her hand.

'Tom Watkins.'

'My father was the judge. He's a doctor.'

'Oh.' Tom, nonplussed at her self-confident air and dazzled by her vivid, pretty face, hunted for something to say. 'I hope I didn't hurt you.'

She shook her head violently. 'Not at all.'

'So this is who you wanted me to meet, is it puss? Did you want to make your apologies to him?'

Isobel looked up at her father, puzzled. 'Whatever for?'

Dr Lansdowne winked at Tom. 'For trying to take his mind off his job.'

'Daddy! I didn't!' she protested.

'Don't forget, I was judging.' He laughed and shook Tom's hand. 'Good show,' he said and moved away.

Tom took a deep breath.

'Can I get you some tea?' he asked Isobel.

*****

The following day Tom was firing 2379 as the goods train made its slow journey to Beesham. George, who was driving, was watching him, first critically, then with growing approval.

'Did all right in the competition from what I hear,' he said. 'In more ways than one.'

Tom grinned and shrugged it off. George watched him a little more then came to a decision. He moved over to Tom's side of the cab.

'Here… give us that… ' he took the shovel and nodded his head towards the driver's side.

'You have a go.'

Tom stared at him, open-mouthed, for a moment, then crossed the cab. George examined the fire and plunged the shovel into the pile of coal.

'Elsie says I'm getting too fat,' he panted.

Tom, nervous at first, then with growing confidence, looked out of the front window and pulled the whistle.

He was only permitted to drive a short distance, with George watching over his shoulder. On their return to the yard they found a busy scene. 5935 'Norton Hall' was being coaled up, 4962 'Ragley Hall' was taking on water and a gang of cleaners were hard at work on 3376. 2843 was being driven towards the sidings, ready to pick up a line of heavily laden wagons.

Fred had stopped at the barrow crossing to let it pass. After it had gone he made his way across the yard towards the shed. He was wearing a suit, not his usual railwayman's uniform and that, as much as his slow, purposeless walk marked him as being out of place amid the noise and bustle around him. He seemed to be smaller, shrunk into himself. He attracted a number of glances but avoided looking at anyone and didn't respond to any waves or greetings. Slowly he went into the shed and made his way to the foreman's office. He knocked on the door.

'Come in!'

As Fred entered, Ben stood up.

'Fred...'

There was a pause.

'How are things?'

Fred shrugged. 'Well as can be expected under the circumstances,' he said dryly.

'Do sit down.'

Both men sat, Fred sitting upright, his face expressionless, while Ben fiddled uncomfortably with some paper on his desk.

'Yes... well... I'm sure you can do without my sympathy, Fred, not a lot of good to you... but if there's anything Vera and I can do...' he glanced up for a moment, '... she sent you her best wishes by the way.'

'That was kind of her,' Fred said after a pause.

Ben hesitated and coughed before picking up a folder. 'I've got your medical reports here...' he spoke more formally, '..and it occurred to me... you know Johnny Prior's retiring?'

Fred nodded.

'Well the doctors' agree that your eyesight is fine for close work at the moment, and I wondered... it seemed to me that you might like to take over from Johnny as time clerk. Keep everyone in order...'

There was a moment's silence.

'Thank you,' Fred said at last.

He stood up, fumbling for the edge of the chair, and left the room. Ben watched him go. Poor old Fred, he thought sadly. It's hit him hard.

When Fred left the office he stood for a moment, staring round the shed. After the earlier bustle and activity, it was experiencing a moment of quiet.

He walked down a row of engines, looking up at each one. On a sudden whim he climbed nimbly up on to the footplate of 3283, the Duke of Cornwall. It was not in steam. He picked up a bit of waste and absentmindedly wiped his hands, staring round the cab as if he would drink in the sight and the smell. He put his hand on the regulator and stood, immobile, lost in a thousand memories.

******

'Mum, mum, where's my best shirt?' Tom yelled as he came hurtling in through the door. He was wearing shoes, socks and trousers, but no shirt.

Nancy was at the stove, her face flushed with heat after lifting the lid of the saucepan to prod the boiling potatoes.

'Did you give it to me to be washed?'

'You know I did!'

'Don't shout. Then I expect it's in your room, or it might be in the basket waiting to be ironed...'

'But I need it mum,' Tom shouted in an agonised voice. 'Now. I'm picking her up at 7.0!'

He went over to the clothes basket and rummaged through it, throwing the contents wildly over the floor.

'Tom! They're clean!' Nancy protested.

'Who's the lucky girl then?' Sylvia asked, pausing in the delicate task of painting her fingernails deep red. She was dressed in her usherette's uniform, ready to go to work.

'No-one you know.'

'I bet it was that girl in the competition. Dai said she was making eyes at you.'

Tom threw a damp towel at her.

'Here, watch what you're doing, You'll mess up my nails!'

He rummaged some more and emerged, triumphant.

'Here it is!'

'My baby brother's first date,' Sylvia remarked. She put the brush back in the bottle, breathed on her fingernails, tested them gingerly then held out her hand.

'Give it to me. I'll iron it, mum.'

'Would you, dear?'

Sylvia plugged in the iron. 'Where are you taking her?'

'I don't really know. Pictures maybe.'

Sylvia pulled a face. 'I wouldn't, not unless she likes horror. It's 'Mark of the Vampire' all this week. She can always hide her head on your shoulder of course,' she added, teasing. 'Why not take her to The Alhambra?'

'I'm not very good at dancing,' Tom confessed.

'Nothing to it.' She took his shirt, held it as if it was a partner, began to dance and started singing the words to the tune of *"Who's been polishing the sun."* Oh Tom, you dance divinely...!

Nancy, holding the colander full of steaming potatoes began to laugh and joined in.

The back door opened and Fred entered. Sylvia and Nancy stopped abruptly. Sylvia returned to the ironing and Nancy to the stove.

'Do you want some tea, Fred?' Nancy asked.

Fred took off his jacket and sat down while Sylvia put the finishing touches to the ironing.

'There.'

'Thanks, Sylv,' Tom took the shirt and escaped.

'What happened?' Nancy asked.

Fred didn't answer for a moment.

'Fred? What happened?'

'I'll be taking over from Johnny Prior,' he said at last. 'Time clerk.'

Nancy and Sylvia glanced at each other.

'Must go, mum or I'll have Mr Pilger on the rampage.' Sylvia picked up her bag, slung it over her shoulder and went out.

******

The band was playing '*Are you having any fun?*' at The Alhambra Dance Hall. The place was full and Tom was painstakingly leading Isobel round the floor, trying to concentrate on what he was doing and avoid the other dancers. Talking was an impossibility. Miserably aware of his failings as a dancer he wondered, ruefully, whether they should have gone to the pictures after all. He misjudged a step and trod on her foot.

'Sorry.'

Isobel smiled and said nothing.

On the other side of the floor Maggie was dancing with Jim. She didn't look as if she was having much fun either.

When the dance came to an end, Tom and Isobel went towards a free table.

'I'm sorry. I'm not much good at dancing.'

'You're all right.' Isobel sat down, composed and divinely pretty, Tom thought. She was wearing a delicate lavender-coloured dress that ended in two flounces just on the knee. When he had arrived at her home at one minute to seven he had caught his breath when she opened the door as she looked so perfect. Small and perfect.

'Now don't be too late home pet,' her mother had fussed, straightening Isobel's hat.

'I'll look after her Mrs Lansdowne,' Tom had said.

Mrs Lansdowne had looked at him and Tom had felt clumsy and ungainly, totally unworthy of being entrusted with her precious daughter.

He came out of his reverie to find her looking at him, an enquiring look on her face.

'Would you like a drink?' he asked.

'Mmm.' She smiled. 'I'd love one.'

Tom stood up and went over to the drinks bar, passing the table where Maggie and Jim were sitting. Maggie looked up, breaking into a smile.

'Tom!'

'Hello Maggie. Jim.'

He brushed past them.

'You'll enjoy the evening now, will you?' Jim asked sardonically.

Maggie looked down and fingered her drink.

'Even if he doesn't speak to you.'

Maggie didn't answer.

'I expect he's other fish to fry...' he glanced over at Isobel. '...very tasty fish I must say.'

Maggie turned away.

'Maggie – he doesn't want to know,' Jim pleaded. 'He never has... why don't you face it?'

Tom returned to Isobel, drinks in hand. 'I never asked what you wanted. I hope this is all right.'

Anxiously he handed over a glass of lemonade.

'Thank you. It's fine.'

She looked up at him and burst out laughing. 'You look like a dog that's expecting a beating.'

'Do I?' Tom subsided into his seat. 'I'm sorry.'

Isobel looked at him over the rim of her glass. 'You've a very low opinion of yourself, haven't you,' she stated.

'Have I?' Tom was embarrassed.

'Yes. You keep apologising.'

'I'm sorry.'

She laughed again and, after a second, he grinned.

'You're not like other chaps I know,' she said, reaching for his hand.

'I suppose you know lots,' Tom said humbly.

Isobel shrugged. 'I have a number of friends,' she said coolly, taking her hand away.

'I didn't mean...'

'There you are, you see. Doing it again. Apologising!'

Tom couldn't think of anything to say that wasn't another apology. He felt he had fallen short – first the dancing and now this - and he couldn't think of a way to redeem himself.

'Most of the chaps I know are studying to be doctors and things,' she went on. 'They're all frightfully arrogant and think they know everything. They either lecture me or try to have an affair with me.'

She aimed to shock and succeeded, although Tom tried not to show it.

I don't go along with that of course, although Susan, she's my eldest sister – there's four of us – she says one should experience as much as possible in life.' She stopped to think about it. 'I'm not sure she meant having affairs though. Lucy might have meant that but not Susan.'

She looked at Tom.

'Do you think she's right?'

'Who?' Tom asked, confused by the plethora of sisters.

'Susan!' she replied impatiently.

'I – I don't really know.' Tom said humbly. 'I've never thought about it.'

'There you see?' Isobel said triumphantly. 'You're not at all like my other friends. You don't think you know everything.'

'No. I'm sure I don't.'

'Do all your sisters live at home with you?' he asked, as the pause stretched out.

'Susan's married,' she said, ticking it off on her fingers. 'She got married last year to a junior doctor. Daddy was awfully pleased. I think he'd like us all to marry doctors – to keep it in the family. Then there's Lucy. She's a bit of a disappointment to daddy I think as she's a bit wild. She wants to go to university but daddy said she's not brainy enough. And then there's Betty.' Isobel pulled a face. 'She's all right I suppose, but always wants to get everyone's attention. And then there's me. I'm the baby and daddy's favourite although he wouldn't admit it. He says he loves all of us equally but I know he loves me best.'

They sat silently then, sipping their drinks as the band resumed playing. Isobel was calm and collected, Tom confused and anxious. Isobel suddenly stood up.

'Let's dance,' she said imperiously, holding out her hand.

Tom got up reluctantly. The evening seemed to be slipping away from him. He wasn't sure exactly what he had expected but it wasn't this sophisticated, modern girl, who, he felt, treated him as if he were a child. He looked at her as she led the way on to the dance floor and caught his breath. She looked enchanting. He hardly dared breathe as he tried to concentrate on what his feet were doing while holding Isobel as if she were a piece of precious porcelain.

A little way away from them, Maggie, to Jim's annoyance, was straining over his shoulder to see who Tom was dancing with.

At 11.00 p.m the band played its final number and, to the strains of *'Goodnight Sweetheart'*, the dancers began to leave. Jim collected Maggie's coat, put it round her shoulders and they left the hall.

'He went five minutes ago. Didn't you notice?' he said sarcastically, as they entered the foyer.

'I wasn't looking for him.'

'Weren't you?'

They went out of the building and began walking up the street.

'You are horrid,' Maggie said, walking quickly.

'What do you expect me to be? You're supposed to be on a date with me, remember?' Jim's anger suddenly boiled over.

'And I don't like playing second fiddle to an under-sized little runt with an over-sized opinion of himself!'

Maggie stood stock-still then turned and slapped his face.

'Such devotion!' Jim mocked, recovering himself.

Maggie hurried ahead and Jim, taking a deep breath, followed.

'Maggie... Maggie... all right, I'm sorry...'

She didn't slacken her pace and he had to walk faster to keep up with her.

'Look Maggs, I don't like the bloke and never have. He doesn't like me either. But it's pretty tough when the girl I love is infatuated by him.'

She didn't reply and Jim grabbed her arm, forcing her to stop.

'Maggie... I said I love you.'

She stood still, silent.

'I think you're brave... and wonderful... the way you've coped... you shouldn't have to... some people are bloody selfish!'

'Meaning my mother, I suppose?' Maggie said coolly. 'Or did you mean dad?'

'I shouldn't have said that,' Jim mumbled.

'No. You shouldn't.'

He dropped his hand and they began to walk on, not speaking.

'You've been very kind to me Jim... don't think I'm not grateful...' she said at last.

Jim stopped. 'Maggie... will you marry me?'

She bit her lip and looked away.

'Maggie...?'

*****

Tom and Isobel, meanwhile, had walked in silence to her house.

'Thank you for a lovely evening,' Isobel said formally when they arrived.

'Can I see you again?'

Isobel shrugged. 'If you like.'

'Friday?'

'All right. Seven o'clock.'

They stared at each other.

'Shall we go and see a film?' Tom suggested.

She smiled. 'Depends what's on.'

'I'll find out,' Tom said eagerly. 'Sylvia, she's my sister, she works there.'

They stood for a moment in silence.

'Well... goodnight then.'

'Goodnight.'

They stayed still for another moment, then Isobel suddenly leant forwards and kissed Tom lightly on the lips. Then she was gone. Tom stayed where he was, dazed, before walking off down the road. Once he turned the corner he gave a great leap in the air. The evening hadn't been a failure. It had been a huge success. And on Friday, on Friday, he would kiss her back!

Chapter Sixteen

Tom rapped on the counter of stores. He grinned as he heard Billy Hughes' monotonous voice from inside, getting progressively louder as he approached.

'...now make sure you weigh it out properly, Sam. Half pounds and quarter pounds, because I've got to account for it and there's no telling...'

He arrived and peered over the counter.

'Hello Tom, what can I do for you?'

'The keys to 5774 and a pair of lamps please Billy.'

'Another firing turn, eh?' He disappeared out of sight but didn't stop talking. 'They'll have to give you firing rates if you carry on like this... how's your dad keeping? I heard he's to take over from Johnny Prior.... Oh, and your mate took the keys.'

He came back with the lamps. 'There you go.'

Tom signed for them. 'Thanks.'

'Hold on a moment, I nearly forgot... there's something come for you from Swindon...'

He fished under the counter and emerged with a brown paper parcel.

'Think it's your jacket.'

He handed it over then waited, expectantly, so Tom felt obliged to tear off the wrapping. It was, indeed, a black jacket.

'Thought that's what it would be,' Billy said with satisfaction.

'Thanks Billy.'

He again turned to go.

'Don't go without signing for it!'

He produced a chit of paper and Tom signed.

'Railway runs on paperwork, not on wheels.'

Tom smiled and went to the door. Billy leant out and called after him. 'You try it on and if it doesn't fit, I'll send it back... those buggers never get things right!'

The cleaners' cabin was empty when Tom came in, holding the coat and the lamps. He put the lamps down, held up the coat and tried it on. It was a little large, but not a bad fit. He squinted down at himself, then picked up the lamps and went out.

Jerry was busy oiling up when Tom arrived, whistling, wearing his new jacket.

'Took your bleeding time, didn't you?' Jerry said sourly.

'Morning Jerry.'

He climbed up on to the footplate, took off his jacket and carefully hung it up.

'What's good about it? And it's not morning. It's the middle of the bleeding night!'

Tom laughed. He glanced at the level of water in the boiler and examined the state of the fire.

******

'...and he gave me my jacket...' Tom was telling Isobel as they walked along the riverside footpath. They had planned to go to the early performance of the film *'Modern Times'* which was showing at The Regal but it was a mild, golden evening, too good, they agreed, to be spent in the confines of the cinema, even though they both liked Charlie Chaplin, so they decided on a walk instead. Besides, Tom was anxious to tell her his news.

Isobel looked at him blankly. 'Your what?'

'My jacket. You get issued with one when you've done twenty-five firing turns.'

'And that's important?' she asked curiously.

'Well... yes...you see it's the first thing the Company gives you, apart from a couple of pairs of overalls and they don't really count...' He glanced at her incredulous face. 'It, it marks something... something you've achieved...' his voice trailed away.

'Well I think it's daft to get so worked up over a jacket,' she said decidedly.

'It's a good jacket...good quality...' Tom tried not to show his hurt.

Isobel took his arm. 'I'm sorry. I just didn't understand. If it's important to you...'

She gave him a kiss. Somewhat mollified he put his arm round her and they went on. As they walked along the footpath a passenger train crossed the railway bridge above them, the late afternoon sun glinting off its carriage windows. Tom looked up at it. The 7.20, a rake of eight coaches headed by the Star class engine 'Queen Victoria', number 4033. Tom wondered who was driving.

Isobel shook his arm. 'Come on, head-in-the-clouds. There's nothing to look at.'

Tom turned and drew her closer. She was smiling at him, a heart-stopping smile. She closed her eyes as he kissed her.

Standing on a path behind the allotments Fred stared at the train as it made its way into the station, an ache of longing in his face. Once the train had gone, he turned and walked away, round the allotments, up Station Road and into the alley running behind the houses.

Nancy was in the garden, unpegging washing from the line.

'Been to the allotment?' She held a pair of trousers up to her face to see whether they were sufficiently dry before adding them to the laundry basket.

Fred didn't reply. He opened the gate with care, closed it behind him and slowly walked up the path and into the house. Nancy watched him. Picking up the basket, she followed him into the kitchen.

Fred was at the sink, gazing at his reflection in the mirror.

'Do you want some tea? Can I make you some?'

Fred didn't speak.

'Fred... please..' She put her hand on his arm. 'Don't shut me out. I want to help...'

'No-one can help.'

There was a knock at the open door and Charlie put his head round.

'Don't mean to intrude but I was wondering whether you'd like a pint before tea Fred.'

'No. No thank you, Charlie,' Fred said slowly.

Charlie came into the room.

'Can't tell you how sorry I am, mate,' he said awkwardly. 'Haven't had a chance to speak to you before. You and me, we go back a long way.'

Fred nodded.

'Cup of tea, Charlie?'

'Don't mind if I do, Mrs Watkins.' He sat down.

'We've been thinking, Maisie and me,' Charlie began, then hesitated. He glanced at Fred, then away.

He took a breath and went on with a rush. 'There's a nice little sweetshop going begging down the other end of town. Lady who ran it, Mrs Simpson, she's a friend of Maisie's, was widowed a couple of years back. The shop's getting too much for her so she's decided to give it up and go and live with her sister in Swanage. The rent's very cheap. So after talking it over with Maisie, I'm going to throw in the towel and take it on.'

'Coming off the footplate?' Fred asked, incredulously.

Charlie shrugged. 'It'd be a job with regular hours and regular meals. Be my own boss,' he added slightly nervously in the face of Fred's disapproval, 'or rather Maisie'd be the boss. Better for the digestion,' he finished firmly as if that settled the matter.

Fred nodded slowly.

'To be honest, mate, I wouldn't have considered it even though Maisie's very keen, not if you hadn't been...' his voice trailed away. 'Fact of the matter is that it wouldn't be the same, firing to anyone else, and that's the truth.' He swallowed hard. 'Besides, it'll give some of those young ones down at the shed a boot up the ladder.'

******

Len glanced swiftly round and gave a short nod of approval. All shipshape. He liked working in a clean and tidy signal box. As he finished writing up the register, the signalman on the next shift arrived to take over. He had a quick word, then climbed down the steps and began to walk home. He was tired. But then he always seemed to be tired these days.

He sighed. A bite of tea then down the 'Western for a few jars. Bound to be a few mates there. Or did he want company? Did he want to see anybody, knowing that they all knew about his wife. Oh, they'd be very kind of course, but behind his back there'd be winks and nudges. He knew. He had already experienced it. He was still turning it over in his mind when he arrived home. He walked round the back of the house and crossed the yard.

'Maggie! Maggie!'

Maggie appeared at the door. 'Don't shout dad – I've just got Joey off to sleep.'

She disappeared back into the kitchen and Len followed.

The kitchen was of the same design as the Watkins' house. Len looked round. It looked to his eyes shabby and neglected. Stands to reason, he thought. Maggie had enough on her plate what with her job and Joey. Then he caught sight of Jim sitting at the table.

'So you're here again,' he said sourly.

Jim stood up. 'Evening, Mr Thomas.'

'Have to charge you board soon, the number of meals we've given you.'

'Dad...' Maggie protested.

''What's for tea then, girl?' Len said, shrugging off his jacket.

'Stew.'

'It's always bleedin' stew. Didn't they teach you to cook at school or didn't your mother teach you?' He laughed humourlessly. 'Ask a silly question.'

He went out of the room and stomped up the stairs.

Maggie watched him go then began to lay the table. Joey, sitting in his high chair, began banging his mug on the side of it.

'Stop that, Joey!'

Joey banged even harder. Maggie grabbed it from him and Joey burst into loud sobs.

'You'd better go, Jim,' Maggie said, her face flushed. She handed Joey a soft toy. 'Here's Georgy-bear come to see you, Joey. Now be a good boy and play quietly.' The sobs subsided.

'Just tell me...' Jim insisted.

'What do you expect me to do?' Maggie said, trying to keep her temper. 'Say yes, I'll marry you in between serving dad's tea and seeing to Joey? For goodness' sake!'

Jim took a deep breath. 'All I want is a straight answer!'

'And I can't give it to you. Not yet. I'm sorry.'

'I can't bear you doing all this...' Jim looked round the kitchen.

'I don't much care for it myself but I haven't any choice right now,' Maggie said with a glint of humour.

'If you married me...'

'Don't crowd me, Jim,' she snapped back irritably. 'I'm feeling trapped enough as it is.'

******

It was a golden autumn that year and, for the first time, Tom began to look forward to and enjoy the firing trips he was given. One bright crisp morning, with the sun swiftly rising but with a nip in the air in a foretaste of winter, Tom was on the footplate of 2379 with a train of goods wagons snaking out behind.

He looked out the side of the cab. Mist was rising from the fields, dispersing in the warmth of the sun, but still swirling round the trees of Chalcote Woods, shrouding them in mystery. Those that could be seen were beginning to put on their autumn colours and a sudden breath of wind sent the first leaves fluttering to the ground. Cut well back from the track, rosebay willow herb vied for space alongside bushes of white Old Man's Beard, their fluffy seed heads, stirred by the movement of the train, floating into the air. Blackberry bushes, thorny brambles laden with fat and juicy berries, sent tentacles outwards, soon to be cut back by the permanent way staff. It was a good to be alive day and he sniffed the air deeply before turning back into the cab and adding coal to the fire.

He had fired to Jerry before, and they were working together very much as a team. Jerry had stopped checking up on him, a measure of how much Tom had improved.

Jerry poured out a mug of tea and handed it across.

'Here.'

Tom took it gratefully.

Jerry nodded towards the woods.

'There's good game to be had there. Want to come along next time?'

'Thanks.' Tom took a deep gulp of tea, put the mug down and got on with the job. For the first time he felt that he belonged. He was where he wanted to be. Life was good. And he would be seeing Isobel that evening.

Once they'd finished the shift and returned to the shed, they climbed down from the footplate after having left the engine over the ashpit and walked companionably to the lobby to book off. They were chatting as they entered.

The shock of seeing his father on the other side of the counter, stopped Tom in mid-sentence.

'Dad... I forgot it was today...'

Fred held out his hand. Tom hesitated for a moment, but a queue was forming behind him, so he handed over his brass disc and moved away.

******

'London is hushed, and all over the world countless millions are waiting to take part in spirit of the last journey of His Majesty, King George V.'

Tom and Isobel sat silently, along with the rest of the audience, as they watched the Pathé newsreel.

'...and so to Paddington Station where the train is waiting to take its burden to Windsor...'

The newsreel ended, the audience stirred, the lights went up and the curtains swished across the screen.

'Poor king,' Tom said, passing over a bag of peppermints.

'We've all got to go sometime,' Isobel replied, taking one and popping it in her mouth.

'I didn't mean him. I meant the new one.'

Isobel took out her compact, powdered her nose and applied fresh lipstick. She giggled.

'Difficult to put on lipstick without swallowing the mint!'
She snapped the mirror shut and returned it to her handbag. 'I
think it would be rather fun being king... all that power...'

'I wouldn't like it.' Tom thought for a moment. 'I wouldn't
mind an impressive send-off like that though. Paddington
Station full of people and a whole train to carry my coffin.'

'You wouldn't know anything about it. You'd be nailed up
inside,' she teased.

Tom was pursuing his own thoughts. 'I'd insist on Western
stock though. Did you see that the coaches were North
Eastern?'

'The what?'

'The coaches.'

'You are funny.'

'Why?'

'All this loyalty. It's only the place where you work for
goodness sake!'

'Oh, I don't know,' Tom said thoughtfully. 'It's more than
that.' He laughed suddenly. 'I sound just like dad.'

Isobel glanced at him curiously for a moment, then reached
over to the paper bag.

'Here – give us another mint.'

The lights dimmed and the curtains parted for the start of
the main film.

It was cold when they came out of The Regal and a sleety
rain was falling.

'Br-rr,' Isobel shivered, turning up the collar of her coat.

'It is winter after all,' Tom teased. 'What do you expect?
Come on – I'll stand you fish and chips in Sid's.'

'Oh, the famous Sid's!' She laughed. 'Are we going there
at last? You've told me such a lot about it.'

'You're in for a treat!'

He took her hand and hurried her up the road. He had never
taken her there because somehow he couldn't see Isobel in the

more rough-and-ready environs of Sid's. Not that it was rough-and-ready, he reassured himself. And now he knew her better he was sure that she would love it. Well, he was almost sure.

Once inside Tom installed her at a table, smiled reassuringly and went to the counter to order. Isobel looked around, wrinkling her nose at the bright cotton-covered tablecloths, the salt shakers and vinegar bottles, the increasing noise as the café quickly filled up with the after-cinema audience, and, over all, the pervading smell of hot fat and frying fish.

'Funny place,' she remarked when he returned with the food. 'Dad would want to know if it's clean. He's very hot on restaurants being clean seeing as how he's a doctor.'

'Well I've eaten here for years and never gone down with anything.' Tom pushed the salt and vinegar towards her. 'Salt and vinegar?'

'Just salt.' She took a chip daintily. 'Still, it's quite fun, slumming it.'

'One of life's experiences as your sister Susan would say?' Tom replied with unusual sarcasm.

Isobel glanced at him in surprise.

'Where does it lead to – your job on the railway?' she asked, changing the subject.

'A driver if I'm lucky.'

'How long does that take?'

'Oh, years and years. I've got to become a fireman first, then a passed fireman, which means that I'm allowed to drive. You go up through the links. First firing small engines, goods and that, then going up to firing on passenger trains. Promotion all goes on seniority you see – that and there being a vacancy at the shed. Or moving to another shed if a vacancy occurs there.'

'I'd get bored doing the same job year after year,' Isobel shrugged, tucking into the fish with relish, despite her initial misgivings. 'And I wouldn't like lots of rules and regulations. You seem to have loads of them on the railway.'

'They're mainly for safety. For the railwaymen and for the passengers,' Tom replied. He went on, a little stiffly. 'I'm sorry if I've bored you about the job. I'll try not to talk about it.'

They ate for a moment in silence.

'I'm thinking of becoming a nurse. Daddy would like me to be one and I rather fancy myself in a starched uniform, soothing fevered brows. I do think those uniforms look nice.' She wrinkled her nose. 'But I wouldn't like the dirty jobs... the bedpans and people being sick... that's not me at all...'

Tom looked at her as she was speaking. She was picking over the remains of the fish. She looked as she always did. Small, delicate features, large blue eyes, brown hair that curled round the edges of her hat. Like a piece of porcelain. Like a statue to be put on a pedestal. When he hugged her, he had secretly been afraid she would break in his hands.

'... so p'raps I'll just stay home like mummy wants and have a good time until Mr Right comes along...'

As he watched her, he felt he was listening to her, really listening to her, for the first time. And as he listened, the magic began to drain away with every word she said.

She stopped speaking and looked at him, pushing away her empty plate.

'Mr Right?'

'My Prince Charming, who'll sweep me off my feet.'

Tom glanced down at the table.

'Finished your meal all right, didn't you, despite slumming it.'

She flushed. 'It was... good... very good...'

He stood up suddenly.

'If you're finished, I'll take you home.'

'Why the rush?' she asked, knowing instinctively that in some unaccountable manner the relationship had changed.

'I've got to be at work in an hour.'

She laughed, lightly, dismissively. 'Oh... work...'

They left the café and walked in silence to her home, both lost in their own thoughts. At the gate she stopped.

'Look Tom,' she said, in the decisive manner he'd grown accustomed to. 'I didn't want to have to say this because I didn't want to upset you, but I think we'd best call it a day, don't you? We've had some fun but it's over. I mean, you're a nice chap and all that but you're not really my sort. Well are you?'

An hour ago Tom would have been devastated. As it was he just smiled, lifted his cap in a formal gesture, then turned and walked away. He was surprised to find that he felt strangely relieved, as if a burden had just been lifted from him.

'I'm sorry,' Isobel said, watching him go, but Tom didn't hear her.

******

It was quite dark when Tom arrived for work. He booked on and ran his eye down the rosters. He had a bit of time before going to stores to collect the keys and lamps to 2373. Might as well go to the cleaners' cabin and put his feet up, he thought. Or maybe he'd have time for a game of cards with Ginger or Les.

It was quiet in the shed and he whistled a tune as he walked down between the ranks of the engines.

He saw Fred as he turned to enter the cabin. His father was standing silently, staring almost hungrily up at the footplate of engine 4041, Prince of Wales, staring as if he would drink in the sight. The large Star class engine towered over him.

'Dad?' Tom called, going over to him. 'Dad what are you doing here? Mum'll be worried.'

Fred didn't look at him. 'Afraid I'll throw myself under an engine is she?' he said wryly. He gave a half laugh. 'I'm not given to that sort of melodrama even if, God knows, I've felt like it at times.'

They stood for a moment in silence.

'Just look at this old beauty, Tom.'

'What's she doing here?'

'Stabled with us for the night.' Fred replied, his eyes rooted on the engine. 'Taking over a special excursion tomorrow. I've only ever driven a Star a dozen times or so...' He stopped, hunting for the words.

Tom glanced at him and was shocked to see tears running unheeded down Fred's face.

'It was always my ambition, see, to drive a Star or a Castle out of Paddington Station. Or even a King. I'd have been so proud... so proud...' He fell silent for a moment. 'See Tom, I've tried to tell you time and again that it's not just a job. Driving is... you're in charge. You're king of these wonderful machines. You're in control, you nurse it, you work with it, you let it know who's boss and it responds like... I haven't got the words for it. But it's a living thing, Tom, a living thing...' He was silent again. 'It's hard, Tom, very hard.'

He wiped his hand roughly over his face.

'So humiliating. Being time-keeper,' he said, almost to himself.

'No-one will think the worse of you...' Tom muttered.

There was a silence.

'I will.'

Tom searched for the right words to say.

'You'll be a hard act to follow,' he said at last.

There was an even longer silence.

'This thing I've got, Tom... this going blind...' Fred began slowly. 'They say it may happen quickly or it may happen slowly... there's no telling and no cure. It's called retin..retinitis... something. I can't remember, Nancy's got the piece of paper. I'm going blind of something I can't even name,' he said bitterly.

He took a deep breath before turning to face his son. 'They say... and I've not told anyone this because I'm ashamed... I'm ashamed because I've always wanted the best for you... tried to give you everything that was best...' he swallowed. '.. but I might have given you this, too, and I don't know how to say I'm sorry. They say it's hereditary and there's a chance... but there's no way of finding out until it happens...'

Tom stood stock still, as the full force of what his father was saying swept over him.

'It's like... walls... closing in... blotting out the light...'

Chapter Seventeen

It was never spoken of again. His father never mentioned it, and, if his mother knew, neither did she. Tom wondered whether she knew. He wondered also whether he should tell Sylvia. But he never spoke and, in time, was able to push it to the back of his mind. He was young, and with the resilience of youth, he shrugged it off. His father had said there was a chance, but then, he reasoned, there was a chance that he might be killed or injured in his work or run over by an omnibus or any one of a thousand chance things that might happen.

In the past he would have gone to Maggie and told her about it, but that was no longer possible. Whenever he saw her, which was not often, she was either with Jim or in a hurry and only greeted him in passing as if he were a stranger. He missed her companionship, he missed her sound common-sense, he also, if he admitted it, missed her heart-shaped face and button nose with its rash of freckles sprinkled over it, and her brown eyes crinkled up in concern, but all that, he told himself firmly, was in the past. Rather like Isobel, who, he was surprised to find, he did not miss. So he took the teasing of his friends down the 'Western about what had happened to his high-class lady friend in good part and soon forgot that he had fallen for a pretty face and little else to commend her.

Some weeks later he and George Southcombe were on engine 5774 pulling a 'down' goods train. They were held at a home signal which was set at danger and they had been waiting there for some minutes.

'Rule 55 Tom,' George said.

'Right mate.'

Tom climbed off the footplate and walked towards the signal box.

Rule 55 meant that if a train was waiting at a signal for three minutes in clear weather the driver had to send his fireman or guard to the signal box to make sure that the signalman knew the train was waiting.

Tom rapped on the door, opened it and put his head round.

'12.10 'down' goods from Gas Works Junction standing at the 'home'. What's the delay Len?'

Len finished entering a note in the register and looked up.

'You'll be going soon. The 12.05 'down' passenger hasn't cleared yet.'

Tom nodded. 'Righto. I'd better sign the book.'

He took a step inside.

Len held up his hand. 'Hey-hey not so fast! I've just washed that floor and I'm not having you tramp coal dust all over it with those bloody great boots of yours! You stay right where you are!'

Tom grinned and waited while Len brought the train register book over for his signature.

'Your mechanical appliances all in order then Len?' he asked cheekily.

Len snatched the book back from him.

'I'll give you mechanical appliances right round your ear-hole, cheeky bugger!'

'Only carrying out Rule 55,' Tom said innocently.

'And you know where you can shove Rule 55 while you're about it. Bloody young firemen. Think you run the railway.'

Tom laughed.

'Invited you to the wedding has she?' Len asked as he took the register back to the counter.

'Wedding? What wedding?'

'My Maggie's of course.'

'I didn't know Maggie was...' Tom's mouth felt suddenly dry.

'Well you're about the only one who didn't then. Young Jim's been hammering on our door trying to persuade her these past few months.'

'When... when's it to be?'

'They haven't named the day yet but no doubt Jim'll get that fixed pretty soon. He's a determined lad, my future son-in-law.'

'I – I hope they'll be very happy.'

'Yes, my Maggie's a good girl and deserves a bit of happiness. The way she's held the home together since the missus left has been wonderful... bloody wonderful.. even if she's not the world's greatest at cooking.'

'Your wife...?' Tom asked, confused.

'Left me and good riddance to bad rubbish I say, though I didn't at the time. My Maggie said she couldn't marry and leave Joey and me to fend for ourselves. "Have Jim live here," I said, "he virtually does now. I'm always tripping over him in the kitchen", but no, she wouldn't hear of it, not to start with. Jim's sorted her out though.' He paused. 'And anyway they might not have to set up home with me. I've other plans in mind.' He grinned and tapped the side of his nose.

Three single bells rang, indicating that the preceding rain was out of the section.

'You'll be able to go now.'

Len offered Tom's train to the next signal box by giving the appropriate bell code for a goods train.

'I'll remind Maggie,' he said, just as Tom was leaving. 'I'm sure she'd want you at her wedding.'

******

287

Maggie turned the sign on the door of Purvis & Purvis, Haberdashery and High Class Ladies' and Gents' Outfitters to 'closed', pulled down the blind on the window and went out, locking the door behind her. She turned and almost bumped into Tom.

'I was waiting for you.'

'Oh?'

'Yes...I... wanted to congratulate you.'

'What for?'

'Your engagement.'

Maggie walked on in silence.

'I hope you'll both be very happy,' Tom said flatly.

'How are you keeping?' Maggie asked.

Tom shrugged. 'All right.'

'And... and... Isobel? She's very pretty.'

'That's over,' Tom said after a pause.

'Oh.'

'When's the wedding?'

Maggie was about to speak but changed her mind. 'We haven't decided,' she said at last.

They turned the corner into Station Road.

'I'm sorry about your mother.'

Maggie didn't reply to that. 'How's your father?' she asked.

'Dad's... all right...' Tom replied awkwardly.

They had reached her house. They stopped and looked at each other, both uncomfortable, unspoken feelings resonating in the air. Tom sighed and held out his hand.

'Well, all the best.'

'Thanks.'

She gave a slight smile as they shook hands. Tom held on to hers for a moment longer than necessary.

'Goodbye Tom,' she said quietly, pulling her hand away.

Once in the house she closed the door firmly and leant against it, her thoughts miles away. She gave herself a sudden shake and looked up to find Jim standing in the doorway to the kitchen, watching her.

With an effort she smiled. 'Hello. I didn't think you'd be here.'

'That's bloody obvious.'

She brushed past him, taking off her coat.

'Been seeing him behind my back, have you?' Jim taunted.

'Don't be ridiculous.'

'Ridiculous? I saw you just now having a heart to heart at the gate.'

Maggie hung up her coat and turned to face him. 'Spying on me? I walked up the road with Tom for goodness sake! There's no law against it. We are neighbours after all,' she finished sarcastically.

'Well you won't "walk up the road" with him again my girl... is that clear?'

'What right have you got to speak to me like that?' she asked, keeping her anger under tight control. She went into the kitchen and Jim followed.

He put his hand under her chin, forcing up her face.

'Every right. The right of a man engaged to be married. I won't have you looking at any other man, do you hear? Not Tom-bloody-Watkins or anyone... I won't have it!'

She pulled away.

'I never knew you were so jealous,' she said levelly.

'Yes, I'm jealous. I'm jealous about my own possessions.'

'I'm a possession now, am I?' she flung back.

'Don't be ridiculous! I didn't mean that. I just meant...'

'You always were a bully at school, weren't you?' she broke in contemptuously. 'You don't love me, you just want to own me.' They stared at one another. 'Well you don't own me. I won't be owned, not by anyone.'

'Except by Tom Watkins,' Jim jeered.

'Not him, not you, not dad, not anyone.' She took a deep breath. 'You... all... suffocate me...!'

She fumbled at her finger, took off her engagement ring and held it out to him. He hesitated then slowly, very slowly, took it.

'Maggie...?' he pleaded. 'Please... I love you... I want to look after you...'

She turned away.

'I'm always the loser,' he said bitterly. He went out of the house, slamming the door behind him.

******

'I couldn't eat another crumb, Mrs Watkins,' Dai said, shaking his head regretfully as Nancy held out a plate of cakes.

'Oh go on, Mr Davies,' Nancy urged. 'I know you drivers have to keep up your strength.'

'Well... if you insist,' he said, taking one. 'Bad as my mam, you are. She's always trying to feed me up. And not so much of the Mr Davies either. I'm Dai to my friends.'

Nancy, Tom, Dai and Sylvia were sitting in the parlour, finishing a lavish tea which had been spread out on a crisp white tablecloth using the best china. A place had been laid for Fred, but he had not come in and although the atmosphere was, on the surface, relaxed and the talk light-hearted, there was more than a hint of anxiety in Nancy's frequent glances towards the door.

Dai finished the cake and sighed. 'That was magnificent.' He pushed his plate away.

'What are your lodgings like in Bristol?' Nancy asked.

'Terrible.' Dai shook his head. 'There's fleas in the bed... no, don't worry, I had a bath before I came... and my

landlady's so mean she even resents me putting salt on my
boiled egg. Not that she offers boiled eggs very often.'

Sylvia shook her head at him. 'Don't listen to him mum,
he's a terrible liar.'

'That's why you know I'm telling the truth. Because I'm
such a terrible liar,' Dai said complacently. 'No-one believes
me if I lie, so I always tell the truth. The food's dreadful too…
the porridge is lumpy and if you ask for a spoonful of sugar she
looks at you as if you asked for a three-course banquet.'

'Don't believe a word of it. I bet she spoils you rotten.'

Dai grinned at her.

'Well…' Nancy rose. 'If you're quite sure I can't offer you
anything else, shall we go and sit more comfortably?'

'I'll help you clear up…' Dai offered, starting to collect the
plates.

'No, no, leave them…'

Her eyes again strayed to the door, but it remained closed.

'I can't think where Fred's got to,' she murmured.

'Perhaps he's down the allotment,' Tom suggested.

'Perhaps.'

'Will you play something mum?' Sylvia asked. 'I've told
Dai how good you are.'

Nancy smiled. 'Now who's telling lies?'

'No, honestly. I'm proud of you. Did you know mum
played at The Regal in the silent days?' she asked Dai.

'What, rising up onto the stage like Venus rising out of the
sea?' Dai asked.

Nancy laughed. 'Walking on to the stage and sitting at an
old piano, trying to coax the right music to go with the pictures
more like. Old Mr Everard, who was the manager then, was
every bit as difficult as your Mr Pilger from what you tell me.
Wouldn't even spend the money having the piano tuned.'

Sylvia pulled a face. 'Nobody could be as bad as Mr
Pilger.'

'Do you play?' Dai asked Sylvia.

'I tried learning when I was little, but I was cack-handed.'

Tom laughed. 'You should have heard her playing scales over and over again. Sent the rest of us out of the house.'

Sylvia pretended to throw a cushion at him. 'I wasn't as bad as all that,' she protested.

'Worse!'

'Children!' Nancy smiled as she opened the piano lid and sat down on the stool, while Dai and Sylvia went to the sofa and Tom added coal to the fire. Nancy chose a piece of music and began to play. She was barely into the piece when the door opened and Fred came in. Nancy stopped playing, Tom straightened up, while Dai got to his feet. Sylvia also stood up.

'Dad...'

Dai put a restraining hand on Sylvia's shoulder then held out his hand to Fred.

'Mr Watkins.'

Fred looked at his outstretched hand, looked up at Dai, at Sylvia, then round to Tom and Nancy. There was a long moment of silence. Then, slowly, he took Dai's hand, more in a gesture of defeat than acceptance. There was a general relaxing of tension.

Nancy got up. 'I'll get you some tea, Fred.'

'No. I'll help myself,' he said slowly. He went over to the table and sat down but did not eat. The others also sat, and Nancy once more started to play.

******

It was evening and, after the bustle of the day, Acton Chalcote Station was quiet apart from a porter loading crates on to a trolley. At the other end of the platform was Maggie. She was sitting on a bench, a large suitcase at her feet. Wearing a shabby olive-green coat and hat and with a brown handbag clutched in her hand, she was frowning, but composed, although her small hands, encased in brown handknitted gloves, were restlessly clasping and unclasping the handle of her bag.

Tom, at the end of his shift, had left the yard and paused at the barrow crossing, looking both ways up and down the track. When he saw Maggie, he stopped for a second, a wave of compassion catching at his throat. He had an overwhelming urge to rush over and take her in his arms.

'Maggie.'

He walked up the ramp to the platform, then stood uncertainly in front of her.

She looked up, startled.

'Why don't you sit in the waiting room? There'll be a fire in there,' he said awkwardly.

She didn't say anything.

'Where are you going?'

She looked up. 'London,' she said defiantly.

'London? Oh, to get your wedding things…'

Maggie said nothing.

'The next through train's not for a couple of hours.'

Maggie shrugged. 'Doesn't matter. I'll change.'

The signal came off with a clang and a small branch line train comprising an engine and three coaches entered the station and stopped at the platform. Maggie stood up and reached for her case, but Tom had already picked it up.

'I'll do that.'

He followed her to a compartment and opened the door for her, lifting her case inside.

'Thank you.'

She climbed in and Tom closed the door.

'There's no wedding,' she said, leaning out of the window. 'It's all off.'

Tom stood still, his hand on the door.

'What...? Maggie!'

The guard waved his flag and blew the whistle and the train moved off. Tom ran alongside it down the length of the platform.

'Maggie...!'

But the train had gone. Tom stood and watched it go then looked around. A goods train was standing in Platform 3. After a moment's thought, Tom raced across to it.

'Alfie...!' he called out. 'You're going to Malcester, aren't you?'

'That's the general idea.'

'Will you give us a lift?' Tom asked anxiously.

'Be my guest,' Alfie replied, waving Tom into the guard's van with an exaggerated bow.

As the goods train wended its slow way towards Malcester, Alfie watched in amusement as Tom paced from side to side.

'Won't get there any faster with you acting like a caged lion,' he remarked.

'Who's driving?' Tom asked absently.

'Sammy White. So you can count on an exciting trip.'

'Oh,' Tom said, not hearing a word. He carried on pacing.

'Come and sit down and have a cuppa. You make me nervous pacing up and down like that.'

Tom sat down obediently, but his mind was far away and after a few attempts at further conversation, Alfie left him to his thoughts.

How could he have been so blind, Tom wondered? Messing with Isobel when all the time Maggie, faithful, kind Maggie, his childhood friend, had been there for him. Maggie, who had always listened to him, consoled him, looked up to him. Did she think of him at all, or was he only the older brother she had never had?

He shifted uncomfortably on the hard wooden seat, keeping his balance with difficulty as the guards' van lurched from side to side. Maggie... he had never once thought to ask how she was. He had never once thought about what her life was like. He had had no idea that her mother had left home, leaving her with her job as well as her father and baby brother to look after. She should have told him, he thought resentfully, but no, he should have asked. And he never had. How could he have been so uncaring, so... He sat with compressed lips, hating himself. He hadn't even behaved towards her as an older brother would have behaved.

And it had been Jim who had seen her worth. Jim the bully, Jim, whose rivalry stretched back to their schooldays. And it was Jim she was about to marry. Or was it? What had she meant by saying that the wedding was off? He got to his feet, unable to sit still.

'How much longer?'

Alfie was hanging over the side, watching for the signal. Tom leant over beside him.

'Nearly there.'

As the driver put in the brake, the effect was felt and multiplied down the train and Tom, in the guards' van at the back, staggered.

'Sammy White at his best,' Alfie said laconically as he screwed down his brake. 'Now you know what we have to put up with.'

Tom wasn't listening. As the goods train crawled into the yard, he was already climbing out.

'Thanks Alfie,' he said. 'Do the same for you some time.'

'Not for me mate. I'm thankfully past all those capers,' Alfie replied dryly.

'Best of luck!' he called after Tom who was already racing down the track.

A quick glance at the destination board showed him that the next London train would be departing from Platform One in forty minutes. Tom ran over the footbridge and down on to the platform. He looked up and down but there was no sign of Maggie.

The newly-refurbished Refreshment Room at Malcester Station with its art deco interior was empty apart from a young couple who were sitting, heads together, talking quietly and intimately at one of the small, round tables. Under the warm glow of the gas lamps, the polished mahogany counter which ran the length of the room, shone brightly, while the glass and chrome display shelves sitting on its gleaming wood surface exhibited plates of tempting buns and cakes. Behind the counter the manageress, short, bright-eyed and bustling in her black dress, was busy polishing glasses, breathing on them before wiping them with a tea towel, while a waitress dried dishes in the sink at the back.

Maggie came in and put her case down with a sigh. She went up to the counter.

'What can I get you miss?'

'Just a pot of tea please.'

'Nothing to eat?'

Maggie shook her head.

You sure dear? Look a bit peaky to me, you do. Like you've lost a bob and found threepence. A nice bath bun would set you up a treat.'

'No, really.'

'Pot of tea for the lady, Glad!' the manageress ordered.

'Right Miss Topham!' came a voice from the back.

Maggie sat down. When the tea arrived, Gladys had also brought a plate with a bath bun sitting solidly in the centre.

'It's on the house, dear!' Miss Topham called across. 'Never get rid of them this time of night and it'd be a shame for them to go to waste.'

'Thank you.'

'And if you can't eat it now, you can always take it with you. Not sure if the buffet service is operating on the next train.'

'Thank you,' Maggie said again. 'You're very kind.'

She looked at the bun with disfavour, then picked it up and took a small bite. She put it down.

Seeing Tom had unsettled her. She'd got everything worked out, it was all going nicely to plan, and then he had turned up on the platform. She wondered if she would ever see him again. Or if she did, he would most probably be married, if not to Isobel, then to someone else. Not that it mattered, she thought drearily.

She was still sitting in front of her undrunk cup of tea and uneaten bath bun when Tom came in. He looked swiftly round the room.

'Maggie...'

She looked up, startled. 'What on earth are you doing here?'

'I had to see you.'

'Cup of tea?' Miss Hargreaves asked, avidly curious.

'No. No thank you,' Tom said impatiently. He sat down. 'I've got to talk to you. I've got to tell you... Maggie, I got it all wrong. Everything. It was when... when your dad said you were getting married that I realised...'

Maggie looked at him.

'What?' she asked flatly.

'That I love you.'

There was a long silence, punctuated by the sound of a train passing non-stop through the station.

'Maggie... I've always loved you...'

Maggie didn't answer for a while. Absentmindedly she put some sugar into her now cold cup of tea and stirred it.

297

'If you'd said that a month ago… a week even…' she began slowly. 'If you'd said that, it would have meant something… everything…'

'That's not fair!' Tom interrupted hotly. 'A week ago you were engaged to be married!'

'Only because I couldn't say 'no' anymore. Jim was there when I needed someone… and all I did was make him see that he could never be more than second best no matter how hard he tried.' She sighed. 'Poor Jim.'

'Second best?' Tom asked, puzzled.

She looked him in the face and her expression hardened. 'You're such a fool, Tom...so blind... I'd have done anything for you...anything...I loved you since I was a kid and you fought off Jim Salter. He gave you an awful beating but left me alone after that.' She stopped. 'I don't suppose you even remember it.' She laughed shortly. 'I'm sure Jim doesn't.'

'I do remember,' Tom said quietly.

Maggie smiled sadly. ''If only you'd gone...not even halfway...just stretched out your little finger...but you never did.' She sighed. 'It's always been one-sided hasn't it? You've always told me all your troubles, but you never once asked about mine... never once...' She looked away. 'All right, so I was the fool.'

'No you weren't,' he muttered. 'I was.'

She looked up at him defiantly. 'Where were you Tom, when my mum went off and I had to cope with dad and Joey?'

Tom was silent.

'The walls have been closing in for a long time now...stifling...housekeeper to dad...mother to Joey...wife to Jim...and you never once asked.'

'Maggie...,' Tom said urgently.

'No, you listen to me for a change.' She sighed again. 'There's only so much love anyone can give and when that's

298

used up there isn't any more. I don't feel anything for anyone, me least of all. I'm tired, Tom...so tired...'

The arrival of a train on the platform outside made them both look up. They could hear the porter shouting.

'Malcester, Malcester, this is Malcester! This train is for Birmingham Snow Hill only. This is Malcester Station!'

The couple at the other table stood up and left the room, his arm around her shoulders. The girl smiled at them as she passed.

When the train had gone, Maggie sat up straight and pushed the tea things away from her.

'I've only got one life, Tom and I'm not going to waste any more of it sitting round waiting for the impossible,' she said determinedly.

'What about your dad...Joey..?'

'Trying to tempt me back? You needn't bother. They're all right. Dad was furious when I said I wasn't going to marry Jim. Thought he was a steady lad, even though he didn't like him "haunting the place" as he put it and us having to feed him. Thought he'd look after the three of us. But he's got a lady friend now so he'll be all right. They'll both be. They don't need me any more.'

Tom listened in silence and with growing respect. Maggie had always been able to look at things squarely in the face.

'Where will you go in London? What will you do?'

'I'm going to my aunt and I'll get a job,' she said, determinedly.

She stood up.

'Let me come and see you...please...' Tom pleaded.

Maggie buttoned her coat and drew on her gloves.

I'm sorry Tom...' she said quietly. 'You're just too late...'

She looked up at the sound of an approaching train.

'That must be my train.'

She picked up her case and walked out. Tom followed.

'Maggie...don't go. Please. You've no need to,' he pleaded as they went out.

'Better than the cinema,' Gladys remarked to the manageress as she went to clear the table.

As they emerged from the Refreshment Room, the express for Paddington drew in, the Castle class engine pulling a long rake of coaches. Once it had stopped, porters sprang into life, opening doors and managing luggage as passengers hurried to get on or off the train.

'Malcester, Malcester, this is Malcester!' shouted the porter. 'This train is for Didcot, Reading General and Paddington only! Change at Didcot for Swindon and West of England stations, also the Newbury branch. Change at Reading General for Slough and Ealing Broadway. This is Malcester!'

The sudden noise and activity was a shock. Tom blinked. Everything had happened too quickly and he felt he was living through some sort of dream. Or nightmare. The swirls of steam from the steam heating system eddied around the platform, turning everything into surreal shapes.

'Maggie...' He caught at her arm. She put down her case and turned on him.

Just give me one good reason why I should stay,' she said fiercely.

'Because I love you.'

'Love?' she said contemptuously. 'You don't know the meaning of the word! You've no idea! You're selfish Tom, utterly and completely selfish! For years I thought I loved you, but I was probably just the stupid kid you always thought me!'

She got on the train and a porter hurried to close the door.

'Maggie...please...'

'Goodbye Tom.'

A wave of the guard's flag and a whistle and the train departed.

Chapter Eighteen

Due to the difficult relationship with Fred, Dai and Sylvia decided that their wedding would be low key, with a small reception to be held in the Railwayman's Club. Nancy had planned it over several months. Despite her deceptive air of vagueness, she was a good organiser. She booked the room, organised the catering, made lists of those to be invited, arranged their accommodation and had invitations printed and sent out by Pearsons, the local printers and stationers.

It was to have been a quiet wedding. However, Dai's family and friends had other ideas. It seemed, to an awed Sylvia and Nancy, that the entire Rhondda Valley would be emptied in order to attend the celebration. Dai's parents, his brother, Gareth, his two sisters, Morfudd and Eunice, together with their respective spouses and children, had all been invited, but in the event aunts, uncles, cousins and sundry distant relations, as well as innumerable friends and acquaintances decided to attend in order to give Dai their support and a good send-off. So they descended on Acton Chalcote by train, by charabanc, even by motor car. The local branch of the Male Voice Choir – those whose jobs permitted – arrived by coach in fine singing voice having rehearsed on the journey, their voices well lubricated by the beer they had thoughtfully brought with them.

Nancy hastily made fresh arrangements for more substantial catering, cancelled the Railwayman's Club and booked a bigger venue in the Great Western Hotel. She also booked the entire accommodation of the hotel as well as many of the guest houses in the town.

There were far fewer members of the Watkins family to invite, but numbers were made up by a strong railway contingent from both the Acton Chalcote and Bristol sheds as well as friends such as Carol, Florence and Mrs White.

Fred took no part in any of these preparations and was rarely seen at home. Both before and after work he would go to the allotment and dig and weed as if his life depended on it. He felt withdrawn, detached from everything, living under a black cloud which threatened to engulf him. The only reality was the thought of the encroaching blindness which seemed to be creeping, inexorably closer and closer.

The wedding ceremony itself, held in St. Peter's Church, went off without a hitch, other than a few muttered comments from some of the more nonconformist of Dai's relatives. Gareth, who acted as his best man, mislaid the ring just before the service but it was soon found safely tucked into an inner pocket of his waistcoat. Despite Nancy's unspoken fears, Fred played his part. He spoke to those to whom he was introduced and walked Sylvia up the aisle, although Nancy had taken the precaution of speaking to Tom beforehand to ask whether he would give Sylvia away if Fred, at the last minute, was not able to face it. Sylvia, radiant in white and wearing her grandmother's veil, held firmly on to her father's arm and did not appear to notice his slight stumble when he didn't see the step up into the sanctuary.

There was a relaxed atmosphere at the reception. With plenty to eat and plenty to drink there was much talking and laughter. Even Nancy, who had been tense with anxiety during the ceremony, was for a short while able to put aside her concerns. At the end of the meal the members of the Male Voice Choir sang, and Nancy's eyes glistened with tears as she saw Sylvia and Dai so obviously happy.

Sylvia squeezed Dai's hand.

'Did you ever sing?' she asked quietly.

'Me? Dai feigned surprised. 'Like a lark. Every Welshman is born to sing!'

Sylvia looked at him sceptically. 'Not sure I believe you. But the Rhondda's done you proud.'

'All in honour of you,' Dai smiled at her. 'Mrs Davies.'

Sylvia blushed.

Once the singing had ended there was a hush as everyone turned to Fred for the traditional toast

'Fred... please...!' Nancy muttered under her breath.

But Fred remained in his seat at the table. He was looking down at his plate, seemingly oblivious to his surroundings. Tom, after a quick glance at his mother, hesitated for a moment, then got to his feet.

He cleared his throat. 'Ladies and gentlemen, I'd like to propose a toast!' he said, nervously to begin with, then gaining in confidence. 'I've known Sylvia, well, all my life, and although she can be a bit bossy at times, she's been a wonderful sister. So could you raise your glasses to my big sister Sylvia and my mate Dai. I hope they'll both be very happy!'

Everyone stood and raised their glasses. 'To Sylvia and Dai!'

Sylvia glanced at Tom gratefully and after Gareth's toast to the bridesmaids, everyone began to move from the tables. The cake was cut, photographs taken and the level of noise in the hall rose.

'A good son-in-law you'll be getting there,' Huw, Dai's father, said, pumping Fred's hand vigorously. 'And a fair beauty he's getting in your daughter!'

'Done well for yourself, haven't you bach!' said Gareth, giving Dai a hearty buffet across the back. 'A good job and a lovely girl.' The big miner smiled down at Sylvia. 'I can't resist a brotherly kiss,' he said, almost lifting her off her feet in a bear hug.

'You put my wife down and stop taking liberties with her!' Dai warned him. Gareth laughed and moved away as Dai's mother approached.

'Well, Sylvia, I hope you'll be very happy with my boy. He's a good lad, mind, and the two of you will always be very welcome in our house.'

Jerry Marshall called for silence.

'Ladies and gentlemen, I've been asked to say a few words about the happy couple... and I assure you they will only be a few...'

There were general shouts of approval.

'I've known Dai ever since he came to Acton Chalcote some years ago. Now I know that some people think of Dai as a bit odd, a bit strange, especially when he quotes all that poetry he's so fond of....' He paused for laughs. Tom glanced at Fred, who was staring at Jerry, growing distaste in his face.

'We've been through a lot, Dai and me, most of which I couldn't recount before a respectable gathering like this...'

'I'm relieved!' Dai shouted.

'...but, being mates, I can let you into a secret. Dai's not odd at all... he's just Welsh...'

This brought both laughter and cries of 'Shame!' from the Welsh contingent.

'... but despite that, or because of it, Dai's a good mate and a good friend, even if he is a bit big-headed,' Jerry went on, '... and if that's what Welshmen are like, I might even consider a transfer to a Welsh shed.'

There was much applause and laughter at this as well as cries of 'They wouldn't have you, bach!'

'So, if you couldn't have a better mate than Dai, what about Sylvia? We all know that Sylvia is beautiful, charming and intelligent – so I can't work out why she chose Dai instead of me! She's also Fred's daughter and Tom's sister so she knows what she's letting herself in for by marrying a railwayman.

And when Dai returns home, exhausted, at four in the morning, Sylvia'll know that it's not another woman. He's just been working a train of coal back from Swansea!'

During the laughter and applause, Fred suddenly turned and began to push his way through the crowd.

Nancy caught his arm. 'Fred…!'

Fred shook her off.

'I'll go, mum,' Tom said quietly and slipped out.

It was a bright day outside and Tom quickly ran down the steps of the hotel looking from one side to the other. He soon spotted Fred walking down the street, one hand shading his eyes as if troubled by the glare. When Fred blundered into a tree Tom raced over to him.

'Dad… dad…!'

Fred regained his balance, glanced back and walked on. He walked quickly, his hands clenched, full of rage, a tightly held-in anger aimed primarily at himself but ready to lash out at anyone.

'Dad, you can't leave…!'

Fred turned on him fiercely.

'Why not? It's a free country.

'But you're spoiling it… for mum…for Sylvie…'

'She's spoiling it for herself… marrying that man…'

'But you mustn't walk out… it's not fair on her…'

'Not fair? Me not fair? You've a bloody nerve! I agree to her marrying the bugger didn't I? You all got round me… your mother and your sister! I gave her away, didn't I? Played my part in church, didn't disgrace any of you.' He spat out the words, trembling with fury. 'But I'll be damned if I give them my blessing and as for staying to listen to that weasel-faced windbag drivelling on about the wonderful man my daughter's been foolish enough to marry… well you can just stick it, d'you hear? You can just stick it!'

He walked on.

'But dad...' Tom called, hurrying to catch up.

Fred stopped again. 'What did you expect? Jam on it? "It's not fair on her"... just who do you think you are to sit in judgment, eh? Who the hell do you think you are?'

Tom was silent.

'Don't spoil it for Sylvie... please... it's her day...' he said at last.

'Her day! Ha! I just hope she doesn't regret it, that's all!'

Tom looked at him curiously.

'You really are selfish, aren't you?' he said quietly.

'You...!' Fred clenched his fists.

'Hit me if you want. That doesn't alter anything.'

Fred stared at him for a moment without speaking.

'You don't have to like Dai in order to see them off on their honeymoon,' Tom went on. 'You don't even have to speak to him. Do it for Sylvie... please dad...'

Fred hesitated, conflicting emotions playing across his face. The refusal of a proud man to admit he was wrong, the slowly growing realisation that he and Tom had subtly changed roles. He looked at his son. Tom had grown, and not just physically. Mature and assured, he stood quietly in front of Fred, waiting...

For the first time, Fred became aware that Tom had grown up. Grown up and passed out of the range of his authority. Worse. The realisation swept over him that whatever authority he had was gone. As he hesitated, the full bitterness of defeat flooded over him.

Sensing this, Tom waited quietly before taking a step closer.

'Dad..?' he asked gently.

'Just don't pity me, d'you hear?' The words were forced out of him. 'Just don't bloody pity me!'

******

The train waiting on Platform 1 had a 'Honeymoon Special' sign hung over the door to a First Class compartment. Mr Elmes, the stationmaster, was standing beside it, spruce and alert, waiting to greet the wedding party. Ribald jokes and a shower of confetti followed Dai and Sylvia as they crossed the platform. Frank Bateson, who was driving, was leaning out of the cab. He blew the whistle as Mr Elmes opened the door to the carriage and Jerry put their luggage in the compartment and swung it up on the rack.

'Thanks mate,' Dai said as he came out.

Jerry nodded in Frank's direction. 'We've bribed him to stop in the tunnel.'

'Better keep him under strong lock and key darling, or I might come poaching,' Carol purred as she gave Sylvia a kiss.

'Now don't forget what I said, Dai!' Mrs White called as she hurried over to him.

Dai gave her a bone-crushing hug.

'I will sweetheart, and you're a darling.'

'I hope your wife likes being crushed to death,' Mrs White's cheeks were pink as she tried to straighten her hat.

'She adores it.'

'Well, the offer's there so you just remember to ask her.' She gave a sudden crack of laughter. 'Not that you will, mind... you'll have better things to do.'

'I'll ask her,' Dai promised.

Nancy came up, and Sylvia pushed her way through the well-wishers to give her a hug.

''Bye mum. Thanks for everything.'

Nancy hugged her tight but didn't say anything. Sylvia looked round for Tom and her father. Failing to see either, she moved, disappointed, towards the train where Dai was waiting, door held open. He touched her arm and she turned. Fred was slowly coming towards her, Tom behind him.

'Dad...!'

She gave him a quick, fierce hug then turned to Tom.

'Thanks,' she as she kissed him. Dai grinned at Tom and shook his hand.

'Take care of her,' Nancy called out.

'Don't you worry!'

He kissed Nancy, climbed into the carriage and more confetti was flung as the door was closed. As the train departed it passed over a large number of detonators which had been laid on the track. The wedding party left behind waved and cheered and began counting the number of bangs. Then the train curved round a bend and was gone.

Inside the compartment Dai turned, laughing at the sound of the explosions. Sylvia took off her hat and shook confetti out of her hair.

'Billy Hughes must have been persuaded to order a special supply of shot,' he remarked. 'God knows what the rest of the passengers are thinking.'

There was one last bang, then silence.

'They probably know, with all the fuss at the station.'

'What, that there's newly-weds on board?' Dai asked lightly. 'Never. Most people are too wrapped up in their own concerns.'

He took half a step towards her, then stopped.

'Hello Mrs Davies. May I say how lovely you are looking?'

Sylvia was wearing a cream dress, with a green and yellow pattern of flowers. Her matching jacket, hat with a green and yellow rosette, cream gloves and shoes completed her outfit. Dai stared at her and caught his breath. He was about to take her in his arms when something stopped him. A slight constraint had fallen between them. Instead, he knelt down and began looking under the seats.

'Looking for booby traps?'

'Looking for your friend, Carol. I wouldn't put it past her to stow-away.'

'Oh... so you heard what she said.'

'I think I was meant to.'

'Perhaps we should try and find her some suitable railwayman.'

Sylvia had sat down in a corner and taken off her hat. She turned to look out of the window.

'I thought you didn't like railwaymen,' Dai said lightly.

She didn't laugh. She didn't answer. He sat in the opposite seat and watched her.

'Little one...' he began hesitantly.

'What?'

'What's wrong?'

'Wrong? Nothing. I'm just tired, that's all. It's been quite a day. Quite the most exhausting of my life.' She leant back and closed her eyes. 'I never knew getting married would be so tiring... did you?

'Not having been married before... no.'

'All those people...'

'Very tiring. Especially the Welsh contingent.'

She smiled. There was a slight pause.

'I wish dad hadn't gone off like that.'

'So do I.'

'Still, he came back.'

'Yes,' Dai agreed, beginning to enjoy himself. 'He came back.'

'It was nice of Tom to jump in like he did with that speech. I expect he hated doing it.'

Dai nodded solemnly. 'Yes, it was nice of him.'

'I wish Tom had a girlfriend. He needs one. He's got a... a sort of empty air about him.'

'Yes,' said Dai gravely. 'Very empty.'

'Do you remember that nasty doctor's daughter he went out with? Do you think he's pining?'

'Who for, her or the nasty doctor?'

Sylvia turned and looked at him.

'Don't make fun of me,' she said simply.

'Sylvia...' He took her hand.

'It's all a bit frightening, isn't it?' she said, speaking rather quickly. 'I mean... we get married and there's all those people wishing us well and we go off and it should all end happily ever after, and at The Regal the credits would come up and the curtain would come across and everyone would stand for the National Anthem and the lights would go up and everyone would go home and I know I'm talking rubbish and I'm sorry but it's not like that, is it? Not really. Not at all. It's not an end, it's a beginning and it's real and I don't even know you that well and... and... I'm scared...'

She trailed off into silence. Dai took her other hand.

'Is it any help to say that I'm every bit as scared as you?' he asked gently. 'That I've gone through every one of the same doubts and fears?'

There was a moment's silence.

'Have you really?' She bit her lip. 'Oh Dai...'

'You know what we both need?' Dai asked, releasing her hands. 'A good square meal. I'm a great believer in good square meals. You never ate a thing at the reception and I know I didn't... I was too worried about the dreadful things Jerry was going to say about my murky past.'

Sylvia laughed and Dai pulled her to her feet.

'They do say, you know, that the first year is the worst. If you can survive that, you can survive anything.'

He slid open the door of the compartment. 'Come on. Food.'

'In the restaurant car?' she queried.

'Where else.'

'It'll be very expensive.'

'If I can't treat my wife to an expensive meal when we've just got married, then what's the world coming to? Mind,' he said as they walked along the corridor, 'the rest of the honeymoon will be done on the cheap. One portion of fish and chips between us, huddled together in one of those shelters along the promenade. You know, the kind of places where old people sit out of the wind. You must remember,' he added severely, 'that a driver's pay won't stretch to champagne and caviar every night.'

Sylvia wrinkled up her nose. 'I've never eaten caviar and champagne tickles my nose so I'll settle for fish and chips – so long as it's as good as Sid's.'

Dai was pleased to see her begin to relax.

'But only one portion between us remember,' he warned her. 'Pity you didn't know I was such a skinflint before you married me.'

The meal was excellent and, together with the wine, did as much to relax Sylvia, as did the flow of inconsequential chat from Dai. When they had eaten, he raised his glass.

'To the first year.'

She raised her glass solemnly. 'The first year.'

'We'll muddle through together.'

They smiled at each other.

'What's Bristol like?' she asked.

'Well, it's big... and there are ships as well as trains.' He looked at her. 'Are you worried about it?'

'A bit,' she confessed. 'I've never been away from home you see, apart from holidays. I know everyone in Acton Chalcote. It'll be funny not knowing anyone.'

'There's a vacancy for a driver coming up at Chalcote,' Dai said after a pause. 'Would you like it if I applied?'

Sylvia took a sip of wine.

'Is the vacancy because of dad?'

'Not directly. But... yes... in a roundabout way. Fred's leaving means that everyone moves up. I'd be at the very bottom of the bottom link of drivers and Fred was at the top of the top link. But I'd be senior to any Acton Chalcote firemen who might apply. I could probably get it – but if only you want me to apply…'

'Where'd we live? I don't think mum and dad…'

'I wouldn't dream of taxing your father with my presence. Besides… it doesn't do to live with in-laws if you can avoid it. There might be a Company house eventually, but to begin with… well, Mrs White said she was looking for lodgers now that Joe's died. The cottage is too big for her on her own… but it's got to be your decision.' He was silent, watching her. 'She can be a sharp old stick but she was very good to me when I stayed with her and Joe and I know she wouldn't want us to be living in each other's pockets.'

He paused. 'You might find it company when I'm away nights. That's worried me a bit as you're not used to being on your own.'

'I thought of asking Carol to come and stay,' she said with a slight smile.

'That might… just might… be grounds for divorce,' he said. He traced the outline of her face with his finger. 'I do love you,' he added.

> *'Then to Silvia let us sing*
> *That Silvia is excelling;*
> *She excels each mortal thing*
> *Upon the dull earth dwelling.*
> *To her let us garlands bring.'*

Sylvia frowned. 'What is that?'
Dai laughed. 'Your English Shakespeare, cariad.'

Chapter Nineteen

In due course Dai applied for the vacant post at Acton Chalcote shed. He was appointed and he and Sylvia moved into Mrs White's cottage. Their arrival gave Mrs White a new lease of life.

'She's trying to persuade me to go to the pictures,' she told Dai one evening, as they sat over a meal. 'The pictures! Me!'

'She's never been Dai, and there's Jean Harlow and Cary Grant on this week.'

Mrs White pursed her lips. 'I'm too old for that kind of junketing around,' she said a little wistfully.

'Old? You? You're in your prime!' Dai said affectionately.

'Oh go on with you and your Welsh blarney!'

Dai laughed. 'Wish I could come with you. Have a lovely time girls!' He gulped down his tea and stood up. 'Must go – won't be back 'til late so don't wait up for me'

After their trip out, which left Mrs White wondering what she had been missing all these years, Sylvia thought about returning to her job as usherette at The Regal.

'What do you think, mum?' she asked when she arrived for a cup of tea, bringing a dozen eggs with her. She put the eggs on the table. 'Here. A present from Lil.'

'Lil?'

'Mrs White asked me to call her that. She said we can't share a house and be Mrs White and Mrs Davies all the time.' Sylvia giggled. 'She said that her real name is Lily and she nearly didn't marry Joe because of it.'

Nancy looked blank for a moment then burst out laughing. 'Lily White! I can see what she means.'

Sylvia looked at her mother who was pale and seemed strained. She was glad to have made her laugh.

'You all right mum?'

'Fine.' She shrugged. 'You know…'

'Dad?'

Nancy nodded. 'He's just lost interest in everything. The doctor he's been seeing said he probably wouldn't go blind. Not totally. But he won't accept it.' She sighed. 'And he gets these headaches. I think it's all part of the same thing. But it's not easy for him.' She poured out two cups of tea. 'Or me,' she added quietly.

She pushed a cup across the table. 'Anyway, enough of that. I think you should go back to your job if you enjoy it. You need an interest, other than just staying at home. And it's not as you've any little ones on the way.'

'Yet,' Sylvia finished. 'I bet you can't wait to spoil the grandchildren,' she teased.

Nancy smiled.

'But it's long hours at the cinema. What does Dai say?'

'I haven't asked him yet, but I popped into The Regal on the way and Mr Pilger said they're short-staffed. He said they'd love to have me back whatever hours I can do,' she added in a surprised voice.

'I always thought you were a bit hard on Mr Pilger.'

That evening Sylvia talked it over with Dai and Lil.

'I didn't think helping Lil's chickens lay the best eggs would satisfy you for long,' Dai remarked.

Lil bridled. 'And I don't want any interference with my girls,' she said decidedly. 'We've a good relationship, my chickens and me and I don't want them upset by any help, however well-meaning. Might put them off laying.'

That settled the matter and Sylvia returned to work. She was allowed one complimentary ticket a week which she passed to Lil, who loved her afternoons out which was followed by fish and chips at Sid's when Sylvia had finished work. She began to read Film Weekly and was soon engrossed in the lives of the stars, much to Dai and Sylvia's secret amusement.

Fred's eyes continued their slow deterioration, with increasing loss of peripheral vision. He was able to continue his job as time clerk but sank into deeper and deeper depression. Each morning he opened his eyes with trepidation, worried that overnight he might have lost his sight altogether. Apart from his weekly meeting with Charlie for a game of chess at the Railwayman's Club he became more and more uncommunicative.

Tom, meanwhile, had worries of his own. Ginger and Les had all been made up to firemen and while he knew that they were ahead of him as far as seniority for promotion went, he was now anxiously waiting for his turn to be summoned to Park House in Swindon for his medical and eye test. He was the longest serving cleaner at the shed and although he was mainly rostered on firing turns, he felt left behind and missed the companionship of his friends in the cleaners' cabin.

'Don't worry, bach, it won't be long,' Dai reassured him when they were crossing the yard after finishing a turn together. 'Quite apart from anything else, there's bound to be vacancies coming up with the number of men who are thinking of leaving in order to sign up.'

For despite Neville Chamberlain's promise of peace in our time following his meeting with Adolf Hitler towards the end of 1938, there were ominous signs of war on the horizon and recruitment into the armed forces had been increasing.

But Tom had a more immediate worry than the remote possibility of war, a worry he did not share with Dai, and that was that he would fail the eye test. It was something he could not share because he did not want to bring his fears into the open.

He often ended up after a shift having a meal with Dai and Sylvia at their cottage. Sometimes he even slept over in the spare room. He loved being there, basking in the warmth and laughter that enveloped him from the moment he took his boots off to leave them inside the back door. He was happy for Dai and Sylvia, but he was also envious.

Ginger and Les both had steady girlfriends and Ginger was seriously considering marriage. Tom had been out with a couple of girls but the relationships had come to nothing for he was haunted by the memory of a short, brave, no-nonsense girl who had been his adoring slave for most of his life but who had now gone to London. He missed Maggie more than he could say, more than he would acknowledge, but it soured the few relationships he had.

******

On a bright autumn morning, Tom was operating the mechanism on the turntable, turning the pannier tank, 5774 round to face in the opposite direction. When the turn had been completed he climbed up into the cab and George drove it into the yard.

'A good trip, mate,' George remarked as he heaved his bulky figure through the gap and down the steps. Tom followed, collecting the lamps as he went.

'How do!' Ginger hailed him as he crossed the yard.

They walked over to stores together.

Tom grinned. 'You're slumming it, aren't you, chatting to a humble cleaner? I'd have thought you'd be above that now you're a fireman!'

'I like to keep my eye on things,' Ginger said easily. 'Can't trust cleaners.'

Tom threw some cotton waste at him but Ginger ducked to avoid it.

'No wonder you're not bloody made up if your aim's as bad as that! Where do you throw the coal? All over your driver's feet?'

They went into stores.

'Keys for 2928 Billy!'

Billy Hughes, bustled forwards, small eyes glinting behind his round spectacles. He was big with news. 'You heard the latest?'

'Don't tell me Joe's been having you on again,' Tom grinned.

'Oh that. Well of course he has. Always trying his tricks that one. He comes to me the other week with a face as long as a fiddle and he says, "Billy," he says, "I've lost the keys to 4912." "Where did you lose them?"' I asks. "Oh, somewhere between Matchurch and Birmingham," he says. "Pull the other one," I says, "it's got bells on it. How did you lose them?" "Well," he says, "I was leaning out watching for the distant and I must have dropped them." "You can go right back and find 'em then," I says. "What does your driver say?" "Oh same as you," he says. Then he looks at the counter. "Hang about," he says, "hang about, that's them there!" And there they were right by my hand and I would have sworn they weren't there a moment before. "You ought to be on the stage," I says. "You'd make a good magician." Billy shook his head. 'Don't know how he does it. But that wasn't what I was going to tell you...'

'What was it?'

'Haven't you heard? It's Jerry Marshall. He's going into the army. Says he wants to be ready on the front line when war's declared.'

'He's crackers,' said Ginger. 'There's not going to be a war.'

'He thinks there is. Seems his uncle or someone does something in the War Office down in London and he tells Jerry there's going to be war, whatever the Prime Minister says. So Jerry's gone and signed up.' Billy shook his head sorrowfully. 'Always been a bit of a hot head that one.'

'When's he leaving?'

'Oh soon. Where've you been, young'un, if you haven't heard the news?'

'We leave it to you to tell us Billy,' Ginger grinned. 'Better than a telegraph system you are.'

Leaving Billy rather pleased at the thought of being the chief disseminator of news around the shed, Tom and Ginger made their way to the booking on lobby.

'Jerry's uncle's probably just one of the cleaners at the War Office, who likes to pretend he knows what's going on,' Ginger remarked.

'A cleaner like me?'

'Not like you. You don't pretend you know what's going on because you walk round with your head in the clouds. I bet you don't know if you're cleaning a tankie or a tender engine half the time!'

Tom threw another piece of waste at him. This time it hit Ginger squarely in the face.

'Oh, very good! With an aim like that you might even make a fireman some day!'

They were both laughing as they entered the lobby and went to the counter.

'Book us on Fred.' Ginger turned to Tom. 'Never mind, mate, your time to leave the cleaners' cabin will come.'

Tom handed his brass disc to his father who took it without comment, then picked up a letter and handed it over.

'For you.'

Tom glanced briefly at his father before ripping open the envelope. He read it quickly then looked up.

It already has,' he told Ginger. He turned to Fred. 'Got my medical next week dad.'

'Have you,' Fred said flatly. He stared at Tom, who suddenly looked down, full of apprehension.

The following week Tom, dressed in his Sunday best, walked nervously up the steps to Park House in Swindon, which housed the imposing doctor's surgery for the Great Western Railway.

He hesitated before climbing the steps and looked up at the austere building. Then, taking a deep breath, he rang the bell.

Once inside, he was directed to a waiting room where he sat with a number of other young men, all looking equally nervous. Nobody spoke. One by one they were called in by a nurse until Tom was left alone. He fiddled with his cap and tried not to keep glancing at his watch. Eventually the door opened and the nurse beckoned to him.

'Mr Watkins? This way please.'

Tom jumped up and entered the medical examination room.

The first part went by quickly and without problem. His height and weight were checked, his reflexes tested and the doctor went through a list of possible ailments which Tom was able to answer without hesitation.

'Good,' the doctor said austerely. 'A very fit young man. All that's left is the eye test.' He handed Tom a pair of spectacles with one lens blacked out, then pointed to a chart on the wall. 'Just read the letters on the lowest line that you can.'

'U – B – Q – R – E' Tom read.

The test continued.

'All right. You can stop there,' the doctor said at last. He made some notes on his pad of paper. 'Now come over here and sit down.'

He shook out a bundle of well-used multi-coloured strands of wool and passed them across the table.

'This test is for colour blindness. I want you to sort the strands into their different shades and colours.'

Tom frowned in concentration and began the task while the doctor sat at his desk and continued writing up his notes. There was silence in the room apart from the ticking of the clock above the mantlepiece. Tom's hands started to sweat as he fumbled to sort the strands.

******

The Railwayman's Club was full when Tom entered it a week later. A noisy game of darts was in progress with spectators, drinks in hand, watching the match, making loud comments on the skill of the players. Tom pushed past them to find Ginger and Les having a pint at the bar.

'Drinks are on me!' Tom said, giving each of them a thump on the back.

'You old bugger! You've been made up!'

They shook Tom's hand vigorously.

There was a babble of voices as people he knew crowded round to congratulate him.

'I said you'd have no trouble.' Ginger said complacently, as Tom took his glass to have it refilled.

'Did you?' I wasn't so sure.'

He looked round the pub contentedly, then caught sight of Fred and Charlie sitting in an out-of-the-way corner of the room, a chess board between them. He hesitated for a moment then went over to them.

'Dad. I've been made up.'

'Congratulations.' Fred's eyes remained on the board.

Tom bit his lip. 'What'll you have? You too Charlie.'

'Nothing for me,' Fred said flatly.

Charlie beamed. 'Good old Tom. I'll have a pint, ta.'

Tom left them to go over to the bar.

'Your move Charlie.'

'Bet you're proud, eh?' Charlie asked, moving his knight.

Fred didn't answer and they played on in silence.

'Here you are,' Tom said, threading his way through the crowds. He handed the drink over, and Charlie took it appreciatively.

'Ta. Well, here's to you. Chip off the old block, eh?'

They both looked at Fred but he appeared to be engrossed in working out his next move.

'How's the shop doing Charlie?' Tom asked.

'Coming along nicely, thanks for asking,' Charlie replied. 'Maisie's that made up with it. She says it's nice having me under her feet all day.' He shrugged. 'Can't understand it. I thought that's the last thing women wanted. To have their men under their feet all the time.'

Tom laughed.

'Your turn, Charlie,' Fred said impatiently.

'What's that? Oh, right...'

Tom hesitated for a moment but as Fred showed no sign of noticing him, he returned to the bar.

Fred stood up. 'I've had enough tonight. Your game.'

'Suit yourself.' Charlie began to collect the pieces together.

'I'll be on my way,' Fred grunted.

Charlie looked up. 'Half a mo and I'll see you up the road.'

Fred bit back an angry retort.

'I'll be all right. You stay.'

Slowly and with care he made his way out of the pub and walked up the road.

When he arrived home he heard the piano being played in the parlour. He lent against the back door and listened. It was Chopin, Nocturne No 2 in E#, a favourite piece of Nancy's. He looked up at the night sky. If he looked hard and squinted he could just make out the occasional pinprick of a star. Surely there couldn't be much wrong with his eyesight if he could see the stars, he thought fleetingly. The hope raised by the thought soon went. He straightened up and the music stopped when the back door banged shut behind him.

'Tom? Is that you Tom?' Nancy called out.

'He's down the Club,' Fred entered the room and sat wearily in his chair by the fire. Nancy turned to him eagerly.

'How did he get on? Did he say?'

'Your son's a fireman.'

'That's wonderful isn't it.'

Fred didn't reply.

'Isn't it? Fred?'

'Oh yes,' he said at last. 'It's wonderful.'

'Fred...? It's what you always wanted isn't it? For Tom to follow in your footsteps? Fred...? What's wrong?'

'What the hell do you think is wrong?' Fred said violently.

'But... this hasn't anything to do with... aren't you pleased... for Tom's sake?'

Fred stared into the fire and didn't answer.

'Oh Fred... that's not fair...'

'Nothing's bloody fair in this world! Nothing! If it was, would I be going blind? Would I? What's fair about that? You tell me? What have I done to deserve that?'

'I know...' Nancy said gently.

'You know! You know! What do you know? You know nothing about how I feel... nothing! There's this... this... anger inside... and it's tearing me up...'

Nancy went over to him and put a hand on his shoulder, but Fred, rigid, unyielding, didn't seem to notice.

'There's other things Fred... it isn't everything...'

'It is everything! To me it is. Everything!'

Nancy turned away and closed the piano lid.

'So our marriage counts for nothing. Neither do our children,' she said sadly.

Fred glanced at her, then away. 'With this... this thing... I'm not the person you married, Nance. I'm not Fred Watkins. What you've got is an old man sitting round the house waiting... just waiting for the darkness to close in. That's what you've got.'

Nancy sat down opposite him.

'To me you're the same. Inside, you're the same...'

'You expect me to believe that? What the hell d'you take me for Nance?'

He got up and went out, slamming the door. Nancy half rose as if to follow him, then sank back in the chair.

******

Much later that evening Tom, Ginger and Les were to be found sitting in a bus shelter opposite the station. Les had fallen asleep and Tom and Ginger had lit cigarettes.

'Y'know Tom mate,' Ginger said after a ruminative silence. 'there's three of us... you... me... an' Les... been through school together... always mates... always chums... now we're all made up to firemen... d'you think we'll be made up to driver together?'

Tom thought about it.

'Don't know,' he said at last.

'Course we will. Next thing is, we'll be getting' married. You thinkin' of getting' married, Les?'

Les snored gently.

'Well I'm thinkin' of it. If Rosie'll have me. I'm goin' to get married. Think I'll go and ask her.'

He stubbed out his cigarette purposefully and made to stand up. Tom pushed him back on to the seat.

'You can't ask her now.'

'Why not?'

'She wouldn't like it.'

'Yes she would,' Ginger said stubbornly.

'She wouldn't. Or her parents wouldn't.'

'I'm not asking her parents to marry me,' Ginger replied with the logic of someone who has had too much to drink. 'I'm going to ask Rosie.'

'It's the middle of the bloody night, man!'

Ginger blinked. 'Is it? Oh. I'll have to ask her tomorrow.'

'It is tomorrow.'

Les grunted, woke, stood up and walked off without a word.

'Think he's all right?' Tom asked watching him anxiously.

''Course he is. Old Les... always all right...' he sighed. 'You thinkin' of getting' married?'

Tom shook his head.

'Why not?' 'S good idea.'

'I haven't got a girl.'

Ginger stared at him in disbelief.

'You haven't... yes you have! What about Iso... whatever her name is?'

'That's over.'

'Is it? You should've told me... that's what mates are for...'

'I did tell you.'

'Did you? Oh yes. Well...' he stopped to think. 'Well, what about Maggie? Little Maggie, who always fancied you. Little Maggie... funny little thing the way she used to trot after us when we was little...'

Tom stood up abruptly and began to walk away. Ginger looked up, surprised, then followed.

'What happened to her? Little Maggie?'

'She went to London,' Tom said briefly.

'What she want to do that for?' He thought about it for a moment. 'Funny things, women.'

324

'Look, just leave it will you?' Tom spoke more sharply than he'd intended. Ginger was taken aback.

'Sorry mate. Didn't know you felt like that. Thought it was all one-sided... her side.'

Tom said nothing.

'You been to see her? In London?'

Tom shrugged. 'Don't know her address.'

'That's no excuse. Old man Thomas'll give it to you.'

Tom walked on in silence.

'She won't want to see me,' he said at last.

Ginger flung his arm round Tom's shoulder. 'Ah...but you don't know 'til you try, mate... you just don't know...'

******

Tom stood across the road from the vast bulk of Whitely's Department Store in West London. It was huge, stretching along two sides of a block, its impressive, rounded corner with its equally impressive entrance looking like the prow of a ship. He shook his head, unable to see Maggie working in such a place. Perhaps he should not have come. It was a mad thing to do, taken on the spur of the moment when he had had too much to drink and in the low that follows the aftermath of euphoria at passing the medical and being made up to fireman. Now where, he wondered, staring up at it, would he find the back entrance – the one used by the staff?

He crossed the road and walked slowly up and down both sides of the building but it wasn't until he saw a couple of girls coming out of a recessed door that he found it. He lit a cigarette and stood to one side, watching as another group of girls left the building, chattering. They broke off their talk to eye Tom appreciatively as they passed.

Tom waited, nervously smoking, plagued by doubts. At last she came out. Thankfully she was alone. He flicked away the half-smoked cigarette.

Smartly dressed in a navy two-piece outfit, cream blouse and matching hat, gloves, shoes and bag, Maggie looked older and extremely sophisticated. Her brown hair had been styled in fashionable marcel waves. At first she did not appear to notice him and, for a second, Tom wondered whether to let her pass without speaking. She looked like a stranger... He swallowed and stepped forwards.

'Maggie...'

She turned, giving a start of surprise.

'Tom!'

'I – I hope you don't mind. I... came to see you.'

She stared at him.

'Look, can we go somewhere...? A cup of tea...?' He broke off, nervously.

'I haven't long,' she said guardedly. 'But... all right.'

'I hope you know where to go. I don't know London at all.'

'There's a Lyons Tea Shop just up the road.'

They walked silently up Queensway, Maggie looking straight ahead, a slight frown on her face and Tom taking small glances at her from time to time, unable to believe that this was the person he had known all his life.

He followed her into the tea shop and they sat down at a table in the window.

Tom beckoned the waitress. 'Two teas please.'

'Anything to eat?' The waitress, sharp-eyed and neatly dressed in black with white apron, collar and cuffs, looked from one to the other expectantly.

Tom looked enquiringly at Maggie, but she was staring down at the table and did not reply.

'No thank you.'

When the waitress had gone, Maggie gave a sigh.

'How did you know where I work?'

'Your aunt told me.'

They were silent.

'How are you?' Tom asked tentatively.

'Very well.'

'You look well,' Tom said. 'Different...' Maggie did not help him. 'Your clothes... and your hair... I nearly didn't recognise you.'

'Not a kid any more?' she asked quietly. Tom bit his lip and there was a prolonged, painful silence.

'Here we are then,' the waitress said brightly, putting the tray down on the table with a thump.

'Thank you.'

'Shall I pour for you?'

'No. Thank you. We'll manage.'

The waitress went and, after a moment, Maggie took off her gloves and poured out the tea.

'Your dad gave me your aunt's address,' Tom explained.

'Did he.'

'He didn't want to. Said you wouldn't want to be bothered...' There was the hint of a question in his voice.

They both fell silent again.

'Look Tom,' Maggie said at last, 'it was very nice of you to have taken all this trouble, but you shouldn't have come. Really.'

'I had to see you.'

'How long are you down here?' she asked after another silence.

'Half an hour.'

'Half an hour,' she echoed in disbelief.

'Well... forty minutes. I'm working tonight.'

'And you came all this way just for forty minutes?'

'I couldn't find your aunt's house to begin with,' he said apologetically. 'Then I got on the wrong bus and then I had to wait 'til you'd finished work. I thought I'd missed you altogether.'

'Oh Tom...' Maggie was touched. 'It's no distance from Paddington Station.'

'I know that now. I sailed past it on the bus. I didn't expect you'd be working anywhere quite so grand.'

Bit of a change from Purvis & Purvis?' she asked wryly.

Tom took a deep breath. 'Those things you said... when you left...'

'I said things I shouldn't have. Things perhaps better never said at all.' She paused. 'I heard you'd been made up.'

'You heard... who told you?'

She didn't answer that.

'You must be pleased.'

'Yes.' He paused. 'Have you been home?'

Once or twice,' she said, not looking at him.

'To see Jim?'

Maggie stiffened.

'I'm sorry. It's none of my business.'

'That's right. It's none of your business.'

'Maggie...'

'I told you. You don't own me. I left because I didn't want to be trapped... I wanted to escape... Besides,' she added with a slight smile. 'They didn't need me any more at home.'

'You mean...'

'She's very nice. Dad's lady. Her name's Dorothy – Dot - and she's really nice. I didn't expect to like her, but I do. Her husband was killed in the war and she and Joey took to each other straight away. I think she wanted children, but her husband died before they could have any. Joey'll be all right. Dad too. I'm glad for them. Really.'

'Was that why...?'

Maggie shrugged. 'Well, that... and other things. Mr Sneller didn't want me to leave but he gave me a reference, which was good of him as I left in a bit of a hurry.'

'And have you...?'

'What?'

'Escaped?'

She evaded the question.

'London's very big. And exciting. Auntie Betty has been very kind. She works at Whiteleys as under-manageress and got me a job. The reference helped. And it's the same sort of thing I was doing at Purvis. I'm in the Haberdashery Department. It took a while to get used to it, but...' she shrugged. 'It's all right.'

He had never heard her speak so much but that was, he realised to his shame, that he had never given her a chance. She was speaking too quickly and her hand, as she took the cup, was trembling. Tom suddenly realised that, despite her apparent sophistication, Maggie was as nervous as himself.

'The girls are very nice and I've made heaps of friends,' she said defiantly.

'I'm glad.' There was a pause. 'I'd better go. Mustn't miss my train.'

Maggie did not reply.

'Can I come and see you again?' Tom asked, hesitantly.

'No Tom... not like this. Please.'

'Will you come back?'

'I don't know. Not yet.'

Tom stood. 'I must go.' He hesitated. 'Have you got to go back to work? Can I walk you down the road?'

'No. I'm...I'm meeting a friend,' she said. It was the first excuse that came to mind.

'Oh. I see... Well, goodbye... all the best...'

He hesitated then turned and left the café. He did not look back. If he had, he would have seen that tears were running down Maggie's face.

The waitress came hurrying over. 'Your young man left without paying.'

'Did he? I'm sorry.'

'Two cups of tea – that'll be sixpence.'

Maggie groped for her bag, took out her purse and paid.

'Had a row dearie? Never mind. They always come back and if they don't there's plenty more fish in the sea I say.'

'No. Not a row. Excuse me.' Maggie got up hastily and hurried out.

Chapter Twenty

When Tom arrived with the lamps he found Dai busy preparing the Collett 0-6-0 goods engine 3205. He looked up and waved the oilcan in Tom's direction.

'Hello there brother-in-law!'

'Hello Dai.'

Tom climbed onto the footplate and inspected the fire while Dai carried on oiling the engine, whistling under his breath. When he had finished, he joined Tom in the cab.

'I think it's all a plot to keep me from my wife,' Dai grumbled good-naturedly.

'What is?'

'A double home turn. But it does mean extra pay which can't be bad.'

'How is Sylvie?'

'Lovely as ever.' Dai looked at Tom with mock severity. 'Now then what bad habits have you picked up? Haven't been rostered with you as my mate for some time.'

'I'm made up I'll have you know!'

'So am I and I'm in charge, so I'll have no back chat from you, my lad.'

Tom laughed.

After they had finished preparing the engine, Dai took it over to the sidings where they picked up a train of goods wagons and waited as Alfie, the guard, came over.

'Busy night ahead of us.' Dai called down.

Alfie grunted.

'I'll be stopping for a moment at Meadows Crossing,' Dai informed him.

Alfie grunted again and walked back down the train, checking that the wagon brakes were off before climbing into the brake van and giving the 'right away'.

'What's up with him?' Dai asked as he drove the train slowly out of the yard. 'He's like a bear with a sore head.'

Tom was checking the water level. 'Told me he's got toothache.'

The sun was beginning to set when they reached Meadows Crossing where Sylvia and Lil were waiting. Sylvia was holding an empty coal bucket which she waved in greeting. Dai closed the regulator and the train came to a stand.

'Hello my lovely.' He lent over the side of the cab, took the bucket and passed it to Tom.

'Fill it up Tom will you.'

He jumped off the footplate and gave Sylvia a quick hug.

'All right?'

'Fine.' Sylvia beamed.

Tom handed down the full bucket of coal.

'Thanks Tom.'

'Can you manage it?' Dai asked anxiously. 'I'd take it up for you but, regretfully, I have this train to drive.'

Sylvia laughed. 'Shame! We'll manage between us. And then we're putting on our glad rags and going to paint the town red. Lil wants to see Fred Astaire and Ginger Rogers. They're showing '*The Story of Vernon and Irene Castle*'.

'Such lovely dancers,' put in Lil.

'Wish we could come with you. Have a lovely time girls, and don't do anything I wouldn't do.'

A quick kiss and he climbed back into the cab.

'Look after yourselves!' Sylvia called as Dai blew the whistle and, with a deep-throated 'chuff' the goods train departed.

As the track curved round, Tom looked back towards the small cottage, nestling comfortably within its surrounding green fields. The evening sun shone golden against the white walls and neat white fence that circled the building and its windows reflected back the glow. Tom could see late rambling roses still flowering around the front door. The sight brought back half-forgotten memories. Behind the cottage, the fields led up the ridge to Chalcote Woods where, high above the trees, clouds were forming, dark against the purpling sky.

Tom glanced at Dai who was smiling as he watched the road ahead, his hand on the regulator, the picture of a contented man. Tom felt a twinge of envy. As if aware of his glance, Dai looked across.

'Watch out for the back 'un Tom, we're almost due.'

The rest of the evening was spent setting down and picking up goods wagons and it was late at night by the time they dropped off the final wagons into the siding at Malmbury, drove the engine on to the ashpit and climbed down from the cab.

'Hope your tooth's better in the morning!' Tom called as Alfie came past.

'A slug of whisky'll soon settle it,' Alfie muttered. 'Been looking forward to it for the past two hours.'

He waved his hand and disappeared into the engine shed.

'Don't know where he thinks he'll get a drink,' Tom commented as they followed Alfie to the booking on lobby. 'The pubs shut hours ago.'

'He's probably left a bottle with his landlady,' Dai replied. 'Always stays with Cissie Brooks when he ends up in Malmbury.' He laughed. 'There was a joke going round the shed that she warmed his bed for him, but seeing Ciss, to say nothing of her twenty stone husband, I can't believe it's true. Anyway Alfie's devoted to his wife and kids.'

They entered the lobby.

'Chalcote men booking off,' Dai said to the sleepy timekeeper, who gave a couple of large yawns as he signed them off.

'Quiet night, here, tonight,' he said in explanation. 'Makes me tired if there's nowt goin' on.'

They said goodnight and left the shed. As they walked along the quiet, deserted street, their footsteps echoed loudly.

'How did Joe and Lil come to live in their cottage?' Tom asked. 'It's not a railway one is it?'

Dai shook his head. 'It belongs to Lil. It was her grandparents' house. They farmed a lot of the land round there but her grandmother had to sell most of it when her husband died young.'

'I'd like to live somewhere like that,' Tom said. 'Out in the country.'

'It's worked out well for us and I'm glad Lil and Sylvia get on. Although the way they gang up on me I'm not at all sure I did the right thing suggesting we move in,' Dai added, grinning.

They turned into a terraced row of houses and a few minutes later Dai opened the front gate to one of them and they went up the path. As they reached the door, two men came out and grunted as they passed Tom and Dai.

'At least the beds'll be warm,' Dai remarked dryly as they went through the hall and into the kitchen.

Dai lit the gas lamps while Tom looked round. It was spotlessly clean but judging by the worn mat and much-darned chair covers, the owner was fairly hard up.

Dai went over to the kitchen range and looked into the fire. It was almost dead. He rummaged in a box at the side, took out a couple of pieces of coal and placed them in the grate.

'Put the kettle on Tom, I'm gasping,' he said as he poked the fire into life.

Tom busied himself filling the kettle. He rinsed out the two cups and saucers that were in the sink.

'The delights of the double home turn,' Dai said wryly. 'To think I could be tucked up cosily in bed with my lovely wife.'

'It's my first trip away,' Tom admitted, hunting for, and finding the tea caddy and spooning tea into the pot.

'Is it now?' Dai went to the sink and washed his hands and face, gasping at the cold water. 'A new experience for you Tom. Your education as a railwaymen is about to be completed. It's my first trip away as a driver but I've stayed here many times as a fireman. Got that tea made yet?'

Tom poured out two cups then took his turn at the sink, while Dai pulled up a chair and stretched himself out with a sigh of relief.

'I'm thinking of writing a poem about double home lodgings. An elegy maybe...' He laughed. 'Perhaps a dirge would be more appropriate.' He reached out for his cup. 'Mind, this one's not so bad. Annie's the widow of a railwayman. She'll give us a good breakfast.'

Tom drew up a chair and sat down. They relaxed in the companionable silence of people who had been working hard together and were tired but needed to unwind before sleep. It was the time for confidences, for letting down the barriers.

Tom stirred. 'Can I ask you something?' he said diffidently.

'Ask away.'

'What's it... what's it like, being married?'

Dai looked into the fire.

'I'm not the best person to ask as I'm so new at it.' He stopped to think. 'It's...finding out about each other...learning to compromise...caring for someone other than yourself...realising just how selfish you really are.' He grinned wryly. 'It's...being vulnerable... All the different masks we hide behind...all the defences we put up... all being stripped away...leaving the things we most despise about ourselves...

the things we spend our lives trying to hide from the rest of the world... leaving those things exposed and liable to be used against us.' He stopped and hunted for the right words. 'It's having enough honesty with each other to recognise that fact and enough trust to believe that it won't be abused... it's not an easy thing...'

He stopped and looked at Tom quizzically.

'Not the answer you expected, is it?'

Tom stirred. 'I went out with someone once. I felt... I felt she knew about those things, the things I try to hide... and despised them... and me...'

'Isobel?'

Tom nodded.

'I hope you're not still going out with her,' Dai said lightly and Tom shook his head.

Dai sighed. 'It's... in one sense... growing up... in another, remaining a child, knowing that one other person in this whole lonely world worries about you, cares what happens to you and loves you, not for what you might be, or for what you pretend to be... but for what you are... and despite all that, still loves you, warts and all.'

Tom thought of Maggie, listening earnestly to him when he had poured out his troubles. How selfish, how utterly selfish he had been. What was it she had said? 'Love? You don't know the meaning of the word!'

Dai broke into his thoughts. 'You should never ask a Welshman to define anything at three in the morning,' he said dryly. He looked at Tom.

'So how's things at home?'

'All right.'

'Fred?'

Tom was silent for a moment.

'I don't know,' he said at last.

'Mmm. I thought it best to keep clear of him since we came back from Bristol.'

'You're probably right. He's built a wall round himself and no-one can get through. Not even mum.' Tom frowned. 'I sometimes thinks he hates me... No, that's not true... I think he hates himself... God knows why, it's not as if he could have helped what happened.'

He swirled round the dregs of his tea. 'Did you know that the disease dad's got is hereditary?' he said at last. 'That I might get it?'

Dai was suddenly still, his cup halfway to his lips.

'What about Sylvia?' he asked, after a pause.

Tom shook his head. 'I don't know. Dad didn't say.'

'Does she know?'

Tom shook his head. 'Not unless dad told her and I don't think he did. I don't even think mum knows. He had to force himself to tell me and it just hasn't been talked about at home. I'm sorry. I never thought...'

'Why should you? But it's time someone thought about her,' Dai said, bitterly. Tom looked at him, surprised. He had never known Dai to be anything but easy-going, someone who looked at the world with gentle, ironic tolerance and self-mocking humour.

'Will you tell her?'

Dai considered it, then sighed. He suddenly looked older. 'Probably. She's a right to know and we don't have secrets from each other.' He squared his shoulders as he came to a decision. 'I'll have to talk to Fred.'

Tom stared into the dying fire. 'It... it shook me up no end when dad told me.' He paused. 'I might go blind and there's nothing I can do about it.' He gripped his cup more tightly. 'I couldn't sleep at nights thinking... especially just before the medical...' He stopped and shrugged. 'Well, if it happens, it happens. There's nothing I can do... nothing at all...'

Dai stood up and refilled their cups. He handed one to Tom.

'Thanks.' Tom gripped it hard. 'It's made me understand a bit what dad's going through. I only wish I could help...'

They were silent for a moment.

'I'll tell you something,' Dai confided, 'but only because it's three in the morning and we're unburdening our souls, but don't pass it around. Sylvia's expecting... we're expecting...'

'Is she? Are you?' Tom did not quite know what to say.

'So you'll be an uncle.'

'Will I? I suppose I will.'

'It's early days and I haven't told anyone else.' Dai grinned wryly. 'Soon as mam and my sisters get the news they'll be on their way armed with stacks of advice and laden with baby clothes. And don't tell Nancy or Fred yet – we want to do it in our own time.'

'Course not.'

Honoured by Dai's confidence, but also slightly uncomfortable at the turn the conversation had taken, Tom stood up.

'This calls for another cup of tea.'

'We'll be floating in it. Pity we haven't got Alfie's whisky.'

Tom boiled the kettle and made a fresh pot.

'How do you know if you love someone?' he suddenly blurted out, handing over the cup and saucer. 'How can you be sure?'

Dai considered it. 'That I can't tell you. It's a bit like asking about the existence of God. You either know or you don't. And even when you do know it's not a once and for all thing. It's not roses round the door and they lived happily ever after. Nothing in life is that simple or that black and white. It has to be worked at and protected and cared for, like anything if it's to have any worth, any meaning, any permanence...'

A coal dropped, unnoticed, in the grate, otherwise there was silence in the room.

'Maggie said to me...' Tom stopped, embarrassed. 'Just someone I know... she said everyone's only got a certain amount of love to give... and when that's used up there isn't any more...'

Dai looked at him.

'Everyone has an infinite capacity to love...' he said gently, 'at least, I've found it so with Sylvia...'

Tom swallowed but said nothing.

'You don't know your danger Tom,' Dai said lightly. 'Given half the chance I'll keep you up all night discussing the meaning of life... but I'll still expect you to fire 3205 with a heavy load on tomorrow.'

He stood and picked up the cups.

'Go to bed. The room's at the top of the stairs on the left. I'll wash these and leave a note for Annie. Is a call at 10.30 all right? We've got to book on at 12.15.'

'That's fine.' Tom got up then hesitated.

'Night Dai. And thanks.'

'Night. Oh..' He called out as Tom was at the door. 'And take your boots off! You won't get any breakfast if you grind cinders into Annie's carpet!'

Tom grinned, slipped off his boots and went to bed.

******

The accident happened the following afternoon as Dai and Tom were on their way back to Acton Chalcote, heading a long train of goods wagons.

Tom was looking out of his side of the cab for the home signal to Crosley Station.

'He's got it on here Dai.'

Dai shut off the regulator as the home signal was set at danger and the train slowed. The signal changed to clear and the train gently steamed into the station.

The signalman was already out of his box and standing by the track, arm outstretched as he held out the token for the next section.

'The passenger's running round at Hampton Lacey,' he said as he and Tom exchanged tokens. 'He should be away before you get there.'

'Righto mate.'

The signalman returned to his box, pulled the starter signal to green and the goods train departed southbound.

After a level stretch of track skirting the river, they turned away and began the climb up the bank. It was slow going and Tom had to work hard to keep the fire up. He stopped for a minute to straighten his back and Dai grinned at him.

'Nearly over the top mate.'

They entered the tunnel and the light was suddenly cut off apart from the glow from the fire and the dim light of the gauge lamp. Shortly after, a pinpoint of light ahead of them grew and grew and the train burst out of the tunnel and into broad daylight. The summit was reached and the train began its descent.

Tom put on the lefthand injector and opened the firebox doors. He examined the fire, then turned to reach for the shovel. Dai turned the blower on and then closed the regulator to cut off power for the descent. Suddenly there was the sound of a very loud bang and flames and much of the contents of the fire shot out from the open firebox and on to the floor of the cab.

Tom was thrown violently backwards towards the tender and cried out as his right arm hit the metal side. Dai flung up his arm for protection against the force of the blast at the same time as he turned off the blower. He was thrown backwards. He hit his head on the front of the tender and collapsed, unconscious, to the floor.

The pain in Tom's arm was almost overpowering. He got to his feet, gritting his teeth as he tried to work out what had happened. He took a deep breath to overcome a rising sense of panic. What to do? What to do first? Burning coals had spread across the footplate and there was Dai...how bad was he? Tom took another deep breath and through the haze of pain and panic he could almost hear the calm voice of Frank Bateson speaking at one of the MIC classes. Brake – put the brake on. He staggered over the coals to the tender handbrake and screwed it on, using his left hand as his right arm hung uselessly. Wonder if I've broken it, he thought fleetingly before grabbing the chain to sound the brake whistle. He began blowing repeated 'pop' whistles to attract Alfie's attention.

The engine began to slow and Tom heard the clank, clank as the loose-coupled wagons bumped against each other.

The floor of the cab was starting to smoulder. Tom re-crossed the footplate and dragged Dai back towards the tender. He bent down to him. Dai was alive but deeply concussed. The burning coals under Tom's boots were beginning to blaze up and he began to feel the heat against his legs. Smoke was obscuring his vision. He grabbed the pep pipe and doused the first flickering flames then reached for the driver's brake handle crying out as he hit his right arm.

The train came to a stand. Tom hung over the side, eyes streaming from the smoke, gasping for air. Looking ahead he saw that the distant signal was set at green.

Alfie, meanwhile, had rushed to the side of the guard's van and screwed down his brake before leaping out and running to the engine, pinning down the wagon brakes as he went. When he reached the cab, Tom was already climbing off the footplate.

'Blowback!' he shouted to Alfie. 'Got to telephone.'

Without waiting for an answer he began running along the track towards the signal.

'Dai...?' Alfie called.

'Unconscious,' Tom shouted back briefly.

Dai. Should he have told Alfie not to move him, Tom wondered as he ran. Never move anyone with a head injury, he remembered from his training. With a sickening sense of shock he realised that he himself had dragged Dai back to the tender, out of the way of the burning coals. But what else could he have done? Say he had injured Dai further, say his neck was broken? How could he ever face him? How could he ever face Sylvia? His breath came in short, anguished bursts.

He reached the home signal. Using his left hand to cradle the telephone to his shoulder he phoned the signalman.

'3205 reporting a blowback.'

A concerned voice sounded in his ear. 'I was wondering what had happened to you. Where are you, driver?'

'About 200 yards before the distant. And I'm not the driver. He's unconscious. I'm the fireman. Fireman Watkins. I've stopped the train.'

There was a moment's silence.

'Right. There's an empty siding at the far end of the station. I'll put you into it if you feel able to drive.'

'Yes... I...' Tom leaned against the signal. Sweat was pouring down his face. The track ahead of him seemed to be moving... shimmering... the light... going in and out... He closed his eyes. The signalman's voice steadied him.

'Fireman Watkins, are you able to drive?'

Tom opened his eyes. 'Yes... yes I'm sure I can...'

'Are you all right?'

'My arm... broken I think... but I'm... all right.'

'Good lad. Get the train in to the siding and help will be waiting. Where's the guard?'

'By the engine.'

'Tell him to travel with you in the cab. Got that?'

'Yes... yes...'

Tom put the phone back and set off back down the track. He went more slowly, suddenly conscious of burning pain around his ankles. His arm, mercifully, was numb.

A concerned Alfie ran to meet him.

'Got to take the train into the siding.'

'I've cleared the coal from the footplate but didn't want to touch Dai,' Alfie replied. 'He looks all right but he's deep in the land of nod.'

'Probably for the best,' Tom said, wincing as he climbed back up into the cab.

'What about you?'

Tom didn't answer that. 'We're on a downward gradient so we'll just roll her into the siding. Can you travel with me in the cab?'

Alfie shot him a worried look. ''Course. I'll just get the wagon brakes knocked off and take off the brake in the van. I'll be straight back.'

He set off at a run.

Tom checked what remained of the fire in the firebox, his movements slow, automatic. He was suddenly so tired... so very, very tired...

He checked the water level then waited for Alfie.

'This'll be one for the history books,' Alfie said as he climbed up. 'A cack-handed fireman and a guard.'

Tom tried to smile. He glanced back down the track, then forwards. All clear. He unscrewed the handbrake, put the engine into forward gear and gave the regulator a slight touch. The train began to move and Tom closed the regulator. His right arm started to throb. Don't think about it, he said to himself. I'm all right. I'm driving this train and we're going to get safely off the main line. He glanced over to Alfie. Was it only yesterday they had taken the train to Malmbury and spent the night...? It seemed like years ago.

'How's your toothache,' he asked suddenly.

Alfie grinned. 'Gone. Nice of you to ask. Nothing like a bit of excitement to make you forget your pains.'

Tom looked ahead, his left hand on the regulator.

Wish I could forget mine, he thought.

As they approached the siding Tom put his hand on the engine brake. He glanced fleetingly at Dai as the train crossed the points, hoping the jolting had not injured him further.

Alfie looked back along the length of the train. 'I'll tell you when we're inside.'

On Alfie's signal, Tom applied the brake. The train stopped.

'Handbrake?' Alfie asked.

Tom nodded and Alfie screwed it down then Tom put the engine into mid gear so that it would not move.

'Quite a welcoming party,' Alfie commented as he took in the waiting ambulance and the group of people who were hurrying towards them.

Tom slowly began to climb down. He missed the step but he was caught and held by firm, comforting hands as darkness swept over him.

******

White. The walls were white, the bed was white, and the lady, standing beside the bed, was dressed in white with a white headdress shaped like wings. Tom gingerly opened his eyes a little wider. His legs hurt and out of the corner of his eye he could see the edge of a white bandage. He squinted down. His arm, encased in plaster, was also white.

'Just five minutes,' the lady said severely and left the room.

Tom turned his head a little and blinked at the sun pouring in through the window, illuminating Nancy and Sylvia. They turned concerned faces towards him and moved towards the bed.

Tom turned his head the other way. Dai was standing by his bedside. He was unhurt, apart from a few scratches and scald marks to his face.

'Dai...' Tom began. His voice sounded strange, even to himself. 'Dai... I thought...'

'Don't try to talk or that dragon of a Sister will throw us out,' Dai said in a stage whisper.

'What happened?'

'Call yourself a fireman and you don't know what happened? The blower pipe burst.'

Tom gave a slight nod and closed his eyes, then opened them.

'Are you alright?'

Dai grinned. 'Apart from a knock on the head which my wife says has taught me some sense.'

'I thought... I thought... I shouldn't have moved you...'

'If you hadn't I'd have probably burnt to death,' Dai said cheerfully. 'There's lucky you were to have turned away from the firebox else you'd have got the full force,' he added sombrely.

Sylvia took Tom's hand. 'Tom...oh Tom...you saved his life...' she said, slightly tearfully.

Tom shook his head slightly.

Sylvia looked up. 'What does he mean?'

'He thinks he's no hero.' Dai explained.

Tom's frowned suddenly as he looked at Sylvia. There was something.. something unfinished.. something that needed to be said...

'Sylvie...?'

'Not now.' Dai's voice was firm as he put his arm round Sylvia.

He was so tired. His eyes wandered round, past the big bunch of flowers on his bedside table to focus on Nancy.

'Mum...'

345

She kissed him. 'I'm here, dear.'

Tom's looked past her. There was someone else in the room...

'Dad...?'

Alfie came forwards, a box of chocolates in his hand.

'Plucky lad you were. I've told them what happened.'

The door opened and the Sister came in, starched clothes rustling with indignation.

'Five minutes I said.' She held open the door.

'We'll look in tonight.' Dai promised as he went.

Tom closed his eyes and slept. He was woken by the sound of rain spattering against the window. It was dark outside.

The door opened. It was his father. Tom watched as he crossed the room, treading heavily. He stopped beside the bed and there was a long silence as they looked at one another.

'Brought you some chocolates,' Fred said, his voice sounding hoarse. 'But I see you've got plenty.' He put them down beside the flowers. There was another long silence. Fred turned away.

Tom pulled himself up in the bed. 'Dad...it's not that bad...'

'I'm sorry.' Fred cleared his throat and turned back to Tom. 'They wouldn't let me see you before... until they'd patched you up, and I didn't want to come at the same time as your mum and the others.'

He stopped again. Tom watched him, conscious of a change in him, then grimaced as a shaft of pain went up through his arm. He moved his legs. They felt as if they were on fire.

'You did a brave thing...Dai was telling me...'

'Dai?' Tom repeated, surprised.

'We've been talking...Dai and me...' Fred stopped again. 'I've been wrong about a lot of things.'

He walked over to the window and stared out at the rain streaming down the pane.

'This has taught me...' he went on in a low voice. Tom had to strain to hear him. 'I've been... so bloody caught up in my own troubles...' He sighed. 'I've had my life... and it's been a good one, by and large. And I've enjoyed it. I've driven some bloody fine engines in my time. Bloody fine... I've got that to look back on...'

'Dad...there's no need...' Tom said urgently.

'There is a need...' Fred insisted. He turned to face Tom. 'I've behaved... badly... to you and to everyone... but especially to you.' He stopped. 'This has taught me... I've had my life... you're only starting. And now..'

'Now what?' Tom asked, feeling a prickle of fear.

'... you might never get the chance...'

There was silence in the room.

'What do you mean... the blindness...?' Tom asked, more urgently.

Fred turned to him. 'Not that. They haven't told you? Perhaps I shouldn't have...'

'Told me...? Told me what...?' Tom demanded.

Fred sighed. 'Your arm's been badly smashed up. They don't know if you'll get back on the footplate.'

Tom closed his eyes as his father went over to the bed, sat down beside him, and placed a gnarled and calloused hand over his.

******

A few weeks later Tom crossed Barney's Bridge and trod the well-worn path of cinders which led across the waste ground towards the end of the station. He was only limping slightly, aided by the crutch under his left arm. His right arm, in plaster, was in a sling, and his legs, which had suffered burns, were still encased in bandages. He went through the gate and along the walkway towards the yard.

He paused to watch a tankie taking on water. It was mid-afternoon and the yard had a sleepy, somnolent feel, shimmering in a haze of summer heat.

He walked on towards the shed and paused again. A 4-4-0 Duke passed, green paint and copper chimney gleaming in the sun, wisps of near-invisible steam disappearing into the blue sky, wheels pounding down on the tracks.

He breathed in the smell of hot oil, smoke and soot and turned into the shed.

Thoughtful and composed, he walked to Ben Goodey's office, knocked on the door and went inside.

Ben looked up. There was a moment's silence.

'Ah Tom. Glad to see you're up and about again.'

'Yes sir.'

'Come and sit down.' He regarded Tom. 'How long before that plaster comes off?'

'Another two weeks, sir.'

'Well that's not too long.' Ben paused. 'And your legs?'

'Mending.'

Ben looked at him in silence for a moment.

'You know about the Inquiry, don't you? You'll be asked to give evidence.'

'Yes. I've been told.'

'Good.' Ben smilled. 'You did very well lad. Very well. We're all proud of you. I expect you'll receive a commendation.'

Tom, embarrassed, looked down, then summoning up his courage, he looked back up at Ben and took a deep breath.

'I will - I will be able to go back on the footplate... won't I?'

There was a moment's silence.

'I hope so lad,' Ben said gently. 'The railway needs lads like you. We'll just have to see how that arm of yours shapes up.'

Tom said nothing.

348

'You want to go back on the footplate, even after what happened?' Ben questioned. 'I wouldn't have been surprised if it hadn't put you off the job for life.'

'I want to go back.' Tom said firmly.

'Well... take it easy for a bit and we'll just have to see... there are other jobs you know... other areas you could go into...'

Tom shook his head.

'I want to be a driver,' he said simply. Then, more firmly. 'I'm going to be a driver.'

He left the office and the shed and stood, once again looking round, drinking in the sights and smells.

5774 came up alongside.

Tom! Here Tom!' Ginger was waving frantically from the footplate. 'Good to see you mate!'

Tom smiled and raised his good hand as Ginger played *'On Ilkly Moor Ba T'at'* on the whistle.

Other people were around and, as Tom crossed the barrow crossing, he was hailed by many of them.

'All right lad?'

'Soon be back back with us, eh?'

'The only one-armed fireman on the Western.'

The comments were affectionate, joking. George, in the cab of 4912 which had just pulled into Platform 2, blew his whistle.

Tom stood waiting at the barrow crossing for the passenger train to depart. He was tired and, despite his firm assurances to Ben, he felt low. Suppose his arm didn't heal well enough for him to return to the footplate? He didn't think he could remain on the railway. Perhaps he would move away from Acton Chalcote. Retrain for another trade somewhere else? The thought depressed him.

He watched 4912 pull out of the station leaving a lingering trail of steam hanging over the platform. He started to cross over the tracks on the barrow crossing but, as the steam cleared, he saw a small figure waiting at the end of the platform. Maggie. It was Maggie.

'Maggie...?'

He took a step towards the platform, then stopped.

'Maggie...?'

'Tom.. oh Tom...!'

She ran towards him then hesitated, her eyes searching his face. Her hand went up and she gently touched his cheek. They stared at one another. Then, with a sob, she flung her arms around him.

'Mind my arm,' he said gently before pulling her close in a kiss.

THE END

If you enjoyed this book you might like...

God's Wonderful Railway

God's Wonderful Railway is the classic 8-part BBC series from 1980. It follows three generations of the Grant family who live and work on the Severn Valley branch of the Great Western Railway.

The Permanent Way tells of the construction of the line in the 1860s. *Clear Ahead* shows the line in its Edwardian heyday in 1906 and *Fire on the Line* shows how the outbreak of the Second World War affected both the family and the railway.

The DVD also includes a film about the making of the series and an item on it on Blue Peter.

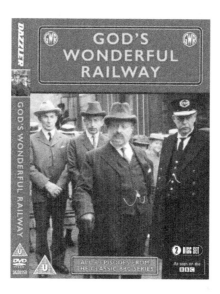

The DVD was released by Dazzler Media and is available from www.amazon.co.uk

The first two books of the series: *Permanent Way* and *Clear Ahead*, can be purchased from www.avrilrowlands.co.uk or email me at avril@laxfordhouse.co.uk.

Avril Rowlands' books for younger readers...

The Magician's Train Set

When Sam finds granddad's model train set had magically come to life, she isn't too surprised - after all her granddad was the famous 'Alfredo, the Amazing Man of Magic'! But when her granddad gets ill and she finds herself right inside the railway, things became altogether different. Who are the strange and frightening mis-shapes? What do they want? Her granddad is in hospital, her parents far away, her brother, Joe, is a pain. Then her unpleasant Aunt Dory and her even more unpleasant son, Craig, arrive, and threaten to dismantle and sell off granddad's train set as well as his home in Mablethorpe. Sam is the only one who can sort things out, both in the actual world and in the magic world of the railway. Time is running out, but Sam is living in both worlds, so which is the real one?

Steam in the Family

Available on Kindle books: www.amazon.co.uk

Shadows on the Wall

Julie can't believe her luck when she's chosen to play a leading part in a children's television drama about smuggling in the eighteenth century. Thrilled at the chance but also rather scared, she arrives on location in Yorkshire and is immediately thrust into the magical, make-believe world of film-making. She's soon made welcome and feels part of the close family of actors and film crew. It's a warm and happy feeling.

But odd things are taking place in and around the film unit and Julie begins to realise that things aren't as they appear. There are the harmless, or perhaps not so harmless, practical jokes; there's the disturbing conversation she overhears, and when she finds Bob, the costume designer, on the beach, victim of a vicious attack, she is determined to find out just what is going on. What's happening in the real world seems to be increasingly like the story in the film. Is present-day smuggling actually taking place? And if so, of what and by whom? What secrets lie in the disused railway tunnel and who, if anyone, can Julie trust? As she gets closer to the heart of the mystery so the danger grows and when at last Julie does find out the truth, is she too late to do anything about it?

Available on Kindle books: www.amazon.co.uk

Milk and Honey

When Nelson and his family arrive in Britain, Nelson can hardly believe that this cold, grey country is their 'promised land'. He is soon homesick for his relatives in Jamaica and for the sunshine, colours and way of life of the Caribbean. It is 1958, and the Vincent family are among the first immigrants to Britain from Jamaica. They soon find out, though, that it isn't easy to adapt to a new country. And although the British government asked them to come over and work, some people in Britain make it very clear that they don't like immigrants.

As he gets used to his new surroundings, Nelson finds a friend in old Mrs Waterman. Wellington, Nelson's older brother, makes lots of friends - though not the sort his parents would approve of - and he starts his own rock band. So they all begin to settle in; but as the long hot summer goes on, tensions rise around them until the situation explodes in violence.

First published by Oxford University Press
Now available on Kindle books : www.amazon.co.uk
Paperback copies from www.avrilrowlands.co.uk
or email me at avril@laxfordhouse.co.uk

Poll

Katie's adventure starts when the supermarket flies into the air, taking her and her little brother with it! She finds herself walking through a strange world of vanishing rainforests, dying rivers, polluted seas and global warming in a real greenhouse. It's not fantasy. It could all be true. It's a place where everything changes and nothing stays the same. Helped by the green tree-frog, Katie knows she must find her brother, Ben. She knows she has to get home. But, most of all, she must discover who or what Poll really is.

First published by Oxford University Press
Now available on Kindle books : www.amazon.co.uk

Paperback copies from www.avrilrowlands.co.uk
or email me at avril@laxfordhouse.co.uk

Steam in the Family

The Shakespeare Connection

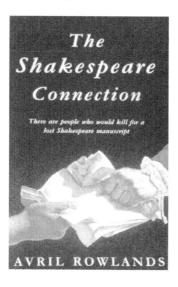

Cal doesn't want to come over to England from America on a school trip and he certainly doesn't want to have to learn all this stuff about Shakespeare. Okay, so Shakespeare was the greatest playwright in history, but what does that have to do with him? It has everything to do with him when Cal finds himself transported back into the past. There is a mystery, and danger, and Cal is thrown into the middle of it all. At first it doesn't seem important. How much would anyone care about a lost manuscript by Shakespeare? Not very much, Cal would have thought, but he soon learns how wrong he can be. Greed. Revenge. Power. There are all kinds of forces and all kinds of enemies that pursue Cal both in the sixteenth century and in the present day. Can the past ever be rewritten?

First published by Oxford University Press

Now available on Kindle books : www.amazon.co.uk
Harback copies from www.avrilrowlands.co.uk
or email me at avril@laxfordhouse.co.uk

******

For more information please go to my website:
www.avrilrowlands.co.uk

Printed in Great Britain
by Amazon

79157040R00210